Shelterbelts

Other books by Candace Simar:

Abercrombie Trail (2009)

Pomme de Terre (2010)

Birdie (2011)

Blooming Prairie (2012)

Farm Girls (with Angela F. Foster, 2013)

Shelterbelts

Candace Simar

NORTH STAR PRESS OF ST. CLOUD, INC.
St. Cloud, Minnesota

To Mom and Dad
Who lived it

Copyright © 2015 Candace Simar
Represented by Blue Cottage Agency
www.BlueCottageAgency.com

Cover design by Riverplace
www.bookcoverdesigns.net

ISBN: 978-0-87839-817-1

Printed in the United States of America.

Published by:
North Star Press of St. Cloud, Inc.
Saint Cloud, Minnesota

www.northstarpress.com

Tia Fiskum

S HE SHOULD PUT IT OUT of its misery.

Tia Fiskum leaned over the side of the calf pen, raising the lantern in the dim light to get a better look at the deformed animal. Another disappointment. Rosy had dropped her calf just as Tia released the other cows from their stanchions after morning milking. They counted on a healthy calf to help pay the mortgage.

Even in the dimness, she saw her duty. The calf's jaw hung at an angle, and stumps showed where its hind legs belonged. Norman was gone to war, and Ma had enough to do planting the garden. A good farmer took care of her animals. Pa would insist if he were alive.

Tia hung the lantern on a nail, lifted the wooden latch and entered the pen. Rosy pawed the ground and tossed her head. Pa always taught caution around animals with newborns.

"Careful, now." Tia patted Rosy's flank. The brown cow humped her back and bellowed. "Hush. Nothing to worry about."

Roosters crowed from the coop, and their yellow lab barked in the yard. Tia shooed away the barn cats feasting on the afterbirth. Glowing eyes of rats showed from the eaves, drawn by the smell of blood.

Getting the damaged animal out of the pen would be tricky. Tia reached toward the calf, but Rosy bumped against her hip with enough force to lift her off her feet. Tia slammed into the watering cup, as Rosy bellowed and butted again.

Tia jumped into the manger, glad for her long legs. As she scrambled over the side of the pen to safety, she heard ripping cloth as Rosy's

1

horn snagged the hem of her skirt. She knew better than turn her back to a new mother.

She wiped her hands on her apron, and rubbed her hip with a grimace. Lucky she'd carry only a bruise. Last year, a neighbor had been gored by a fresh heifer. Needed ten stitches and was laid up for a whole month. He only escaped by pushing the animal away with one of his crutches.

Somehow, Tia had to hold Rosy away and pull the calf out of the pen. It was a two-person job, but Tia would not trouble Ma for help. Asking would only prove Tia couldn't manage as well as a man.

As she fetched the pitchfork, she glanced out the open barn door, looking across the pasture toward the lights of the Hanson's barn. Every window glowed like a Christmas tree. Tia promised herself she would put in the electric, too, after the war ended. She would buy a tractor and baler, add another hog barn, and replace the roof on the machine shed. She would build up the dairy herd, maybe get some of those electric milk machines. Someday, her farm would be as modern as any in *The Farmer Magazine*.

Tia re-entered the pen with a scoop of grain in one hand and the pitchfork in the other. She dumped the grain into the manger. While Rosy nuzzled it, Tia slipped backward through the gate, dragging the calf by one hoof, holding the pitch fork ready with the other hand. Rosy bellowed and lunged against the gate just as Tia, with the calf, slammed the gate behind her.

Tia wiped her hands on her apron, and caught her breath. The smell of blood, the deformed calf and the bawling cow had unnerved her more than she cared to admit. "Hush now. Everything will be all right." She didn't know if she talked to herself or the animals.

Tia leaned the fork against the wall, and fetched the stone maul hanging on a peg. A farmer had to do the hard things. If she used all her strength, she could land one fatal blow. She faced the calf. Lifting the heavy maul with both hands, she clenched her eyes and gritted her teeth.

Foolish. She lowered the stone maul to the ground, resting its flat edge against her shoe. She must keep her eyes open. If she didn't aim just right, she might need more than one swing. She couldn't bear to hit the poor thing more than once.

She lifted the maul again, and positioned her stance for the blow. It was no different than butchering hogs, or cutting the heads off chickens, something she had done many times. Of course, she could do it.

But then, the calf flopped his head toward her, and opened his brown eyes. He seemed to look right through her. A pitiful, mewing came from his mouth. Bits of straw stuck to his wet skin, and smears of blood and manure streaked over his back.

The Nazis killed handicapped children and helpless old people. Mercy killing, they called it, if one could believe the newspapers. The calf bleated again, sending Rosy into a frenzy of kicking and bellowing.

Tia lowered the maul. She knelt and brushed a fly away from its eyes. "*Stalkers liten.*" She wiped its back with a handful of clean straw. "Poor little one."

Norman would label her a sissy for being so squeamish. He always said girls belonged in the kitchen.

But Tia was a farmer whether or not Norman approved. It's what she always wanted to do with her life. The calf stuck out a healthy, pink tongue, and pushed up with its front hooves, trying to stand. It fell back.

It was bad luck all around. If Tia killed the calf, she would have to deal with Rosy's anguish. Milking a fresh heifer for the first time was always difficult, even with a healthy calf at her side. Tia couldn't imagine how hard it would be to milk Rosy if she were wild with grief.

Why not let nature take its course? Either way, the calf would die. At least she would be spared the gruesome task. Tia hung the stone maul back in its place with a curse, and reached for the milk can. No one would know. The calf couldn't stand up without hind legs to suckle on its own. It wouldn't last.

She hefted the heavy milk can, and splashed a bit into a smaller bucket. Tia knelt beside the calf, dipped her fingers into the milk and let the quivering calf lick her fingers. Its tongue felt rough, but determined.

"*Bya, bya, litte gut,*" Tia crooned as she dipped her fingers into the milk again.

Someday Tia hoped to have a husband and children. She was only twenty-nine; it could still happen. She imagined holding a newborn to her breast, how it would feel to be a mother. She imagined childish voices giggling in the haymow, and small arms snuggled around her neck. Even plain women found the right kind of man, one who looked beyond outward appearances to the real person inside.

Rosy saw her calf out of reach, kicked the sides of the pen and bucked like a bronco at the fair. She hurled herself against the gate, humping her back, and bawling with wild eyes.

Tia didn't have time for this. She pulled the calf as close as it could be without being inside the pen. The barn quieted as Rosy licked her calf with her long tongue. The silence a sweet relief.

Tia lifted the milk can and stepped out of the stuffy barn, shivering as the chilly air hit her face. The sun painted a scarlet lip over the eastern horizon. *Red sky in morning, sailors take warning.* A clear day—a good day to be planting corn.

Tia carried the milk into the house where Ma already washed the morning eggs. Tia would deliver the cream to town as soon as Ma finished separating the morning milk. Ma had been on edge lately. They hadn't heard from Norman since Christmas and now already May Day. A POW camp should be safe enough.

"Oatmeal on the stove," Ma said, as she emptied the milk bucket into the top of the separator bowl. She wore a deep frown and it seemed her hair was grayer than it was at Christmas time. Her Bible and prayer book lay open on the table.

"No time," Tia said. She wouldn't mention the calf. "Tank is empty."

The morning burst into full light as Tia reached the pump house. Green blades of grass pushed through the spongy soil. She sniffed the aroma of spring as she worked the handle of the pump until the water splattered into the holding tank. She wished for a gale of wind to turn the windmill, but the tail vane hung limp and useless. Someday, they would have an electric pump like the Hansons.

At least gravity drained the water down to the hog shed and barnyard tanks. As the water gushed out of the pump, Tia cupped a hand beneath the icy stream, and drank her fill while pumping with the other. Pa always bragged their well gave the best water in Tolga Township.

Tia watched Pet and Pat, their team of work horses, graze alongside the small lake as she filled the tank. The clump of birches next to the lake leafed out in Tia's favorite shade of green. She rested her eyes on the color, feeling the hopefulness of spring, in spite of the calf and her guilt over not doing the right thing. She hoped the team was strong enough to make it through another season. They weren't young anymore. Impossible to buy a tractor with the war on, even if she had the money.

Beyond the lake lay the Hanson farm. Black furrows stretched behind Clyde's plow as he rounded the corner on his John Deere and began another row. His father must be doing the milking to give Clyde such an early start. Though she was too far away to see Clyde's face, she imagined the chocolate brown of his eyes, and the way he cupped his cigarette in the curve of his thick fingers. He always carried a dime novel in his back pocket. She wondered what he was reading. Reading the same book would be almost like having a conversation.

Tia worked the pump handle again and again. Most of the men were gone soldiering, and Clyde Hanson remained one of the few eligible bachelors left in Tolga Township. He'd invited her to the Farmer's Union dance last fall. They twirled across the floor to schottisches, polkas, and waltzes. It had been the happiest evening of her life. Funny, he hadn't called on her since.

Of course, he was busy. His mother told everyone Clyde wanted to improve their farm before he took a wife. Only sensible.

Above the tree line, beyond the Hanson farm, the steeple of Tolga Lutheran poked into the clouds. The steeple showed from every corner of their farm. Tia looked toward the church many times a day while doing her work. She couldn't put it into words, and would have been embarrassed to try, but she found a quiet strength in her faith. How else would she have gotten this far?

Tia straightened her spine, rubbing her lower back with the back of her hand, once the tank filled. She squeezed her eyes shut, and hoped with all her might that the calf would die, Rosy would settle, the war would end, Norman would return from the prison camp, and Clyde would come calling. It wasn't exactly a prayer—but close enough.

She lugged a bushel of corn cobs to the hog pens. Six Yorkshires, almost market ready, pushed to the troughs, jostling for better position, their snouts black from digging in the dirt, their ears erect as if listening for a warning. In a separate pen, the sow flopped on her side, nursing a litter of eleven piglets. Hormel paid good money for pork bellies, and claimed Spam was winning the war. In that case, her pigs would soon be soldiers.

Ma met Tia at the kitchen door, her face wrinkled into worry lines. "The postmaster telephoned–chicks are in."

Tia hated Ma's old, shapeless dress. It reached to the tops of her shoes, and was faded to the point of being colorless. For once, she was glad Ma didn't drive. Tia didn't want her to go into town looking like a *gamle* from the Old Country. Tia made a mental note to stop at the store and buy the prettiest sacks of flour she could find. A new dress required two sacks, and it wasn't easy to find two of the same pattern. Anything would be better than what Ma wore most days.

Ma counted out change from the sugar bowl to pay the C.O.D. charges for the chicks, as Tia pulled on her favorite gray sweater.

"I think it's enough," Ma said, "if you add the egg money."

A quick worry intruded. Baby chicks required heat, and the old kerosene heater proved temperamental. Someday they would have the electric and a modern heat lamp like the Hansons. Tia would tend a large flock of hens for steady egg money, and kill a rooster for Sunday dinners. She looked out the window towards Clyde's field. It didn't cost anything to dream.

"The cream check comes Tuesday," Tia said. "We'll be all right until then." Tia glanced out the window, and saw a moving cloud of dust. "Oh, no!" A dirty, green truck nosed into the driveway.

"Clarence must have taken a day off the mail route to put in his crops," Ma said. The worry lines between her eyes furrowed deeper. "Maybe Tillie won't stay long this time."

Tillie parked behind the DeSoto, blocking any hope of Tia's exit. Ma moved to the stove and poked another stick of wood under the coffee pot. Tia answered the door. Tillie's eyeballs bulged like a rat terrier's, and her red hair swirled into a fashionable up-do. She wore lipstick and a new dress. Tia tucked a loose strand of hair behind her ears, and smoothed a pilly spot on her sweater.

Tillie started talking before she stepped over the threshold. Norman called Tillie a giggle puss behind her back, and named her twitchy and skittish as a heifer in heat. Tia steeled herself. Last year, Tillie reported Lucinda Petterson's death three times before Lucinda actually died. Gunda Olson brought a hot dish to the mourning family only to find Lucinda, not only alive, but canning pickles.

"You won't believe it!" Tillie dropped her pocketbook on the table, and plopped into a chair by the kitchen table. "I saw Vera Sonmor at Rorvig's Store." She paused with a dramatic flair worthy of Veronica Lake. "Guess what?"

Tia couldn't guess. She took a chair across from Tillie, as Ma fussed with the coffee pot. A town girl was as foreign to Tia as a German or Japanese might be. She knew Vera from Rorvig's, of course, but had never talked to her outside of asking the price of sardines or *gjetost* cheese.

"She's sewing a silk wedding dress with pearl buttons and a lace insert at the neck." Tillie paused for a breath. "Her brother mailed a parachute from France. Real silk." Tillie placed both hands on the table, palms down, and leaned forward. "A fancy dress and a church wedding. Planning the date around the peonies."

"Nice," Tia said, as Ma pulled cups and saucers off the shelf. Tia noticed that Ma used the everyday dishes, not the good ones.

Daylight burned. Chicks needed food and water within twenty-four hours of shipment to survive. She and Mildred always split an order to save on postage and get a cheaper rate per bird. She'd stop at the Moberg farm on the way home to deliver Mildred's birds.

"Aren't you going to ask who she's marrying?" Tillie lowered her voice and leaned close enough that Tia could smell bacon grease clinging to her hair. "Clyde Hanson. Can you believe it? His parents are fit to be tied that he settled for a town girl." Her words came out so fast a splash of saliva hit Tia's face. "After all these years, Clyde's finally getting married."

It couldn't be. Clyde had said nothing about a fiancée when she greeted him in church last Sunday. He came alone to the Pentecost Dinner. He hadn't called because he was busy building the new shed. Surely this was another of Tillie's wild stories.

"I always thought you and Clyde would get together," Tillie said. "Your farms next to each other. And together at the harvest dance." She stared directly into Tia's face reminding her of the rats eyeing the afterbirth. "I knew you'd want to know."

It was as if a winter wind blew through the room and sucked the air out of Tia's lungs. Everything slipped into slow motion except for the twitch in Tillie's left eye that fluttered like a hummingbird's wing. It was impossible. Tillie stared until Tia thought she would scream.

Ma plunked down at the table. The look of pity on her face was more than Tia could bear. She wouldn't let them see her disappointment. Wouldn't let her ragged feelings lie naked for Tillie to gossip about across Tolga Township.

She could hear it all now. Tia Fiskum, the heartbroken old maid, lost Clyde Hanson to a town girl. Ugly old maid, Tia corrected herself. Tia Fiskum, tall and gawky, tongue-tied with a long nose and big feet.

"Sorry, but I have to get the cream to town." The bitch. The gossip monger. She wouldn't give her the time of day. Tia stood, and yanked her sweater closer around her. She crossed her arms and crimped her mouth. It felt good to lash out. "Your truck is blocking my way."

Ma shook her head in protest at such rudeness, but Tia wouldn't back down. Tillie didn't deserve good manners. "We have chicks waiting at the post office."

Tillie raised her eyebrows. For once the Nosey Nellie was speechless.

"*Mange takk* for stopping." Ma stood to her feet. "Come again soon."

Tillie wore a bewildered look, but gathered her pocketbook, and headed toward the front door, her heels tapping a quick staccato, blabbering about Ingeborg and Olaf Hanson being upset about their son's choice. "Vera can't cook an egg." She kept talking as she climbed into her truck and started the engine. "The only thing she knows how to make is chocolate cake. Can you imagine?"

Tia hefted two filled cream cans from the reservoir next to the windmill. Tillie's voice shrilled from the open pickup window as she backed into the driveway. "Let's throw a bridal shower."

Tia didn't answer. She heaved the wet cans into the trunk, and fished for a piece of twine to secure the gaping lid. She jumped into the car, slammed the door and gunned the motor. Gravel sprayed up around the car. A stone smacked the windshield. The De Soto veered onto the township road, and then Tia remembered the irreplaceable, balding tires.

Helvete! She wiped her eyes with the sleeve of her sweater, and slowed to a normal speed. Driving like a crazy woman wouldn't help anything.

She breathed deeply and counted the facts. Clyde wasn't stupid. He wouldn't put their farm in jeopardy by marrying a town girl. A smart farmer chose a wife who would be a helpmeet rather than a detriment. Clyde was smart. He always had his nose in a book. He had always bested her in school. Had won the spelling bee every year, and got A's in arithmetic and history. Besides, Vera was younger than they. Much younger. Maybe a dozen years. Their parents always wanted Clyde and Tia to marry. It only made sense with their farms so close together.

Her grandfather often quoted a favorite Norwegian saying. *Bonde trivst mellom boender best.* Farmers thrive among farmers best.

Tillie once whispered that *True Story Magazine* said men did not think with their brains. Tillie laughed as she said it, a coarse chuckle that explained the phrase. Was Clyde like that?

Tia drove the winding road into town keeping both hands on the steering wheel and her eyes on the road. She would have to hear it from a more reliable source than Tillie before she really believed it. She swerved around a rut, and jolted to a stop beside the brick creamery at the edge of town.

The egg room sat opposite the Tolga Creamery, though in the same building. The sour stink of the creamery filled the air. The first budding lilac leaves showed around the wooden steps to the office, and Eddy Root played with something under the bush as a little child might do. Eddy was a grown man, but feeble-minded. Tia had always been a little afraid of him.

"How you doing, Eddy?" Tia untied the twine holding the trunk lid. She took care to stay out of his reach. One never knew when dealing with a lunatic, although Ma said he was a gentle soul and perfectly harmless. After Pa's death, Eddy and his father helped put their hay up, and refused any payment. No one was stronger than the Root men.

"Lizard's talking—says snakes will kill a chicken," Eddy said. She could see now that he played with a lizard. You never knew what he might do. His hair clipped so close to his head that he looked bald, and his face grizzled with gray stubble. A blue chambray shirt hung limply over ragged overalls. He didn't make eye contact, just tied a thread around the lizard's leg and dragged it through the weeds. "White coats mean as snakes."

"How's your ma feeling these days?" Tia hefted the cans out of the trunk. If Eddy's father had been outside, he would have made Eddy help with the heavy lifting.

Whoops and hollers erupted from inside the creamery before Eddy had a chance to answer. Too early for a baseball game. Must be something about the war. Eddy crawled deeper into the lilac bushes, dragging the lizard behind him.

Tia lugged the heavy cans to the conveyer belt, and wrinkled her nose at the smell of disinfectant coming from the creamery. More cheers came from inside. She placed the case of eggs on the landing and hurried into the office.

"What's happening?" Tia said.

Harvey Root, Nels Carlson, and Pastor Hustvedt huddled around a radio on the counter. They shushed her, and motioned her to come closer to hear the words pouring out of the speaker.

10

"Report confirmed. Adolph Hitler committed suicide yesterday, April 30, 1945." The announcer paused with emotion. "A date to remember."

Nels thrust one of his crutches into the air and cheered. His son, George, fought in Germany. Nels carried a crippling wound from the Great War. His hatred for Germans was well known throughout Tolga Township.

"The Huns are out." Nels thrust the crutch up again as a victory sign. "Down for the count, by God."

Harvey jigged until he coughed and clutched his chest. He leaned on the counter to catch his breath. "Now get the hell out of Norway," Harvey said, and shook his fist at the radio. "*Drittsekk Nazis!*" He cast an apologetic glance toward Tia and the minister. "Excuse the language."

"The war can't last, thank God," Pastor Hustvedt said. "And Roosevelt not alive to see this day."

Tia watched his Adam's apple bob up and down. No wonder the Luther Leaguers called him Ichabod Crane behind his back. Pastor Hustvedt looked out from wire rimmed spectacles, blue eyes floating behind thick lenses. "Your brother coming home." He reached out and gripped Tia's shoulder. She stood eye to eye with him. "George and all the boys."

Nels crutched out of the creamery to tell his wife, Olga, the news. The boys, gone so long, finally coming home. Tia had waited for this day, and yet found it overshadowed by Tillie's terrible news.

Tia hauled the egg case toward the candling room. Olga Carlson came out leaning on her husband's arm.

How frail and thin she looked. Her dress hung on her like a sack on a fencepost. Only her blue eyes seemed alive, and they filled with tears. Tillie said Olga was deathly sick and wouldn't live past summer. Anyone could see Olga looked unwell.

Tia set the case of eggs on the ground. Olga grabbed Tia around the neck and hugged her. She smelled like a feather pillow left out in the rain. "Such good news for our boys," she whispered into Tia's neck. Tia felt as if she were holding her upright, so heavily did Olga lean against her. "Thank the Good Lord, it will finally end."

Nels urged his wife to hurry. He said they needed to get home to the radio. "You bet your life, this will crush those heinie bastards once and for all," he said, with a face set hard and sharp as the tip of his crutch. "Let Hitler burn in hell, and every German with him."

Tia looked toward the creamery office. Rumor had it Pastor Hustvedt's mother was German. No one knew for sure. It could be she was Bohemian or some other foreign ancestry, but Tia hoped the minister hadn't heard Nels speak that way.

"Did you hear about Clyde Hanson?" Olga spoke as if it took all her energy. "Going to get married. Forget her name. The pretty girl at Rorvig's Store." She paused and took a few deep breaths. "Ingeborg says she and Olaf will move upstairs, and let the newlyweds take the downstairs. Work the land together."

A black film dropped over Tia's eyes. It was true, then. She had to leave. Had to get alone and think. Her shoulders stooped, and she straightened her spine in an effort to appear normal.

She waved goodbye. "Work to do." She didn't trust her voice to say anything more.

Eddy Root pulled the lizard by the string in the dirt. He never looked her way as she climbed into the car. She backed out, stomping on the foot feed, almost hitting Pastor's car in her hurry to leave.

She drove down Main Street. Though she vowed not to look, Tia craned her neck, and caught a glimpse of Vera through the front window of Rorvig's General Store. Vera was standing in front of the window, and laughing with a customer. She must set her hair in bobby pins every night for it to curl over her shoulders that way.

Tia jumped the curb when she parked in front of the post office, cringing as she remembered the balding tires. She backed onto the street, determined to finish her business and get home.

Tia heard the chirping chicks as she opened the door. Tia avoided conversation with Eddy's mother who was mailing a package to her nephew in the service. Tia counted out the C.O.D. charges, and toted the flat box with air holes on the sides out to the car.

She was just about to drive away when the postmaster came running out with a letter in his hand. "Mail for your mother," he said.

Tia didn't even glance at the letter, but shoved it behind the visor. She felt cold as ice although the sun burned overhead. She rolled up the window, and turned on the heater full blast. She drove out of town and onto the country road leading to Mildred's house.

The car grew hot as an oven, and Tia's blood began to circulate again. Vera Hanson. It couldn't be. Tears coursed down her face. She sobbed like a baby, great wails coming out of her chest, almost frightening in intensity. She wept and drove, swerving alone on the country road, chicks peeping from the back seat.

Clyde chose a pretty girl. Of course, he would want someone younger and prettier. Tia felt so tongue-tied around him that she barely said a word that time he took her to a picture show. She should have asked about crop rotation. Anything to prove she wasn't a complete idiot. They danced well together, but lots of people were good dancers. How foolish to dream Clyde would love her. Naïve. Stupid and naïve and foolish. *Helvete!*

She cleared her throat, and fished a handkerchief from her pocket. She hadn't felt like this since the day she found Pa slumped over dead in the hay barn, as if the earth had shifted beneath her feet. For her, there was only Clyde. Living in Tolga Township meant she would never meet anyone else. She didn't want anyone else.

As she steered around a washed out place in the road, she remembered what Pastor Hustvedt had said about the boys coming home.

He was wrong. All the boys would not be coming home. Willy Moberg lost in the Pacific. The paper reported terrible casualties from places with unpronounceable names. The thought consoled her somehow, that she was like one of those wounded soldiers or sailors.

Tia turned into the Moberg driveway where Mildred planted potatoes in the garden plot beside the barn. A gold star hung in the window.

Mildred waved and brushed the dirt off her hands and house dress. A red bandanna handkerchief covered her hair, just like Rosie the Riveter in the defense plant posters.

She was Tia's oldest friend, and also unmarried. She, Mildred and Clyde were the only students in their grade at country school. Mildred's brother and Norman followed a year behind them. Their mothers had shared a deep friendship.

"Something wrong?" Mildred said with a look of concern. "Not Norman?"

Tia shook her head and wiped her eyes on her sleeve. She told of the radio announcement of Hitler's death. They agreed it meant the end of the war. Then they slipped into silence. Mildred didn't mention Willy. Tia thought to say something about Clyde and Vera.

They carried the box of chicks to the brooder house beyond the garden, Tia on one side, and Mildred on the other. They passed the old tire swing where they used to play as children. A sharp memory of Willy climbing the rope brought a catch to Tia's throat. The roar of a tractor in the nearby field almost drowned out the sound of peeping chicks. Mildred's father almost finished with his corn planting.

"I cleaned the brooder house last week," Mildred said, as she opened the door with her free hand. "Newspapers all ready. I'll plug in the lamp."

Tia bumped her head on the low door frame. She knelt and counted one hundred wiggling balls of black fluff, as Mildred stretched an extension cord through the open window to an outlet at the nearby pump house.

"They're adorable!" Mildred said when she returned to the building.

"Good layers, good meat production," Tia said, though her voice trembled.

"Time for coffee?"

Tia shook her head. Her throat parched until the words almost scraped out of her throat. "There's more." She cleared her throat. "Clyde is engaged to Vera Sonmor. You know, from Rorvig's."

Mildred didn't say a word. She looked down at her shoes. Her silence told Tia everything.

"You knew?"

"Saw them together at Elbow Lake when I went to the dentist last month." Mildred looked up. Her lip twitched the way it always did when she was nervous. "And at the show last week. They were pretty chummy."

"Why didn't you say something?" Tia wanted to blame someone. Mildred should have told her. She knew how Tia felt about Clyde.

"Nothing to say. Just saw them together. That's all."

Then Tia remembered Mildred came home from her dental appointment to find the telegram about Willy. Tia's anger melted. It wasn't Mildred's fault. It was no one's fault.

Mildred promised to phone later in the week. Tia's tears started again as soon as she was in the car. She was the last to know.

Back on the road, she swerved to miss a red fox darting across the gravel road. Pebbles bounced on the windshield like a load of buckshot. A wicked and evil thought scurried across her mind the same way the pebbles skittered across the glass. She hated herself for even thinking such a thing. She was a horrible person. She saw how hard Willy's death was on his family. Yet in spite of this knowledge, Tia faced the stark truth.

If she could choose between marrying Clyde or her brother coming home, she knew which one she would pick.

* * *

THE NEWS OF HITLER'S suicide shaved five years off Ma's face. "Are you sure?" Ma walked over to the kitchen calendar, and turned the page from April to May. "It could be over then, maybe this month."

"Pastor says it won't last much longer."

"Norman coming home." Ma dabbed her eyes and sniffed into her handkerchief. "Wrong to be glad for a suicide, I know, but after all Hitler's put this poor world through." Ma straightened her shoulders, and a hard edge showed on her jaw. "Vengeance is mine, I will repay, saith the Lord."

"Got work to do." Tia had to get out in the field where she could be alone, or she would explode. "Help with the chicks."

They were at the car when Tia saw the corner of the envelope in the visor. She reached for it. "Almost forgot."

She handed the letter to Ma, and was reaching for the box when Ma screamed.

"No! It can't be." Ma stood with the envelope in her hand, staring as if she'd seen a ghost. "It's from the War Department."

Norman might be hurt—or worse. "What does it say?" Tia said.

"I can't open it. I can't . . ."

Tia grabbed the letter, and tore it open. She unfolded a thin sheet of paper with typewritten words. "He's been found." Tia's hands trembled until the letter shook.

"What do you mean?" Ma's voice rose to a near screech. "He wasn't missing."

Tia read aloud. "This is a follow-up to the previous letter concerning the missing prisoners of war." The Nazis had evacuated Norman's camp before Russian troops arrived. American soldiers recently found the few survivors in Germany, hundreds of miles away from Poland. Many Americans died of starvation and exposure. Norman recuperated at a military hospital in England. He would transfer to a stateside hospital as soon as transport could be arranged.

"We never knew he was missing," Tia said.

"I didn't need a letter," Ma said. The years climbed back onto her face. She looked haggard and drawn. "I've known for weeks that something was wrong."

They stood by the car for a long moment without speaking. Such a mixed up day. The calf. Norman lost, then found. Hitler dead. Clyde marrying a town girl.

"We might as well keep busy," Ma said at last. "It's good news overall. The Lord answered our prayers. He'll survive this war." Tears

16

traveled the wrinkles in her cheeks. "All those poor mothers learning their boys didn't make it."

Ma made no mention of Clyde's engagement, although she must know Tia felt as desolate as those gold-star mothers must feel. Instead, Ma chatted about her plans as they carried the chicks to the brooder house. She would call Pastor Hustvedt with the good news, and they must write letters to Norman at the English hospital.

"Things will change, once Norman's home." Ma removed the chicks from the box, and placed them beside the watering dish. She was trying too hard to be cheerful. "He'll take over the outside work and you can be a girl again."

Tia felt her jaw drop. She snapped it closed. "What do you mean?"

"Why, the farm." Ma reached for a scoop of chicken feed, and sprinkled it over the newspapers. The chicks pecked at the tiny bits of grain. "You've done your share, but it's Norman's responsibility, after all. The farm will be his someday."

"Why should anything change? I like farming," Tia said. Would every dream she ever had die on this terrible day? "I won't give it up."

She remembered the time in eighth grade when Mrs. Tingvald presented Clyde with the prize for agriculture. Tia's experiment and research paper on egg production had earned an A+. Clyde only copied a magazine article on contour plowing. Pa said it was only right a boy be recognized in the field of agriculture.

"You're still young." Ma chattered about Tia having time for the church choir, and joining a canasta club. She was as irritating as Tillie Stenerson. "You'll keep out of the sun and spare your complexion." She didn't say the words, *find a husband*, but they were there. "You won't have to work like a man."

Tia jerked the kerosene heater a little rougher than needed. Her thumb went through a rusted part, and kerosene dripped onto the clean newspapers spread for the chicks.

"*Uffda, fyda,*" Ma said with a cluck of her tongue. "You're always in such a hurry. Look what you've done."

"Maybe it can be fixed," Tia wiped kerosene on her apron but didn't give a thought to repairing it. Let Norman worry about it when he got home.

"It's ruined. We'll have to find another," Ma said. "Can't risk burning the place down."

A chick sprawled flat on its belly, and Tia picked up the little bird, barely bigger than the palm of her hand. She held the poor thing close, feeling its heart pound like the insistent bell on a wind-up alarm clock.

"I'm sorry, Ma," Tia said. No matter how hard she tried, she always did something wrong. "Maybe when we sell the hogs."

"See what you've done?" Ma bit her lower lip. "We'll take them into the kitchen, for now. Put the box on the oven door. They need ninety degrees to survive."

Tia could tell she was angry by the set of her jaw. It always happened like that. Never enough money. Never the equipment they needed to improve themselves. One step forward and two steps back. The chicks came unsexed and they could expect at least half to be hens. Fifty hens adding two hundred eggs each per year meant another eight hundred thirty-three dozen eggs for the creamery. Enough to make a real difference, to get ahead. But they had to raise them first.

"Ingeborg Hanson has an old kerosene heater." Ma nodded a quick nod as if the entire issue were solved. "Go over and borrow it."

"I need to start planting corn," Tia said. Surely, Ma wouldn't be so cruel.

"Your problem." The set of Ma's jaw showed she wouldn't back down. "I'll call and tell her you're coming."

* * *

INGEBORG MET TIA in the yard fifteen minutes later. They walked to the storage shed next to the granary. The Hanson buildings showed fresh paint. A mother duck waddled by with a line of new babies snaking behind her wherever she went.

"Your ma told me the good news about Norman," Ingeborg said. "I'm glad for you."

Hercules, their rat terrier, yapped and nipped at Tia's ankles until Ingeborg picked him up, and carried him on her thin hip. The door creaked open to piles of broken screens, hoes without handles, a rusty garden tiller, leftover planks, unused chicken feeders and empty bushel baskets. Ingeborg plopped the dog on the floor. It scurried under a pile of junk.

"Catch a rat," Ingeborg said. "Good doggie."

Ingeborg barely came up to Tia's chin. She was slight and quick, and known for her strong opinions. She rummaged until she pulled out the heater, brushing cobwebs off her crown of gray braids. "I suppose you heard our news."

Tia nodded, not trusting her voice. Ingeborg pulled a rag out of her apron pocket and wiped off the heater. She checked the wick. "Looks like it will work."

"*Mange takk.*"

"You teach a child how to get on in life, and then he goes ahead and does what he wants anyway," Ingeborg said with a bitter laugh. "*Betre ugift enn ille gift.*" Ingeborg shook her head disapprovingly and pursed her lips into a tight circle. "Better unmarried than badly married."

Tia nodded. Anything she said would be wrong. Ingeborg and Olaf were newlyweds when they bought this farm next to her grandparents, and had been close family friends down through the generations. Tia's grandmother acted as midwife when Clyde was born. They had quilted together, canned together, shared strawberry and raspberry crops, hayed together, threshed together, and during the Dirty Thirties, almost starved together.

A marriage between the two families would have been a natural thing, like combining fields or breaking down a fence between pastures.

Marriage to a town girl would be like harnessing a Shetland pony with a work horse.

She turned her thoughts away from what might have been. It was too late now.

"You should get the electric when this damn rationing ends," Ingeborg said. "It's the best thing we ever did."

They talked about Hitler's death, and the war. Clyde's mother said they listened to the news on the radio every morning and night. Tia couldn't imagine what it would be like to wake up in the morning, and turn a dial to hear the news even before the newspapers were out. When she got the electric, she would get a radio, too.

The phone rang as they lugged the rusty heater to the De Soto. They heard it through the open kitchen window. Ingeborg ran inside. Clyde came out of the granary, and walked over to Tia while pulling off his gloves. Chaff sprinkled across his curly hair. His rolled-up shirt sleeves showed muscular arms. Grain dust thickened his heavy eyebrows and lashes.

"What breed chicks did you get this year?" he said.

Tia's tongue tangled. After the first words squeaked out, the rest of them tumbled like a waterfall. First, she told Clyde about the letter about Norman, and how he was coming home soon. She then talked about how she and Mildred split shipments of chicks to save on postage, and get a better rate per bird. She chattered about the Golden Wyandotte's hardiness, temperament, meat and egg production. Then she launched into a spiel about the broken kerosene heater, and the news of Hitler. She, who had never been able to talk to Clyde about anything, felt helpless to stop her torrent of words. She was as chatty as Tillie.

He didn't seem surprised. "I'm getting married, you know, and would have liked Norman for best man."

The words, naked and blatant, gouged her heart like the talons of a hawk. She felt the blood drain away from her face. She opened her mouth to speak, but all that came out was a feeble squeak. "He'll be home soon. You could wait 'til then."

Clyde laughed, and pulled a cigarette from his shirt pocket. "When the love bug bites, it bites hard." He struck a match on the back of his overalls. The smell of sulfur burned her nose, as the match burst into flame.

She widened her mouth into what she hoped was a smile. He didn't care at all for her. She saw it as plain as the nose on her face. He never had. The dam rose up again, and she couldn't say another word.

"Plant more cucumbers," Ingeborg said, coming out of the house, and waving her apron to shoo the hens out of her flower beds next to the sidewalk. "That was Gunda Olson. Said the pickle factory is short of growers this year. Good money but lots of work."

Tia thanked her for the use of the heater, and left for home. In the rearview mirror she watched Clyde walk back to the granary.

She wouldn't allow herself the luxury of another weeping spell. At least not now. If she was going to be a farmer, then she had best face her responsibilities. She and Norman would run the farm together. She would deal with Ma later.

Ma waved as Tia drove into the yard. Ma had noon dinner in the oven, but Tia only grabbed a glass of milk and a honey jumble. She spent the afternoon planting corn with Pet and Pat pulling the old corn planter that had belonged to Grandpa Fiskum.

The back and forth trips across the field calmed her mind. Farming was always a mystery, how a seed thrown into the soil would die, and yet spring back to life. And then yield a harvest of more seeds.

She had once read a novel about a broken-hearted woman who entered a convent to assuage her grief in prayer and isolation. Tia wasn't Catholic, so that option was out of the question, but even if she were, she wouldn't leave Tolga Township. No one could make her leave. Not her mother, not Norman. She was a good farmer. She would work to improve herself and the farm.

Tia planted corn until milking time. She would have rather kept going until the field was finished, but she noticed how Pet's head drooped with fatigue. Ma limped towards the watering trough where Tia watered the team. Ma held a hand to her lower back, looking pale and tired.

"Your lumbago acting up again?"

"*Nei*," Ma said with a shake of her head. "It's the dark of the moon. The root crops had to go in." She urged Tia to stop for supper, but Tia shook her head. She doubted she could eat a thing.

"Lots to do before dark."

Tia headed straight for the barn. The calf bleated pitifully, and Rosy bellowed. The cows came in from the pasture, winding toward the barn in a single, snaking line. Tia would have just enough time.

"Hush now, Rosy." Tia tenderly lifted the calf and placed it farther away from the fence, out of Rosy's sight. Rosy bellowed and stomped, kicking against the fence until Tia feared she would hurt herself.

Tia fetched the stone maul. Flies buzzed around the calf, and crawled over its face and mouth. It was weaker now, barely able to hold up its head. A rat scurried in the gutter. The lowering sun coming through the barn door gave full light to even that far corner of the barn.

Tia raised the maul high over her head. She killed the calf with one blow.

Tia finished the milking, and took the milk can into the house for Ma to separate. "Rosy dropped her calf," she said. She hoped Ma wouldn't ask for details, and for once she didn't. Probably too preoccupied with thoughts of Norman. "It didn't live."

* * *

AFTER SHE FINISHED eating her late supper, Tia carried the calf out to the small clearing next to the shelterbelt where their former pets were buried. The air cooled quickly. It was still too early for mosquitoes.

Tia remembered her father and grandparents with each shovelful of dirt. She thought of Norman, thanking God he had survived, wondering what he had seen and endured these last months. She was wrong to think she would choose Clyde over her brother. Blood was blood. For the first time she looked forward to Norman coming home.

Norman had planted the struggling row of Chinese elms and balsam firs into a much-needed shelterbelt along the driveway. Somehow, she kept most of them alive through the dry years, hauling water to the surviving trees. She had often walked among them in the evening, pulling the weeds around the saplings, willing them to survive as Norman wanted. She thought of them as a hedge against all the bad things that might happen, not just the whirling snow drifts of winter.

She checked the chicks one final time. They snuggled under the heater, a mass of fluffy potential. She prayed no fox or weasel would find them in the night.

She crossed the cow yard stepping from one hummock to another, pausing to check the gate lest the young stock escape. All quiet in the pig house. The horses stood sleeping in the pasture. An owl swooped down upon a mouse in the grass with a whoosh of wings that startled her into slipping off a hummock into the black mud.

The Hanson place blazed electric lights in both levels of the house. She imagined them listening to the radio, and making plans for the wedding. Maybe they would mention Norman's name. She doubted they would think of her.

Then she turned her face toward their little house on the hill, and started home.

No light showed in the windows.

Nels Carlson

IT WASN'T AS IF he had time to lollygag. Olga slumped on the davenport after she finished supper dishes. Nels got up from his favorite chair and clicked off the evening news on the radio. He hitched his suspenders, and reached for his crutches. "I'll be back before you know I'm gone."

Olga looked at him with what he thought was accusation. She leaned back and closed her eyes. He knew how she hated his evenings at the tavern.

"Be home before dark."

"Oh, Lord," Olga murmured a cooing prayer that reminded him of setting hens. "Dear Jesus." This irritated Nels more than a reprimand. Olga had been raised in a Holy Roller church, and her prayers were not exactly words. Nels suspected she spoke in tongues. He didn't dare ask.

Maybe she wasn't as sick as she let on. But Olga couldn't fake the blue ring around her mouth, or the way her weight had fallen away.

He opened the door, and looked back to say goodbye, but she spoke first.

"I love you," she said. "But sometimes I hate you." She didn't open her eyes. She returned to that strange humming prayer. "Forgive me, Lord. Help me, Jesus." The words followed him. He slammed the screen door on his way out.

Patsy greeted him in the yard with a wagging tail, but he pushed her out of the way with one of his crutches. He didn't understand why Olga made such a stink. He would have a couple of beers, and come right home. Nels worked hard. Surely he deserved a little reward. He enjoyed visiting with the other men, playing cards. Something to pass the time and get his mind off his troubles.

Nels pulled up in front of the Lower Joint in Dalton as Sylvia Anderson, a pretty woman from Elbow Lake, walked down the sidewalk toward the tavern. Loud laughter and music from the juke box poured out of the tavern.

Three young boys played on the sidewalk near the door. The boys held their stomachs, bending over and mouthing laughter, mocking the barkeep's famous belly laugh. They gave a perfect imitation. Nels bit back a grin.

"Get the hell home," Nels said with a growl. "Have a little respect." He shook a crutch their way, and chuckled as the boys scattered.

Just then, a dusty green pickup drove up the street. Nels groaned. Tillie Stenerson all dolled up for some kind of hen party, wearing a fancy hat on her red head. White gloves showed on the steering wheel. She slowed to a crawl and craned her neck out the window to get a better look. It would be all over the township that he had gone drinking and left Olga home alone.

"Goddam gossip," Nels muttered. He resisted the urge to give her the finger. She was his second cousin, after all, and Nels didn't want to stir up the family. Instead he looked away, and followed Sylvia Anderson into the tavern as another roar of laughter erupted.

Sylvia joined a pair of grass widows from Ashby already sitting in the far corner. Nels took an empty stool at the bar beside two of his neighbors. Mansel Jorgenson had served in the Great War, as Nels had. Count on Mansel to shoot the breeze and share a bottle once in a while. Poor Mansel had a crippled daughter and a crazy wife. No wonder he needed to get away from the house. Julius Olson stayed on the farm when most young men joined up. At least he showed a little common sense, unlike Nels' son.

George enlisted right after Pearl Harbor. Nels pleaded with his hot-headed son to stay back. The draft board would have easily given an exemption, especially with Nels' crippled leg. They'd almost come to blows over it.

Talk was they'd be sending George's unit to the Pacific now the Huns were licked. The radio predicted a million of our boys would die invading Japan. The thought sickened him. Damn Germans, dirty Japs. Goddam dirty bastards.

"Mr. Carlson," the barkeep's voice boomed. "Thirsty again, I see." He slid cold bottles of Hamm's Beer across the counter to Mansel and Julius, and poured a shot of whiskey for Nels.

Nels eyed the glass before him, watching how the amber liquid reflected the light. It would be different this time. Only one drink, maybe two.

* * *

At closing time, the barkeep shook Nels's arm. "Time to pay up and go home." Nels shook his head and tried to remember where he was.

An empty bottle stood in front of him. The juke box sat silent. Everyone had left. Nels pulled money out of his pocket and belched.

Olga would be furious. "What time is it?" Nels said as he counted out the money.

"Almost midnight," Wendell said. "You all right to drive?" He held the door open, and motioned Nels outside with a nod of his chin. "Looks like a storm moving in. Want me to call somebody?"

"I'm fine." Nels wobbled onto his crutches, and stepped out into the darkness. If George were home, he could have come for him. If it weren't for the dirty Huns, he wouldn't need the crutches, would have his son home where he belonged and wouldn't need to spend his nights drinking at the Lower Joint. Lightning flashed across the dark sky as a roar of wind blew through the shelterbelt planted on the west side of town. His head cleared in the cold air and smattering raindrops. He had driven in worse condition.

The same boys hovered in front of Gamble's, throwing stones at a stray dog. The dog yelped a pitiful cry, and someone yelled out from the apartment window above the store. The boys ran across the street toward Nels.

"Get home." Nels slurred his words in spite of his best efforts. "It's going to storm."

"Go home, boys," they mocked in slurry voices, and imitated Nels staggering with the crutches.

They must be the juvenile delinquents the newspapers talked about. Someone should take them in hand. Nels shook a crutch at them as his legs gave way. He fell in a heap. The boys gathered closer, taunting and teasing, the rain falling hard enough to make his back and shoulders damp.

"I'll call your pa," Nels said. "You're too young to be out so late."

"Can't, mister," the oldest said. In a flash of lightning, Nels saw his ragged clothes and gap-toothed grin. "He's fighting Japs."

"Then I'll call your ma," Nels said. Terrible for these children to be raised without their father. Growing up to be criminals.

"You won't find her. Works nights at the loony bin," the smallest boy said. "With all the crazies."

"Go home," Nels said. "It's late. Your ma wouldn't like it."

He fished three nickels from his pocket. "You boys help me into the truck and I'll give you this money."

The two older boys each took an elbow and pulled Nels to his feet, while the youngest boy pushed from behind. Nels staggered to find his balance, and grabbed for the door frame of the truck. They pushed him into the cab, tucked his crutches in beside him, and whooped and hollered down the empty street, holding their nickels gripped in their hands. Nels tried to imagine George running wild at that age. He shook his head. Damn war. They weren't bad boys.

Nels gunned the motor and ground the gears, lurching out into the empty street. He must be drunker than he thought. The truck swerved across the middle of the street, and it took all his concentration to turn at the main road. He yanked the steering wheel to the right, as the rain fell in great sheets. In his confusion, he slammed on the foot feed instead of the brake.

The truck lurched up on the curb and smacked into a walnut tree, right in the middle of the parsonage lawn.

"God no." Nels moaned, and rubbed his head where he had bumped against the steering wheel. He had to think. He gathered his wits, and turned off the motor. Lights flickered in the windows.

The parsonage. Of all places for a crack-up. He opened the door and pulled himself out of the cab, pulling the crutches into position. He rubbed his bum leg to loosen a cramp of pain. No real damage though it was too dark to see well. A bent bumper for sure. A broken headlight.

"Are you all right?" Pastor Hustvedt charged out of the house wearing a striped bathrobe and carrying a flashlight. "What happened?" Nels held up an arm to shield his eyes from the probing beam.

"Sorry, Preacher. Nothing to worry about," Nels said. He straightened his spine and kept his voice steady. "I slipped on the wet road, that's all."

"Nels Carlson," Pastor Hustvedt said. "Is that you?"

Nels searched his mind for something to say that would explain why he was out so late and smashing into walnut trees. A strange hissing sounded. Pastor Hustvedt must have heard it, too, because he turned the light to the front of the truck where the tire flattened into a slab of flabby rubber.

Good God, and not a new tire to be found at any price. What would Olga say?

Tillie Stenerson

TILLIE STENERSON LEFT THE DISHPAN, swiped her hands on her apron and lunged toward the ringing telephone on the wall by the door. Two longs and a short meant a call to the Carlsons. Everyone knew Olga had been poorly all winter. Maybe the doctor calling.

Tillie picked up the telephone with great care, holding the receiver down with her finger as she lifted the ear piece, releasing the receiver ever so gently to prevent the click that trumpeted a listener on the line. She stood on tiptoe to get closer to the receiver, and pressed the phone to her ear.

Then the tea kettle shrieked from the kitchen stove.

"Rubbernecker," Nels Carlson's voice roared through the receiver. "Get off the line!"

Tillie hung up, and hurried to the stove, tripping over Irene's dollhouse and stepping on Punky, the orange cat. Punky yowled louder than the shrieking kettle.

"Hush now!"

Tillie scooped up the cat with one arm and turned off the gas with her free hand. At least Nels wouldn't know who it was. Eight neighbors shared the party line.

Tillie needed news to share at tomorrow's appointment at Fern's Cut & Curl. She always planned topics ahead of time to fill awkward gaps in the conversation. She bounced the cat on her hip, and worried as she poured boiling water through a strainer of used tea leaves into her favorite mug. It brewed a weak cup. She liked it that way.

With all the shortages of recent years—first the Depression and then war rationing, Tillie learned how to get along on less. Underwear sewn from old flour sacks never wore out. The children complained about Red Mill Flour stamped across the seat of their drawers, but it faded in time. She rendered chicken fat for cooking. Stacks of smoothed brown paper collected on the kitchen shelf for reuse. She balled every bit of string. Tin cans had a million uses. By skimping on little things, Tillie enjoyed a few luxuries along the way. The beauty shop was one of them.

How she loved having her hair shampooed and styled by Fern Hauge every Friday. While she sat in the stylist chair, Tillie felt beautiful and important, as lovely as she had felt on her wedding day ten years before. With her hair done, she no longer felt invisible. Well worth the expense—at least in her mind.

Tillie stirred in a half teaspoon of sugar and splashed a little cream from the ice box, still holding the cat. Punky meowed, and Tillie poured a bit of cream into the dish on the floor beside the stove. "Good kitty." Punky dropped to the floor with a thud of paws.

Tillie took a sip of tea before diving into the stack of dirty breakfast dishes. She looked out the kitchen window to make sure the kids weren't dawdling on their way to school. She glanced at the clock. She was right on schedule.

Punky rubbed against her legs as Tillie scrubbed dried egg yolk off a plate. Tomorrow's appointment filled her mind. She might tell how the minister's drawers flapped at the front of the clothesline for all to see, his wife not having the decency to hide them behind a row of sheets or towels. Bernice said that Mrs. Hustvedt rarely did her wash before noon. To think she would be so lazy in spite of having no outside chores. Bernice even witnessed Mrs. Hustvedt buying store-bought jam at Rorvig's Store. And all those lovely plum bushes behind the parsonage! But Mrs. Hustvedt was old news. She was a city woman who didn't know better.

In a pinch Tillie supposed she could discuss war news, but people were tired of it. Everyone just wanted the boys to come home. Last week they discussed Vera and Clyde's engagement, and Tillie's suspicion that

Tia Fiskum was secretly in love with Clyde. All old news. No one cared about stodgy old Tia.

Tillie poured scalding water over the clean dishes in the drainer, and looked toward the telephone. It wasn't polite to rubber. Her mother had taught her that. But maybe they were still on the line. She lifted the receiver again. Bingo!

Olga was speaking to her grown daughter, Lilja, who was married to a storekeeper in Underwood.

"Are you sure?" Lilja's voice choked.

"That's what the doctor said."

Tillie waited for more, hardly daring to breathe, but their conversation switched to the Norwegian language, a sure sign they knew someone was listening. Tillie hung up. The juicy news out of reach. Her parents had insisted they speak only American growing up. Knowing a little Norwegian would surely be handy sometimes.

Something was desperately wrong with Olga. Dropsy? Heart failure? Polio? The possibilities were endless. She could telephone, of course. She had known Olga all her life, and was related to Nels. Their grandmothers were sisters making her and Nels second cousins. Better to drop by, casual like, maybe bring some *sweet soup*.

Tillie looked with distaste at the horsehair sofa, the patched rocking chair, and the dusty upright piano in the front room next to the kitchen. If only she could spruce things up with a new rug or curtains. The place felt gloomy as a tomb in spite of the electric bulb hanging from the ceiling. It looked nothing like the parsonage with its bright colors and blue davenport. She grabbed a dust rag and bottle of furniture polish from beneath the sink. After she dusted the furniture, she reached for the broom and swept cobwebs from the corners of the high ceilings.

If only they lived in town. She would enjoy a life of ease like Mrs. Hustvedt, getting the wash out by noon if she felt like it. Buying jam and to heck with the plum bushes. If she lived in town, she would join a canasta club, maybe help with the local 4H. Her three kids would attend town school, and walk home for dinner break. She wouldn't be home alone all day with only the cat for company.

She looked toward the phone again, anxiety rising in her chest. Tillie lifted the receiver but heard only silence. "Darn."

"Is that you, Tillie?" Gertie, the switchboard operator said.

"Sorry," Tillie said, and her ears burned at being caught on the wire. "Just remembered Olga Carlson has an appointment with Doctor Sorenson. I'll try later."

"Her appointment was yesterday," Gertie said. "It's a shame, isn't it? I could ring her up but she's probably taking a rest now before dinner."

Tillie hung up in humiliation. That Gertie! Rubbering on the phone all day and getting paid for it. Why even the switchboard operator knew more about her cousin's wife than she did. The frustration made her let loose a stream of Norwegian words sometimes spoken by her father when he had thought he was alone. She didn't know what the words meant, and she couldn't ask without looking foolish, so Tillie only used the phrase when she was alone and in great agitation.

She scrubbed and peeled potatoes and carrots. A rooster, killed and dressed yesterday, roasted in the oven for dinner. Of course, Clarence heard the news on the mail route, but he didn't talk about his work. Didn't talk much at all.

"I won't be contributing to the rumor mill," he often said.

The rumor mill. The very idea made her teeth ache. She saw herself as a vital cog in the township chain of communication. She opened the oven door and poked the raw vegetables around the roasting bird, sprinkling salt and pepper, then drizzling melted fat over the browning skin.

Tillie tied a kerchief around her hair, and slipped into an old sweater hanging in the entry. If she hurried with chores, she'd be ready to leave right after the noon meal. But as she stepped toward the door, she decided to check the line once more. Sometimes Gunda Olson and Ingeborg Hanson avoided rubberneckers by setting a time when each would pick up the receiver without going through Gertie. Tillie learned about their scheme a while back when she tried calling Bernice Hegdahl about the Pentecost Dinner and discovered the two friends already in conversation—in spite of the fact that Tillie had been in the kitchen baking pies, and hadn't heard their ring. It was a brilliant idea, but Tillie figured it out.

Caught them again! She almost salivated into the mouthpiece. She hoped for something worth bringing to the Cut & Curl.

"Isn't it terrible?"

"Couldn't be worse."

A tickle rose in Tillie's throat. She felt a sneeze coming on. She held her nose in an attempt to stop it, but was too late. A huge explosion burst out of her.

Dead silence. The conversation resumed in Norwegian. Tillie hung up in disgust.

She considered her dilemma, as she lugged water and feed to the hen house. Their farm, taken over from Clarence's parents, had a beautiful barn and decent outbuildings. They had started out with fields under tillage, fences up, electricity installed in the house and basic farm equipment bought and mostly paid for. They were in good shape compared to most, but the drought and now frozen war markets set them back.

If she were single, she would join her friend, Nedra Johnson, used to be Ingvalstad, at the Ammunition factory in the Twin Cities, or travel to California shipyards like Nedra's parents. They made good money. It wasn't fair that farmers were held back while others profited from the war.

Tillie gathered the eggs into her apron, holding the corners into a loose bag. She had already picked the eggs once, but wanted a full case. She needed the money for her hair appointment.

Tillie checked the telephone line again before she washed the eggs, but found it silent. She cooked fresh coffee, and laid the table as Clarence pulled into the yard, brakes squealing and door slamming. He pulled off his coat and hat, hanging them in the mud room.

"Smells good." He rubbed his hands together, and reached for the coffee pot. "Chicken?"

She nodded, and bit back the burning question. She mustn't appear too eager. It was best to ease into the subject.

Clarence poured a cup of coffee, holding the icebox door open with his hip as he searched for the cream pitcher. Punky meowed, and he poured a bit into the saucer on the floor.

Tia asked about the weather, and if he had seen any ducks or geese in the river. Tillie knew her husband appreciated wildlife. They talked a few sentences about a mallard and babies walking across the road by Tolga Lutheran Church.

Tillie's question burned in her throat, an almost physical sensation, like the pressure building up before the sneeze earlier that morning.

"Any news?" The words released the pressure.

Clarence looked at her with what she interpreted as disappointment, and mumbled something that sounded like nothing. Tillie swallowed a hard knot.

What was wrong with them? Clarence had once been the best looking boy in Tolga Township with his thick curls and flashing eyes. He danced the *Halling*, winning prizes and ribbons everywhere. Now he was bald like his father, and carried an extra paunch over his belt. The job with the post office meant early milking before the mail route. He couldn't stay awake after evening chores long enough to read the newspaper or listen to the radio. He didn't do anything but work and sleep. He withdrew even more after her miscarriage last summer—when she needed him the most.

It had been a hard spring. First her mother's death, and then morning sickness. Then there had been that pesky Fuller Brush man who started coming around. At first she admired his jet-black hair and confident manner, maybe even encouraged him to stay a few minutes longer than needed after she paid for her order. But then, he started coming real often. Scared her almost to be alone in the country with a strange man who was somehow too familiar. She told him to go away and not come back.

She never told anyone, not Clarence, or even Fern at the Cut & Curl. It was too embarrassing to admit that she might enjoy a harmless flirtation.

Tillie helped Clarence as much as she could, but farm chores never ended. Milking cows morning and night, feeding the calves, cleaning the stalls, caring for the chickens, cutting wood, and now all the spring work of plowing, picking stones, spreading manure, planting, cultivating, haying, and then harvesting. And the never ending washing, ironing, cooking, baking, gardening, canning, sewing, cleaning, and caring for their three children.

She hadn't known it would turn out this way. She felt as trapped as the chickens in their coop or the cows in the stanchions. She had imagined a life with Clarence like town people enjoyed: well behaved and beautifully dressed children, family time at the picture shows or State Fair. She thought she and Clarence would work with the 4H program, vacation to California, visit Duluth and fish off the North Shore.

Life was passing them by. Randolph already nine, Irene seven, and Dickey in first grade. She had miscarried the terrible day of Pearl Harbor and then again during last year's wheat harvest. A bitter taste filled her mouth.

* * *

THE NEXT DAY at Fern's Cut & Curl, Tillie told Bernice Hegdahl, who also had a regular Friday appointment, that Olga Carlson stood at death's door.

Bernice looked with skepticism, a wordless reminder of the embarrassing mix up concerning Mrs. Petterson. Last spring, Tillie thought Mr. Petterson told his sister in Evansville, that his wife had died. How was Tillie to know he spoke of his horse? She had never known a horse named Sweetie and everyone knew Lucinda had the cancer.

Hair dye dripped down the sides of Bernice's face and onto the *True Story Magazine* in her lap. She wasn't a young woman, and the black dye did not soften her gaunt features. "Hope it's nothing catchy."

"Well," Tillie said in a conspiratorial tone. "Maybe it is. They whisper about it only in Norwegian—must be something terribly embarrassing." Then a flash of inspiration. She didn't know if she dared say it out loud. It might backfire and cause trouble. Bernice looked at her expectantly, and Fern peeked out from behind a hair dryer to listen. Tillie felt the pressure building up within her. She tried to hold back, but the words burst out of her.

"Nels has a wild side, you know." Tillie spoke slowly to accentuate the drama, drudging up the ancient history about Nels taking up with a barmaid in Elbow Lake. Tillie embellished a few critical details. "I hope Nels didn't bring something home—you know—something embarrassing." She licked her lips and winked a slow dramatic wink. "You know—to his wife."

Bernice sat up ram-rod straight, and dropped the magazine. "Oh, my God," she said. "I've read about that." She dipped her head toward the magazine on the floor by her feet. "I heard that Sylvia Anderson, you know, Stinky's wife, the one who works at that road house over by Elbow Lake. Well, I heard that Nels Carlson . . . you know . . . liked her." She mopped her face with a wadded handkerchief leaving black stains on the white fabric. "Why, my sister saw him out late at night with someone who looked like Sylvia." She dipped her head again in a quick nod. "And Olga such a saint."

Tillie's conscience zipped a sharp pang. "I don't know for sure, mind you," she said. But it was too late.

Clarence always warned that loose lips sink ships. She pursed her lips as tight as they would go.

* * *

"Gunda Olson is throwing a wedding shower for Clyde and Vera this Friday," Clarence said. He dropped their postcard on the kitchen table along with the light bill. "Sent invitations to half of Tolga Lutheran—going to be at the Hanson place. A surprise."

Tillie's mind whirled a mile a minute thinking what dress she would wear, what they could give for a gift. "At least my hair will be done."

She telephoned Bernice Hegdahl for the details. Bernice had talked to Ingeborg Hanson who had spoken to Gunda Olson.

"Gunda says they're having it at the Hanson's so the young couple won't suspect," Benice said. "I can hardly wait!"

She told Tille everyone was to bring a plate of sandwiches, a hotdish, or pickles to share. Bernice would bake a layer cake but asked for contributions of ration stamps or sugar for the frosting.

Tillie was hardly off the phone when Gunda called. Tillie almost swooned when Gunda asked her to be in charge of decorations.

Tillie loved to decorate, and still had leftover pink and white streamers from the Root golden wedding the year before. Her kids could make paper bells to hang around the table, and use lilacs and lily of the valleys from her yard in a centerpiece. Thank God they were in bloom.

"I've asked the men to toast the couple with old Norwegian sayings," Gunda said. "It's something we used to do before folks got so American. Be sure and tell Clarence to come prepared."

Tillie hemmed her best dress. *Farm Wife Magazine* advised readers to show patriotism by wearing shorter skirts. At Fern's Cut & Curl they talked of nothing else. Clarence's sister would babysit for the kids. Clarence milked the cows an hour earlier than usual so Tillie would arrive in time to decorate.

Clarence and Olaf ambled off to the barn to take a look at the new calves with a stern warning from Ingeborg to come inside when the company came.

Tillie climbed on a dining room chair and draped streamers from the light fixture over the table. Ingeborg's was the nicest house in Tolga Township. Tillie ogled the sliding French doors, and chandelier with four light bulbs. Not a speck of dust anywhere, and she got a good look from her perch on the chair.

Ingeborg must have stayed up all night getting ready for the party. Tillie would have liked a look at the back stairway but didn't know how to ask without appearing nosey. The stairway, patterned after a North Dakota bonanza farm where Ingeborg had worked in her youth, was the talk of Tolga Township. A grand staircase led upstairs by the front door, but a smaller one connected the pantry with the second story.

Tillie fixed a large crepe-paper bell at the bottom of the light fixture to hang directly over the lilac centerpiece. Tillie clambered down and twirled the pink and white streamers before pinning them to the four corners of Ingeborg's best linen tablecloth. The flowers filled the room with a glorious perfume that almost covered the odor of manure wafting in through the open window.

"How did you keep the party a secret?" she said as she pinned the last streamer.

"Invited Vera and her parents for supper and sent Clyde to pick them up." Ingeborg chuckled. "Gave him strict orders not to bring 'em 'til seven o'clock. Said I was poorly and had to rest." She broke out into a hearty laugh. "Never sick a day in my life, but he fell for it."

Tillie stepped back to admire her work. The bell from the chandelier hung in perfect proportion to the vase of flowers beneath it. She sprinkled a few lilac petals around the vase. It was perfect.

As good as any town woman. And to think it hadn't cost her a penny. She used the leftover streamers, flowers from her yard, and pins from her pincushion. It just proved a person could better herself if she tried.

Tillie finished hanging smaller paper bells and streamers around the sewing machine where the gifts would be displayed. She hoped someone would ask who did the decorations, smiling to think of the comments that would surely come.

Ingeborg greeted guests at the front door: Gunda Olson and her son, Julius; Nels and Olga Carlson; Harvey and Blanche Root with Eddy in tow; Pastor and Mrs. Hustvedt; Selmer Moberg and Mildred; Beryl and Bernice Hegdahl; Hannah Fiskum and Tia; Elmer Petterson; Vera's parents; Vera's cousin who would be her maid of honor; Clyde's cousin who would be his best man; and Mansel and Ada Jorgenson. Ada's sister agreed to stay with Minna to give them a night out.

Tillie cringed when Ingeborg moved the lilacs to the side to make room for Bernice's three-layer cake. The cake, decorated with chocolate icing and small paper parasols, upset the balance of the table décor. The cake should have been placed to the side of the flowers instead of the other way around. Tillie looked for a way to change it back, but didn't dare. Ingeborg was strong minded, and heaven help the one who crossed her. The aroma of egg coffee filled the house along with smells of soap, sweat, and cow manure. People were laughing and talking about crops and weather.

A mound of gifts piled on Ingeborg's sewing machine. Tillie grimaced as Harvey Root deposited a large box on top of a paper bell. Women bustled to arrange the *smorgasbjord* on the sideboard where most of the guests would eat cafeteria style. Tillie laid the dining room table for the wedding party and close relatives using Ingeborg's best china, a lovely white pattern with a silver rim. She saw an opportunity to move the flower arrangement back to the center of the table, but when she picked it up, she was interrupted by Ingeborg.

"You're right," Ingeborg said with a cluck. "It's too big for the table. Move it into the front room."

Tillie's mouth dropped open. Only city women appreciated decorations. Instead she moved the vase, an arrangement as beautiful as something out of a magazine, to the sideboard beside the napkins and silverware. It wasn't a perfect location, but at least everyone could still enjoy it.

To her relief, Tillie saw that Ingeborg didn't notice.

Tia filled a tray of fancy glasses with Olga's dandelion wine, and her mother's chokecherry wine. The men gathered in the front room and talked war news, weather, and crops.

Clyde and Vera finally came walking hand-in-hand into the house amidst whistles and well wishes.

"What's this?" Clyde said.

"Surprise!" everyone shouted. Clarence pulled Tillie aside into the front room.

"Nels wants to talk to us after the party," Clarence said in a hoarse whisper. "Looks sober as a judge. Said to meet him out by the silo because he doesn't want Olga to know."

Tillie's heart dropped. Bernice must have blabbed. Even though she was Nels's second cousin, she could expect no mercy. Nels said what he thought, and wasn't afraid to hold a grudge. Why, oh, why, did she open her big mouth? She was sunk. If Nels didn't kill her, Clarence would.

"What's it about?"

"How should I know," Tillie said with a shrug. "I have to help in the kitchen."

Only Tia Fiskum stood in the pantry, slicing dill pickles into a cut-glass serving dish. She wore an old-fashioned navy-blue dress that reached half way to her ankles. The Old Maid of Tolga Township looked the part with her long hair wound in braids around her head, and lack of lipstick. Tia looked downright grouchy.

"Need some help?" Tillie said, feeling young and stylish in her shortened skirt and red lipstick.

Tia shook her head and barely looked up.

"Any word from your brother?" Tillie said.

"Still at the Army Hospital in Ohio," Tia said, never looking up from the pickle dish.

Tillie folded a dishtowel lying across the back of a kitchen chair and placed it on the side of the sink. Then she straightened the chairs around the table and checked the coffee pot on the stove. Finally, she grabbed the broom from the corner and pretended to sweep the already-clean floor. Gunda stuck her head through the swinging kitchen door.

"Come, girls. We're ready to start."

Gunda seated the honored guests around the table. Vera Hanson's face glowed, and Clyde looked happier than Tillie had ever seen him. He draped his arm around the back of Vera's chair, and leaned in to whisper in her ear. She giggled and looked at him as if he were the most wonderful person in the world. Even Ingeborg and Olaf looked relaxed and hopeful.

Julius passed the wine tray, a toothpick hanging out of the corner of his mouth as usual. The remaining guests gathered close around the table, standing in a big circle. Tillie made it a point to stand as far away from Nels as she could.

"Before we eat, we'll toast the happy bride and groom," Julius said in a booming voice as he used his toothpick to point at Clyde and Vera. He was usually so soft spoken. Why, he could be a preacher with that voice, or a politician. She had always thought him too shy to speak in public. "And only in Norwegian!"

"How will we know what they say?" Tillie blurted out. She couldn't help herself. It was a handicap, not knowing the language shared by so many.

"Each will toast the bride and groom," Julius said, "and provide the translation. We'll drink together after the last salute."

The room quieted, everyone looking at his neighbor, no one volunteering to be the first. Julius nodded encouragingly at the minister.

"*Ver sikkert paa aa svare om kjaerleiken banker paa.*" Pastor Hustvedt raised his glass. "When love knocks, be sure to answer."

Mansel Jorgenson leaned over and slapped Clyde on the back. "You be listening for that knock, now. It comes night or day, so be ready."

Harvey Root guffawed and elbowed Nels in the ribs.

"*For kvinner er den hoegste tilstanden ektestanden.*" Julius raised his glass. "For women the highest state is the married state."

"That's for sure," Harvey said. "Keep them pregnant and barefoot."

The men snickered and winked, nudging and jostling like school boys, while their wives cast dirty looks in their direction.

"*El aerleg knoe er ein skatt som varer,*" Olaf said, and raised his glass to his soon-to-be daughter-in-law. "An honest wife is a treasure that lasts."

"Thank you," Vera said, with a demure laugh. Long hair curled over her shoulders and her high forehead with its widow's peak reminded Tillie of Ingrid Bergman. Vera's front teeth showed a small gap that made her pretty and sweet.

Olaf pulled his wife over and kissed her wrinkled cheek. "I ought to know!" He kissed her again. "I found a good one."

Ingeborg turned bright red and pushed him away. Everyone laughed.

"*Nei*, enough of that!" she said. "There's no fool like an old fool."

"*Aldri saa klein ei kraake at den ikkje vil ha ein make,*" Nels Carlson said while balancing on one crutch and holding his glass with the other hand. "There never was so bad a crow that it did not want a mate."

"Are you calling my bride a crow?" Clyde raised his fist in mock anger and pretended to get to his feet. "You'll answer to me behind the barn."

"*Nei*," Nels said. "Not talking about your bride, Clyde, but you!"

The men hooted and women giggled. Tillie felt Nels's icy stare turn her way, and she tried to duck behind Tia in the corner.

Clarence raised his glass to the couple but looked at his wife. "*Den som giftar seg blir glad for ein dag; den som slaktar ein gris blir glad for eit aar.*" He paused a long moment before translating. "Who gets married will be happy for a day. He who butchers a pig will be happy for a year."

"You ought to know, Clarence," Nels said.

The room erupted into raucous laughter. Tillie felt her cheeks flame. So that is what he thought of her. After ten years, it had come to public humiliation. Lately, she worried about how unhappy she felt. She never considered that Clarence might feel the same.

"We can't top that one so let it be the last," Julius said. "Let's drink together, good friends and neighbors. Join in wishing Clyde and Vera the best of luck and many happy years together. *Skaal!*"

They emptied their glasses with a great smacking of lips. Tillie had chosen Olga's prize-winning dandelion wine. It tasted bitter in her mouth.

"And a baker's dozen of children," Olaf said with a grin. "All boys to help with the farm."

Vera giggled, and Clyde kissed her straight on the lips in front of everyone. The men whistled and stomped with lewd and whispered remarks.

Tillie tried to remember how it felt to have an adoring bridegroom. It had been so long ago. She looked for Clarence, but he was talking to Eddy Root in the entry way. Nels flashed a cold stare. Her knees wobbled. If only she could sneak away.

Julius clanged a spoon on his glass, and asked the minister to say grace.

Pastor Hustvedt led in singing the table prayer in a high and quavering tenor.

The melody died out, and Gunda signaled for Tia to begin serving the head table. Julius motioned for Pastor and Mrs. Hustvedt to start through the buffet line. Someone had moved the vase of lilacs to the floor in the far corner. An ugly chipped crock of pickled beets replaced it. Tillie felt too worried to care.

* * *

AFTERWARDS, CLARENCE and Tillie headed out to their truck parked behind the silo. She desperately looked for a way out of what she knew would be an awkward confrontation. Nels followed with his crutches. As soon as they were out of sight of the house, Nels turned to Tillie.

He leaned so close she could see the hairs in his flaring nostrils. "I have something to say and I want Clarence as witness."

Clarence stepped back a half step leaving her exposed to Nels's anger. A chill went through her, and she crossed her arms.

"Olga has breast cancer," he said, and Tillie thought she heard his heart pounding. "It's killing her." Maybe she heard her heart beating. It was hard to tell above the sudden roaring in her ears. "It would destroy her to know the filthy and low thing you said." He choked and swallowed hard. "How could you kick her when she's down?"

"Tillie." Clarence said in a sharp voice. "What did you do?"

She couldn't meet his gaze, couldn't find the words to explain. Cars pulled out of the driveway, people shouted good-byes. Loons called from the lake. Mosquitoes whined around her head. Eddy Root scurried out of the hay barn carrying baby kittens. Tillie stood mute and helpless before Nels's rage.

"And Lilja. Think of our daughter." Nels's neck corded as he repeated the conversation from the beauty shop, a few juicy details added along the way. "I heard it from the barber who heard it from his cousin." He looked at Tillie with disgust. "The barber said Stinky Anderson beat

43

the shit out of his wife when he heard the rumor at the feed store in Elbow Lake." His words felt like hammering blows. "I hardly know Sylvia. She has nothing to do with Olga's cancer."

It was like a bomb dropped. When she dared peek at Clarence, she saw a vein throbbing in his temple, and his hands clenched into fists. He had never laid a hand on her in all their years of marriage, and she had a sudden fear he might follow Stinky Anderson's example. A wave of nausea cut through her, and she felt her breath sucked out of her lungs.

"How could you?" Clarence's lips curled in disbelief. "Apologize."

Before Tillie could say anything, Nels interrupted.

"No apology," Nels said, in an icy tone. "It would only make it worse."

Tillie felt caught like a rat in a trap. Her loose lips had sunk her. "I'm sorry . . ."

"*Rasshoel!*" Nels spat toward her feet, and spittle lobbed on her shoe. He had such hatred in his face that she stepped back, and raised her arm to ward off a possible blow.

"We want nothing to do with you. If you come to the house, I'll sick the dog on you. If you telephone, I'll shove it down your goddam throat. God help you if I catch you rubbering." He took a breath. "If you so much as look at Olga or mention her name to anyone . . . even to the preacher . . . you will regret it." His shoulders shook. "She deserves better than this."

Her mouth turned to dust. She felt like a guilty prisoner hearing the sentence.

"And when she passes," he took a sharp inward breath, "don't show your ugly mug at the funeral."

"You're right. I'm sorry . . ." She fumbled for the words that would make it go away.

"I'll show you sorry." With that he stomped away, poking his crutches into the dirt with every step.

* * *

CLARENCE DIDN'T SPEAK on the way home. Didn't look at her. He took his pillow and slept in Dickey's room where they kept an extra bed. In the days to follow, he ate his meals, did his work, and kept his normal routine except that he didn't speak to Tillie at all. Didn't touch her. Each day seemed longer than the day before, and such heaviness settled on Tillie's chest, that she worried about TB.

She stayed home from the Ladies' Aid meeting on Thursday, telling Bernice Hegdahl she had a cold. She spent a lot of time holding the children, reading books to Dickey, teaching Irene to embroider, and all the while trying to think of a way to make amends.

Bishop Fulton Sheen spoke on the radio about finding absolution at the confessional. There was no denying she was in the wrong. She had hurt Olga and Nels, even Stinky and Syliva. She was a terrible person. She didn't dare speak to Pastor Hustvedt.

If only she could find a Catholic church and talk privately to a priest. The nearest was miles away.

On Friday, Clarence finally spoke. She had been ironing Dickey's good shirt, and looked up in surprise at the sound of his voice. Her heart quickened. Maybe he was done being mad, and they could go back to the way it used to be.

"You'll not use the truck today." His voice sounded easy, like it used to sound when he loved her. She still loved him. Loved the way he did his work, so meticulous and steady. Loved the way he carried little Dickey in his lap while he drove the tractor in the field.

"You going someplace?" Her voice came out too eager, and she tried to tone it down, tried to be casual—like a town woman would be in a similar situation.

"Nope. Cultivating corn in the south field." He made eye contact and she saw the anger in the clench of his jaw. "You're not going to the beauty shop anymore."

"What?" Her head struggled to figure out what he was talking about. "I always go on Friday."

"You're going to cancel today's appointment and next week's and every week."

She smelled something burning, and lifted the iron from Dickey's shirt where a scorch mark the size and shape of the iron branded the fabric.

"Me or the gossip. You choose." His words came out faster then, like a river of hate pouring out of him. He stepped nearer. "You go back to that goddam gossip parlor and I'll divorce you."

He fairly spat out the words, words she never dreamed would be said in their home, words that were only spoken in other people's marriages, in town people's marriages.

"You can't be serious," Tillie said. She couldn't be hearing right.

"Out on your ear. You'll lose your kids and everything you have." His words like pummeling fists. "I'm tired of being the laughingstock of this township."

"You have no grounds." Divorce. The word rang worse than the Norwegian word Nels had called her, far worse than the swearing her father used.

"Oh, don't I?" Clarence said. "You like rumors so much? I heard one last year you might like." He sniffed and hitched up his suspenders. "Heard the baby you lost last summer wasn't mine. Belonged to some goddam Fuller Brush man who came by when I was on the route. Beryl Hegdahl said he saw the car coming by real regular last spring."

"It's a lie." Sobs welled in her chest.

"In my own house," Clarence said. The agony in his eyes broke her heart. "How could you? He blabbed at the Foxhome Tavern. Bragged to Mansel Jorgenson that I'd be surprised when a little black haired eye-talian baby was born into our family.

"I didn't . . ." To think people would say such terrible things about her and their little baby, the baby they wanted so much. "You have to believe me."

"You know how it is." He reached for his barn coat, and headed toward the door. "People always believe gossip over truth."

"What's wrong?" Randolph and Irene stood in the doorway. "Why are you fighting?"

Tillie felt a pain rip through her chest. Her legs turned to wooden stumps, and her tongue thickened. "Sit up to the table, children, and have some cookies." She put the jar on the table, and followed Clarence out to the porch, careful to close the door behind her so the kids wouldn't hear.

"You have to believe me." Tillie's knees shook until she thought she might tumble over. Divorce. Her children growing up in a broken home. It couldn't be happening. "I would never do that to you."

He looked at her for a long time.

"Don't you see how hard you make it for me?" he said. "I've lived here all my life, rub shoulders with these people. I can't pick up and move away. I've got a farm to tend. How can I face them when you keep everyone stirred up like you do?"

She hadn't really thought about it before. She hadn't considered how her actions affected Clarence, or her children. Her marriage.

"I don't know why I did it," she said. "I've felt so lost and sad since the babies . . ." She couldn't go on. "But I would never . . ."

They stood on the porch as the mourning doves cooed in the shelterbelt built along the north side of their driveway. Their song usually cheered Tillie, but today it seemed more like a funeral dirge. A cool wind blew across the field and Tillie felt goose bumps raise on her arms. Dark clouds gathered in the west, and it felt like rain moving in.

"I've made such a mess of it."

"You sure have." Clarence took a deep breath. He leaned against the porch railing and stuck a toothpick in his mouth. "My parents warned me, said you'd never be satisfied on the farm. Said you'd be my downfall."

She had always known his folks didn't like her. Had always felt that she didn't measure up, even though their criticism remained unspoken. Bernice said Clarence's folks had wanted him to marry Tia Fiskum. Maybe Clarence would take up with Tia once Tillie was out of the picture. Maybe he already had.

Tillie knew a few divorced women, stylish dressers, loose maybe, working out of the home and named *grass widows*. Worse yet, she had known children without both parents.

"Think of our kids," Tillie said, mopping her face with her twisted handkerchief. The sobs so strong she could barely speak. Clarence loved his children more than anything. "Who will take care of them when you are on the mail route or out in the barn?"

"I've been thinking about them," Clarence said. He pulled the toothpick out of his mouth and jabbed it toward her like a pointed finger. "All year I've kept my mouth shut thinking it best for the kids. But then this whole thing with Nels. I can't live like this."

He stepped off the porch and headed for the machine shed, his long strides covering the ground in big gulps. Tillie knew he would go out in the field, do the chores and then sleep.

"Wait." Tillie followed, almost running to keep up to him. It wasn't just the beauty shop, or her gossip. "We need to talk."

"Work to do," Clarence said, not turning around or slowing down. "Seems there's been enough talk."

"I won't go back to the beauty shop," Tillie said, touching his arm. He slowed down and didn't pull away. "But I have to do something. I can't just sit at home waiting for you to finish the work that never ends."

"What do you mean?" Clarence stopped and looked at her. "I'm working myself to death for you and the kids. I can't do any more."

"You're a good man," Tillie said, feeling for the words to explain how she felt. "But the kids are in school and I get lonesome out here all by myself." She might as well lay it all out on the table. "I'll give up the beauty shop, but I need something from you, too. Maybe we could join a card club or work with the 4H." She pulled in her breath and searched his face for a sign that he heard what she was saying. "Bowling or square dancing. Anything."

He pulled the toothpick out of his mouth, and stuck it in his shirt pocket. A burst of wind puffed through the trees and rifled her apron. Thunder rumbled in the west.

"I've ruined everything." Tillie swallowed choking sobs. It was too late. She saw it in his face. Knew his stubborn streak once he made up his mind about something. She had destroyed her marriage. It was her fault.

"You've really done it this time, Tillie Girl," he said.

He pulled a handkerchief from his pocket and handed it to her. Then he turned and headed toward the tractor.

Norman Fiskum

THE STIFLING GREYHOUND pulled to a stop in front of the Minneapolis Bus Depot. Norman Fiskum pushed back his army cap and licked dry lips at the thought of a cold beer.

He had enjoyed a seat to himself since Cincinnati by pretending to sleep sprawled across both sides of the upholstered bench. In spite of his thirst, he would not risk his seat by running inside for a drink. The last thing he needed was some nosey old hen beating her gums all the way to Tolga Township.

He would face enough questions from Tia and his mother once he got home. Besides, he had known thirst before, and could hold out a while longer. A runny-nosed, skinny kid paused by his seat. Pale blue eyes beneath red hair sprouting in all directions. He wore bib overalls with a patched knee and was barefoot. He must have been about twelve or thirteen and reminded Norman of kids he had known from his childhood.

"You getting back on the bus after the stop?" Norman said.

"Yup." The boy looked at Norman with suspicion. "What's it to you?"

"Want to earn a nickel?"

Norman tossed the boy a quarter. "Bring me a bottle of cold pop and all the candy this will buy. I'll give you a nickel when you come back."

The boy brightened and shoved his way out the door along with other passengers. Everyone in America looked so well fed. He had forgotten their easy affluence and their casual way of speaking. And he had forgotten how short the skirts were being worn during war-time. He eyed a tall blonde wearing a sequined hat and tottering down the aisle on high heels. As she passed, he noticed one nylon seam meander across the back of her calf like the winding Rhine River.

Norman reached for his canteen, and tipped the last swallow of tepid hooch into his mouth, tapping the bottom to drain every drop. The bus already felt hot as a hayfield. The drink burned his throat until sweat beaded on his upper lip. His own stink mixed with the diesel fumes drifting through the open windows. He rubbed his stubbly chin. Gone three and a half years, and now it seemed as if he would never get home.

Norman hung his head out the open window and counted the trees around the parking lot. He had learned to do this in the prison camp, and though he never admitted it to anyone, not even to the headshrinker at the army hospital who signed his discharge, Norman credited counting trees with keeping him sane. He had counted the date palms at the Tunisian oasis where he had been captured. He counted the trees around the holding camp in Italy and the German prison camp in Poland. By night he had dreamed of the thousands of seedlings he had planted with the Civilian Conversation Corps back in Minnesota before the war. He blamed the weight of those heavy water buckets for stretching his arms well below his cuffs. He had counted the trees during the death march across Germany. Too many damn trees to count during that "shoe leather brigade."

He eyed five evergreens and a straggly oak beyond rows of jalopies and dirty buses clustered around the depot. An elm towered higher than the others. He rested his eyes on its leafy branches before turning his gaze across the street where four box elders, two flowering crabs, and a dozen lilac bushes grew alongside a wooden fence and a metal gate.

Norman hated gates. He hated locks. Most of all Norman hated Germans. The Italian guards were almost human, but the Nazis were sadist pigs.

He sat down and pulled his cap over his eyes with shaking hands. He stretched across the seat as passengers filed into the bus. He needed another drink to steady his nerves. The shrink advised deep breaths when the memories became too much. All around him soldiers and civilians jostled suitcases into overhead racks. A baby cried. It grew even hotter. The air filled with the sickening smell of stale tobacco, cheap perfume and unwashed bodies.

"Shove over, Mac," a gruff voice said.

From under his brim, Norman spied a noncom on crutches who wore a starched uniform splendid with stripes, ribbons and patches. His rotten luck to end up with a gimpy NCO breathing down his neck.

Norman started to move but the gimp had already taken the seat behind him. Almost immediately an older woman with a whiney voice asked about the soldier's injuries. Listening to them converse was almost as bad as making small talk himself. It seemed they believed the war was over. Fools. Lots of fight left in the Pacific even if Hitler had swallowed his gun.

Norman roiled with a sudden burst of anger toward the woman and the noncom and the stupid Bosch who allowed a lunatic to ruin the world. For a brief moment he wished he still believed in God. It would be a comfort to think Hitler burned in hell.

Norman had once believed the teachings of Tolga Lutheran Church. He kept his faith through the Dirty Thirties when drought stole their crops, and killed his father with dust pneumonia. Norman prayed during the landing in North Africa. He prayed when he was captured by those sonofabitches, for all the good it had done. But by the end of the war, the Nazi bastards had driven the faith out of him. How could anyone believe after being marched across Germany, starved, gone without water, given no decent clothes in sub-zero temperatures? Norman saw too many good men slaughtered like so many hogs to market. No one could believe in God after that.

The boy pushed back onto the bus, and shoved an icy bottle of Hires Root Beer into Norman's hands with a sack of candy: Necco wafers, Bit-O-Honey, root beer barrels, a black licorice whip, and a Hershey bar. How long it had been since he had eaten his fill of candy? He downed a quick swallow of root beer, savoring the sweet fizz, and pressed the sweaty glass against his neck. The boy's face split into a grin when Norman tossed him the coin. "I almost got you a Baby Ruth but the Hershey bar was bigger."

The bus engine coughed and backfired. Norman flinched and gripped the pop bottle until his knuckles turned white. It sounded like an exploding *schu* mine. He struggled to remember the name of the guy in Tunisia. He couldn't recall his face, only his gushing stump and anguished screams. Norman squeezed his eyes to block out the image, and counted from memory the trees that lined the lot next to the Veterans Hospital. He willed his lungs to breath and heart to slow. He drained the bottle and stored it on the floor to return for a deposit, pleased to remember this detail. Maybe there was hope for him yet. He opened the Necco package and popped a purple wafer into his mouth, savoring the taste of cloves as his thoughts turned toward home and the trees planted along the driveway on their Otter Tail County farm.

Norman had filched the seedlings from the CCC the day he was called home for his father's funeral in 1937. He read the telegram telling of his father's death and strode out to the storage barn at the camp where he helped himself to a gunny sack of Chinese elms and balsam fir. Norman had never stolen anything before, and was surprised at how easy it could be. No one questioned him, not even when he climbed aboard the truck heading into town where he would catch the train for home.

Immediately after the funeral service, Norman grabbed the old spade and headed to the driveway. It was an open spot where winter winds roaring in from North Dakota always plugged the road with drifted snow. Chinese elms grew almost as wide as they were tall, and were the best defense against eroding winds. Norman loved the smell of balsam fir and the way they stayed green year round.

He had not even changed out of his church clothes, but tossed his suit coat across a fence post. He would plant three rows, taking great care to make the rows straight and precise, envisioning how they would grow into a shelterbelt to last long after all of them were buried in the churchyard.

Clyde Hanson joined him that sweltering August day, although Norman had not asked. The afternoon sun blazed and tormented, but the labor felt a solace after the morbid morning at the church, and was far better than sitting in the house with the crying women folk. Together

52

they toted water from the windmill, a bucket for every three saplings. By milking time they were black as coal miners, but the little trees stood proudly among the horse tail weeds and wilting blue stem grasses.

They shook hands before separating to do their evening chores. Norman had no words to thank his closest friend but nodded his gratitude. Such gestures made up the language of farmers. Words seemed unnecessary between lifelong friends and neighbors.

Norman had threatened Tia with bodily harm if she didn't keep the trees alive while he was in the army. Norman often thought of that shelterbelt and had written home asking about its survival more than once. Neither his mother nor sister answered his questions. Maybe they didn't get the letters, or the censors had thought the information dangerous to national security. Maybe the trees had died in spite of Tia's promises.

"May I sit?" A girl's muffled voice with the musical lilt of his Scandinavian people jarred him from his thoughts. "It's the only seat."

Norman jerked his feet over to his side and curled against the window with closed eyes as the bus lurched forward and merged into traffic. His luck had run out, and he dreaded the polite conversation required of him. Maybe she would leave him alone if he pretended to sleep. He reached into his candy bag keeping the rustling to a minimum and pulled out a Bit-O-Honey. He would suck on it to make it last longer. It was as if his body could not get enough food. Starvation did that to a man.

He drew a deep breath and tried to think of something positive. The headshrinker had advised him to make the best of things. At least he was on the home stretch, only six hours until Tolga Township. He would make the trip bearable by pretending Vera Sonmor sat next to him. If he didn't look at the girl's face, he could pretend.

Daydreams of Vera had kept him going. His guts still ached from the sawdust bread that chewed up his insides. Prison camp food was bad enough but that march . . . Norman had willed himself to survive by pretending that Vera would be heartbroken if he died. He made it somehow but emerged thin as a ghost, barely a hundred pounds. He knew he was one of the lucky ones.

Although he'd added a good ten pounds at the hospital, Norman was still skin and bones. When he looked in the mirror, he was startled to see feathers of gray hair above his brown eyes. He was an old man at twenty-eight. Old and beaten down and used up, like their old mule after the dust storms.

Vera once held his hand while returning change at the grocery store in Dalton. That was before he shipped out in '42, but his hand still burned when he thought of it, and his face warmed remembering how she smiled up at him. He had fallen in love that very minute.

They'd exchanged few letters. It was all pretend but still a kick in the belly when his mother wrote of Vera's wedding to Clyde Hanson. Clyde had enough sense to stay on the farm instead of enlisting. And he was smart enough to make his move on Vera while Norman was gone. The draft dodger. The low-life. Clyde lived it up while others did his share, while good men lost their lives.

The woman beside him sniffled. Norman pulled closer to the window. Then her sniffling turned into great gulping sobs.

Norman cringed. He hated a scene. He pulled a clean handkerchief from his pocket and peeked out of the corner of his eye. Then he stared with both eyes wide open. He knew her. Nedra Ingvalstad had attended the same one-room school. Their farms were only a few miles apart. Norman's father had been confirmed with her mother. In Tolga Township everyone knew everyone.

God, she looked terrible. Nedra's hair carried a ghastly yellow hue and pulled tight from her pale face until her freckles popped large as kernels of corn. She was skinnier than he remembered and her face, though not beautiful, had a chiseled look that might be considered handsome. She wore a drab skirt and blouse, ankle socks, and sturdy shoes. A smell of cordite clung to her and Norman realized with a start that she must work at the ammunition factory. His mother had written about her marriage to a carpenter from Fargo. Sure enough, a wedding band gleamed on her ring finger.

Norman groaned. If he acknowledged her, he would have to be polite the rest of the way home. He fingered the handkerchief and tried to ignore her heaving shoulders.

Poor Nedra. She had always been gawky. One year she knocked over the Christmas tree at the Sunday School program. Luckily, Mansel Jorgenson stood handy with a bucket of water, or the church might have caught fire from the candles. Nedra's face turned first red when everyone stared, and then white when she realized she had ruined everything.

Someone must have died. He didn't want to know. People looked their way and whispered. He couldn't stand it. Norman held out the handkerchief.

"Here, Nedra."

She grasped the handkerchief and covered her face. Norman slumped back into his seat and counted the trees along the highway, his daydream of Vera more out of reach with each mile closer home.

They drove west into the glaring sun, leaving the hazy smog of car exhaust and clamoring traffic. Norman breathed a sigh of relief as they left the outskirts of the city and Nedra's sobs subsided. The corn crop looked decent and farmers were making hay, must be a second crop, maybe third depending on the rains. He hoped they appreciated it after so many droughty years. But of course, they would. Everyone across the country had suffered during the Great Depression.

Black-and-white Holsteins trudged single file toward red barns. Farm kids manned vegetable stands along the roads. Large wheat fields spread like golden carpets. It looked like a bumper crop this year, maybe thirty-five bushels to an acre. Of course, he was not close enough to finger the kernels or chew them into sticky gum. He imagined the nutty flavor of ripe wheat. He put another Necco wafer into his mouth and counted the apple trees in a roadside orchard until the bus left them behind. Pheasants scurried in the ditches. A gray cat streaked across the road and a red fox looked at them from the ditch.

For the first time Norman realized he was really going home. He could go wherever he wanted, eat when he was hungry and change his plans at a whim. He reached for a root beer barrel. The quack had said everything would fall into place once he got back home.

A stab of conscience reminded him of his situation. He couldn't stay in Tolga Township as his mother expected. He couldn't take over the family farm that had been his grandfather's dream. He couldn't bear the thought of living next door to Clyde and Vera. Their marriage felt too much like failure.

Nedra kept her face buried in the handkerchief though her shoulders no longer shook. It was a relief. At the St. Cloud Bus Depot, Norman returned the empty bottle and bought more candy, as well as an extra Salted Nut Roll and Coca Cola for her. She didn't thank or acknowledge him but took a sip of Coke and pressed the cold bottle to her face. The candy bar lay on top of her purse in her lap.

"Are you all right?"

She nodded without looking at him. He couldn't tell if she recognized him or not. Maybe the war had been harder on him than he knew, changing him from the boy who had left, returning him as a stranger.

Darkness settled though it brought no relief from the oppressive heat and humidity. A baby wailed at the back of the bus. A sailor snored in the front, his head resting on the shoulder of a buxom woman wearing a big hat. Heat lightning flickered on the western horizon. A woman declared her aching bones predicted a coming storm. A man across the aisle said that a soaking rain would be a welcome relief to farmers with corn coming into the milk stage.

Norman's head bobbed awake, and he wondered how long he had been sleeping. He had been dreaming about the march again. He wiped his mouth and hoped he hadn't called out in his sleep. The doctor said nightmares were normal and would pass in time. The Underwood water tower stood in the glare of the headlights. They were almost home.

"Do you smell it?" Her voice startled him and at first Norman thought she was asking about the odor of cordite on her clothes. "Black dirt and growing things." A boom of thunder and a jagged bolt of lightning shot through the night.

He felt his composure slip away with the crescendo of thunder and stabs of lightning. Like mortar fire. Fat drops splattered on the windshield and fell as a hammering deluge on the metal roof. A sheet of cold rain surged through the windows as they turned south towards Dalton.

Then a great swooping wind blasted inside just as he jerked the window up. Cold water drenched him. He wiped his face on his sleeve. His hair dripped water. It felt good. Like breathing the cold air of January after being stuck cleaning the cow barns.

"Oh, no," the woman behind him whined as ice bounced off the glass. "My cousin lost his wheat last year to hail."

The bus crawled along the gravel road, its feeble headlights probing a small path to follow through the night. The roar of the storm drowned their voices. Norman couldn't recall if the skies had looked funny before darkness fell. Usually before a tornado the skies turned a strange yellowish-green. It would be just his luck to be killed by a twister when he was two miles from home.

The bus finally slowed and squealed to a stop. He and Nedra gathered their things and moved toward the front of the bus. Rain poured out of the sky. Thunder boomed.

The bus driver opened the door and closed it with a snap. He looked at Nedra, then at Norman and back at Nedra. "You gonna be all right, ma'am? The Dalton Hotel's open—you could telephone for a ride from there."

"It's a short walk," Nedra said with a voice barely heard above the storm.

The driver glared at Norman as if he were an axe murderer and cranked open the door with seeming reluctance. They stepped out into the deluge. Lightning crashed and in the brief illumination Norman saw Nedra splashing through a puddle, wrestling her heavy suitcase with one hand and shielding her face with the other, heading west toward her parents' farm which was a good mile off the main road, over the hill behind the Olson farm.

Norman paused. He knew these roads like the back of his hand and could navigate his way anywhere he wanted, even in the darkness. Gunda Olson and her son would welcome them with open arms if they sought refuge at their house. Hell, he'd be lauded as a war hero. The thought sickened him.

The Carlson place directly south of the Olson's showed a light. Perhaps Nels was up tending his wife. Ma had written she was doing poorly. Clyde Hanson lived directly across the road from the Carlsons to the east. Their house sat in a hollow down a long driveway. Norman's home farm lay beyond Clyde's farm farther east toward Tolga Lutheran Church, in the opposite direction of the Ingvalstad home. The closest path home for Norman was through Clyde's fields.

"Your folks know you're coming?" Norman raised his voice loud enough to carry above the rain. Nedra was already ten rods down the gravel road. The sensible thing was to bang on Nels's door and seek refuge until the storm ended. His light was on, and it would be less of a bother. But Nels would have questions—questions about Tunisia, his prison years, polite but still nosey. Nedra didn't seem anxious for questions either.

Norman made a sudden decision and ran after her, grabbed her suitcase while balancing his duffle bag across his shoulder. "Better run before we drown."

They cut through the corner of the Olson hayfield and across the pasture. The flashes of lightning showed the worn path across the hummocks. Norman's shoes and trousers squished water and rain dripped off the brim of his cap. He was surprised how weak he felt. The headshrinker had promised that good food and familiar surroundings would make him normal again. Norman no longer remembered what normal felt like.

Nedra's teeth chattered, and it seemed she was crying again. It was hard to tell in the rain. By the time they reached the dark Ingvalstad farmhouse, he felt the rain slow to an icy drip. His legs trembled and the muscles of his back relaxed as he set the heavy suitcase on the sidewalk. Thunder growled to the east as the storm moved away from Tolga Township.

Nedra tripped up the porch steps, and Norman reached to steady her. She shook off his hand. As the moon peeked through the dissipating clouds, it cast enough light so that Norman saw her kneel and fumble for a key under the door mat. She spent a long time fitting the key into the lock.

He had never known anyone in the township to lock his house. He doubted his ma owned a key. Norman followed Nedra into the house and waited as she searched for a lamp. Everything smelled musty and stale. No dog greeted them. Even without a light Norman could tell the place had been empty a long time.

Norman searched his pockets and came up with a lucifer. He struck it on the door jamb and in its flickering flame saw the ancient cook stove, the kitchen table, wood box, and limp curtains hanging at the windows. He lit the wick of the dusty kerosene lamp. A mouse scurried under the stove. He slapped a draping spider web away from his face.

"Where are they?" He thought maybe her parents had died. He steeled himself for her answer.

"California—working in the shipyards."

She shivered and slumped into a chair by the table. Norman turned the damper of the stove and lifted the lid to the firebox. He fished for kindling from the wood box and dug out an old newspaper with a bold headline, "BATTAN FALLS TO JAPS." The smell of burning wood filled his nostrils. A rusty dipper hung on the wall alongside an ancient coffee pot.

"I'll fetch some water," he said. "You better change your clothes."

When he returned, he saw that Nedra had not moved from the table. She stared with blank eyes when he offered her a dipper of water. Her teeth chattered and she spilled most of it. He had seen soldiers in shock during the war.

"You have to get out of those wet clothes before you catch your death."

She didn't move or look at him. Water pooled around her feet from her dripping clothes. She looked like the muskrats he used to pull out of the traps on Stalker Lake. He added another stick to the fire while trying to figure out what to do.

He could only imagine how she might act if left alone without food, car, or telephone. An almost-empty *Postum* jar sat on the table alongside salt and pepper shakers shaped like miniature beer bottles. *Hamm's* stamped over the *S* and *P*. *Postum* would be better than nothing, although Norman would have rather had the *Hamm's Beer*. He set the coffee pot on the stove to heat and went looking for blankets.

Norman pulled a quilt off the bed in the downstairs bedroom. A picture of Nedra's grandparents hung on the wall. Most likely their wedding photograph since they were young and smoothed-skinned. Their faces stared back in frozen solemnity, as if knowing the hardships that lay ahead of them. He remembered them from his childhood as stern pioneers, gnarled and crippled from the back-breaking work of wresting a farm from the wilderness. Once Old Man Ingvalstadt had given him a peppermint stick and called him a good boy for helping his father tend the graves of his grandparents on Decoration Day.

But Norman knew that Old Man Ingvalstad had a mean streak. Some folks said he was the one who turned in poor Eddy Root to the sheriff, sending Dumb Ed to the Fergus Asylum.

In the closet, Norman found a ragged nightshirt that must have belonged to her father. He handed it to Nedra. "Take off your wet clothes and get into this."

She didn't answer, and he didn't know if she would have sense enough to follow his directions. He led her by the hand into the bedroom and set the lamp on the dresser. "Change your clothes while I make Postum."

He should change, too, before he caught pneumonia. He searched his duffle for his driest uniform. It was stinky and wrinkled but it was the best he had. When he got home he would burn all his uniforms. He hurriedly changed behind the cookstove. No sign of Nedra. The stove smoked and he adjusted the draft.

He'd give her a little time. He added more sticks to the firebox. A quart of popcorn seeds stood all alone on an empty shelf. His mouth watered as he measured kernels into a metal popcorn popper on the shelf and placed it over the hottest burner. Soon the sounds of popping corn filled the room with a homey rhythm. He dumped the popped corn into an old metal roasting pan, sprinkled it with salt and pushed a handful into his mouth. Nothing had ever tasted so good. He shoveled it in as fast as he could swallow, and then forced himself to slow down, and set aside a small dish for Nedra.

He yanked opened the kitchen window and breathed the rain-washed air. Whippoorwills called from the yard, and bats dipped and soared against the light of the waxing moon. Complete silence except for night birds and crickets. By God, it was beautiful. He had been around the world and never once saw anything like the rolling hills of Tolga Township. Here the prairies met scattered patches of hardwood forest. Lakes and sloughs reflected blue sky. Tolga Township's black dirt could grow anything. The light blinked out in the Carlson house. He counted the trees in the Ingvalstadt grove.

He had just decided to check on Nedra when she came out of the bedroom with her hair wrapped in a towel. The nightshirt dragged almost to the floor. She wore a pair of gray wool socks with holes in both toes. She was pale and her lips were blue but she no longer shivered.

He draped their wet clothes over the wood box. Nedra didn't speak and he couldn't think of anything to say. Instead he poured hot water into cracked cups and sprinkled Postum. "Eat. You'll feel better."

To his surprise she obeyed, nibbling a kernel of popcorn and taking a small sip of Postum. She looked every bit as miserable as when she had knocked over that Christmas tree.

"I should be getting home." He wished he had a stiff drink before facing his mother. He imagined the way her face would crumple when he told her he wouldn't be staying to take over the farm. Liquor would make it bearable. It was five miles to the nearest town—too far to walk.

"Don't go yet." Tears welled in Nedra's eyes, and he feared she would start in again with the weeping. He couldn't take it if she did. He sat on his trembling hands and pulled up the memory of the trees at the Cincinnati hospital. He counted them over and over in his mind. First the six arbor vitae and then the four flowering crabs. Then he counted the three hickory trees and the row of fifteen elms along the street, remembering how at suppertime the hickory bark had reflected the sunlight.

They sat at the table until Norman's eyes drooped. It had been a long day and the worst lay ahead. He looked at Nedra and fully intended to tell her that he had to leave. She dozed in her chair with her chin resting on her chest. No harm would come from waiting a little while longer.

Nedra cried out in her sleep and jerked awake. She looked around with wild eyes and slipped from the chair to the floor as if in slow motion. She didn't pull away when he helped her to her feet.

"No, not Steven." She twisted her face and tears gushed from her eyes. "He's gone."

Steven, the carpenter from Fargo, no doubt killed on some God-forsaken battlefield.

The newspapers were filled with news of the Philippines and the sinking of the *Indianapolis*. He didn't want to know where Steven died.

Without thinking he scooped her up into his arms and carried her to the bedroom. She was as light as a wet bird, her bones hollowed with grief. He gently laid her on the bed and pulled a blanket over her amidst squeaking springs and clouds of dust.

"Hush now," he said in the soothing voice he used with injured lambs or new calves. "Rest yourself."

She clutched his arm. "Don't leave," she called out in a panicky voice. "Please."

He sat on the edge of the bed, but she pulled him closer. He knew what his mother would say about him staying with Nedra longer than necessary. He knew what Nedra's parents would say about him being in her bedroom, what Pastor Hustvedt and the people at Tolga Lutheran would think.

She looked so pathetic. "Please." He hesitated before stretching out beside her. He didn't get under the covers. She clutched his hand and fell asleep almost immediately but Norman lay awake for a long time. He should be home looking at the shelterbelt and answering his mother's questions about the war.

Once Nedra woke up and called out, clutching at him wildly, like a drowning person struggling to stay afloat. He thought she had fallen asleep when she spoke again. "I don't remember his face."

"You must have a picture."

"In my purse," she said. He could hear the relief in her voice.

Norman crept from the bed to more squeaking springs. He fetched the lamp from the kitchen table and placed it on the dresser. The unopened candy bar lay inside her purse alongside his soiled handkerchief. He found her billfold and held it up to the lamp light. A few folded bills. A rattle of coins. A ration card and an identity card for the New Brighton Ammunition and Artillery Factory. A weathered photo. Steven smiled up wearing a big smile and his Marine cap and uniform. *To Nedra With All My Love* scrawled across the bottom in a strong masculine hand. Norman swore under his breath. He handed the picture to Nedra. She kissed it and pressed it to her heart.

Norman lay down beside her again and dozed. Just before morning, he woke to find his head resting on her chest and both of her arms around him. He realized with horror that he had awakened her with one of his nightmares. She rocked him back and forth, patting his back and kissing his head. "It's all right," she said. "It's over now." He tried to pull away but she stopped him. "You're home now. Everything is all right."

She was crying. He felt her tears on his face. He reached up to wipe them and realized they were his.

The next time he woke up it was the full light of day. A rooster crowed in the distance. His throat felt dry as Tunisia. It took a moment to remember where he was. Nedra was gone. His cheeks flushed to remember how he had slept beside her, how he had lay on her chest. Somewhere far away a tractor's engine sounded. He went into the kitchen, blowing out the lamp as he passed the dresser. The smell of kerosene mingled with the dusty smell of the house.

In the kitchen, Nedra knelt beside her open suitcase, still wearing the night shirt. Her feet were bare. She had discarded the holey socks. It was already warm in the kitchen, and a pot bubbled on the stove. She held Steven's photograph in her hand. The candy bar lay on the table, divided in two.

"You had a nightmare," she said calmly. "Do you remember?" Then she raised her face and looked directly at him and pointed to red marks on both sides of her neck. "You grabbed me. I thought you were going to kill me."

Norman looked in horror at the imprints of his hands still visible. "I'm sorry." He wasn't well enough to leave the hospital in spite of what the doctor said. He should be locked in a loony bin somewhere. He dropped onto a kitchen chair.

"Who is Milton?"

Milton Torgerson. His face bloomed clear in Norman's mind. Milton laughing as he shot craps with Nebraska Bohunks on the troop ship.

Norman sat on his hands, the ones that hurt Nedra, the reason she had held him during the night. He thought to care for her and she ended up taking care of him. He was the wreck. He was the ruined one. They looked at each other for a long moment without speaking as the sound of a tractor drew closer.

"Some things have no answers," he finally said. What he meant to say was that the world was a ruined mess without sense or reason. He had learned that only too well in the chaos of war, and the stupidity of governments and armies. But what he meant to say and finding the words to say it were two different things entirely.

"I didn't care if you killed me," Nedra said at last in a quiet voice. "Let me be done with this misery."

"You can't think that way." Norman thought of all the platitudes he might say that were supposed to make her feel better. They never worked. They didn't work for him.

"We were going to come back to Tolga Township after the war," she said at last, and pushed a lock of hair behind her ear.

In the distance a dog barked. The tractor rumbled louder and Norman looked out over the fields. The corn waved in the breeze, tassels like flags above the green leaves. He didn't see anyone.

"What will you do?" she said.

He imagined the hundreds of times that same question would repeat over the next weeks. He had practiced with the psychiatrist. He knew what he should say. But the words wouldn't come out.

"Don't know," he lied. "Have to figure it out."

"Take over your mother's farm?"

He flinched and gripped his hands into fists that dug into the underside of his thighs. "Maybe."

"You're lying." Her voice was quiet and practical. Unsentimental. "You called for Vera."

Norman's heart sank. It was worse than he thought. "Battle fatigue, the doctors call it." He counted the trees outside the kitchen window. Three box elders, the same number of years he had spent in prison camps. The number of months they were marched across Germany in the cruel dead of winter.

"Vera Sonmor from Dalton?" Nedra said.

"She married someone else." It felt good to speak it aloud. It was as if a weight lifted off his back. Not exactly the full weight, but a small bit of weight lifted. He took a deep breath and lifted the cup to his mouth. His hand trembled only a little.

"And you?" he said. "What now?"

"San Pedro to stay with my parents," she said as tears filled her eyes. "We were hardly married, only a week before he shipped out." She wiped her eyes on the sleeve of the night shirt. "Nothing to show for it."

A tractor roared over the hill and stopped in front of the kitchen door.

"I can't go to the door in my nightdress," Nedra said with a worried look, and Norman realized how it would appear to a stranger. They would be the gossip of Tolga Lutheran.

"Get dressed," Norman said.

Julius Olson stood on the steps. He pulled a toothpick out of his mouth when he realized who Norman was.

"Norman?" He reached out a grubby hand. "Well, it sure is good to see you home again. What are you doing here? I saw the smoke from the chimney and thought I better come over and chase the bums away."

"Came last night during the storm." Norman noticed Julius's eyebrows shoot up in a questioning manner, as he stuck the toothpick back in his mouth. It was a stupid thing to say as the Fiskum place would have been no farther from the bus stop, only in the opposite direction.

Nedra came out of the bedroom buttoning the last button on her blouse. Her hair was combed back from her face and she was barefoot.

The only trouble was that her blouse was buttoned wrong and she looked thrown together.

"Hello, Julius," she said. "Thanks for stopping but everything's fine."

Julius scratched his head and took the toothpick out of his mouth, using it as a pointer to point first to Nedra and then to Norman. "You're together?" And so it begins, Norman thought, the country way of ferreting out every detail, of fitting the pieces together and fueling the gossip machine at the merest hint of impropriety.

"Nedra's husband was killed in action." Norman's words sounded harsh to his ears, and he winced for Nedra's feelings as he spoke them. "She just found out yesterday and by chance we met on the bus coming home. She needed help carrying her suitcase."

That was the way to handle the gossips. Everything up front in a straight forward way that eliminated the need for further questions.

Julius clucked his tongue and sighed. "Sorry to hear it." He stuck the toothpick back in his mouth, as his blue eyes filled with sympathy. He was a tall man, and slim. A shadow of blond beard covered his lower face and his clothes were clean, though patched and worn. Julius and his ma were decent folks, hard-working. Widow Olson would know what to do. The neighbors would reach out to Nedra with a helping hand. Folks would ask a million questions, but when push came to shove they would do everything they could to help one of their own.

Nedra sniffed and reached for the handkerchief.

"I'm heading home now," Norman said. "She shouldn't be alone."

"Come," Julius said to Nedra. "Ride with me on the tractor. Ma will help you figure it out."

Nedra gave Norman a hopeless look and nodded. She turned to gather her suitcase. Norman saw the red marks fading on her neck. Julius left to unhook the hay mower after first explaining how he planned to begin another cutting soon as the fields dried. Norman pulled the damp clothes off the chair and stuffed them into his duffel bag. Nedra stood with her suitcase.

"The worst part is telling someone," Nedra said at last. "After that, it's not so bad."

They walked outside and Norman pushed her suitcase up to Julius and helped Nedra climb up behind the seat.

"Hang on tight," Julius said in a voice louder than the tractor.

Nedra hung on with both hands. She didn't say good bye but as the tractor bounced down the lane she looked back at him and mouthed, "Thank you."

She didn't wave.

Norman squared his shoulders and hoisted his duffle bag over his shoulder. Only a wisp of smoke came from the Ingvalstad chimney. The air smelled as fresh and clean as only a Minnesota morning after a rain could smell, like the world was washed clean again. The heaviness of yesterday's heat replaced with a lightness that felt hopeful and new. Robins hopped across the yard looking for worms and orioles trilled from the grove. Across the cornfield came the sounds of a barking dog and mooing cows. The gentle coos of mourning doves sounded from the lilac bushes. The grass glistened in the morning sun and light reflected off the standing puddles from last night's rain. A few broken branches scattered across the yard.

Tolga Township was about as far from North Africa, Poland, and Germany as one could get. He would burn his uniforms before his mother could decide to use them in a quilt or other such nonsense. He sniffed the stinking bag. He would burn the duffle, too. By the end of the day there would be nothing left to remind him of the war. At home, Tia would be milking the cows, and his mother making real coffee. If he hurried he would get there in time for breakfast.

Eddy Root

WORMS CRAWL IN THE WET GRASS next to the milk house and talk to me in wiggly voices. Dumb Ed they say want to go fishing?

I rub my hands together and dance a little jig. It's early before breakfast and Ma says I can squirt milk at the barn cats after I'm done milking. Pa is too old for heavy work now. Ma is old too and sometimes falls over her own feet. It isn't funny but sometimes I laugh. She has trouble making her tongue work. Ma says that I'm a good boy though I'm fully grown and not a little boy anymore.

Here kitty. I splash through mud puddles to the barn and the cat comes running. A whole bunch of robins chase the worms in the grass and fly away because of the cat. They have pretty red bellies and look a little bit fat. Come to Dumb Ed I say to the kitty and hold it close enough to hear its engine rumbling.

I look back to make sure Pa isn't listening. Pa and Ma never call me Dumb Ed. My name is a joke. Old Man Ingvalstad called me Dumb Head at the Sunday School picnic when I was little. He wasn't Old Man Ingvalstad back then but only plain Mr. Ingvalstad. He was real mad because I picked flowers off the graves. Nels Carlson thought Mr. Ingvalstad called me Dumb Ed. That's because my name is Edward. People laughed and call me Dumb Ed ever since.

Pa doesn't like the joke. Pa says Mr. Ingvalstad was a nosey sonofabitch. He says I won't be dumb if I work hard and keep out of trouble. Pa says if he ever hears me call myself dumb he will take the belt to me though I am bigger than he is and Pa is so old he has to hang onto the door frame to stand up.

The night crawlers talk the whole time I do the milking even though I holler out the door for them to shut up. The cows say Pa is too old for fishing. They say it but I think if I have a can of worms Pa might change his mind like he did before.

I squeeze a tit and squirt a long stream of warm milk at the cats' little faces. They twist their mouths and stretch tongues and lick all over. The cows laugh with funny moos, and Bruno our rat terrier dog dances on his hind legs until I squirt him in the face too. Then I strain the milk into the cream can and set the lid. Ma wants me to hurry because she has to run the separator before Pa takes the cream to Dalton.

On the way into the house I see the worms wiggling and set the can of milk on the ground so I won't spill it and kneel in the wet grass to smell them. I put a few into my bib overall pocket for fishing. They slide all around and stretch like rubber. Bruno yips and jumps up and down. His tongue is soft and wet, and he smells like rotten eggs. That reminds me of the chickens. I run to fetch a bucket of feed. On the way back from the granary I find a piece of old rope lying in the weeds by the coop.

The rope talks to me. I drop the pail, and the hens swarm over the spilled feed pecking at my feet and flapping their wings. I don't like mean chickens. The rope talks again, and I leave the bucket and the mean hens and drag the rope behind me like a big snake. It leaves a slithering trail in the wet grass that sparkles. This makes me laugh, though I peek over my shoulder to make sure Pa isn't watching. He says I am too old to play around like a little boy.

It's a snake. I grab the end of the rope and run out to the gravel road dragging it behind me. Bruno nips my heels. The barn cat chases the rope, batting its wiggly end and hanging on for a ride. The faster I run the more the rope snake wiggles.

I don't notice the man walking toward me from the Ingvalstad pasture until Bruno barks and growls to protect me.

Hush the man says. You've got a different dog. What happened to old White Dog?

I stop and eye him. Short hair frizzes around his forehead and out of the top of his shirt where the buttons hang open. He's skinny and wears a soldier's cap like the one in the newspaper picture hanging on our wall. Ma says the picture is my cousin from Fairbault, and he won a medal for being a hero. This isn't my cousin but he looks like someone I should know.

Don't you remember me? The soldier drops his bag on the road.

I worry it might squish the worms. Don't be scared I whisper. It's all right.

It's me Norman Fiskum home from the war. He breathes hard like he has been running and his white face is sweaty though it's not even hot yet. You know me.

The worms tell me it can't be Norman because he used to be a little bit fat in his tummy. This soldier man is skinny like a snipe and his nose sticks out a long way. I get ready to run away. But then Norman smiles and I know it is him because of his broken tooth.

Playing with the rope?

I shake my head. Pa doesn't like me playing. Then the worms wiggle in my pocket and I hold a few in the palm of my hand.

Going fishing.

Norman helps me gather night crawlers until my pocket fills to the top. He wants to know about Ma. I tell him she is holding her own. That's what Ma always says when folks ask. She is always nice to women-folk who ask how she is even though Pa calls them nosey bitches.

With Norman right there in his army clothes, the worms don't talk. They are afraid of him I think but I'm glad they're quiet. Pa says he'll whip me if I talk back to worms or crows or any other critters. I can say come boss to the cows and sic 'em to the dog and here kitty but that's all. He says not to talk to the chickens or the birds. He says people will think I'm crazy and send me back to the Fergus Asylum. I don't want to go back there. Some of them white coats are mean as snakes.

Nightcrawlers is what Norman says and time on my hands and my old rowboat on Stalker Lake. He lets out a long sigh. Good to be home.

The worms tickle and I tell Norman how White Dog died and Bruno is our new dog. He kills rats and eats paper. Norman has been gone a long time. I helped him plant trees along the cemetery fence a long time ago and helped him dig the grave when Old Man Ingvalstad died. Norman never calls me Dumb Ed though it wouldn't matter because it's a joke. Willy Moberg is too dead to come back from the war. His grave stone is at the cemetery but he didn't need a hole because his body is in the ocean.

Sometimes I am real smart. Even Ma says so. Norman says he is coming from the war but he comes from the Ingvalstad's.

Is the war at the Ingvalstad place?

Norman tips his head back like one of the robins swallowing a worm. Instead of swallowing a worm Norman makes a loud and scary sound. Maybe he is laughing but I back away ready to run to the house.

No the war is far away he says when he quits making that sound. Across the ocean. His face goes from white to red. Just visiting at the Ingvalstad's.

I look up the road half expecting to see the war come over the hill. I'm not sure what war looks like but Bruno barks at a flock of crows over the cornfield. Old Man Ingvalstad died a long time ago. Then I remember Jesus on Easter.

Is Old Man Ingvalstad still dead? I brace myself and get ready to run. I don't like that nosey sonofabitch. The grave flowers were pink and smelled sweet even though little ants crawled on them. The ants talked to me and told me to pick the flowers for Ma. But then that mean old sonofabitch came running out of the church.

Keep away from those flowers you dumb head or I'll give you a *chilliwink* you won't forget he said. He grabbed and shook me until my teeth rattled. Nels Carlson yelled for help and grabbed Mr. Ingvalstad around his ankles to stop him. Nels said help help real loud.

Pa said stay away from that mean old sonofabitch but it was hard because sometimes I helped him with getting up wood or cleaning barn or picking rocks or chasing cattle or something like that. He always gave me a pretty silver penny that I gave to Ma. She called me her good boy and kissed my forehead. I was glad to dig the old man's grave even though he was our neighbor and Ma says not to speak bad of dead people. Old Man Ingvalstad liked to wrestle.

Norman gets real quiet and shakes his head. No need to worry. He looks me over and takes a cigarette from his pocket. He won't be back. He strikes a match and sucks until smoke swirls out of his mouth.

What for you smoking now I say.

All soldiers smoke Norman says. The whole damn war runs on cigarettes. But look at you—your hair turned gray. How old are you now?

Norman asks the hardest questions. Run away a crow caws overhead. One time Mrs. Hegdahl asked my age and when I answered three she nearly laughed her head off. Pa says she's a nosey old bitch and tells me to stay away from her. He says I should never answer a question with a number answer. He says something else I should say but I forget what it is. Pa is real smart.

Then it comes to me. I remember. Old enough to know better I blurt out in a stream of words so fast it sounds like swearing. Pa says I can remember if I put my mind to it. It must be a good enough answer because Norman doesn't laugh at all.

I've got to get going. Norman gathers his pack and smiles a smile that shows his broken tooth and makes me glad he is isn't dead. Ma and Tia are fixing breakfast he said. Can you smell the side pork?

I sniff the air like Bruno but can't smell a thing except a lake stink coming from the slough. That reminds me of the milk can sitting on the grass and Ma making pancakes. The pancakes tell me to hurry up. They talk louder than the crows and louder than the worms in my pocket. I turn toward the house but the rope yells my name. I go back for it. Wait I've got a present for you Norman says. He takes off his nice army cap and sets it on my head. Now you're a soldier.

If I hadn't been a dummy I could have been a soldier. That was the last war when Ole Stenerson and Nels Carlson went to France. Nels came back but Ole was too dead to come home. Thinking about Ole makes me sad but Pa says just forget about him because someday I'll see him in heaven. Nels hurt his leg in the war and has to walk with crutches.

That makes me sad too but everyone calls him the Potato King and his name is a joke too though I don't know what's funny about potatoes.

I want to give something to Norman too because he gave me his hat. The rope talks real loud when it sees what I am thinking and tells me it wants to stay with me. I reach into my pocket and pull a bunch of wigglers.

Norman looks at the worms and his eyes get red and his nose runs with snot. Thanks Eddy but you catch a fish for me instead. It's been a long time since I had a fish fry. Snot drips until he wipes his nose on his sleeve and he coughs a little cough. Use the old boat if it still floats.

Norman looks sad and I look at the rope. No he doesn't want me the rope says. It's time to eat.

Ask him the worms say when I'm half way across the ditch. The wet grass makes my pants wet around the bottom. Ask him the rope says and the crows too.

Ma calls from the house and I'd better hurry before Pa gets the belt. Pa gets mad when I talk about it because he says they'll send me back to the asylum but Pa is too far away to hear.

Norman I say. He is already walking down the road. The cap fits real good on my head. I yell out. Do you like to wrestle?

Not much Norman says and looks back with a wrinkled up nose like he is thinking real hard. Going to be wrestling matches at the County Fair next week he says. Saw a poster at the bus depot.

Norman starts walking again real fast. Pa says the fair is full of nosey sonofabitches and a good place to find trouble. He won't take me to the fair even if there is wrestling but he might take me fishing. The worms wiggle in my pocket and I hurry toward the house dragging the rope behind me like a big snake.

Harvey Root

HARVEY ROOT HATED HOT WEATHER. He hated the way August nights felt like a heavy quilt across his chest, robbing his breath. Not even a breeze stirred through the open windows, just sweltering heat and buzzing mosquitoes. Always hottest during haying season, this year, as the war was finally grinding down to an end, felt more oppressive than usual.

Harvey had been up most of Sunday night, August 5, first with the heat and then with the storm. There was nothing he could do to protect the crops from the weather, but it always made him feel better to be up and worrying, instead of trying to sleep.

His wife, Blanche, said he should pray instead. Harvey put no faith in superstitions. Besides, *boener flest gaar trass alt utan svar*, most prayers go unanswered anyway. He kept such opinions to himself, just to be on the safe side. It could be Blanche and Pastor Hustvedt were right, after all.

Last week, Harvey made another trip into town to visit Doc Sorenson about a cough that had plagued him all summer. Harvey worried he might be getting TB, but Doc Sorenson said it was his heart.

Harvey reached for his medicine bottle from the cupboard over the kitchen sink and poured a spoon of the bitter potion. He swallowed it down and slumped into a chair by the breakfast table. The truth was he was a dying man. He had lived a long life. Doc Sorenson warned him to get his affairs in order.

Easier said than done. The mortgage was paid off, thank God, but the crops were still in the field. He couldn't leave Blanche alone. And then there was Eddy.

"What's keeping him?" Blanche stood with the mixing bowl propped between the crook of her left arm and hip. She blew tendrils of gray hair out of her eyes and stirred a few times. She stopped to rest before stirring again. His wife, once the fastest runner at the school picnic, stumbled through life leaning forward like a rose in a vase. "Pancakes almost ready."

She wore a shapeless blue dress made out of flour sacks and a patched apron. He should have provided better for her. She should be wearing new dresses and have an easier life.

Harvey looked out the front window and saw Eddy shaking his fist toward the skies. No doubt talking to the birds again. "Good Lord!" Another day, Harvey might have laughed at the antics of his fifty-year-old son but not today. "You have to watch him every minute."

"Eddy don't hurt nobody." Blanche slurred her words since her stroke. "He's a good boy." She dropped a spoonful of batter on the sizzling griddle beside strips of side pork.

"We won't be here forever." Harvey felt a heaviness fill his chest, and his voice came out with a strange wheeze. "Then what happens to him?"

"You haven't talked to the judge." Blanche turned to look at him. Her hand reached up to pinch the loose skin at her throat like she always did when she was worried. "Like Pastor Hustvedt said."

Harvey stiffened his spine. Pastor Hustvedt was a nosey sono-fabitch who recently told him to sign papers so Eddy would be cared for after their passing. He said it bold and plain-spoken as if he were a blood-relative instead of a pissant preacher.

Pastor Hustvedt said to name Blanche's nephew as guardian to take over the farm and care for Eddy. As if Harvey would be so foolish as to turn his farm over to a town kid who spouted mechanization and modernization. Lordy, Lordy. War hero or not, Gordon Swensrud would not get his paws on the Root farm. Harvey and his father before him hadn't worked themselves to death building it up to turn it over to some egg head who would run it into the ground.

Besides, Gordon never paid the least attention to Eddy except to call him Dumb Ed and tease him about talking to crows and cows. No,

Gordon Swensrud would have nothing to say about Eddy's future, even if he was Eddy's only relative.

Eddy finally came into the house wearing an army cap and babbling about the war over the hill at the Ingvalstad place, of all the crazy ideas, and that Old Man Ingvalstad would come alive like Jesus at Easter. Blanche finally pulled it out of him that the cap came from Norman Fiskum. That's how it was with Eddy. You had to listen close to figure out what he was saying.

"Hush," Harvey said. "Eat your breakfast. There's work to do."

But Blanche egged him on by asking questions about Norman Fiskum and why he was coming from the Invalstad's instead of being home with his mother.

"He doesn't like to wrestle," Norman said as he slathered pancakes with butter and brown sugar and poured heavy cream over the top. "I've got worms for fishing."

The doctor had said Harvey needed to avoid all exertion, as if that was something a farmer could do. In recent years, Harvey had turned most of the heavy work over to Eddy, but his son needed constant supervision, or he would run off and chase ducks or some foolishness. Even the constant watching and bossing was getting too much for Harvey's failing strength.

They were down to a few steers for butchering and a hundred hens. Harvey sold off the hogs last fall and culled the dairy herd. The cream check from their few cows kept them going. He had thirty-five acres in corn just coming into milk stage, and a nice looking forty of wheat. Promising, but he had learned long ago to put no hope in a crop still in the field. Harvey didn't know how he would get the harvest in. Always before he had driven the team to cut the grain or pull the threshing machine, but this year he felt too weak to do it.

Nels Carlson, their closest neighbor and the one Harvey usually turned to for help, was down with a bad leg and a sick wife. The young men in the township were off to war for the most part, and the ones left behind had their hands full with their own crops. The thought came to him that maybe Norman Fiskum would be looking for a little work now that he was home again. Harvey had always liked Norman. Thank God he made it home alive.

Norman kept a rickety rowboat at Stalker Lake. If Eddy rowed the boat, there was really no work about fishing. Maybe after the chores were done and the back fence fixed. Last night's rain meant a day off from the hay field.

"Why should I take you fishing when you forgot to pick the eggs?" Harvey tried to look stern but softened when he saw Eddy's lower lip quivering. It was always hard to stay mad at him. "You know better. Your ma needs your help."

"I couldn't help it," Eddy stammered. "The worms talked to me—"

That did it. Harvey unbuckled his belt. "By God, I tell you and tell you, but you don't listen." He pulled off his belt with a snap, and laid it on the table. "Do you want a whipping? Go on about worms talking to you or birds or anything else and I'll take the belt to you." His voice lowered to a near whisper as a pain pushed under his chest bone. "Remember the white coats? If you talk about the voices, they'll send you back."

By then Eddy was blubbering like a baby. He promised he would be good, and wouldn't talk to worms anymore. Then he rambled about nosey sonofabitches at the fair, and how he wouldn't go to the fair even for the wrestling.

Blanche shushed him and kissed the top of his balding head. "You're my good boy." Her eyes glistened. "That's enough now." She glared a warning at Harvey, and kissed Eddy again. "You're all worked up. Finish your pancakes."

"We won't always be around," Harvey said, while trying to control his voice. "You have to be good."

Bits of chewed pancake hung out of the side of Eddy's mouth, and rivulets of white snot dripped onto them. He wiped his nose on his sleeve and swallowed the pancake. "I can say sic 'em to the dog and here kitty, kitty to the cats."

"Of course you can." Blanche cast a warning glance at Harvey that made him thread the belt through his loops again. "Just don't make trouble," Blanche said. "Promise you'll always go to church and never drink beer or smoke cigarettes, even after we're gone."

"I can say come boss to the cows."

"Quiet!" Harvey said. It was no use. Eddy would never learn. "Not another word."

They ate their pancakes then, forks scraping on plates, and flies buzzing on the screen door. Blanche was the first to leave the table. She poured the milk through a strainer into the separator, and motioned for Eddy to turn the crank. Harvey switched on the Philco for the morning news. He was digging in the roll top desk for a check blank when the news bulletin came over the radio.

"Single bomb dropped on Japan destroyed the city of Hiroshima." The reporter listed grim statistics. "Missile equals 20,000 tons of TNT. Truman warns a rain of ruin unless they agree to unconditional surrender."

"War?" Eddy blinked his eyes and tucked his hands under his armpits, letting the separator handle swing to a halt. "I'm a soldier now."

"Hush!" Harvey moved closer to the sideboard and bent his ear to the radio. Static muffled the words, but it was clear something big had happened. No country could stand such destruction. This would end it once and for all. He should be glad the boys would be coming home. It seemed the world was coming to an end. A single bomb destroying a city. A single heart attack ending his life. A conversation with worms threatening Eddy with the asylum. Time was running out.

Harvey sat down in his easy chair and tried to gather his wits. He saw it clearly. He couldn't wait any longer. Blanche asked him a question, but he shook his head and sat listening to the announcer talking of the city of a quarter-million people, now destroyed.

"The *Enola Gay* dropped *Little Boy* on the unsuspecting city. President Truman says hundreds of thousands of American lives will be spared by the drastic move."

Harvey had been to Minneapolis once when he was a young man. He remembered the bustle of traffic on the streets, the crowded street cars, the children playing on the sidewalks. Minneapolis was nowhere near the size of Hiroshima. He tried to picture every person in Minneapolis dead or dying. He couldn't imagine.

Blanche said the cream was ready for town. Harvey snapped off the radio and found his cap. He thought to mention something to Blanche, but couldn't find the strength to form the words. Instead, he made his plans as Eddy added the fresh cream from the morning's milking into the can hauled out of the spring where it kept sweet, and loaded it into the back of the old Model T.

Harvey gave Eddy a list of chores. Eddy nodded and smiled, but was already gawking toward the slough, no doubt hearing some bird talk to him. Then Harvey drove to Nels Carlson's place just over the hill and down the road. Harvey had known Nels' since he was a baby and his parents before him. Nels was about Eddy's age, a few years older maybe. They had always been good friends.

Blanche didn't approve of Nels. She didn't like his drinking or his open skepticism about religion. There were rumors that Nels ran around with other women. She always said Olga deserved better. It was rare for Blanche to speak ill of anyone, but she made an exception with the Potato King.

Nels was better than the other nosey sonofabitches around. Nels at least told you what he thought to your face without going behind your back. He dared to plant potatoes instead of wheat during the dry years, and had done better than most. He had his faults, Nels's handshake was as solid as the bank. It was Nels who pulled strings to get Eddy out of the asylum after Old Man Ingvalstad filed a gripe with the sheriff back in the '20s. Nels knew something about the old sonofabitch. Harvey didn't know the details, but Nels was always sharp that way.

It had been a set up from the start. Ingvalstad hired Eddy to help with his field work. When the harvest was in and the manure spread and fall plowing done, Ingvalstad complained to the sheriff that Eddy had made "improper" remarks to his wife. Hell, everyone knew Eddy was too simple minded to know an improper remark if he heard it. Ingvalstad was a mean sonofabitch, that was all. Had it in for Eddy. Harvey shouldn't have let Eddy work out. But nothing would change it now. Somehow Nels strong armed Ingvalstad into withdrawing his complaint.

The dog barked a welcome, and Nels came out of the barn balancing on crutches. He wore bib overalls and a faded shirt with rolled up sleeves. A lock of gray hair fell over his face from underneath a John Deere cap. His boots were caked with manure and chaff. Harvey could see the grimace of pain on his face as Nels maneuvered toward him. No wonder the man drank. Blanche would have sent a loaf of bread or a jar of sauce had she known he was stopping by with Olga sickly. It wasn't as if he came empty handed, Harvey reminded himself.

"By God, did you hear the news?" Nels said. He sat down on a hay bale near the barn door. The dog laid his shaggy head on Nels's leg. "A whole city with one bomb. Damn Nips asked for it. They started it at Pearl Harbor, but we finished it, by God."

Harvey clucked his tongue and shook his head. "War will end for sure now."

Nels swore a blue streak. "Wish they'd drop one on Germany while they're at it, and finish those dirty bastards once and for all." Nels spat in the weeds by his feet.

Nels said that Bertha Olson phoned with the news that Nedra Ingvalstad's man had been killed in action, and that Norman was home.

"A crying shame to lose her man just when it's ending," Nels said with a sigh. "But Norman home. His folks must be glad."

"I need someone to watch out for Eddy after we're gone," Harvey blurted out as a pain started in his left arm. "Keep him out of the asylum and I'll sell you the farm like you've always wanted." He felt the tightness ride up into his neck and jaw. "I'll draw up the paperwork to make you guardian." His voice weakened. "If something happens before we can transfer the title, I'll put it in writing that you are to have it." It would be something if he died right there before he had a chance to see the judge.

Nels looked at Harvey, and then reached into his overall pocket for a small flask. He unscrewed the cover and wiped the mouth of the flask on his shirt sleeve, and passed it to Harvey.

"It's a big responsibility," Nels said. "Sometimes I can barely manage myself, let alone Eddy."

"He's a good worker if you keep at him," Harvey said. "Strong as an ox but flighty."

Liquid fire burned Harvey's tongue. He felt the heat surge through his body as the chest pain eased. He returned the flask. He needed his wits about him.

"Our place has served us well." The liquor slurred his tongue. "I turned you down before, but I've changed my mind."

"I don't know with Olga sick." Nels took a nip, and then another. "What price did you have in mind?"

They talked land values and acreage. The Carlson family had been staunch friends and neighbors throughout Harvey's entire life. They had shared good times and bad.

"George will need a place when he gets home," Nels said. "He was sweet on that Karlstad girl over in Elbow Lake, and I wouldn't be surprised if he takes up with her again." He tucked the flask back into his pocket. "We'll need more acreage to support two families." Nels reached down and scratched the dog's neck.

Harvey nodded. There was a time when he had dreamed his son would take over his farm as he had taken it over from his father. But that dream, like so many others, had disappeared into thin air.

It was over too fast, his life. Blanche's life. It seemed they would live forever and now it was almost finished. His pa always told him that was the way it would turn out, and he was right.

"You got crops in the field." Nels said. It wasn't a question. "And you're poorly."

Again Harvey nodded. Sweat trickled down his back.

"I'm shorthanded but I'll find help for the harvest." Nels's face turned sharp. "Lower the price and it's a deal."

Harvey felt the pain start again in his chest.

"You pay this year's taxes." Nels pushed the dog away and pulled himself to his feet using the crutches. "I've a little put away for a down payment. The rest on shares." Nels put the flask back in his pocket. "Clear title. And I'll give Eddy a roof over his head and keeps him out of the loony bin. Those are my terms."

A panicky feeling came over Harvey that it was happening too fast. He wasn't dead yet. Maybe he would recover in spite of Doc Sorenson's predictions. "Could we stay at the house?"

"Eddy's starts tomorrow. You can stay in the house as Eddy's wages."

Nels was a sharp dealer. A small down payment, shares of the crops, Eddy's labor, a free title. He was making out like a bandit. But cash money would keep them afloat. He'd watch over Eddy. Would provide for Blanche after . . .

They talked down payment and legal arrangements. Harvey would have access to the south pasture and the vegetable garden. Eddy could have Sundays off. Nels had him by the short hairs.

"It's good sense, that's all," Nels said.

Harvey could barely answer for the lump in his throat. "It's good for Eddy to get used to working with you." He reached out and shook Nels's hand.

He climbed into the Ford, and as he bounced over the ruts in the driveway, Harvey tried to imagine Eddy living with Nels and working his fields. At least Eddy would be working the home place, too. Harvey hoped his father would approve of the arrangement if he were alive. Somehow he thought his father knew. He rolled down the window and let the wind blow in on his face.

Although Harvey could almost catch a glimpse of the future, he couldn't quite fathom a world that did not include him in it.

* * *

"Take him fishing, Harvey," Blanche said that night at supper. "You promised and I'd like a mess of sunnies for Sunday dinner."

When she called him by name, she meant business. Harvey dared not refuse, although the events of the day had left him exhausted. He hadn't told her about the sale of the farm. Had thought to sleep on it, and tell her in the morning before he sent Eddy to Nels' place to begin work.

Eddy rowed them to a shady spot in the shallows of Stalker Lake. Harvey stole a nap while Eddy wet his line, but woke when Eddy whooped over a tug at his line. Eddy pulled in a tiny perch that had to be thrown back. It splashed in the water. Eddy sniffed his hands and giggled—he always liked the smell of lake and fish.

"Son," Harvey said as Eddy baited the hook again. "I've been thinking." Harvey pulled a toothpick out of his shirt pocket and shoved it into his mouth. "If something happens to me, you'll have to take care of your ma." Harvey's voice sounded weak even in his own ears, and he made an effort to strengthen it. "Doc Severson says my heart's bad. I won't be around much longer."

Eddy tossed the line into the water and watched it sink beneath the blue surface of the lake. Then he looked up and examined the sky. "You going to heaven?"

The question unnerved Harvey. How was he to answer? Who knew about such things?

"Angels watch us," Eddy said. "Ma says we can see them in the clouds if we look real hard."

Then he started humming, something he did to stop the voices. No amount of whippings or scolding or bossing would change a single thing about him. Lord knows, Harvey had tried for fifty years without success.

"You'll have to keep up with the work and do as Ma says." Harvey pushed the toothpick until it was a wobbly twig hanging between his teeth.

Eddy kept looking at the sky without seeming to pay the slightest attention.

"And when we're both gone," Pa cleared his throat and continued. "Nels Carlson said he'd watch out for you."

"Potato King?" Suddenly Eddy was all ears. His voice shrilled and his face took on a look of excitement.

Harvey nodded. "He's always been good to you. Remember how he helped get you out of the asylum?"

"He fought Old Man Ingvalstad that time at church." Eddy giggled and rubbed his free hand on his pant leg. "He grabbed him around the legs and said help, help."

Harvey explained about Nels taking over the farm and that Eddy would be going to Nels's every day to begin working. Eddy squinted at the worms and whispered to them when he thought his father didn't notice. Then he pulled up the hook to look at the worm dangling on its sharp barb.

"Nothing to worry about," Harvey said. "It's all settled." He leaned back in the boat and pulled his hat over his eyes again.

The smell of lake and fish filled his nose, and the setting sun felt warm on his face. Harvey dangled his hand into water as warm as a bathtub. The gentle splash of waves against the boat and the buzz of flies and mosquitoes. A turtle swam by and Eddy called out to it along with the fish, worms, and sea gulls. His voice melted into a soothing stream of sounds and words that made little sense. When Harvey really listened, he heard him talking about White Dog, Ma, and Ole Stenerson who died in the Great War. Willy Moberg didn't need a hole in the cemetery and Old Man Ingvalstad comes alive at Easter.

Harvey thought to warn him to never mention the voices. Suddenly it didn't seem to matter.

Adjustments

IN MY DREAM, CLYDE STANDS with me at the altar of Tolga Lutheran Church. He's tall enough to make me feel feminine and petite. Warm sun streams in through the stained glass windows and spills across us like a spotlight. He's handsome in a new suit and Windsor tie. Pearl buttons on my silk dress and Hardanger lace.

Ma hands me a clutch of pink peonies from our garden and reaches, laughing, to tie a ribbon around their stems as their fragrance fills the country church. Pa, alive again, smiles from the front pew and my brother, Norman, home safe from the war, stands as best man for his best friend and only sister.

Clyde's eyes are melted chocolate pools. He takes my hand and I feel the old scar on the tip of his ring finger where he once caught it in a gopher trap. I rub my finger back and forth across the scar until the heat rises in my veins and melts the strength in my knees. I lean into the nap of his jacket, tuck my head beneath his neck, smell the shaving soap on his face. His arms wrap around my waist.

He looks at me and words form on his lips, loving words—I know they're coming, but just before he speaks, Norman has another of his nightmares. His scream slaps me wide-awake.

Ma meets me in the hallway by Norman's room, her hair near white down her back, her eyes wild and worried. Her flashlight pierces a pale beam into the darkness. She tries to gather him in her arms but he pushes out blindly, still asleep, and knocks the flashlight out of her hand. I fear he might strike her, shove her down on the floor or hurt her like last time he had a nightmare.

85

"Norman!" My voice rings harsher, crueler than I mean, but Ma's face is whiter than her gown. "Wake up!" I grip his arm. "You're dreaming."

His eyes open, wild birds scattering before a gun, and when he sees Ma crying, his sobs are worse than the screams.

I remember a time in first grade when Clyde chased me across the school yard with a dead gopher, the tail already chopped and stored in his pocket for the township's two-cent bounty. Although I've never been afraid of wild things, alive or dead, I held both hands over my eyes and screamed myself hoarse.

I want to scream again. Scream until Norman's dream goes away and mine comes back.

* * *

Ma's voice is too cheerful the next morning and she's fighting a head cold. Outside drips dismal sleet. She sets a pan under the leak in the corner. The wood stove is stoked to a warm glow and a kettle of oatmeal bubbles on the back burner. Lucy, the house cat, curls next to the wood box. The room is filled with the smells of fresh coffee, burning oak, and the smoky kerosene lamp lit on the checkered oil cloth. Ma already has a sponge set for bread and has washed this morning's eggs.

"Wind's switching to the north." Ma sniffs into a red bandana handkerchief. Her hair is braided into a limp crown, held in place by hairpins and an old net. She's wears two sweaters and Pa's old carpet slippers like she always does when she's sick. "Expect it will turn to snow."

"You'd best go back to bed," I say. "I'll help Norman with chores."

She doesn't argue or mention the night before. For that I am grateful as I down a bowl of oatmeal and drink a cup of weak coffee. Ma uses the grounds over and over until they barely color the boiling water. I grab Pa's old barn coat from the entry and twine a tattered red scarf around my head and neck.

The wind cuts through my coat and slaps the scarf ends around my face. The sky is settled upon the trees and buildings like a shroud of gray wool, and I can't see any lights from the Hanson's, though I know Clyde is up doing chores as we are. They have electric and their lighted barn windows are usually visible across the pasture.

Rex sniffs my jacket and wags his tail. Maybe he smells my father in the old cloth though he's been gone almost seven years. If Pa were alive, things would surely be different. Familiar grief clutches my throat tighter than the scarf around my neck.

I head first for the outdoor toilet, behind the summer kitchen, hidden from the front door by the lilac bushes. Ma has already swept the floor and spread yesterday's newspaper to collect today's dirt. In the corner is a neat stash of old peach wrappers and the Sears catalog for toilet paper. Ma keeps it spotless clean though the odor of sprinkled lime does not entirely cover the stench from the three holes in the long wooden seat. Pale light shines through the crescent-mooned window but I crack the door open so I can see across the barnyard.

Hoarfrost paints the farm into a fairyland. Like a page out of *Good Housekeeping*. The log barn, chicken coop, brooder house, granary and corn crib are all built from original timber. They're solid as ever though needy of paint. I like to finger the gouges left on the wood from Grandpa's axe. How did it feel to leave Norway and start over in the wilderness, I wonder. He's only a shadowy figure in distant memory, but I think of him often.

Sometimes I imagine how my grandchildren will think of me. They will finger the peonies bushes I planted, walk the familiar pathways through the pasture to fetch the cows, and climb the piles of stones we picked. They'll hear the same church bell and stand as Confirmands at the same communion rail. Our farm is smaller and less modern than others in the township, but it has dark, rich soil. The well water is pure and ice cold. Pa said the farm held his very breath.

It's all I've ever wanted. To work the land for children and grandchildren, so Pa's and Grandpa's lives will count for something besides living and dying.

The cows bawl to be milked. Norman isn't around though he should be. The cows stand dripping and lowing in their stanchions. I promise to tend them as soon as I find my brother. I light the lamp hanging in the alley and call his name. I climb the ladder to the hayloft, check the back stalls where the draft horses are housed for winter, peek into the henhouse next to the barn, and finally find him slumped in the corner of the granary, sipping from a half-empty whiskey bottle.

Smoke from his cigarette curls like a question mark above his head.

I hang the lighted lamp on the nail and slip to the floor beside him. He offers me the bottle and when I shake my head, he tips it up, swallowing the rest of its contents in one gulp. He pitches the empty bottle against the wall so hard that it shatters into a hundred pieces.

"That will make everything better." I jump to my feet and grab the broom in the corner to sweep up the shards of glass. "You think you're the only one with problems?" My voice shrills and I hate myself. "You made it home. A lot of others didn't."

"Goddamn it, Tia," he says. "Don't start."

He pulls himself to his feet and lurches out the door while I sweep the glass onto a page of an old calendar torn from the wall and throw it into the trash barrel outside, taking care to close the granary door tight against rodents. Pa always said the granary is a farmer's best banker. A granary guards the best seeds for next year's planting. It holds our future.

Farm work never ends. I'm used to the heavy work and don't mind. I'd rather do the outside work than be stuck inside. Norman starts the milking while I measure grain into the troughs for the six Guernseys held captive in their stanchions, throw a little extra to the heifer soon to freshen. I pitch hay into the horse pen and feed the chickens. I pump and carry water from the outside well to fill the watering troughs. The barn cleaning will wait until after the milking is finished and the cream separated.

Then I pull the milking stool beside Rosy, the last cow to be milked. Her flank is warm against my cold cheek and she doesn't mind my tears. Warm milk pings into the pail between my knees and the smell of fresh milk mixes with the odor of manure in the gutters. Tabby, the barn cat, rubs against my legs, begging. I squirt one teat into her face and she blinks and licks the milk, wiping her face with white paws. Then all is quiet except for the sound of milk rhythmically stripped into pails, grinding cuds, the occasional stamp of hoof and the bleating sound of the newest calf.

His voice surprises me. I'd been thinking again about last night's dream.

"They killed 'em," his voice cracks. "Shot down like dogs."

I hold my breath, and forget to milk.

"You dreamed about them last night."

His silence is my answer. The pinging of the milk in the buckets starts again. We finish the milking without talking.

* * *

That night we leave Ma nursing her cold and go to the Farmer's Union Hall for the monthly meeting. The building sits across the yard from the one-room school house on the edge of the flatlands known as Dane Prairie. A fresh layer of snow covers everything except the tire tracks in the road and foot prints on the path leading up to the door.

Hanging lanterns light the doorway and line the sides of the open hall filled with wooden folding chairs. The place smells of damp wool, sweat, and cow manure. Cigarette smoke hazes over the crowd of men like a blue cloud.

The old building holds mostly good memories for me. Pa taught me to dance here by letting me stand on his feet. We went to Easter egg hunts every spring. At the fall harvest dance we danced the *schottische*. Tillie Stenerson spread a rumor that Clyde and I would surely marry.

Norman hangs his army jacket on a row of nails alongside the door. His face carries that hunted look he's worn since his return.

"Norman." I bite back the words just in time. He heads toward a cluster of young farmers bunching around the barrel stove in the corner. It's not my job to mother him but a quick worry rises when I see Julius Olson offering him a paper bag. Maybe if we leave before the dancing . . .

When I step behind the wooden table that separates the make-shift kitchen from the rest of the hall, Tillie Stenerson stops talking in mid-sentence, looking first at me and then at Vera Hanson. No one says a word, not Bernice Hegdahl heaping doughnuts on a chipped tray, not Blanche Olson spiking pickled beets into a dish, and certainly not Vera Hanson.

Vera holds a key and fumbles with a red Arco coffee can, trying to unwind the metal strip holding the cover, in her store-bought dress with a blue Peter Pan collar. She holds a hopeful expression that reminds me of a little girl trying to please her teacher. A kerosene lantern hanging from the ceiling casts a feeble glint off the rings on her left hand. She's a town girl with knuckles small enough to wear such a treasure. I shove my hands into my apron pockets. What does Clyde see in her?

I didn't cry at their wedding last summer, and I refuse to cry now.

"Tia," Tillie's voice chatters. "What a lovely apron."

It's flour-sack cloth, no embroidery, nothing new or pretty about it. I pretend I don't feel the tears press hard against my lids and frantically search for something to do. The kitchen is just a wooden table, a rickety shelf holding a mish mash of odd or chipped dishes, an empty slop pail and a wood cook stove. The stove is rusty and smoky and a metal dishpan heats water on the front burner. A clear bowl on the table holds brown eggs coated with bits of straw and dried chicken manure.

"I'll wash the eggs," I say to no one in particular. Odd that someone would bring dirty eggs for the coffee. Then I see the piece of white tape labeled "Vera Hanson" sticking on the side of the bowl. Only a town girl wouldn't know to bring washed eggs.

I dip an old rag in water and rub each egg until the manure and dirt is gone, careful not to press too hard, rinsing with clean water and thinking the whole time how fragile the shell that holds in the white and yolk, separate but together.

Murmuring voices signal the start of the meeting in the adjoining room. Vera reaches over to pour water into the huge blue-speckled coffee pot.

"Don't lift such a heavy thing!" Bernice whispers so as not to disturb the men, her voice fairly oozing with importance. "Not with the baby coming." She speaks to Vera but looks at me while saying it.

Blood drains from my limbs, and I gather my wits as the women cluster around Vera and pull a folding chair away from the wall for her to sit down. I grasp the heavy cream can filled with water from the Olson well, and hoist it onto my bent knee. I wrestle the sweaty can until it balances on my leg, and then pour a stream of water so steady that not one splash messes the painted floor laid with old newspapers for the November mud.

I heft the coffee pot up onto the wood cook stove.

Clyde once teased that if we married and merged our two farms, we'd own the biggest acreage in Tolga Township. "We could do it," he said and my eyes couldn't move away from watching how his hair curled around his ears. "You're as strong as any man."

Although I'd known him all my life, my tongue felt like lead that day before everything changed, and I couldn't say a word, just stood there gaping like a complete fool.

"Norman's looking good," Tillie says. "Put on some weight."

"Ja." My throat cracks from dryness.

"Your ma must be relieved." Blanche slices a loaf of homemade bread into thick slices and slathers them with butter. "And proud he done his part."

Vera flushes. Clyde's exemption from the draft to help with his father's farm . . . Ma had begged Norman to do the same. With Pa gone, the Draft Board would surely have let Norman stay back.

I measure two heaping cups of Arco into a bowl, drop two eggs over the grounds, and mix them together with a fork, half listening to the women chatter about the need for the men to return home now that the war is over, the farm work undone with so many gone and the late fall rains that set the corn picking back. I crane my neck and spot Norman sitting beside Clyde. At least Clyde won't give him booze.

The pot boils. I scrape the grounds into the boiling water, and toss the empty shells in for good measure. Then I pull the pot away from the heat with a screeching sound that turns heads from the hall toward the kitchen. Or maybe it's the smell of egg-coffee wafting through the air. I feel Clyde's eyes on the back of my head.

"You stayin' for the dancing?" Tillie says.

"It's up to Norman," I murmur. "He's got to ring the church bell in the morning."

"Ride home with us," Vera says. "We're neighbors, after all—it's not out of our way."

"No thanks." As soon as the words are out of my mouth I realize I spoke too quickly. I feel my cheeks flush and busy myself with setting another dishpan on the stove to heat. "I should be getting home, Ma sick and all."

When I catch Norman's eye after the business meeting is over, and motion that we should leave, he gives me a flushed scowl and shakes his head. The fiddler scrapes a squeaky note, and the drummer taps a steady beat while men push chairs away to clear the dance floor. It's hot and crowded and men outnumber the women.

I elbow my way closer to Norman and mention again the need to leave.

"What's your hurry?" His eyes shine with drink. "We've got all night."

"I'm sick." The lie comes easy. "Catching Ma's cold."

* * *

In the morning, I sip coffee by the dry sink while Norman eats his eggs. Ma is already out in the hen house. I scrape the frost from the window with the back of my thumb nail and look out. No lights this morning either. "It's snowing," I say. "We'd best leave a little early."

"And the world will end if I don't ring that damn bell on time." Norman's eyes are red-rimmed and his shirt is buttoned wrong. A cigarette hangs out of the corner of his mouth though he knows how Ma feels about smoking in the house.

"We don't have to be there for two hours." Tears well in my eyes. "I'll help with the milking."

"Maybe you could ring the goddamn bell, too."

The idea of ringing the church bell because my brother is drunk jars me to action. "It's your job." I set down the cup and reach for the barn coat. "But I'll go with you and dust the pews between first bells and service."

We don't speak on the short drive to the country church. New snow glazes the gravel road. The DeSoto slides on bald tires.

"Tire rationing is ending—maybe we can buy new ones," I say.

His silence scares me. Ma locked up all the guns last week and hid the key in the good sugar bowl.

"Have you heard when tires will be coming in?"

"Don't start, Tia." He wipes the inside of the windshield with the back of his hand. "For Chrissake."

He parks in the churchyard and hurries to fire the furnace, going through a side door directly into the basement. After a week without heat, the sanctuary will be an icebox but at least without running water, there's nothing to freeze up. I look toward the western side of the cemetery beside the church. Grave markers hide beneath a layer of snow. Naked trees stand ghostly white guarding the perimeter. The oak tree nearest Pa's grave dangles a few rusty leaves that shiver in the wind.

The church is Tolga Township's proudest achievement. Built on a hill in the middle of fields and pastures, its cross and bell tower can be seen for miles. The dead sleep in the earth they loved, this place where they spent their lives. Pa lies next to Martin Hegdahl, his lifelong friend and neighbor. Grandpa and Grandma lie a little to the north closer to the fence. A new stone for Willy Moberg stands by the sidewalk.

I wipe my feet before entering the unlocked doors, pull off my rubber overshoes and line them up on the mat inside the door. It's too cold to remove my coat, gloves, and scarf. Complete silence greets me except for the clanking stove door in the basement and the creak of my shoes on the floorboards. To the front is the carved pulpit and communion rail. A large painting of Jesus praying in the Garden of Gethsemane stretches from floor to ceiling. His eyes are gentle and I stand there, feeling His agony as the comforting odor of burning oak fills the sanctuary. It's still cold enough to see my breath.

I dust the pews as Norman clops up the wooden balcony steps and rings the bell exactly one hour before the service. It's old fashioned, I know, but beautiful to hear the bell ringing over the fields, reminding the farmers to finish up the chores and ready for church. As the chimes drift to silence, Norman grabs the snow shovel to clear paths to the outhouses, wood shed, steps, and sidewalks.

As I dust, I pray for Norman. Looking around to make sure I'm alone, I kneel at the communion rail and ask Jesus to rescue him. At first I pray he'll give up liquor, but deep inside I know it's more than the liquor—more than the drinking and the swearing and the cigarettes. Something dark and terrible has captured him as surely as the Nazis captured him in North Africa. I pray my sweet brother would somehow be set free from this prison as well.

Mildred always comes early to practice the organ. I jump up and busy myself with the dust rag, as she enters the foyer. I think to mention her brother's stone, but I don't have the heart to talk about it. Instead I call out a greeting, wave and go upstairs to dust the balcony pews.

I'm sick of the war, talking about the war, and hearing about the war. It's over. We won. Let's forget, and move on.

As if we will ever forget. Too many graves. Too many lives ruined. Mildred's beautiful music fills the sanctuary.

We always sit in the balcony so Norman can be near the belfry. It seats only a handful of people and is rarely crowded. I tuck the dust rag into a cleaning bucket stored under the back pew in the belfry and find a seat. I don't want to talk to the people straggling into the main floor of the building. I don't want to explain or defend Norman's behavior. I bury myself in the pages of the *Concordia Hymnal* as if they were my lifeline, reading the words of the old hymns, gathering comfort in the printed liturgy and responses at the back of the blue book.

Downstairs in the sanctuary, the church fills with hushed whispers, stomping feet at the door, talk of weather, hoarse coughs. Norman should be finished with the shoveling. I glance out the belfry window. No sign of Norman but Clyde and Vera drive up in their Ford. Heat rushes to my cheeks.

The footsteps on the stairs belong to Vera and Clyde. They shuffle in and sit in the pew in front of me. They unbutton their coats. Vera turns and smiles my way and mumbles something about my mother feeling better.

"Ja, she's better." I can hardly be rude in church. "Many thanks for asking."

Clyde drapes a muscular arm over the top of the pew around Vera's shoulders and whispers something that makes her giggle. I turn back to the *Concordia Hymnal* until a loud noise clatters on the stairs.

Norman trips but catches himself from falling backwards. His eyes are glazed and rheumy, his nose red, and he reeks of alcohol. When he reaches the top step, he trips again. His eyes lock on mine as he starts to go down. This time there's nothing he can do to right himself. He raises his hands in surrender and falls flat on his face.

It's as if I'm seeing him go down on the battlefield. Seeing the bullet rip into his body. Seeing him lie helplessly on the ground, bullets flying all around. It's as if I share his moment of humiliating defeat.

His crashing fall turns all eyes toward the balcony. Mildred pauses briefly in the middle of the organ prelude. Pastor Hustvedt looks up from his notes. Tillie Stenerson cranes her neck for a better look. Dumb Ed, always afraid of trouble, bolts from his pew and runs out the door like a scared rabbit.

Norman just lays there until Clyde helps him to his feet.

Once upright, Norman staggers to the belfry, grabs the thick rope with both hands and pulls it down to the floor. I hold my breath as he rides the rope a few inches off the floor as the bell rings, and then his feet clomp back down on the wooden floor. Pull. Ring. Ride. Clomp. Over and over. He's taking too long—surely it's past time for the service to begin. I fear he will never stop ringing the bell.

But he does. Silence fills the church and everyone stands for the opening hymn. Norman leans against the belfry. His face twists in naked agony. He lurches toward the pews as "Onward Christian Soldiers" sounds. Norman's knees thump hard on the wooden floor as he falls beside Vera Hanson. Norman's sobs are louder than the organ. Heads turn again toward the balcony.

I feel like a gopher caught in a trap, frantically looking for something that will stop the disaster happening before my eyes. I'm frozen in place and can't look away. Thank God Ma is home sick. Thank God she doesn't see this.

Vera Hanson sits down, touches Norman's shoulder and then reaches into her pocket and pulls out a clean handkerchief.

"It's good to have you home again, Norman." Her voice is gentle and easy. She hands him the handkerchief and Norman wipes his eyes and nose. His shoulders heave, and he buries his face in her lap. She pats his back.

Tillie Stenerson once said that Vera had a rough life because her father is a drunk.

"Of course you can sit by us." Vera moves over and makes room for Norman, who pulls himself from the floor and slouches meekly beside her in the pew ahead of me. She puts her arm around him and he lays his head on her shoulder. His sobs continue, quieter now, until he finally dozes against her, snoring.

What if Norman loses this job? The note at the bank is due in March. We count on his wages from Tolga Lutheran. The deacons won't put up with this. We'll have no way to get by. No jobs for women with all the returning vets looking for work. Maybe if we sell the heifer, we can make the note but we need to increase cream production to cover taxes and roof repairs.

I force myself to focus on Pastor Hustvedt, recite the familiar liturgy and sing the songs. I don't hear one word of the sermon.

During the benediction, I reach over and jab Norman awake. "It's time to ring the final bells."

Norman's face is deathly white and his jaw hangs slack. He looks like an old man, much older than Clyde though they are the same age.

Clyde visits with Norman after the bells are quiet and the sanctuary empties. Through the window I see Dumb Ed playing with the Hegdahl dog in the cemetery, pulling a rope behind him for the dog to chase. Pastor Hustvedt hurries toward his car. He has to be at Parkdale Church for the next service.

Vera snugs a blue silk scarf around her head. The scarf brings out the blue of her eyes, and I tower like a giant over her. I tuck my hands into my coat pockets.

"Tia, won't you come over for coffee sometime?" Her smile is timid, like a schoolgirl, though her lips are painted red and she wears matching earrings. The buttons on her coat are snug with the coming baby. "I don't know many neighbors."

It's as if time slips into slow motion. Norman leans against the door and Clyde keeps him talking until everyone else is gone. Clyde laughs at something Norman says, and Norman smiles and looks toward Vera, who gives him an encouraging nod.

Vera is my nearest neighbor. I'm not going anywhere, and Clyde will never give up their place. Lonely years stretch into the future.

She isn't so bad.

"I'll stop by this week." I'll only go when I know Clyde is out in the field or away from the house. I can stand it if Clyde isn't around. "When Ma is better."

Miracle Valley

IT WAS AN ANGRY DAY with gray clouds spitting pebbles of ice. North-west winds howled around the eaves of the house, defying the shelter-belt that separated the home place from pastures, calling out like the soldiers in the trenches. Wind like the moans of the dying.

Nels Carlson steadied himself on his crutches and cursed. He once considered himself lucky to muster out of France with only a leg wound. It had always been a fierce weather predictor, forecasting every drop of rain before a cloud showed in the Minnesota sky. But lately arthri-tis had set in the old wound with a vengeance.

"What's wrong?" Olga called from the bedroom, her voice slurred from the medicine the doctor insisted she take. Without it, the cancer left her quivering and weepy. Slurring was better than weeping, better than sending her to live with Lilja.

"Nothing," he called. "Go back to sleep." He bit back another curse and eased himself over to the cook stove. Balancing on his left foot, he jiggled the stove lid, and pushed a dried piece of oak into the firebox. The coals pinked and burst into a smoldering smoke that streamed into the room and stung his eyes until he reached up and adjusted the draft. It had been smoky in the trenches, too.

Ole Stenersen, his boyhood friend, took the gas at Flanders. He had moaned and coughed all night, gasping and calling out for his mother. Nels turned his thoughts away from Ole's mother. Whenever Old Lady Stenerson had seen him throughout the years, at church or at the store, Nels had the guilty feeling she blamed him for Ole's death. Of course, it was all long ago. And now another war barely over.

By God, war made a man old before his time.

Olga mumbled something in her sleep. Nels listened to see if she was praying but it seemed she was only mumbling. How long could she last? The doctor said she wouldn't make it past threshing, and here it was after Thanksgiving. You never knew the strength of a person. Ole had lasted all night after the gas. Sonofabitches. Damn Germans. Papers said they used gas in this war, too, but against civilians. Damn them all to hell. They should have wiped them out while they had the chance.

Nels touched his foot to the floor, and pulled the coffeepot over to the hottest burner, taking care not to screech against the lid. There was enough in the pot to carry him through the long evening. Enough to share with the good doctor when he stopped by to check on Olga.

He eyed Olga's medicine. The doctor said it would ease his leg, but Nels quickly turned his thoughts to something else. Anything else. He needed his wits to care for Olga. They had promised until death do us part and by God, he'd keep his end of the deal.

He reached instead for the aspirin bottle and downed three tablets. Sometimes it took the edge off. He tipped it again and took another of the bitter pills.

The telephone rang two longs and one short. Maybe Lilja calling to check on her mother. Nels crutched his way to the doorway, hurrying to reach the wooden receiver fastened to the wall before it could wake Olga.

"Carlson's," he said into the mouthpiece, turning away from the open bedroom door and speaking as low as he dared.

"Nels?" the doctor's voice sounded tinny and far away. "Is that you?"

"Hello," Nels repeated, louder this time. "I'm here." He could hear kids arguing in the background. Damn Tillie, rubbering again.

"How's Olga?"

"'Bout the same."

"The Olson baby . . ." His voice faded out, and Nels didn't catch the rest of the sentence. "Won't be out your way until tomorrow."

Nels hadn't realized he had been waiting for the doctor to come. Anyone to come. The nights were so long. He couldn't work with the stock, couldn't shovel snow, couldn't do a damn thing but wait for his wife to die. He tipped the metal pot and poured thick coffee into a chipped cup. It bubbled, but he sipped it all the same, burning his tongue. He stifled another curse as he pushed the mug across the table within reach of the radio.

He settled in his favorite chair, checked his pocket watch and leaned forward, twisting the knob of the old Philco. Sometimes on cold, clear nights he could pull in stations from far away St. Louis or Chicago. The signals whined in and out as he twisted through the static to find 590. WOW from Omaha was usually dependable.

"This is Reverend A A. Allen, God's Miracle Man." Nels pulled his chair closer and turned up the volume. "Coming to you tonight with a power packed, Holy Ghost, sin-killin', devil chasin', camp meeting revival."

Nels glanced at Olga's door. It was always a relief when she dozed off, anything to keep her from the pain. Although he knew that Olga would not mind listening, too, Nels liked being alone when he listened to the radio preacher. There was something about his voice. Something bold and kind—not like the tedious sermons of Pastor Hustvedt. No, there was something about the Reverend A.A. Allen that pulled a deep yearning from Nels's heart. Maybe akin to hope. God knew there was no hope in the good doctor or Lutheran liturgy. But when A.A. Allen spoke of healing, Nels could almost believe.

He tried to imagine Olga back on her feet with the energy and beauty of former years. Tried to imagine her with strength and health. He remembered her face when she met him at the train after he returned from the war. God, she was beautiful. Her eyes blue as the Atlantic, her hair twisted in a bun, just begging to be loosed over her shoulders. He took another sip from his cup.

It would be enough if only she could live out the rest of her days without cancer. Without pain.

"Jesus said come unto me," the preacher said, "and I will give you rest." Nels reached for his coffee with trembling hands. "There's nothing in your life that God can't fix. There's no sickness beyond his healing hand. There's no sorrow he can't relieve."

It was a sorrow, thinking about Ole and the Great War. And sorrow upon sorrow that Olga was dying. More sorrow with George stuck in Germany without enough discharge points to come home, though the war was over. Thank God for that, thank God. But it was a sorrow, nonetheless, that George would miss his mother's funeral. Miss saying goodbye.

"Jesus was a man of sorrows, acquainted with grief." The radio whined, and Reverend Allen's voice strained through the miles. "He carried your pain to the cross. He took a whipping for your healing."

He'd been thinking about it all day, and Nels was ready with pencil and paper when Reverend Allen gave the address where people could send for handkerchiefs. "We've prayed over these cloths and anointed them with oil." The receiver howled and Nels leaned over and adjusted the dial. "Lay it on your body where you have pain. The prayer of faith will raise the sick. They shall recover in Jesus' Name."

Miracle Valley. It's where the letter would go along with a folded dollar to help with expenses. Nels eased back to his feet, fetching a stamp from behind the sugar bowl in the kitchen cupboard.

He'd lay the cloth on Olga's chest, while she slept. He'd tell her about the handkerchief only after she was healed. He wouldn't raise her hopes by speaking about it ahead of time. She'd be well when George came home, would return to her duties around the house, and start singing again. By God, he should have done it months ago.

The mailing was a problem. Nels didn't care to answer Lilja's questions about an unexpected letter to Reverend A.A. Allen in Miracle Valley, Arizona. She'd think he had lost his mind and might insist on taking Olga as she had been hinting for weeks. If he put the letter in the mailbox, Clarence might gossip about it all over the country, might even tell Pastor Hustvedt. Now that would be a situation. He doubted very much the preacher would approve of anointed handkerchiefs sent through the United States mail to heal sick Lutherans.

To hell with them! With all of them. What mattered was that Olga would be raised from her sick bed like St. Peter's mother-in-law and the ten lepers. She'd be well again. Jesus was the same yesterday and today and forever, just like the preacher said. If the Lord raised her up, what could anyone say? They wouldn't think him a lunatic after Olga was healed. Why, last week there was a man on the radio who received a new gold tooth after anointed prayer. There could be no argument with that. A tooth was a tooth. You either had one or you didn't.

Nels jammed his cap on his head and fastened the earflaps under his chin. He shrugged into an old barn coat hanging in the entry, the cloth radiating cold through his shirt and union suit. He tucked the letter into his coat pocket. He buckled his overshoes, and pulled on mitts smelling of cow manure. Foolish to go out so late. If he fell . . . He cast a final glance toward the bedroom and pushed through the storm door out into the darkness. A feeble light glowed through the kitchen window and a weak moon shone milky through the cloudy sky.

A few stars above, not many. And a howling north wind at his back as he limped through frozen ruts, carefully planting the crutches so he wouldn't slip, inching his way down the driveway to the letterbox. It was colder than he had expected, the wind burning on his cheeks and watering his eyes. He crutched a little faster while Patsy, the old collie, whined at his side. "Good girl," Nels said. "Sorry to get you out of your warm bed."

Thank God for short driveways. Nels reached the box, steadied himself and placed the letter inside, pulling up the red flag that signaled mail to be picked up.

"God," he looked up into the dark skies. He didn't deserve anything. Had made a mess of most things. A few flakes swirled down, more ice than snow, more like hail against his face. "You know I haven't asked before—but I'm asking now."

The only sound was the howling wind and Patsy's shivering bark.

* * *

As he crawled into bed beside his sleeping wife, Nels touched a finger to her arm. He wouldn't wake her, wouldn't risk waking her, but he touched her nonetheless. Just a finger on her arm, feeling the heat of her skin through the flannel of her nightgown, assured that she was still breathing. He felt nearly frozen but the smell of cancer, hideous and fetid, caused him to pull away from the furnace of her body. Her cheeks sunken, her hair gray and thin, her skin like peeling bark from an ancient birch.

Nels thought again of the radio preacher. There was something about his voice. It came to him as he dozed off. That voice, the peculiar timber of A.A. Allen's voice over the airwaves, carried the authority of one acquainted with sin. It was the voice of someone who knew what it was like. Nels dropped into the blackness of sleep.

Olga's stillness woke him while it was still dark. Later, when he tried to remember, he couldn't recall any particular noise or movement. The clock read a quarter of four, and Nels knew she was gone. He reached out and touched her.

She was cold.

Nels thought again of Ole Stenerson, how he had frozen into a block of ice before the stretcher bearers could reach them, his passing a quiet affair—moaning one minute and still the next as the shells fell around them in bursts of stink and screams. No doubt the bombardment drawn by the smoky fire Ole had begged for, that Nels had built against direct orders. Death always inconvenient, always at the wrong time. First too soon and now too late.

By God, he needed a drink. He dragged himself to his feet and tried not to look at Olga's body. He pulled a sheet across her face—at first he thought to spare her the humiliation of being seen in such a grotesque sight. But then he realized he could not bear to look at her, not his beautiful Olga, reduced to bones and horror. The tears came when he realized how dead she had been—dead long before she finally died.

* * *

Lilja wanted him to move in with her, and insisted he couldn't live alone. But Lilja's man and Nels had never quite seen eye to eye and there was the stock to tend. Eddy needed watching, in spite of his many promises and good intentions. *Nei*, Nels would stay at the farm until George came home.

George's last letter said that he had enough points but waited for passage. The army having a dickens of a time getting the boys home from all around the world. He said the wounded had top priority. It almost sounded like George wished he would have been wounded to get home quicker, but Nels was glad his son had been spared that misery. A purple heart came with too high a price.

Nels couldn't let his mind go beyond George coming home. God alone knew what George had been through. D Day. The Bulge. Finding that terrible camp with its living skeletons.

Nels fried an egg for his noon meal. Lilja had left a loaf of fresh bread. He wasn't hungry but pushed the food into his mouth, swallowed, washing it down with coffee. He took his time reading the *Farmer's Almanac*. Looked like a dry spring. Maybe an early end to winter. He was scrubbing his plate when Patsy's bark warned of visitors. Nels wiped his hands on a ragged towel and pushed back the curtain. It was Pastor Hustvedt with a carload of Luther League carolers.

Christmas. They came every year and it was nothing out of the ordinary, though Nels was startled by their appearance. He had forgotten all about Christmas. Of course he knew it was coming, but it seemed the entire world had paused with Olga's death. But of course it hadn't. Only his world in pause. Only his.

Rosemary Hegdahl carried a Swedish tea ring baked by her mother. By God, he was now numbered among the pitiful old ones needing charity from church people. And Mrs. Hegdahl at that! A snooty woman who never gave Olga the time of day. He wanted to refuse the bread, to slam the door on their smiling faces, but instead he invited them in, laid a newspaper on the floor for them to stand on while they sang the old carols. He knew Olga would have insisted. Their eyes bright, their voices young and hopeful, their skin so smooth and innocent. Their overshoes dripped onto the newspapers, smearing the print.

He crutched to the pantry. On the shelf sat the last two bottles of Olga's dandelion wine. Olga had been known throughout the community for her wine. Although it pained him to waste a bottle on the carolers, he had no choice. He carefully poured a thimbleful of the yellow liquid into the fancy wine glasses Old Lady Stenerson had given them as a wedding present so many years ago. It was the old way, giving small sips of wine or brandy to the carolers at the door. Pastor Hustvedt might frown upon it in this modern time, but to hell with him. The kids came to sing, and by God, they would have a treat.

"The mailman stopped when we drove up," said Rosemary while he passed out the small glasses. "Here's your mail." She laid a small stack of envelopes on the kitchen table. Nels barely noticed, so intent he was on not spilling. It was a chore Olga had always done, always such a happy time. Listening to the old Norwegian songs, Olga would tear up and smile. He missed her. He concentrated on the task at hand, refused to let his mind think of her right then.

He didn't look at the mail until after the young people left in a flurry of coats and excitement. He lowered himself to a kitchen chair, and pulled it over in front of him. By God, his leg hurt today. It was like a sore tooth, agonizing in its persistence, relentless.

A slightly bulging letter postmarked Arizona huddled between the REA bill and a notice about the Farmer's Union New Year's party.

Nels took his penknife from his pocket and opened it with clumsy hands, carefully slitting the top of the envelope. Too late. He had waited too long to send for the prayer cloth. Here it was, but Olga in her grave more than three weeks.

He pulled it out. It was just an ordinary handkerchief, maybe cut in two as evidenced by one ragged edge. He touched it and smelled it. Nothing out of the ordinary. Dear God, why had he let his hopes be raised by a charlatan?

Nels threw the handkerchief to his side, and brought the wine bottle to his favorite chair by the radio. He swigged it right from the decanter, wishing he'd kept the whole bottle for himself, immediately stricken to realize that there would not be another batch of Olga's dandelion wine. Maybe Lilja knew the recipe. He'd ask her the next time she called.

He would save that last bottle for a special occasion. Maybe when George came home. Or when he married that nice girl from Elbow Lake. A momentous occasion required a celebration.

A drawing force moved his hand to the radio dial, and WOW whined in from Nebraska. ". . . the miracle working man of God . . ." then faded out again. "Have faith, Brother, the Lord God has not abandoned you . . ."

Nels pulled a flask of brandy from beneath the cushion of his chair and tipped it up. The heat of the liquor burned through his veins and flushed his face. By God, if George weren't coming home, he'd end it all. But George couldn't return to both parents dead. Nels took another swig. He'd tough it out, as he always had, and take it as it came. It couldn't get any worse. The pain in his leg, the hurt in his heart, the agony of his spirit.

Nei, it couldn't get any worse.

"God has a good plan. Your future is filled with hope. Turn to Him. Confess your sins."

Nels snorted and propped his throbbing leg on the ottoman. He reached over and picked up the handkerchief from the floor. It didn't look like a miracle. He placed the handkerchief over his sore leg, thinking how he deserved nothing but hellfire. He had been a horse's ass to Olga. She deserved better.

He drained the bottle, and dropped into a deep sleep, barely hearing the words from the radio, "He is closer than a brother. Don't despair."

Nels didn't stir until the room was cold as an icebox. The fire had gone out. He roused himself and put a birch log in the dying embers. Then he added a stout block of oak, closed the lid, and stumbled into the bedroom. Not bothering to crawl beneath the covers, Nels lay on the bed and pulled a quilt over himself.

The crowing rooster woke him while it was still dark. Damn bird belonged in the stew pot. He turned over and pulled the quilt over his head. Then he realized with a start that his leg didn't hurt. He was sleeping on his left side—the side that usually caused the most pain. He stretched his leg. Twisted over on his back.

It didn't hurt.

He looked for his crutches, but they weren't by his bed. He saw them through the bedroom door, still propped against the kitchen table. What the hell. He had left them in the kitchen the night before. It couldn't be. He tried to remember. He had been drinking. It all blurred in his memory.

He sat up, pulled his knees to his chest and stretched out his legs. He touched a toe to the floor and leaned his weight onto his foot. Then he stood on both feet. He squatted down and stood up, then danced around the room. Hopped on one foot and then the other. Bent over and touched his toes. His knee and hip as limber as before the war. He examined the old scars half expecting them to be gone. They blazed across his hip as they had for thirty years—but without pain.

By God, he was healed. Dear Jesus.

Nels picked up the handkerchief lying next to his chair and buried his face in the plain cloth. Only cloth. The prayer of faith would heal the sick. He tucked it inside the top button of his shirt. Then he eyed the crutches.

He picked up the hatchet from the wood box and chopped the crutches in pieces while both laughing and crying. It wasn't easy—diamond willow dried rock hard. Nels stopped often to wipe tears from his face. The sobs almost blinded him and he had to be careful not to chop a finger off. He laughed at the thought of being healed and then cutting his finger off in stupidity. God must be laughing, too. He stuffed the last length of crutch into the firebox, adjusted the damper and watched the wood catch on fire.

It should have been Olga. If he had acted sooner she would still be with him. Olga deserved a touch from the Almighty. He didn't. Why, the things he had done in his life. The war. The petty meanness. The selfishness. The greed.

As Ole lay dying, he had said something that seemed so strange. Ole looked up at the dirt walls of the trench and at the faces of his friends and said, "It don't matter now. None of it matters."

Sometimes when Mrs. Stenerson had looked at Nels with that accusing glance that made him feel responsible for Ole's death, Nels thought to tell her what Ole had said. He had imagined a hundred times the way her mouth would crimp and the tears would well up in her eyes. He thought how easy it would have been to hurt her.

Now he realized what Ole meant. By God, he finally understood. After all these years it was as if a light bulb had been turned on. Ole meant that nothing mattered compared to what comes next. Of course, why didn't he see it before?

Sweet Jesus.

Healed

IT WASN'T THAT TILLIE WANTED to go to church, but Bernice Hedquist, wearing her title of Sunday School superintendent like a feather in her hat, scheduled an extra practice for the Christmas program right after services.

Dickey knew his angelic lines by heart. "Fear not," he practiced with a lisp that would melt the hardest heart. "I bring you tidings of great joy."

Tillie stepped closer to the mirror next to the kitchen sink where Clarence filled buckets with hot water. She peered into the mirror and plucked bobby pins from her hair. She frowned as she reached for the hairbrush.

"Are you sure you won't go along?" Tillie said as she ran the brush through her straggly hair. Without her weekly appointment at Fern's Cut & Curl, she looked like an old farm-woman. Faded, out of style and washed up. As outdated as Tia Fiskum.

"How can I show my face?" The muscles of his jaw worked, and he jerked the buckets out of the sink, splashing water on her clean floor. "By God, I'm the laughingstock of Tolga Township."

"It'll blow over," Tillie said. "It's all lies. You have to believe me."

"I'll believe you when you figure out how to fix this mess." He pulled on leather mittens. "Make it right with Nels, at least. Mend fences with the neighbors." His face looked more like his father's instead of the man who fathered her children. "If you don't, I'm seeing a lawyer after Christmas." His rubber boots squeaked on the linoleum. Steam from the buckets swirled around his angry face.

She had never seen him like this. The rumors started again just when things were getting better. That damn Fuller Brush man went on another toot, and bragged about his supposed exploits. Said her baby had to be his because Clarence was incapable of fathering another child. Of all the crazy lies! Vera's father heard him at the Lower Joint, and told Clyde. It got back to Clarence. She swallowed a knot in her throat.

"But Nels won't talk to me." Tillie's voice took on that pleading tone she hated. "You're asking the impossible." Nels was the best grudge-holder in Tolga Township. He still carried bitterness toward the Huns who had wounded him back in the Great War. He wouldn't trade at Schmidt's Meat Market because Schmidt was a German.

"It's not my fault," she said, though she knew it was her fault. She hadn't committed adultery, but her loose tongue and big mouth ruined everything. They were no closer to reconciliation than when the big mess happened last June. But divorce! For once she was glad her mother wasn't alive.

She watched Clarence through the window. Billows of steam spouted out of his mouth and swirled above the buckets of water. It was below zero. She hated to be out on the roads alone.

She called for the children, and helped them bundle into their heaviest coats and rubber overshoes. Irene clutched her favorite doll under her arm. The doll would star as Baby Jesus in the pageant. Tillie reached over and wiped a smudge of toast crumbs off Dickey's chin.

"Where's Daddy?" Dickey said. "Isn't he coming?"

"Not today," Tillie said. "Pipes froze up in the steer shed."

"He'll come to the Christmas program, won't he?" Irene chewed the end of her pig tail like she always did when she was worried.

Tillie tied Irene's scarf tighter around her neck but didn't answer. They climbed into the truck as Clarence trudged back into the house for more hot water.

"You kids behave yourself," he said. He didn't look at her.

At church, she and Clarence usually sat near the front, on the right side of the sanctuary. Without him, she sought the farthest corner of the belfry, but it overflowed with young families there for the practice. The church crowded, too, and she headed toward an open pew towards the back, behind the Root family. A strange smell of old cheese wafted from Dumb Ed.

"Phew!" Irene said. "What's that smell?"

"Hush!" Tillie said.

Mrs. Fiskum and Tia slipped into the pew beside Dumb Ed. Tia, mousy and tall, wore a faded coat with sleeves too short. Her mother seemed an invisible gray shadow.

A feeling of gloom settled over Tillie, and she snuggled Dickey next to her until he pulled away in protest. Soon she would join the ranks of widows and old maids, drunks and lunatics. The divorce would cling to her like Dumb Ed's bad smell. Sitting alone. How would she make a living? Worst of all was the thought of life without her children. Clarence was firm about that. He had the law on his side. His mother would move in and keep house.

Mildred Moberg started the organ prelude, "Joy to the World." Eddy Root grinned and sang along in a monotone, looking back at the children, and showing a splash of dried egg yolk on his stubbly chin.

"We're not supposed to sing yet," Dickey said.

"Hush." Tillie pulled out the *Concordia Hymnal* from the rack, and paged to the first hymn listed on the board at the front of the sanctuary. Pastor Hustvedt stood behind the pulpit next to the Christmas tree.

"Look," Tillie whispered to the children as Norman Fiskum crawled around back of the tree, and plugged in the lights. The tree reached all the way to the ceiling and the Sunday School children had decorated it in red and green streamers. Underneath a few wrapped packages already covered the floor.

Dickey clapped his hands. "Pretty!"

The organ transitioned to Clarence's favorite Christmas carol, "O Come, O Come Immanuel." Tillie prayed a desperate prayer for Jesus to come into their situation before it was too late. "Come, Jesus," she whispered. "Please, for the sake of my children."

"What did you say, Mama?" Randolph tugged on her coat sleeve.

She pulled herself back to reality and shook her head. She was as bad as Dumb Ed, talking aloud in public. "Nothing," she said.

Clyde and Vera Hanson squeezed into the empty pew directly ahead of the Fiskum women. It was sickening the way Clyde draped his arm across the back of her seat. Newlyweds. Just give them a few years and see if they still ogled each other that way. Vera flashed a smile at Dumb Ed, as if he were totally normal, and greeted Tia and Mrs. Fiskum as if she hadn't a clue that Tia was in love with her husband. Tillie stuck in her nose in the hymnal, and didn't look up until they all stood for the opening hymn.

Pastor Hustvedt looked tired. Tillie noticed the droop of his eyes, and the way his vestments wrinkled across the front. Bernice said his mother was sick, and he had made a trip to the Crookston Hospital.

Tillie didn't care if he was tired or not. She would catch Pastor Hustvedt after church, and ask to see him privately. Maybe he would know a way to save her marriage. She was desperate. She doubted he would have any influence on Nels, but maybe he could talk to Clarence. The Romance magazines talked of "counseling" and "therapy." It was far-fetched, but she had to do something.

They finished the second verse of "O Little Town of Bethlehem" when someone clattered into the sanctuary. Mrs. Fiskum and Tia both flinched at the sound, and turned their heads toward the door. Tillie turned to look, too, and then froze in horror.

Nels stood in the aisle near the back of the church looking like a wild maniac, his hair standing up in all directions. His shirttail stuck out through his unbuttoned fly. It couldn't be. Nels never attended church, certainly not without Olga.

The only open seat in the whole church was in the pew beside Tillie's family.

Tillie looked around, wondering how she could get out without bringing attention to herself. She felt trapped in the corner. She must walk right past Nels if she tried to leave. Instead, Tillie pulled as close against the wall as she could and pulled Dickey closer to her side.

"I've been healed!" Nels shouted above the organ music. "Look."

He hopped first on one foot and then the other, clutching a white handkerchief in his hand. He bent over and touched his toes. Tillie stared in disbelief. He must be drunk. Or crazy.

"A miracle, by God, healed by the radio preacher from Miracle Valley."

Tillie gasped. No one sang. Mildred quit playing the organ. A murmur swept through the congregation like a prairie fire through a field of dried corn stalks.

"For shame. Drunk," Bernice said loud enough for everyone to hear. "And Olga barely in her grave."

"I'm not drunk," Nels said. "Healed." He waved the handkerchief. "Not a pain."

"Where are his crutches?" Irene said. "What happened?"

Nels jumped up and down, kicking his heals and making a spectacle of himself. It seemed impossible, but there was no denying it. He walked without crutches. Could it be that he was really cured? By a radio preacher?

Pastor Hustvedt stood ashen faced and slack-jawed. He cleared his throat and motioned for Mildred to resume playing. She fluttered with the hymnal, and in her confusion, knocked it off the music stand. Pastor Hustvedt rapped on the pulpit. No one paid him a bit of attention.

Pastor Hustvedt frantically motioned for Mildred to start playing. "'Angels from the Realms of Glory,' page 113," he said loudly. "Please stand." No one listened.

"It should have been Olga." Nels said. He worked his jaw and swallowed until his Adam's apple bobbed. "I'm a sinner." Nels broke down in tears. "Didn't treat her right. Broke all the commandments." He stumbled forward to the communion rail at the front of the church and fell to his knees. The bottoms of his shoes showed need of repair.

"I think the old buzzard's going to faint," Clyde said in a loud whisper. Tillie couldn't help but overhear. "Look at him."

"You mean Nels?" Vera raised the hymnal a little higher to hide their conversation.

"Nope," Clyde howled with what sounded like glee. "The preacher."

"Mama," Irene said. "Mr. Hanson called Pastor Hustvedt an old buzzard."

Tillie tried to hush her children, as the church service took on a near-carnival atmosphere: Nels wailing at the altar; Pastor Hustvedt clinging to the lectern; Elmer Petterson beckoning for Selmer Moberg and the other deacons to join him at the front of the church; Clyde laughing; Bernice Hegdahl asking for someone to call the sheriff because Nels was drunk.

As soon as Bernice mentioned the sheriff, Dumb Ed bolted from the pew and fled the sanctuary, slamming the door behind him.

"Nothing to worry about," Blanche said to no one in particular. "Eddy is scared of sheriffs, that's all."

It was certainly the most excitement Tolga Lutheran had ever known, at least since Old Man Johnson took an axe to the pulpit over some ancient doctrinal dispute. She wished Clarence were here to see it for himself. He would never believe her.

A strange flicker of hope stirred. Nels would forgive her, now. He had to if he had gotten religion.

Pastor Hustvedt left the pulpit and walked over to the communion rail. Tillie thought he looked helpless. Nels and the deacons prayed at the altar. Mildred sat at the organ as if in a trance. Pastor Hustvedt shook his head and his shoulders slumped. He looked to the belfry and motioned for Norman to ring the closing bell, though church had barely started. It was unheard of for a service to end without a sermon. Not even an offering.

As the bells pealed, Tillie watched for her chance to speak to Nels. She tried to imagine Clarence's face when she told him that Nels had forgiven her. Her heart thumped within her rib cage. The forgiveness would be as much a miracle as Nels' healed leg.

"Children meet in the basement for practice," Pastor Hustvedt said loudly. He clung to the pulpit as if he would collapse.

It was as if no one knew what to do next. Mildred pounded out the recessional as the children hurried to the basement. Harvey and Blanche were among the first to leave, saying they worried about Eddy waiting out in the cold. Most of the adults waited for their children to finish practice. A humming sound stirred among the congregants.

Bernice Hegdahl craned her neck to get a better look at what was happening around the communion rail. "He's drunk, I tell you." She crossed her arms and sniffed loud disapproval.

"Do you think he's drunk?" Vera whispered to Clyde.

"Of course." Clyde pulled the buttons of his overcoat and reached for his hat. "I've known the Potato King all my life." He stood to his feet with a last glance toward the front of the church. "Just don't know how he's managing without his crutches." He reached for Vera's hand. "I'm starving. Let's get home to that roast beef."

Tillie gathered her things and moved to the front pew next to the organ. She would catch Nels before he left church. It could all be over in just a few minutes.

"I tell you," Nels said. He stood up and kicked his leg up as high as it would go. "I'm cold sober. I was drunker than a skunk last night, but not today."

Norman unplugged the Christmas tree lights, and the church dimmed. The smell of pine filled the room, and the sound of children singing came from the basement. "Fear not!" Tillie heard Dickey saying his lines above the hum of conversation. Poor Dickey deserved to have both a mother and a father in the same home.

"I've got to get to Kvam for the next service," Pastor Hustvedt said. He seemed glad to leave.

Tillie hesitated. She had to choose. She could nab Pastor Hustvedt and ask for a meeting. But he was in a hurry. If she could speak to Nels, she wouldn't need to tell the minister the sordid details of their situation. She didn't know what to do. Then Pastor Hustvedt left and the choice was made for her. She must speak to Nels. Her children's future hinged on his forgiveness.

With the preacher gone, everyone else gathered around Nels at the front of the church.

"How did it happen?" Mrs. Olson said. "Did you see an angel or anything Catholic?"

"I can't explain it," Nels said. "I was drinking, and listening to the radio preacher. I sent for this prayer cloth when Olga was real bad. I woke up healed."

Nels stretched his leg out and then ran in place. "I haven't been able to do this in twenty-seven years."

"I'm glad for you." Mrs. Fiskum kissed Nels' cheek. "I only wish Olga could see this happy day."

Bernice Hegdahl shook Nels' hand, but leaned in close to sniff his breath.

"You've been drinking," she said. "I knew it."

"Goddamn it, Bernice," Nels said in exasperation. "I told you I was drunk last night. I'm sober as a judge today."

Tillie stood to the side, waiting for her chance. The church emptied except for Norman who was sweeping dried pine needles from underneath the Christmas tree.

"Nels," Tillie said. "I'm glad for you."

Nels's expression hardened. He didn't take her outstretched hand. Tillie felt the knot return to her throat. She swallowed and forced herself to speak.

"I'm sorry for everything last summer." Fear not. She wouldn't be afraid. "I'm more sorry than you could ever know. I was wrong, terribly wrong, and I'm sorry. Please forgive me."

"You've got to be kidding."

"You've been touched by God," Tillie said. "You have to forgive me now."

"I don't have to do anything."

"Please." She swallowed hard. "Clarence is going to divorce me unless I can work this out."

Nels looked at her a long moment. She thought he might be softening. "It's about time."

* * *

The rest of the day turned into a blur of remorse and hopelessness. Clarence cut a small spruce tree from the shelterbelt and left it propped against the porch. He spent the afternoon in the barn. The children talked only about Christmas, decorating the tree, if Santa would come, and the program.

Tillie pulled out a box of leftover wrapping paper and crayons. "Make chains for the Christmas tree." They seemed happy, glad, even.

"Cut snowflakes and angels from the white paper—careful with the scissors."

Clarence's mother would take over. She was old fashioned, more of a disciplinarian than the children were accustomed. Grandma wouldn't have patience with Irene's habit of chewing on her hair. Dickey sometimes wet the bed. Clarence said she had whipped him for wetting the bed when he was a Dickey's age.

Tillie tried to ring Pastor Hustvedt, but hung up when she heard someone, probably Bernice, rubbering on the line.

She thought of driving over to the parsonage. She hesitated leaving the kids alone in the house, what with the danger of wood stoves and house fires. It was getting colder, the thermometer showed four below. Too cold for the children to play in the barn while their dad did chores. Dickey's lungs were weak, and she didn't want him catching cold.

Instead, she set the table with the good dishes and used her mother's crocheted tablecloth. She fixed a roaster of scalloped potatoes with ham, Clarence's favorite, and put a squash in the oven. When she arranged things just right, she found room in the oven for an apple crisp.

* * *

It was already pitch-black, the shortest day of the year, though barely five o'clock, when Clarence finally came into the house. The thermometer read ten below and Clarence's face showed traces of frost.

Irene and Dickey hung on his legs, as Clarence washed up at the kitchen sink.

"Are the kittens all right?" Irene said, chewing on her pigtail.

"The gray one caught a mouse today," Clarence said, "and the spotted one fell asleep on top of Bingo's back."

If Clarence was surprised by the fancy table, he didn't mention it. It seemed like a normal day, a day before everything went to hell. They had just sat down when headlights flashed through the kitchen window. Bingo barked a welcome.

"Who could it be?" Clarence said with noticeable irritation. "Can't even eat in peace."

Tillie went to the window, scraped frost and peered outside. She looked and then looked again. "It's Nels Carlson's truck." Her heart sank.

"He was healed by a radio preacher," she said, surprised at the calmness in her voice. "Came to church this morning without crutches." She had planned to tell Clarence, but had forgotten. There would have been a time when she would have remembered.

It would be over. Nels would tell her off, and Clarence would give up. Maybe it was time to end this agony. Even divorce would be better than subjecting the children to their acrimony. She would just have to make the best of it. Tears welled.

Nels stood in the doorway, face red from the wind and holding a decanter of Olga's dandelion wine. He and Olga had always given wine to all the relatives at Christmas.

Tillie stared. It couldn't be. She looked at his face and then down at the wine again. She stood speechless.

"Won't you invite me in, Cousin?" Nels said. He thrust the wine into her hands as Tillie looked in astonishment. "Colder than a witch's tit outside."

Julebukking

THE DOG BARKED A FRENZIED WELCOME. Tia pulled back the gingham curtain and peeked outside. "I can't see who it is." She scraped frost with her thumbnail.

Unexpected visitors were rare. It might be another visit from Pastor Hustvedt about Norman's drinking. Dear God, she prayed. Anything but that.

Tia could tell Ma was nervous, too, by the way she bit her lip. Maybe Ma worried about a preacher's visit as well. The kerosene lantern sputtered on the table, the evening shadows filling the corners of the old farmhouse. Norman swallowed his last bite of cake.

"It's too late for the Watkins man," Ma said.

Tia heard giggles and stomping feet. Norman pushed away from the table, his bib overalls stained and greasy from fixing the pump. "I'll get it."

Two people dressed as trolls stood in the doorway. The taller wore an old buffalo coat with swirling black curls. A feed sack with cut-out eyes and nose draped over his face, and a tall pointy hat topped his head. The other, smaller by a foot, huddled beneath a horse-hide blanket and wore a carved wooden mask. Both held straw baskets made in the shapes of goats. Their breath puffed vapors of cloud as they shifted their feet to keep warm, hunching their shoulders against the east wind.

"*Julebukkers!*" Ma motioned them into the kitchen with a delighted chuckle. "*Velkommen!*" Ma's face lightened and she more resembled the woman Tia remembered from her childhood.

119

Tia relaxed. It was only foolery, something done between Christmas and New Years, an ancient Nordic custom that went back to the days of Thor.

"Who be you?" Ma hurriedly cleared the table. "And on such a night."

Ma kept asking questions. "East wind means snow, don't you think?" Tia knew it was the old way—asking questions until one of the visitors answered. A voice was hard to disguise in a small community.

Tia fed a chunk of wood into the range and adjusted the damper. It had been a long while since anyone had come *Julebukking*—before the war at least. She remembered being afraid of the costumed neighbors— and her relief when her parents guessed who they were and the masks came off. Usually the *Julebukkers* took someone along from every house. By the end of the night, large groups traveled house to house.

Most of all, Tia remembered the laughter over coffee and lunch afterward, a vivid image of her father's face framed in lamplight. Such happiness they had shared before Pa died, before the war, before Norman was prisoner, before Clyde married Vera. Not like now. Nothing like now.

Tia filled the coffee pot from the water bucket.

These *Julebukkers* didn't fall for the bait. They kept silent. The taller stood at a gawky angle, holding his arms away from his body in an ape-like manner. The shorter brayed like a donkey.

"Tia, can you guess who they are?" Ma said.

Before Tia could answer, Norman cut in, "I'd know you any- where, Clyde Hanson, even without hearing the engine of your new Ford. Your big feet give you away every time."

Clyde and Vera removed their masks. Envy, like a choking hand, cut off Tia's voice.

Tia busied herself getting lunch. She pulled a crock of rosettes, crispy fried cookies, from the top cupboard. The heavy smell of lard wafted into the room when she lifted the lid. Clyde always made a big deal about Tia's being the best in the township. She hesitated. Clyde only deserved plain honey jumbles—or none at all. But Tia would not be rude to their neighbors. She dusted the rosettes with sugar and arranged them on the good cookie plate—the same as always.

Vera barely came up to Clyde's chin. Tia watched Vera's feet, small and dainty, pull from the big overshoes of her disguise. As she looked away, Tia saw Norman's unmistakable look of longing. She and her brother made a good pair. She and Norman, Mr. and Miss Fiskum, forever the bachelor and old maid, each in love with someone out of reach.

"Sit and have coffee," Ma said. She fluttered around, trying to be jolly, talking about old times and *Julebukkers* from the past.

It came to Tia Ma was desperately unhappy. Ma expected everything to be normal when the war ended. Instead, everything was even worse.

Vera only sipped her coffee but Clyde ate five rosettes, almost the whole plate. "These are delicious," he said and hooked another with his index finger. "Vera, get this recipe."

A warm flush crept up Tia's neck and cheeks as she stirred sugar into her cup.

"Who'll come with us?" Clyde said. "We're going to the neighbors."

Tia frantically searched for reasons to stay home. There was mending. She was reading a good book. The last thing she wanted was to parade through the neighborhood with Clyde and Vera.

"Please," Vera said, "We'll have fun."

"I'm too old," Ma said. "It's for younger people."

Though Ma said the words, Tia had the feeling Ma didn't believe she was too old at all. It was Ma's way of coping with the sadness of Norman's drinking and all the rest.

"I'm reading *The Yearling*," Tia said. "Ma gave it to me for Christmas. But you should go, Norman."

"Only if you go along," Norman said.

They all looked at her. Ma gave that encouraging nod she always used when she wanted Tia to do something against her will. Vera's face lit up like an electric bulb. Tia supposed Vera expected they would soon become best of friends.

Tia didn't need a friend. But Norman did. Since his return from the war, Norman was changed. Maybe the old custom would be good for him. Tia would do anything to help her brother. It was good of Clyde to think of it.

She finally nodded, and Ma flurried to gather costumes.

Ma pulled a shirt from the mending basket, and helped Tia into an old pair of bib overalls that had belonged to her father. They fit her well, not too long or tight. Norman handed her a wool cap. With the ear flaps pulled down and the cap's bill tugged forward, identification was impossible. Ma helped Tia into men's work gloves and then into Norman's barn boots, still crusted with dried manure. Vera suggested she tie a bandanna handkerchief over her mouth like a cowboy.

"Swell!" Vera clapped her hands. "Like the Lone Ranger."

"You'll fool them," Clyde said. "They'll never guess."

Ma fished in the closet for her oldest dress. It hung on Norman, tight across the shoulders but covered his legs down to his feet. Ma tied an apron around his waist. Norman pulled on a bulky barn coat, swathed his face and head in a wool scarf and topped it with Pa's old fur hat.

"All you need is lipstick." Clyde elbowed Norman in the ribs.

Ma's eyes glittered. "Have fun," she said. "Oh, to be young again."

Tia hurried to Clyde's Ford parked behind the lilac bushes. A million stars winked above them with a waning moon. She crawled into the back seat, expecting Norman to follow. Instead, Vera scrambled in beside her. Tia's legs crowded against the seat. She scrunched to the side trying to fit her legs at an angle.

"We gals will sit in the back so we can gab," Vera said. Headlights reflected on drifted snow. "The men need the leg room." Their breathing steamed the inside of the windows as the heater battled the bitter cold.

"For Christ sake," Norman said, and Tia hoped he wouldn't change his mind. "You could have picked a warmer night."

"Your Ma's right about snow moving in," Clyde said. "It was tonight or never." Then Clyde entertained them for the first cold mile by telling how he woke up to a gnawing sound and discovered a porcupine eating the new machine shed. Tia hung on every word, the timbre of his voice, his measured cadence in drawing out the story.

"Hercules went after it," Vera said, "got his mouth full of quills." Her voice trembled. "Terrible."

"Any damage to your shed?" Tia said. Strange that Vera cared only about the dog.

They talked back and forth about buildings and hazards to them. Vera told how her father had once driven through the wall of a garage when he was drunk. Conversation lagged.

"Any porcupines in Germany?" Clyde said.

Tia held her breath. Norman avoided all questions about his time in Eruope. A heavy silence filled the car.

"Didn't see any." Norman finally said. His voice stretched and strained but he answered the question. "A few squirrels. Birds."

Tia let out her breath with a sigh. It was good for Norman to be out with people, even if they had to dress up as fools to do it.

The feeble gleam from the dashboard cast an eerie light in the car. At least she could hide in the darkness of the back seat where Clyde couldn't see her. She could look at the back of his curly head all she wanted without him knowing. She had always admired the way he tilted his head when he talked.

"Before we get to the Olsons'," Vera said from her side of the backseat, "we'd like to ask you and Norman something." She had that child-like look on her face that Tia had grown to expect. "Do you want to ask them, Clyde?" Her voice sounded breathless and hesitant, as if unsure of his response.

"Go ahead," Clyde said.

"My sister, Selma, lives in California," Vera said, "or we'd ask her." She fiddled with the carved mask on her lap, scraping a sliver away from the nose with the back of her fingernail. "We're expecting, you know," she said. "We'd like you two to stand as godparents."

Norman's jaw dropped open with a snort. Tia had dreamed of standing at the altar with Clyde—but never as godmother for his child. A mental image of them together at the baptismal fount skittered through her mind. Standing exposed before the whole church, fueling gossip about her broken heart. Of taking responsibility for Clyde's child although he had chosen a town girl. Tia's throat turned dusty and she doubted she could answer even if she had words to speak. The warming car reminded her of the manure on Norman's boots.

"I'm not much of a Lutheran," Norman said with a gruff voice. He reached up and scraped frost off the inside of the windshield with his gloved hand. "Not too much of anything, I guess."

"I can think of no one better," Clyde said, and his voice carried none of the usual teasing banter. "We've been friends since diapers and our parents before us. You and Tia are like brother and sister to me."

"Please say yes, Tia." Vera clasped mittened hands in front of her.

Vera looked like Shirley Temple waiting for applause. She was only a child. Not sensible enough to be a mother.

Tia should have told Clyde how she felt about him when she had the chance. He wouldn't have asked her to be a godmother for his child if he knew her feelings for him.

"We'll think about it," Norman said at last.

Tia sent a silent thank you to her brother, mental telepathy though it was. Emotion clogged her throat, robbed her of breath, and stopped speech.

"Don't know I'll stay in this country," Norman said. "Been thinking of moving on."

The road slicked icy with soft drifts gathered in the curves. Across Olson's field, the snow mounded like ocean waves, whipped by the wind. Snow fences stretched across the western lip of the road in a futile effort to keep the road open.

"Need a shelterbelt down this stretch," Norman said. "Or at least better snow fences."

"Selma says California is warm and sunny year round," Vera said.

"Don't," Clyde said.

Norman started to say something, but the car turned into the Olson driveway.

"Time to put on your mask, Kemosabi." Clyde pulled the Ford to a halt a short way from the Olsons' door. He pulled the hand brake and turned out the headlights. "Tonto and Lone Ranger are *Julebukking* tonight!"

Widow Olson greeted them in her bedclothes, her white hair loosed from its crown and falling down to her waist. She held the lantern higher to glimpse their faces.

"*Julebukkers!*" she said, and burst into a toothless smile. "Uff da! Come in out of the cold wind."

They stood on newspapers. Clyde took the same ape-like stance he had used at their house, standing with his elbows cocked and shoulders hunched. Vera looked like a little kid behind the carved mask. Tia towered at her side. Norman made an unlikely woman with his wide shoulders and stubbly chin.

"George Carlson, is that you?" Mrs. Olson poked Tia in the arm. "I know it's you." She reached to hug Tia. "Welcome home, George. I hadn't heard you were back."

Tia shook her head and pulled back, humiliated. No one would ever mistake Vera Hanson for a man.

"Tall strapping boy." Mrs. Olson chortled with happiness. "I'd know you anywhere! When did you get home?"

Norman unwrapped the scarf around his face. "It's just us, Mrs. Olson," he said in a flat, soft voice. "Clyde and Vera and Tia and me."

Tia gave him a grateful glance, and he nodded to show he understood. They had always been close. At least until he went away to war. It was as if her brother left for war, and a stranger came home wearing his face.

"Norman!" Vera said. "You spoiled it. She wasn't even close!"

"Stand on the rug and I'll get your drinks." Mrs. Olson placed the lamp on the edge of the table and rummaged in her cupboard until she pulled out a wine decanter. "This will warm you!"

Mrs. Olson's chokecherry wine was acclaimed throughout Tolga Township. Tia watched Norman's eyes light with anticipation.

"Julius will be sorry he missed you," Mrs. Olson said as she poured the wine into thimble sized glasses. "He went to a picture show. Something with Spencer Tracy and Katherine Hepburn."

"Don't mind if I do." Norman reached for a glass.

"Nothing too good for our soldiers," Mrs. Olson said. "So glad you're home safe and sound. I suppose you're going to take over your ma's farm."

Norman didn't answer her question. He downed the wine as Mrs. Olson passed the glasses to the rest of them, and then refilled Norman's.

"Your ma must be glad," Mrs. Olson continued. "Will you be adding to your herd? Butterfat prices are only going higher."

Norman did not answer. Clyde stuck out his empty glass, and then Norman held his out for another refill. Mrs. Olson motioned toward Vera and Tia, but they shook their heads.

Tia had a hard time emptying her glass. Since Norman's return from the war, his drinking had caused enough heartache to make Tia consider joining the Women's Temperance Union.

"We used to go *Julebukking*," Mrs. Olson said. "All the Hexums and the Hegdahls. We made our own fun."

If Julius had been home, no doubt they would have taken him along, but not Mrs. Olson already in her nightgown. Instead, they said their goodnights and trudged out to the car. The cold a bitter slap after the warmth of the house.

"Another for the road?" Norman pulled a flat bottle from his pocket and held it out to Clyde. "Might as well take a nip."

"I'm driving," Clyde said. "Maybe the girls want some."

"None for me," Vera said and patted her stomach.

Norman did not offer any to Tia. Instead he tipped the bottle and guzzled a long swallow. Where did he find money for liquor? They needed every cent to pay their mortgage. A sharp anger rose up within her, anger at Norman for bringing a bottle along, anger at herself for being unable to stop his great thirst.

"Nosy old hen." Norman took another swig from the bottle. "None of her business what I do. None of anyone's damn business. "

"She meant well," Vera said. "She's a nice old woman."

Norman kept drinking. He was almost staggering by the time they arrived at the Moberg farm.

"Think we can squeeze Mildred into the car?" Clyde said.

"Good old Millie," Norman said with a slur. "Sent me cookies while I was a jail bird."

Tia wanted to slump under the seat.

They fitted their masks in the yard as the dog circled and barked.

"It's all right," Tia said, and reached out to pat the dog. "Good girl."

Selmer opened the door and ushered them into the kitchen. Clyde postured, and Norman stood like Betty Grable with his chest stuck out and hip pushed forward. Vera brayed like a donkey, and Tia wanted only to melt away like the frost on the windows.

The piano music ended when Mildred joined them. The kitchen felt homey with its warm electric lights, gas range and smell of fried onions.

"*Julebukkers!*" Mildred said. "Don't mind your overshoes."

Selmer eyed them for a long moment, and scowled at Norman. "Norman Fiskum."

"How did you guess?" Vera said. "He has a great costume!"

"Should I fetch the brandy, Daddy?" Mildred said.

Selmer shook his head. "Looks like they've had enough already."

Tia wanted to run out of the house and go home. Selmer was on the Church Board. So far the community had been tolerant of Norman's behavior. It couldn't last.

Mildred took their coats. They sat around the kitchen table. Mildred put the coffee on the stove, and pulled cookies from a stone jar.

"Will you come with us, Mildred?" Vera said.

Mildred nodded when Selmer interrupted. "Not tonight." Selmer sat with his arms folded across his chest. "We're busy."

Mildred looked in surprise.

"I'm driving," Clyde said. "It won't be late."

"Not tonight," Selmer said. "Another time."

The talk switched to hog prices, the cost of seed corn, and the snowy forecast verified by the easterly wind. Mildred kept cups filled. Vera asked Mildred about the Luther League social coming up, and prattled about an electric butter churn that could be purchased with green stamps. Tia listened to the men's conversation. She wanted to ask Clyde if he thought it wise to build up the dairy herd or diversify into beef cattle. Farming always interested her more than housework.

Finally Clyde pushed away from the table and stood.

"Sure you don't want to come, Mildred?" Tia asked.

Mildred looked toward her father, and shrugged one shoulder while shaking her head.

"We'll talk tomorrow," Mildred said to Tia. "Have fun."

"Good old Millie," Norman said when they were back in the car. "Her dad won't let her out with a killer. Folks are like that, you know. Sent us off to kill Nazis but then look down on us."

"Norman," Tia said. "That's enough."

"Don't be too hard on Selmer," Clyde said. "Willy . . . you know."

"Ain't my fault." Norman took another swig. "Lots of boys bought it."

"Where next?" Tia had to turn it around somehow. If she said the right words, it might turn out all right. "The Hegdahls?"

"First the Carlsons." Clyde turned the wheel and the tires slipped. Vera squealed. "For Christ's sake, Vera," Clyde said. "I'm a good driver."

Tia wished that she had stayed home. She didn't like being with Clyde and Vera, didn't care to see them squabble over petty things, and didn't like the side of Clyde she was seeing. He had grown bossy.

"Vera," Norman said with a loud belch. "Tell me about California."

Vera chattered as Norman emptied his bottle, rolled down the window and threw it out into the ditch. Clyde didn't say anything, just pulled a fag from his pocket and lit it with the lighter.

"Damn the Germans." Norman leaned against the car door and groaned. "All to hell."

"It's all right," Vera said. "You'll—"

"Quiet!" Clyde said with a twist of his head to see the back seat. Tia saw the angry look on his face from the light of the glowing dashboard.

"Do you need to stop, Norman?" The car hit a drift of snow and swerved to the side. Clyde turned his attention back to the road, and turned the steering wheel to keep them on the road. "Don't be sick in our new car."

"I'm sick, all right. Sick of everything." A gush of vomit spewed over the dashboard, the car door, and the front of Norman's coat. A sour smell filled the car.

Clyde smashed on the brakes, parked the car, and leapt out. He ran around to Norman's door and opened it. Norman struggled to get out and Clyde grabbed him by his coat sleeve and pulled him out, just as another wave of vomiting erupted. Tia and Vera scrambled outside.

"Christ!" Clyde said. "You could have told me to stop."

Tia grabbed handfuls of soft snow to clean off the dashboard. She undid the bandanna kerchief around her neck and wiped at the soiled upholstery and the door handle. The night had turned into a disaster.

Norman lay in the snow, slobbering and crying. "None of her damn business. I'm not in prison. I'll leave if I feel like it."

"That's right," Vera knelt by Norman's side, and wiped his face with her handkerchief. "No one can force you to do anything."

Tia choked back tears. What would happen to Norman if he didn't stop drinking? What could she do to help him? "Clyde, take us home."

"But what about the Carlsons and the Hegdahls?" Vera said with a childlike wail. "I wanted to ask Nels about his healing. It's too early to quit."

The Blizzard

THE STORM KEPT TIA AWAKE with its howling winds and icy pellets tinkling against the window. The farm house groaned and cracked in the cold. At first, Tia worried about chimney fires. Ma had added dried oak to the fire until the stovepipe glowed red. You'd think Ma would know better, but sometimes she was downright stubborn. Downdrafts pushed puffs of acrid smoke and creosote into the house, each time waking Tia with a start.

Finally, when she had almost fallen asleep, Tia heard Norman calling out in his sleep. His strangled voice felt colder and more frightful than any blizzard. She tried to quiet him before Ma woke up, but failed. Tia suspected they all lay sleepless in their individual rooms, listening and worrying. So near, and yet each so distant and alone.

Tia lay in her narrow bed, and imagined how it would feel to be married. No fears with someone close beside her, the noise of the storm creating a private world for just the two of them. Though Tia knew it was a sin to covet another woman's husband, she allowed herself the luxury of putting a face on the imaginary spouse.

In the morning, Tia woke to intense silence, common in the wake of a storm. The winds finally gone. Every sound muffled by the mounded drifts. Ma stirred the firebox in the kitchen and the scent of burning pine wafted up the stairs along with the smell of cooking coffee. Tia hurried into her clothes, every breath a burst of vapor in the frigid room, and rushed to warm herself by the kitchen range. Norman pulled on woolen socks in front of the open oven door.

130

"Is it still snowing?" Tia said, as she cracked open the kitchen door for a better look. Arctic air swooped in like a sharp knife. Snow glittered in dazzling brightness.

"Good Lord!" Ma said. That was as close as she ever came to swearing. "Shut the door!"

Tia hadn't planned on leaving the door open, just wanted to check the temperature. She obeyed her mother and scraped a small peep hole in the frosted window pane "Brrrr. Thermometer says twenty-six below," she said.

"Norman, pull your ear flappers down," Ma said. "And bundle up in Grandpa's buffalo coat."

Norman added another sweater, and pulled on the old coat worn only on coldest days. He tied a red, wool scarf around his nose, and stood round and fat as a snowman. He didn't say anything, but Tia suspected he was biting back words the same as she. Ma was too bossy this morning. The restless night had them all on edge.

The phone rang two shorts and two long. Tia reached for the receiver and struggled to understand the hysterical voice on the other end of the line. It took Tia a long minute to realize it was Blanche Root.

"What's wrong, Blanche?" Tia said. "Slow down and tell me again."

Harvey was lying in a snow bank by the pump house. He wasn't breathing.

"We'll be right over," Tia said. Her mind went in a million directions, remembering when she found Pa in the hay barn, the shock of losing him. "Stay in the house 'til we get there." Then another worry intruded. "Where's Eddy?"

"Ran off," Blanche said, her voice a quivering wail. "He'll freeze in such weather."

Tia was about to hang up when Tillie Stenerson spoke on the receiver. Rubbering again. "I'll call the neighbors," Tillie said. For once, Tillie would be useful. "Maybe the sheriff."

"Not the sheriff," Tia said. "You know how Eddy is."

Tia hung up, and scrambled for a plan. Drifts piled as high as the eaves of the house. Roads blocked. Snowplows wouldn't clear the side roads for days. It seemed the storm had passed, but one never knew. Sometimes it wrapped around and hit again, even harder than the first time.

"I'll go if you do the chores," Norman said to Tia. "I'll hitch the cutter."

"Blanche needs a woman," Ma said. "You'll go along, Tia. I'll do the chores."

"The work's too heavy for you," Tia said. "I'll do the chores. Norman can go alone."

If the truth were told, Tia dreaded being with the grieving widow. She never knew what to say in difficult situations. Tia could cook, clean barns and milk cows, but she didn't have a clue how to comfort someone in need.

It came to her that Ma should go with Norman. She was Blanche's friend, after all.

"I couldn't stand the trip in such weather," Ma said. "Hurry now."

Tia looked toward Norman for support, but he shrugged. "We'll fill the stock tank before we go." He left the house. Tia hurried into her coat and followed.

The cold bit into her lungs. She and Norman took turns pumping water. Their mittens stuck to the frozen iron pump handle. "At least we don't have to deal with frozen pipes," Tia said.

Tia fetched the small sledge behind the barn door. It was little more than a stone boat on runners, something Grandpa had built. Tia wiped cobwebs with her mittens. Two ancient bells hung from the front. It was old fashioned but the only way to travel until the snowplows cleared the roads. The livestock huddled in the steamy barn, their breath and body heat making it feel as warm as the house. Norman collected Pet.

The cows mooed in their stanchions, full udders dripping, while cats lapped drops of milk beneath them. Ma would be out soon enough to do the chores. They had to hurry.

Norman led the gelding out of the barn, Pet's coat shaggy against the cold, his huge hooves plunging through the snow. Tia hugged his neck, sniffing the horse-smell, his nicker a soft vibration through the thickness of hide. She loved their horses more than she could ever love a

John Deere tractor. She must ask Clyde if he missed their old team. The horse stomped and huffed against the cold, but stepped into the traces.

"Good boy." Norman petted his nose, giving him a lump of sugar from his pocket, as he secured the harness. "Always willing."

"I'll fetch the robes," Tia said, a sudden lump in her throat because Norman sounded for that brief moment like his old self. "You get the scoop shovel."

Ma had the horse-hide blanket ready. She wrapped old blankets around rocks heated on top of the woodstove. "Put these at your feet," Ma said. "Wish there was time to bake potatoes for your pockets" She asked about long underwear and extra socks. Tia gathered extra mittens, another blanket and the basket of food Ma had already packed for Blanche.

"Poor Blanche," Ma said with a cluck of her tongue. "Stay as long as you're needed. Norman and I will get by without you."

Tia widened her eyes, but bit back her retort. She couldn't be away from the farm for any length of time, even if Blanche needed someone. Ma couldn't do the heavy winter work. Ma didn't know how Norman hid in the granary instead of doing chores. She didn't understand that Norman was unreliable.

"Hurry now," Ma said as she peered out the window toward the horizon. "Before another storm."

Tia would have liked to have driven the horse, but Norman held the lines. Their shoulders touched as they sat side by side on the only seat. They adjusted the robes and blankets, and placed the wrapped stones under their feet. Tia felt the welcome heat through the soles of her rubber overshoes. The old robes smelled of mice. Norman flicked the lines. The bells jingled with each lurch through the snow, a tinny sound that bounced over the snow banks. The shelterbelt barely showed above the drifts.

"Damn this weather," Norman said

"It's not the weather," Tia said in her most cheerful voice, "it's not wearing enough clothes." She pulled the horsehide blanket higher over her face to block the wind. "That's what Grandpa always said."

"It is the goddamn weather," Norman said with a growl. "This godforsaken country."

They bounced across the pasture, the township roads no better than the prairie, taking the shortcut. Pet churned through the snow, stumbling and falling through the frozen crust. Norman steered around the worst snowdrifts, driving with one arm shading his eyes from the glare of sun on snow. The horses passed gas with every step, groaning and popping like the house during last night's storm.

"Poor Harvey," Tia said. "So sad."

"Falling asleep in the snow isn't bad," Norman said. His voice took on a strange timbre. "It isn't the worst way to go."

She knew he meant the war. So many questions that she didn't dare ask. She couldn't imagine what he had lived through, and he wouldn't speak of it. Maybe if he did, he would get some relief from the torment. Her poor brother, wounded inside though no one would know it by looking at him. She leaned closer toward him, feeling the comfort of his presence.

They hit a level stretch where the horse pulled easier. They would go right through the Hanson farm. Her mind drifted back to her daydreams of Clyde, but Norman interrupted her thoughts with more complaints about Minnesota winters and his plans to move away.

"Don't just piss and moan," Tia said. "What's keeping you here if you hate it so bad?"

Pet stumbled and the sledge lurched. "Whoa, boy," Norman said, as he pulled the lines. The sleigh evened out and the bells jingled again. The horse passed more gas.

"Ma thinks you're staying," Tia said. "Why don't you tell her your plans?"

She had a million questions but a sharp memory intruded, stopping her flow of words. Last year, an old Luther League friend moved back to Tolga Township after her husband lost a leg in Italy. Tia had been trying to make conversation at the Ladies' Aid meeting, and almost blurted out something unthinkable. She stopped herself in the nick of time from saying that at least her husband, known for his temper and cruelty to animals, would no longer be able to kick their dog. Thank God, she hadn't put voice to it. Anything she said to Norman would be equally misspoken.

They were in sight of the Hanson barn when Pet stumbled again. The sledge tipped to one side, throwing Tia across the snow. She had a wild thought that Norman flipped the sleigh on purpose to get back at her.

Tia jumped up, brushing snow off her coat and face. Icy shards found bare skin around her stockings and between her mittens and coat sleeves.

"You all right?" Norman said. He bent down and dug snow away from the runner with the shovel. "Lodged in a root."

"Like sliding down the Moberg's hill," she said. "Remember Willy's birthday party?" She tried to keep her voice light, trying to picture the old Norman who loved sliding and sleighing, the brother who claimed winter as his favorite season.

"Don't start," he said. "I hate it when you go on about stuff." He grumbled, cursed and reached for a bottle inside his coat. She gritted her teeth until her jaws ached, and grabbed the shovel and dug the snow away from the sleigh. Blanche needed them. She dug as fast as she could.

They had to do what was needed at the Roots, and get back to the farm before dark. Norman watched her work, tucked the bottle back into his coat pocket, lit a cigarette and took a deep drag.

He grasped the runner with the cigarette dangling from a corner of his mouth. His words slurred with the effort of holding the cigarette in place. He motioned for her to lift on the other side. "I've said all along that I'm not staying."

"Ma doesn't know," Tia said. Her voice sounded as sharp as the wind picking up from the north. "She's convinced I'll find a husband and you'll take over the farm."

Norman snorted. "That'll be the day."

She didn't know if he scoffed at her finding a husband, or him staying on the farm. He was right—either way.

"Norman, promise me that you'll tell her."

"What's the difference?" He snorted again. "Just sparing her the truth a little longer. She'll find out soon enough."

"No," Tia said. "I mean it. Just tell her. She needs to know."

"Goddamn it, Tia," Norman said. "I don't want to be pushed."

"Daylight's burning," Tia said. Her feet ached and her disappointment and frustration sat like a stone on her chest. Talking to Norman was like talking to a brick wall. "The faster we get there, the sooner we get home."

Together they jerked the runner free. Norman climbed on the cutter, and urged the horse to pull ahead. Tia grabbed the robes and blankets spilled across the ground, and followed behind, stumbling in the tracks until Norman pulled to a stop. She climbed in, and searched for the hot rocks. The blankets were there but the rocks must have fallen out when the sleigh tipped over. She adjusted the robes again. It felt colder. She couldn't stop shivering.

They finally reached the Hanson's yard. Clyde waved from his tractor seat where he plowed snow with a v-blade attached to the front of the tractor. "Back to horse and buggy?"

"At least our pipes don't freeze up," Norman shouted. His words blew away in the wind. Pet shied from the roar of the tractor. Norman held him firm, talking in a soothing voice.

"Going to open Blanche's road," Clyde shouted over the tractor's rumble. "Leave the sleigh and ride along. Pa's in the barn."

The horse, sweaty from his effort, quivered with exhaustion. Tia looked at Norman and shrugged. Made sense to spare Pet when they could.

Olaf came out from the barn carrying a bucket of milk. His face wore a serious look that reminded Tia of his life-long friendship with Harvey Root. It was a sorrow to lose a good neighbor. A loss to everyone.

"They're riding with me," Clyde said. "Take care of the horse?"

"Road's open," Olaf said. "Tia can ride with us."

Norman jumped up behind Clyde, hanging onto the back of the tractor seat like a fat tick on the back of a dog. The tails of his red scarf blew straight behind him. They roared down the driveway without a backward glance. Tia led the horse toward the barn.

Olaf set the milk bucket to one side and took the lines. "You're shivering," he said. "Take the milk into the house and warm up. I'll be right in."

She couldn't feel her feet. She took the bucket and trudged to the house, thinking the whole time how she'd rather stay in the barn with

Olaf. Ingeborg's little dog stuck his head out of the doghouse to bark a greeting. She rapped on the kitchen door.

Vera threw the door open. "Tia, I'm so glad to see you!"

Vera was crying, her eyes puffed red, and she dabbed at her eyes and nose with a pretty, lavender handkerchief. The kitchen felt like an oven after being outside. Tia's nose ran. She pulled off her mittens, sniffed and searched for a handkerchief in her coat pocket.

"Stand on the floor grate," Vera said, as she wiped her eyes again. Vera bit her lower lip with her perfect front teeth. "Don't worry about your overshoes." Why was Vera so upset? She had only known Harvey a few months. "Warm up while I put my lipstick on."

The warm air rising from the basement furnace brought an ache to Tia's cheeks and feet. She'd be lucky to escape without chilblains. Dirty cereal bowls cluttered the kitchen table beside a box of corn flakes and a jar of store-bought jelly. Tia could have written her name in the dust on top of the refrigerator. Of course, Vera probably couldn't see that high. Tia resisted the urge to clean it for her.

"Isn't it terrible?" Vera said, returning to the kitchen with her lips freshly painted. The tears started again. "I'm heartsick."

Tia looked up in surprise. She felt badly about Harvey's death, and worse about Blanche's predicament. She worried about Dumb Ed. But she had not felt like crying. To be honest, Tia didn't cry very often. Vera was different. Tears pooled in her eyes, and ran down her face.

"Just think of Blanche." Rivers of tears dripped down her face. Her shoulders heaved as sobs started. She sat on down at the table and covered her face with her hanky. When she finally looked up, her bright red lipstick smeared across her fancy handkerchief.

"Can you imagine how sad it must be to lose someone you love? How terrible to be all alone?"

Tia felt a sudden urgency. She pulled off her overshoes. "Can I use your water closet?"

"Of course," Vera sniffed into her handkerchief and motioned Tia to follow. "It's this way."

She led Tia through the dining room and past the staircase that went upstairs. She pointed to a door. Tia opened the door into Clyde and Vera's lilac-colored bedroom. Lavender walls with lacy curtains at the frosty windows. Tia passed their unmade bed to get to the little half-bath tucked under the staircase. She stepped over Vera's sheer nightgown and a pair of Clyde's dirty socks.

Tia finished her business, admiring the flushing water that eliminated the need for chamber pots and slop pails. She fingered Clyde's shaving brush on the sink beside several tubes of lipstick and a jar of cold cream.

Vera had everything: electricity and indoor plumbing, a coal furnace in the basement, a modern tractor, and a nice dairy herd. She slept next to someone she loved during the storm. Vera didn't know to treasure such luxuries. Tia would have kept the house as neat as a pin, making their bed before she thought about lipstick or other foolishness. She would fix a hot breakfast every morning, and wash the dishes before going out to the barn to help with the chores. She and Clyde could have been so happy.

Suddenly Tia felt the walls closing in. What was she doing? She washed her hands and wiped them on a purple hand towel monogrammed with a fancy H. She set her jaw and refused to look at their bed on the way out. She stepped right on Vera's slippery, sheer nightgown. She wouldn't stay in Vera's house a moment longer than necessary.

* * *

They piled into Olaf's 1936 Packard, Vera still sniffling into her handkerchief. Ingeborg held a basket of baked goods in her lap. She shook her head in disapproval at Vera's tears. "He lived a good life," Ingeborg said. "Nothing to cry over."

"I can't help it," Vera said, burying her face in her handkerchief.

Tia couldn't believe a grown woman would act so foolishly. Vera didn't have a lick of sense, was no better than Dumb Ed. Tia could see Ingeborg's disapproval of Vera.

"Have you put in your order for chicks?" Ingeborg turned part way around in the front speak to speak directly to Tia, obviously excluding Vera from the conversation.

They talked about chickens and egg production, following the single track Clyde had cleared to the Root farm. They slid off the track once, but Olaf steered the car back onto the path.

"He should have made a wider track," Vera said.

"We're lucky to have this one," Olaf said.

He spoke too quickly, showing that he, too, was running out of patience with Vera. They turned into the Root driveway where Clyde plowed snow away from the hay barn and outbuildings, making huge mountains of snow. Tia didn't see Norman, probably out doing barn chores. She looked toward the pump house where Blanche said Harvey had dropped. Tracks in the snow where he had fallen, but no sign of Harvey.

Clyde waved to them as they climbed out of the car. He loved to use machinery of any kind, and loved pushing snow. Tillie said he hoped to work for the township someday, driving the big plows.

Eddy stepped out from where he had been hiding behind the lilac bushes. His stubbly cheeks blazed red from the cold. He wore only one mitten. Tia figured he must have been watching Clyde on the tractor, and wondered if Blanche knew her son wasn't lost anymore. Eddy shifted his weight from one foot to the other, his mind as slack and weak as a snowflake tossed in the wind. "The frogs are talking," he said.

"Frogs sleep all winter," Vera said. "Come inside and warm up."

"Frogs say Pa is in heaven with Old Man Ingvaldson." He sucked in his breath as a worried look crossed his face. "Stay away from that nosey old sonofabitch."

"We've brought treats." Vera walked over to Eddy, and took his cold hand in her mittened one. "Come inside and have cookies."

Inside Blanche sat at the kitchen table, her white hair sticking out in all directions like a dandelion gone to seed. She wore a thin, cotton dress more suitable for hot July than freezing January. When she saw Eddy, she burst into loud weeping.

"Eddy, where have you been?" Blanche motioned to her son to come to her. He tracked snow across the kitchen floor, mumbling about frogs in the swamp. "I've been worried sick about you." Blanche didn't seem to see anyone else, just grabbed Eddy around the neck and cried into his chest. "You're freezing." She pulled him closer, and kissed his forehead.

They all removed their overshoes and wraps. When Eddy took off his stocking cap, his ears showed enough dirt to plant potatoes. Tia hung up everyone's coats in the entry way. Vera fetched an afghan from the davenport and draped it around Eddy's shoulders, then fetched another for Blanche from the bedroom. Through the open door, Tia glimpsed Harvey lying stiffly on the bed. Seeing his body, unnerved her. Made her feel the same dread she had about killing the deformed calf last spring. Tia stood awkwardly to the side, wishing she could find something to busy her hands.

"Let's start a pot of soup," Ingeborg said, and handed Tia a paring knife. "You can peel potatoes."

It felt good to be useful. Tia peeled slowly, wanting the chore to last as long as possible.

"Papa's called to heaven." Blanche rubbed her gnarled fingers over Eddy's bald head. "My good boy, you have to be strong. The Good Lord called him."

"Is he dead like Ole Stenerson in the war?"

"That's right," Blanche's voice cracked, and she dissolved into more weeping. She slumped into a kitchen chair and Vera sat beside her.

Ingeborg poured a dishpan of hot water from the tea kettle on the stove to soak Blanche's feet. Then she poured another for Eddy. Tia shied away when she saw Eddy's toe nails, long and curving over the top of his toes.

Olaf fired the wood stove, and Blanche told how Julius skied in like an angel of mercy to move Harvey out of the snow bank and into bed. "An angel, I tell you, like a flying angel coming to help me and Eddy."

Ingeborg asked where their brandy was hidden, and Vera fetched it from a cupboard. Vera poured a shot into Blanche's cup, and a little nip in Eddy's. Ingeborg cut slices of fresh bread, and set out the jam pot.

The kitchen quieted except for the whooshing flames going up the stovepipe and the loud sounds of Eddy's chewing.

"What happened?" Vera said. "We still don't know what happened to Harvey."

Everyone in the room flinched. Leave it to a town girl. Tia looked at Ingeborg who shook her head in apparent disgust.

"His heart," Blanche said. "Strange such a good-hearted man would have a bad heart. I begged him not to shovel. Doc Severson said heavy work would kill him. But there's no telling him anything." She released a huff, paused, reached across the table, and touched Eddy's arm. "He promised Eddy would do the shoveling."

"Didn't you help him, Eddy?" Vera said. Again the room flinched at her directness.

"Colder than a witch's tit." Eddy rubbed his hands together and grimaced. "Frogs talked to me. Goddamn sonofabitch snow."

"I did the dishes up. When I looked out later, Gunda's chimney smoke went straight up behind the trees so knew it were cold. Couldn't see the men. Then I spotted red against the pump house."

Vera leaned forward, just as if she were watching a moving picture show. Fat tears hung like icicles on her dark lashes. She laid her soft hand across Blanche's twisted fingers. Vera's nails painted bright red.

"My mind mixed up. I didn't even put no coat on." She looked at Vera and squeezed her hand when she noticed Vera's tears. "When I saw he was gone, I prayed for God to take me, too." She wrung Vera's hand until it blanched white. She lifted it to her face and kissed it. "Don't cry so, honey. He had a good life."

"What for you cried so loud, Ma? Did a bee sting you?" Eddy's face smeared with chocolate frosting from the cookies. He reached for another off the plate.

"Seeing my Eddy put my mind back to rights. Seeing my good boy so worried about me stopped such selfishness. My boy needs me."

Eddy pushed the whole cookie into his mouth. He chewed a while and swallowed hard. "Pa said damn you, Eddy, I'll get the belt if you don't start shoveling."

Norman and Julius stomped their feet on the doormat and stepped into the kitchen, their cheeks as red as Vera's nails. A toothpick hung out of Julius' mouth. They set a basket of eggs on the floor by the door. The potatoes were peeled so Tia began washing eggs.

"We did the chores up and watered the young stock," Julius said. "Is there anything else you want us to do?"

"*Mange tusen takk.*" Blanche shook her head. "You've done too much already."

"Don't be silly," Ingeborg said. "That's what neighbors are for."

Outside, Mansel Jorgenson skied into the yard and Nels Carlson drove up in his truck. Tia watched them greet each other as Mansel stuck his skis into a snow drift. They grabbed shovels and dug out the pump house, the job that toppled Harvey only hours earlier.

"I'm going home to fetch Ma," Julius said. "She'll stay with you a few days."

A wave of relief washed over Tia. They could leave without guilt. She set the bowl of clean eggs on the sink.

"That's too much!" Blanche said, her face dripping with tears. "I could never repay such kindness?"

"No need," Julius said, removing the toothpick and holding it like a pointer in his hand. "Do you remember how good you were to us when my father died?"

Tia had always known Julius to be a clear-eyed boy. He was a man now, tall and good looking. It came to her that Clyde plowed the snow but Julius moved the body into the house, and now it was Julius who said the words that eased Blanche's burden.

"Harvey and Eddy came after the funeral." Julius shifted his weight and dipped his chin. "We must have picked a million cucumbers that day, had to—or lose the crop."

"I did it." Eddy stuck out his chest. He squeezed his eyes shut and rubbed his hands together in front of him. "I picked those goddam sonofabitches pickles."

"None of us have forgotten," Julius said. "*I dag til meg, i morgen til deg, vi er alle i det saman.* Today to me, tomorrow to you, we're all in it together."

The truth of it settled over Tia as the snow had settled over Tolga Township.

Mildred Moberg

MILDRED PULLED THE BENCH closer to the Wurlitzer organ and flipped on the switch. She tentatively slipped out of her left shoe, and stepped on the ice-cold pedal. The organ moaned a low C in protest, growling louder as the instrument warmed. Almost as if called back from the tomb for its weekly duty at Tolga Lutheran—and not happy about it.

She slipped back into her shoe and blew on her fingers to warm them. Her breath puffed short clouds. Two below on the thermometer, and Norman only now firing the basement furnace. Her father had commented on the lack of chimney smoke when he dropped her off to practice before church service. In fact, her father had recited a litany of Norman's short comings: he didn't value his mother's farm, left heavy work for his sister, smoked and drank too much, didn't appreciate his job as sexton. He stopped short of comparing Norman's war experience to her brother's.

Dad didn't say Willy should have come home instead of Norman.

The stove door clanged as logs thudded into the firebox. A smoky scent wafted up from the basement through the floor grate with the first hint of warmth.

Norman should have been here earlier. Probably out drinking last night and late because of it. He'd made a complete fool of himself before Thanksgiving when he fell down the belfry steps. Anyone else would have been fired, but after what Norman had been through in the war, the deacons looked the other way.

With that thought, Mildred crimped her lips and firmly pressed a full G chord. The loudness echoing through the empty sanctuary startled her, and she quickly readjusted the volume. The old pump organ had responded only to her pumping feet. She thought about it with a twinge of longing. But progress was progress, and she did love the new Wurlitzer. No reedy exhalations, no clunk of pedals, and no bellows to work until one became exhausted.

She kicked off her shoe again, felt the draft on her stocking, and reached for the corresponding pedal to accompany the chord. Mildred followed the beautiful harmonies and melodies of the Concordia Hymnal that carried her to a different time and place. While the music flowed she forgot the mundane life she led, the loneliness. She forgot and was transported to what she always thought of as God's presence. A kingdom of order and harmony splashed across the page in quarter notes, half notes and melodies both exuberant and measured.

When she finished the last stanza of "Blessed Be the Tie That Binds," Mildred noticed Norman leaning against the arched doorway, listening. He wore an old barn jacket, four-buckle overshoes, and held a plaid wool cap in his burly hands. His face drooped with eyes that reminded Mildred of their old collie. Like he had seen too much.

Mildred felt a blush rise up in her cheeks and delved into an interlude of "Beautiful Savior" in the key of F, her favorite from her collection of sheet music. For congregational singing, she chose arrangements for lower voices. Few farmers could scale the high notes to ecstasy. But during the prelude, she was free to choose any key she wished. Always she aimed higher, thinking how the high notes drew them to look beyond their ordinary lives, higher than their work with cattle and fields.

The door pushed opened and Pastor Hustvedt swept into the sanctuary with a whoosh of cold air. Others began to trickle into the church.

She smelled Herman Gilbertson before she saw him. A dairy farmer, Herman used an expensive teat wash that permeated his skin in spite of soap or washing. Years ago, long before he married Nora Jenkins, Mildred once went with him to the picture show in Dalton. The smell of his clothes and hair had watered her eyes. She avoided him ever after.

The odor didn't seem to bother Nora. Herman's son sat on his lap, round eyed and drooly, while two little daughters snuggled close. Farm prices had been good with the war, and Nora boasted a new hat. The girls sported matching gray storm coats, all the rage with their fur collars.

Mildred looked away from what might have been. She knew the song almost by heart. She glanced up at the balcony where Norman's mother sat with closed eyes next to Tia. She and Tia had played together as children while their mothers picked raspberries or quilted for the church bazaar.

Norman had been the little brother, a year behind them in school. He'd been quiet and shy, maybe a little slower at his studies than he should have been. To be honest, Mildred hardly knew his existence other than a pesky tag-a-long. She nodded at Tia who smiled back. Of course she had sent him V-mail a time or two, as was only proper, and had shipped a box of peanut butter cookies at Christmas.

Dr. Sorenson dozed beside his plump wife in the back pew. A new baby, maybe, or a flare-up of scarlet fever might have kept him up last night. The paper said a family from Dane Prairie was quarantined with measles. The name sounded Catholic, certainly not from their congregation.

The chords beneath her fingers plunked a flat and lifeless rendition of "Sweet Hour of Prayer."

She was almost thirty years old without a prospect in sight. It wasn't exactly her fault, with all the men off to war. She would have liked to have joined up with the WAVES or WACS or moved to Minneapolis to work in the ammunition plant. Nedra Ingvalstad had done it. Mildred might have met someone if she had left Tolga Township.

But Dad depended on her to keep house since her mother's death. Like him, she was tied to the farm. Tied to the old house and the chicken coop and the vegetable garden and the apple orchard and the milk room. And tied to Dad. He'd be as lost as Nels Carlson if left alone. Especially with Willy gone.

She was as shackled as any married woman, but without someone to love and call her own. Without children. She gave another quick look at Herman's drooling baby, and transitioned to "Rock of Ages."

She was as bound to these neighbors as she was to Dad. The thought both terrified and surprised her. These neighbors were farm folks, committed to the land. They weren't going anywhere, and she couldn't get away. Even without matrimonial vows, they were as married as married could be. Common-law, she guessed. Living together without benefit of a wedding.

The years stretched before her like a prison sentence. Cooking and canning. Caring for the poultry. Gathering and washing eggs to sell to the creamery. Washing the cream separator. Planting and harvest. Playing the organ every Sunday and for every funeral. Maybe a wedding once in a while. Ladies' Aid Society. Teaching Sunday School. The Christmas program. Threshing crews to feed. The county fair. The Pentecost Dinner. Knitting. Tatting. Until Dad died.

And then what. She'd be too old to study music then, or travel abroad. Too old to find a man. Too old for children.

Mildred crashed the chords for "A Mighty Fortress Is Our God," as Pastor Hustvedt stepped into the pulpit. His white collar askew above his black vestments.

Norman rang the bell. Mildred delved into the music and was lost for all five stanzas. Lost and blissfully happy for the brief period of time it took for the little flock to struggle through the verses.

Pastor's New Testament text dripped like icy water down her back. "Children obey your parents in the Lord for this is right." Then he turned to the Old Testament reading. "Honor thy father and thy mother that it may be well with thee."

Easy for him to say. His parents lived with his sister in Crookston. Pastor Hustvedt didn't know what it meant to care for a parent. Why, Dad was only fifty-one years old. She heaved a heavy sigh, and Dad looked her way. She turned the corners of her mouth into a forced smile.

She wasn't up to duty and obedience. Instead, Mildred daydreamed about traveling to New York and taking in a concert at Carnegie Hall. Then she dreamed she was an organist performing in Paris with the Philharmonic Orchestra.

It didn't cost anything to dream, and she might as well dream big while she was at it.

Dad elbowed her for the benediction. Mildred stumbled to the organ and plowed through the final liturgy, and a very mediocre rendition of "God Be with You till We Meet Again."

She'd never see Carnegie Hall—she could barely play well enough for Tolga Lutheran. She transitioned into the postlude as the congregants filed out, feeling depressed and out of sorts.

"We need to get home," Dad stood by the organ. "Can you cut it short?"

"What's the hurry?" The last chord lingered in the empty sanctuary. She usually kept playing until the parking lot was empty, giving a musical goodbye to the parishioners of Tolga Lutheran.

"Bossy is calving." She could tell he was worried by the way he kept hitching up his trousers with the insides of his wrists.

"Start the car." She gathered her music into a brown accordion folder tied with a shoe lace. "I'll be right there."

The wind slammed into her as she pushed the heavy door and stepped outside onto the cement stairs. She pushed away the ends of her scarf slapping into her face as the frigid cold sucked the air out of her lungs.

Snow lay heaped in great mounds around the headstones in the churchyard cemetery and piled against the wooden snow fence. She looked toward the farthest corner where her mother's grave lay cold and lonely, too far away to read her name on the blue granite marker, then gathered her courage and looked toward the spot where her brother's new stone lay buried beneath the snow. Willy always hated winters. Millie pretended Willy preferred a watery grave in the Pacific over frozen Minnesota.

Mildred reached again to push the scarf out of her eyes, and the music folder fell out of her hands, dropped down the steps, and the loose knot gave way. Sheet music flew out with the wind, dodging her grasping hands, sailing over the cemetery, some catching on the cold stones.

Norman had done a piss-poor job of shoveling, she thought as she grabbed for thin air. Mildred lost her balance, slipping and tumbling down the icy steps. The next thing she knew, she was lying on her back at the bottom of the stairs.

She couldn't catch her breath.

Nels Carlson and Norman called her name and knelt beside her. Dad left the car idling and rushed over as Tia joined the small huddle around her.

"Can she move her legs?" Tia said, always the practical one. "Where's the doctor?"

Mildred's breath returned, and her legs felt fine, but when she tried to get up a pain in her left wrist caused her to black out for a brief second. Doctor Sorenson had already left for home. Norman urged her to lie down. Someone covered her with a woolen blanket that smelled of moth balls.

"Pastor Hustvedt!" Nels called, his voice a foghorn above the wind. "We need prayer out here."

It might have been comical had her arm not hurt so much, and if she hadn't felt so embarrassed. Pastor Hustvedt came running, still in his vestments, the wind whipping the black robe into billowing clouds.

Pastor Hustvedt mumbled the Lord's prayer with lowered eyes and folded hands. Everyone joined except Mildred who was fighting to keep from crying, and Norman who fetched a stout branch. He untied her scarf and used it to stabilize her arm to the branch.

"I'll drive you to Doc Sorenson's," he said, after the amen.

"No need," Dad said.

"But Bossy," Mildred said.

"I'll take her, Selmer," Norman said.

Dad hesitated for a moment, Mildred nodded, and soon she was bundled into the DeSoto with her throbbing left arm stretched across the seat tied to a branch with her best scarf. She looked out the window, anything to avoid looking at Norman.

"He'll fix you up in no time." Norman scraped at the inside of the windshield with the back of his hand. "You'll be back at the organ before you know it."

Until then she had not considered what a broken arm might mean. What would she do if she couldn't play the organ?

A wave of condemnation rolled over her. Just a few minutes ago she had compared her life to a prison sentence. Without her music, she would really be in prison. The tears came in spite of her best efforts to hold them back, as the car jolted in a pot hole.

"Sorry!" Norman fished a blue bandana handkerchief out of his coat pocket and handed it to her. "It must hurt like the . . . the blazes."

"It's not that," Mildred said when she could control herself enough to speak. "It's just that my music . . . means so . . . you know." She gulped back a sob and clutched her arm to steady it, feeling the rough wood of the splint.

The fields mounded with white drifts, swirls of wind-whipped clouds blew over the roadway. Gray clouds hung low above them, a portent of more snow.

"Your music is everything," he said after a short silence.

She nodded, the tears dripping again. It was cold as a meat locker, and she tugged at the blanket, pulling it up to her chin.

"You play," he said. "with your heart more than your hands."

She didn't know what to say. It was the nicest compliment she had ever received.

"Like the robins," he said. "Singing their hearts."

The tires slid across a strip of icy road, and Norman reached out to steady her. His arm was strong, surprisingly gentle.

"You like music, too."

"I sang hymns in the camp." Norman's voice had a tight sound to it, like a fiddle string tuned to high E. "Recited the Bible and Luther's Catechism." He slowed to turn into Dr. Sorenson's driveway. "The Highwayman," "The Village Blacksmith . . ."

"Me, too." Mildred winced. "I quote "Paul Revere's Ride" every April 18th whether I need to or not."

Dr. Sorenson's black lab greeted them with a ferocious bark. "Don't worry." Norman's voice was lower now, an easy B. "See his tail wag."

* * *

Afterwards, Norman escorted her to the car, and shielded her new cast. The ether used for the bone setting weakened her joints and loosened her tongue. She rolled her head back against the seat.

"Does it hurt bad?"

"Nah," Mildred said. "I don't want to go home."

"The doctor said you need rest."

"Maybe go to a picture show. *Rhapsody in Blue* is playing in Fergus." Her words tumbled out, slurred and rapid-fire. "Don't you love Gershwin?"

"Show's already started." Norman looked at his wristwatch with a frown. "Too late."

"But I want Paris." Mildred knew she was saying too much, but it was impossible to stop the torrent of words. "And Gershwin."

Norman rubbed his chin, and Mildred suppressed a giggle. It seemed he was trying to make her laugh.

"I'll tell you about Paris." Norman's voice lowered to a lovely baritone in the soothing key of A major.

She hadn't known his voice so musical. Hadn't thought of him other than Tia's pesky brother. She never thought of him at all, certainly not as someone who had been to Paris. Her giggles switched to sobs. "You've been there?"

"In the army." His eyes blue as irises planted around their chicken coop. But there was a sadness in his face, something that hid behind the color of his eyes. She wanted to reach out and smooth it away. She raised her hand to reach toward him but pulled it back and tucked it beneath the blanket.

"I'd do anything to see Paris." Mildred fought an overwhelming urge to sleep, and leaned her head on Norman's shoulder. "Nothing happens here."

It seemed only a minute until the car turned into their driveway, and Mildred jolted awake. She sat up, and felt a sharp throb in her left wrist. Her head ached. She had forgotten to elevate her arm. She was sure the doctor had told her to keep it up.

"Are you all right?"

"Uh-huh." Mildred wiped her mouth with her mitten. She had actually drooled while she slept.

"How about going to the show when you're feeling better?" Norman pushed in the clutch, stepped on the break and slowed towards the house. "Right now you'll have to settle for Gershwin on the radio."

"Phonograph," Mildred mumbled. "I have all his records."

"Good," Norman said. "We'll play 'Rhapsody in Blue' and I'll tell you about Paris. I loved the beautiful trees of Paris."

He didn't ask permission, but she didn't mind. She didn't mind at all. Dad poked his head from the barn door, and headed toward them.

Norman went around to the passenger side and helped her out of the car. He cradled her arm to prevent jostling, and tucked a strong arm around her waist. He smelled of sweat and shaving soap. How gentle his touch. Dad held the door, as Mildred wobbled into the kitchen.

While Norman told Dad about the broken wrist and the cast, Mildred thought how lucky she had baked yesterday. Honey jumbles, nothing fancy, just plain farm food made with honey from their hives. It wasn't something she'd normally fix for company, but Norman wouldn't mind. They'd eat honey jumbles and drink coffee and warm by the wood stove. She'd tell Norman where the records were kept. "Rhapsody in Blue" in the key of E flat soared like a flying bird. She imagined how the chords would fill the room.

"Thanks, Norman," Dad said as they eased Mildred to a kitchen chair. "It was a bad day for me to be away from the herd." He grasped Norman with a firm handshake and opened the door for him to leave. "I appreciate it."

"I was glad to help," Norman said with a helpless glance toward Mildred.

"We'll be fine now," Dad said, and opened the door wider. "Thanks again. Millie-girl needs to get to bed."

He fairly pushed Norman out the door. Bitter tears burned Mildred's eyes and dripped down her face. He had wanted to stay. She thought to call him back, but it was too late. Norman was down the steps and heading toward the DeSoto.

Dad turned toward her and inched up his trousers with the insides of his wrists. "Are you all right, Millie-Girl?"

Mildred took a deep breath and thought suddenly of Pastor's sermon. It wasn't that she disrespected Dad, but she was a grown woman.

"It wouldn't have happened had Norman sanded the icy steps," he said. "It was like an icebox in the church. He's a drunk."

With great dignity Mildred stood and cradled her casted arm. He reached to help her, but she shook him off.

"Please don't call me Millie-girl. I'm a grown woman." Dad looked bewildered as Mildred walked toward her bedroom. "Things are going to be different around here."

She paused at the old phonograph, and carefully placed the needle on the record. Then she cranked up the volume as high as it would go.

Gershwin's rhapsody carried her to her room.

She looked at her single bed with the white coverlet, her eighth-grade graduation photo on the dresser, and the hand-tatted doily on the back of the chair. Her Bible and catechism rested on the bedside table beside a copy of *The Sun Also Rises*. The book had been a Christmas gift from Willy his last Christmas home, though he knew she wasn't much of a reader.

"I'll see the world," he'd said as he handed her the book without wrapping or ribbon. "You can read about Paris until I get home and tell you about my adventures."

She'd put off reading it because of the chores and the Easter cantata. She picked it up after the Pentecost dinner, but had read only a few pages when they got the telegram about his death.

She'd not opened it since.

She wasn't sleepy. Instead of going to bed she'd sit in her chair with her casted arm propped on a pillow, and see for herself what Hemingway had to say.

The Box Social

ALL THAT MORNING TIA BAKED. She and Ma always packed lunches for the Valentine's Day box social at their country school and baked cakes for the cake walk. With the war over, they could make whatever they wanted without worrying about sugar. Tia had poured over the old cookbook, and settled on a Lady Baltimore cake with seven-minute frosting. Ma made her favorite orange-kiss-me cake, her three-day buns for barbecues and fetched pickles and relishes from the basement.

Tia worried as she tied purple threads around the handles of forks and spoons. Each family brought extra dishes and silverware to share. A different colored thread made identification easier at the end of the evening. As Tia tied the threads, she tried to think of a way to decorate her lunch box. Every woman wanted to bring the prettiest box with the tastiest food. The most beautiful creations brought the highest bids. Tia knew how to cook and bake, but in a plain, down-to-earth farm way. She knew nothing about decorations.

Fresh doughnuts lined the table, and the aroma of Ma's buns filled the kitchen. Tia placed the marked silverware in a box next to the cakes. She might cut a geranium blossom, or use a hair ribbon, but anything she did would look pathetic and ordinary. She reached for the old picnic basket. Some older women packed their lunches in baskets to avoid the need to decorate. It would have to do.

"Did you hear that the preacher wanted to send any money raised at the social to the Squint Eyes?" Norman dropped an armload of kitchen wood into the wood box with a clatter. "Called it a symbol of reconciliation."

153

"Where did you hear that?"

"Oh, I know things," Norman said. "You'd be surprised what comes through those heating vents at the church. But Selmer Moberg put his foot down."

Tia wasn't surprised. Pearl Harbor was too fresh. Mildred claimed her father couldn't rest with Willy's body at the bottom of the Pacific. Even the stone at the cemetery hadn't helped. The war had changed Selmer. It had changed all of them.

Norman knelt down to buckle his overshoes. "Do you know if Mildred's going?"

"You sly dog," Tia said with a grin, and slapped the last spoon on the table. "So it's Mildred?"

"Of course not," Norman said with a flustered look. He unbuckled his overshoes and buckled them again, a trick since childhood to avoid looking at someone. "But last time I got stuck eating with Tillie. Not an experience I'd care to repeat."

"It's only about avoiding Nosy-Nellie?" How perfect if her brother and best friend would get together. A feeling of hope stirred. Norman could forget about California and settle down here where he belonged.

"Is she going?"

"Everyone will be there," Tia said. "And I know for a fact she's bringing apple dumplings and potato salad. Her mother's secret recipe."

Norman unbuckled and re-buckled his overshoes again. It seemed obvious to Tia he wanted to ask what Millie's box looked like so he would bid on the right one. All the girls kept their boxes swathed under towels or newspaper until the auctioneer readied them for auction. Very hush-hush. The Valentine's tradition sparked more than one local romance over the years.

"Last two years she's tied her box with a green, plaid bow," Tia said. "I expect she'll do it again."

That night, everyone crowded into the school house. Bruce Hegdahl, Beryl's brother, was back from Germany. He smoked on the school steps with one of the Hexum boys, just returned from the Pacific. Both men wore uniforms, looking tanned and lean, young and handsome.

Dumb Ed stumbled in from the outhouse, still tucking his shirt and buttoning his pants. He stopped at the water fountain in the entry-way, covering the spigot with his mouth and licking at the water squirting over his face and shirt. The young Stenerson girl eyed him in horror.

"Teacher says not to put your mouth on it," she said. "It spreads germs."

"Eddy," Blanche Root said from where she had been hanging up her coat. Blanche seemed thinner since Harvey's passing. "That's enough."

Dumb Ed wiped his mouth on his sleeve and stepped away from the fountain. He headed back to it as soon as his mother went into the main school room. Dumb Ed. He was always getting into something. Mildred said that he had been hanging around their farm one day. When she asked him what he was doing, he rambled some nonsense about soldiers drinking beer.

Ma took a seat by Blanche Root while Tia and Norman hauled the food to the make-shift serving table underneath the blackboard.

Pastor Hustvedt always played auctioneer to the row of baskets and boxes lining the teacher's desk. One box sported a green, plaid bow. It was clearly the most beautiful box on the desk. Tia tucked her plain basket toward the back.

"Get your money ready," Tia whispered to her brother. "It will go sky-high."

Norman fingered coins in his pocket. "I only have two seventy-five. Do you have any I can borrow?"

"A dollar," Tia whispered back in irritation. Norman had plenty of money for the tavern, plenty for smokes, but nothing for anything else. She needed her money for the cake walk. Ingeborg Hanson and Gunda Olson sold chances on a log cabin quilt that would look beautiful in her room.

She followed Norman to empty chairs beside Clyde and Vera. The room so crowded, they had no other choice. Norman sat next to Clyde, and Tia sat beside Norman, grateful she didn't have to sit by Clyde.

Vera wore a heart-shaped pin on a red dress that matched her lip-stick and nail polish. A red comb held curls away from her face. With her widow's peak, her face looked heart shaped, too.

Mildred headed toward them, and Clyde pulled Vera onto his lap to give Mildred Vera's chair. Mildred looked especially nice in a blue dress that matched her eyes and brought out the pink of her perfect complexion. Of course, Mildred wasn't as pretty as Vera, but she had a restful way about her that Tia always admired.

Pastor Hustvedt called for order.

Dickey Stenerson stood on a chair and lisped a memorized welcome. Everyone applauded. Dickey grinned, showing a dark gap where his front teeth should have been. Pastor Hustvedt wished everyone a happy Valentine's Day, and opened with prayer. He thanked God for the end of the war, the safe return of the veterans and prayed for those still deployed in Europe and Japan. He prayed for those suffering in Europe and Asia. He didn't mention Japan by name, but Norman poked Tia in the ribs anyway. He ended by praying for good crops the coming season to feed the starving people of the world.

Then school children sang "God Bless America" and led the crowd in singing "Let Me Call You Sweetheart." Olaf Hanson made a show of putting his arm around Ingeborg and singing directly to her, making everyone laugh.

"It's not just for the young, you know," Olaf said. The men elbowed their wives and smirked. Clyde squeezed Vera and kissed the back of her neck. Tia looked away.

It grew hotter as the crowd pressed in and the wood stove blazed red hot. Julius Olson cracked a window in the entryway. Dumb Ed splashed at the water fountain. Tia looked toward Blanche, but she seemed oblivious to Eddy's behavior.

"Gentlemen," Pastor Hustvedt stood on a stool, and banged a gavel on the teacher's desk. "These boxes smell mighty good. Fried chicken, if I'm not mistaken, and fresh bread." He leaned closer and sniffed loudly. "Here's your chance to eat with a lovely lady, and help our suffering brethren at the same time." He paused for effect. "All money raised tonight will go to Lutheran World Relief for Norwegian war orphans."

A murmuring approval rippled around the room.

"You've read in the papers how Trygve Lie, a Norwegian, is the first Secretary General of the United Nations." Applause and cheers filled the little school house. Clyde whistled through his teeth and stomped his feet. "What you may not know is how Norway suffers, even though the jack-boot has lifted. They're short of food, clothing, even blankets. Your generosity will make a difference to our people across the sea."

Tia offered a silent prayer of gratitude that America had been spared occupation. It was bad enough sending the boys away to war. She shuddered to think of sleeping without blankets or firewood. Nazis stripped everything they could carry away. There were wild rumors of Nazi programs breeding Norwegian girls with Nazi soldiers to produce Aryans for the Master Race. It seemed unbelievable, though Mrs. Hustvedt told Tillie it really happened. Maybe these were the orphans needing help.

"We'll auction off the boxes first. The rest of you can buy lunch from the Mother's Club. Ten cents for adults and a nickel for children. Twenty-five cents for families. Fish pond for the kids at one cent a ticket. Cake walk in the basement. Don't forget the quilt chances. There's something for everyone."

He picked up a white box decorated in pink, celluloid roses. "Now I know you men are tight-wads—I count the offering plate every week!" Laughter rippled through the room. "But open your purses for the orphans. Do I hear twenty cents?"

Julius Olson and Mansel Jorgenson bid against each other, raising the price to a whole dollar.

"Look at this beautiful box, Gentlemen!" Pastor Hustvedt said. "Surely worth more than a dollar."

Mansel jumped in with a dollar and ten cents. Clyde offered a dollar and a quarter. Tia suspected the box belonged to Vera. It looked like something she'd come up with. Then Julius bid a dollar-thirty.

"Going once, going twice," Pastor Hustvedt bent low, pointing the gavel at the different men, urging them to loosen their purse strings for a good cause. "Sold to Julius Olson for a dollar and thirty cents."

Tillie Stenerson waved to indicate it was her basket. Tia felt Norman relax. At least he wouldn't get stuck with Tillie's non-stop chatter. If

Julius was disappointed, he didn't show it. Tillie said that Julius had taken up with a girl from Battle Lake but didn't have the guts to tell his mother. No doubt Tillie would ferret more details while they ate.

The auction proceeded. Selmer Moberg bought Ma's basket for sixty cents. Pastor Hustvedt bought Blanche Root's for fifty cents. Herman Jenkins bid on his wife's box with unusual enthusiasm, holding a baby on each arm, and declaring her the best cook in Tolga Township. Clarence Stenerson bought Mrs. Hustvedt's square basket with heart shaped cookies tied to the handle. Only a half dozen lunches remained on the desk.

The preacher held up Tia's basket. Tia tensed. What if no one bid on it?

"Is someone hungry?" Pastor Hustvedt leaned down and sniffed. "Hmmm. Smells like doughnuts."

"I'm hungry," Eddy Root called from the doorway. "Talk to me, doughnuts!"

Everyone laughed. Tia cringed. Dumb Ed smelled funny, and manure covered his worn shoes. His shirt was wet and his fly was open. Mildred said he had reached over and touched her necklace last Sunday in church. Her dad named him dangerous.

"Who'll give me twenty-five cents?"

Mansel bid a quarter, and Olaf raised it to thirty cents. Tia let out a breath. At least someone would buy it. Clyde bid forty cents. Elmer called out seventy. Olaf made a joke about the young men hogging the best food, and bid seventy-five cents. It looked like Nels' eighty-cent bid would hold. Tia wouldn't mind eating lunch with the Potato King—she would ask about his healing. Lots of rumors circulated, but she wanted to hear it from the horse's mouth. She still couldn't get used to seeing him without crutches.

"One dollar!" Clyde called out.

Oh, no. Tia felt her heart sink. Anyone but him.

"Sold!"

All eyes turned to Tia as she raised her hand. She tried to smile at Clyde.

"I knew it!" Clyde said with a teasing voice, then looked back to Vera with what seemed like adoration. "I hope she made rosettes!"

What it must feel like to be loved. Her food mattered though she didn't. There was nothing to do but pretend it didn't matter.

Pastor Hustvedt wiped his brow, and picked up the box with the green bow. "Look at this, gents. A delicious feast for the man with the deepest pockets."

"Fifty cents!" Elmer said.

Norman bid sixty cents and Elmer Petterson seventy-five. Mansel raised to a dollar.

"A dollar and a quarter," Norman said.

"A dollar and a half," Elmer said.

Mansel shook his head and dropped out of the bidding.

"Two dollars," Nels said. A murmur went through the crowd, it being the highest bid of the evening. "That's as high as I'll go."

"Two fifty," Norman said quietly with a slight nod of the head, as if at a real farm auction.

"Too rich for my blood," Elmer said.

"Sold!" Pastor Hustvedt said.

Tia looked toward Mildred, but she didn't move a muscle. Instead Vera jumped from Clyde's lap as if she had won a prize.

"Norman," squealed Vera. "It's swell that you bought mine!"

"I fancied that nice bow," Norman said. He looked toward Tia with a raised eyebrow.

"I got it from Mildred," Vera said. She chattered about the bow, the box and the lunch until Tia wanted to wring her neck. She was as bad as Tillie.

The bidding continued. Olaf Hanson bought Bernice Hegdahl's box. Elmer Petterson bought Mildred's blue box with a red satin bow for ninety cents. Mildred cast a distraught look toward Tia.

The four together again: Tia with Clyde, Norman with Vera. In Tolga Township one could never get away from the neighbors.

Pastor Hustvedt led in singing the table prayer, and the couples untied ribbons and bows to eat the boxed lunches, while the rest of the people crowded around the lunch table for barbecue buns and orange nectar.

Vera chattered about Norwegian orphans, as she unpacked sandwiches made with boughten bread, potato chips, and store-bought cookies shaped like windmills. They drank bottles of Coca-Cola, Norman fishing in his pocket for a church key. Clyde and Tia ate in silence though Clyde leaned toward Vera, and told her she needed Tia's doughnut recipe. Across the room Mildred nibbled sandwiches with Elmer Petterson. It didn't look like she was having a good time, either.

"Have you thought any more about California?" Vera said to Norman.

Not California again.

Norman shook his head. "My head is stuck in the wood pile. Almost finished with Ma's wood but have the church's to do."

"Have you planned your spring crops yet?" Clyde asked around mouthfuls of doughnuts. "I'm thinking to put in more barley."

"We're trying flax in the lower forty," Tia said. She felt as if she spoke too quickly, but somehow she couldn't stop the words. "And we're planting soybeans. Aren't we, Norman?"

"Whatever you want," Norman said. "Where did you say Selma lives?" Norman turned his back on Tia.

A selfish thought sneaked into Tia's mind, as Vera gushed about the benefits of living on the West Coast. If Norman moved to California, the farm would be hers, and she'd be free to do as she wanted. Ma couldn't say a thing if Norman moved away.

The music for the cake walk sounded in the basement. Mildred helped the teacher set up the fishpond in the corner of the main school room.

"Ready to go home?" Norman said to Tia. "I've had enough."

"I have to sell tickets," Tia said. "And I promised to clean up."

He ambled over toward Bruce Hegdahl and the Hexum boy lingering by the door. Tia took her place behind the table selling chances for the quilt and tickets for the cake walk. She looked toward the door, but Norman and the other men were nowhere in sight. Dumb Ed played in the water fountain.

"It's all gone," Dumb Ed said, leaning over the spigot and working the lever. "Where did it go?"

"Needs to be refilled." Tia pointed to the empty bucket. "Why don't you fetch another bucket?"

Kids swarmed around the fishpond. For a penny, they could cast a fishing line over an old sheet hanging diagonal across the corner. Little Lucy Petterson squealed with delight when she got a box of new crayons. Poor motherless thing.

The fish pond ran out of prizes, and the kids ran to the basement for the cake walk. Crumbs, bits of candy wrappers and peanut shells littered the floor. Wet footprints from overshoes and Eddy's antics at the water fountain puddled into muddy tracks. Mildred folded the fish pond curtain. Tia pushed a mop over the floor.

"Idiot! Look what you've done," Selmer said.

He had come up from the basement carrying Tia's Lady Baltimore cake when Eddy charged through the outside door with a full bucket of water. The two collided on the landing. Water sloshed over the cake and down the front of Selmer's clothes.

"I'll call the sheriff," Selmer sputtered as he eyed the soggy mess of cake. "You don't belong here."

At the mention of the sheriff, Eddy threw the bucket at Selmer and ran outside. Tia hurried over with the mop.

Selmer slammed the door, and threw the cake into the garbage bin, plate and all.

"It was an accident," Norman said as he stepped into the room. "No reason to get your undies in a bundle."

"Wasting food when poor people are starving!" Selmer grabbed his overcoat from the coat hook and called for Mildred. "We're going home!"

"I'm not finished," Mildred said. She gestured to the classroom. "Can't leave it all for Tia."

"She won't mind," Selmer said. "We're going now."

"We'll take Mildred home," Norman said. Tia knew he was angry by the way his jaw twitched, but his face set hard and quiet as a stone. "No trouble at all."

"You've been drinking," Selmer said with an indignant sniff. "She'll go with me."

Tia wondered if it were true. Norman and the other soldiers had been outside. Tia hoped they were only smoking.

Mildred looked at Norman with an exasperated shrug, and fetched her coat. Tia pulled her plate out of the garbage bin while Mildred picked through the dirty dishes on the table, finding the forks and spoons tied with her green threads.

"I'm sorry," Mildred mouthed the words to Tia, like they used to do when they were school girls. "Dad ruins everything."

Of course the night was ruined, but Tia didn't blame Selmer. It was ruined long before the incident with the Lady Baltimore cake. She may as well have saved herself the bother and stayed home.

"Good Night Ladies, Good Night Gentlemen," sounded up the basement stairs in four-part harmony.

"Keys are in the car," Norman said. He came close enough that Tia could smell the liquor on his breath. "I'm going to town with the boys."

"Don't go," she said before she could stop the words.

"I'll do what I want," he said. "None of your damn business."

His words felt like a kick in the gut.

Send Him Back
to the Asylum

THE NEXT MONDAY NORMAN tackled the church's woodpile. A cold north wind carried a bite as sharp as the axe in his hand. Wood split easier in cold weather. A hollow sounding pop landed with each blow of the splitting maul, and the sweet fragrance of freshly split oak pleased him. A low bank of dark clouds clustered in the western horizon, proof the radio forecaster might have been right for a change.

Actually, Norman was relieved to leave the house where Tia toiled over laborious diagrams of crops, gardens, and pasture. It reminded him too much of the endless escape plans in the prison camp. Never ending plans that didn't materialize. Besides, it mattered little to him whether she planted flax or barley. She acted like it was a matter of life and death. It wasn't.

He had been working only a short while when Pastor Hustvedt drove up in his Chevy. "Deacon Board today," he said. "Fire the woodstove?"

Norman filled the stove, and went outside for another armful of wood, as the board gathered in the church study. Good Lord, couldn't they find better men than Selmer Moberg, Elmer Petterson, Beryl Hegdahl, and Doc Sorenson?

Their voices filtered down through the heating vent when he added wood to the furnace. He listened as he adjusted the draft.

"Something has to be done," Selmer said. "Nels has gone fanatic. It's sacrilegious, the way he carries on."

The voices melded together, Norman strained to hear the preacher's response but couldn't make it out. Selmer's voice drowned out the others. He must be facing the heating vent. Norman heard snatches about confirmands, a reference to the electric bill and utter dismay about Nels' plan to host home Bible Studies. They were quick to pass judgment on something they didn't understand. Norman decided he might go to the Bible Study, just to flaunt them.

"Let's face it. Nels is a problem," Selmer said. "He's not fit to watch over Eddy."

"Harvey set it up," Elmer said. His voice distinct. "It's legal."

"But that was before all this nonsense," Selmer said. "Harvey never had time for religious nuts. Eddy would be better off in the asylum."

"We shouldn't go rushing into anything." Norman recognized Beryl's whiny voice. "There's nothing to worry about until Blanche is gone."

"There are women folk who might think different," Selmer said. His words muffled. Norman strained to hear. "He's a walking time bomb, I tell you. Eddy can't help himself. It's human nature."

More words that Norman couldn't distinguish.

"If anything happens, we'll shoulder blame," Selmer said. "Better safe than sorry."

Norman leaned too close, and bumped the metal door of the firebox. The men grew very quiet.

"Is someone in the building?" Pastor Hustvedt said. Footsteps sounded in the study above the furnace. "These meetings are private."

Norman slammed the furnace door, and left the building in two, huge strides. The frigid air felt good after the political stink inside. Pastor Hustvedt's face showed in the study window, as Norman shouldered his axe.

He split and stacked wood all afternoon, thinking how Eddy's days as a free man were numbered if Selmer had his way. Selmer bossed Mildred within an inch of her life. Mildred's brother joined up to get away from his pa. Norman had seen it in the army, in the camps, even in the hospital. Someone always stepped up to be the boss. It wasn't fair that Selmer would now try to rule Eddy's life. Eddy had done nothing wrong.

Norman had acquired a vivid vocabulary in his army days. With every swing of the axe, he used this vocabulary in imaginary conversations with Pastor Hustvedt, Selmer Moberg, and the church board. Then he started counting the trees alongside the cemetery and alongside the township road that led up to Tolga Lutheran.

It would be best if Nels watched Eddy a little closer until the ruckus blew over. Norman would visit Nels and make sure that he knew folks were complaining about Eddy roaming around the township and bothering people.

The men ended their meeting, and left the church. Doc Sorenson waved to Norman as he climbed into his car. Selmer looked his way but did not wave. Norman had a sneaking suspicion they plotted to get rid of him, along with Eddy. Let them. Hypocrites. If Jesus came to Tolga Lutheran, and Norman doubted He had ever visited before, Jesus would certainly take Eddy's side.

Stacked wood filled the woodshed attached to the outbuilding. One side of the building held the outhouses and the other a locked storage shed holding the lawnmower and grave digging tools. It also held the corpses of those unlucky enough to die when the ground was frozen too hard to dig a grave. The only coffin in the shed belonged to Harvey Root.

Norman filled the woodshed. Then he stacked a tier of split oak alongside the entry way to the basement at the back of the church.

Norman hated firewood that wouldn't burn properly. As a soldier, he'd tried too many times to keep fires going with wet or poor quality wood. Piss elm. Wet pine dripping with sap. Dried sticks or grass that wouldn't hold a fire. He covered the stack by the door with an old canvas tarp, holding it down with heavy logs, and the rock used to prop the door in summer.

He had done a good day's work. And though wood overflowed from the storage places, the church would still need more before the winter gave up. He'd like to have next year's drying over the summer. Several dead trees from the Hegdahl's shelterbelt lay waiting in the corner of the cemetery for another day of axe work.

Norman looked around to make sure he was alone, and pulled a bottle from a hiding place behind the back door. He deserved a bump. He took a nip, thinking he must cut back soon or he would have a problem. He eyed the bottle, but tucked it back in its hiding place after only one sip.

The temperature plummeted. The woodpile lay on the east side of the church, and Norman had worked mostly sheltered from the wind. He felt its blast when he stepped around the corner to replace the axe and maul in the storage shed. There he found Eddy Root huddled in the alcove next to the men's outhouse, wearing Norman's old army cap.

Eddy looked at him with a guilty expression, and pushed something behind his back. His nose ran, and red ears poked from under the cap. He held a mitt with a partially burned thumb.

"Hey, Eddy," Norman said. "What happened to your mitten?"

"A soldier now," Eddy said. "Don't smoke or drink beer, Pa said. Go to church and work for the Potato King."

"Smart man, your pa," Norman said.

"What for Pa in the outhouse?" Eddy pointed to the locked storage shed where the coffin waited for spring burial.

"Ground froze," Norman said. "In the spring, we'll dig him a nice grave, Eddy. Don't you worry about that."

Norman didn't like the idea of coffins locked in the outhouse building. As a boy, he had been fearful of ghosts. Once he wet his pants rather than go to the outhouse near where a coffin was stored.

"How is your Ma?"

"She cries," Eddy said. "Might have the toothache."

Norman lit a cigarette and blew the warm smoke toward his face, a trick he had learned in the army. "Want a ride home?"

Eddy pulled himself to his feet. A small pile of dried leaves and sticks littered the ground behind him, along with burned matches and broken cigarettes.

"Your Pa said not to smoke," Norman said. "Fire is dangerous."

"Soldiers smoke." Eddy jammed the army cap lower over his ears. "Bruce Hegdahl smokes."

"You're right," Norman had to agree. "But your pa wouldn't like it."

* * *

A storm kept everyone at home the next day, dumping a foot of snow on Tolga Township. Tia planned next year's crops, pouring over farming magazines and plotting the coming spring work.

166

"There's so much to think about," Tia said. "Crop rotation, weather patterns, markets, soil samples. I don't know what to do." She slammed the magazine closed with a slap. "Wish I could go to Ag School and learn how to do it right."

"Maybe you should go to Ag School, Norman," Ma said. She wore a worried expression and Pa's old sweater. She sat darning socks by the kitchen stove. "You've got the GI Bill."

Norman shrugged, and didn't answer. He did not want to disappoint Ma, but he hated the farm. Bruce Hegdahl planned to attend the Morris Ag School, but Norman would die first. He didn't suffer through those years in prison to spend his life doing something he hated. He once considered studying forestry, leaving these flatlands and moving north among the lakes and pines. But only an eighth-grade education meant four years of high school before he could even start college. His mind cluttered too much with memories from the war. He had lost his ambition somewhere in Poland.

He wouldn't stay in Tolga Township. Norman had seen the worst, and held no illusions about the future. That bastard, Stalin, said another war was inevitable. Nels wouldn't survive another war. He wanted only to find a warm place where he could rest his mind. Away from Ma and prying neighbors.

Tia tapped the end of her pencil on the paper in front of her with a definite frown on her face. It must be just as hard for her when Ma pushed for him to take charge. He wasn't Selmer Moberg. He wouldn't rule over anyone.

"Ladies' Aid today," Ma said. "Don't forget."

"There will be hell to pay if I don't shovel the sidewalks and fire the furnace." He pulled on his warmest cap and mittens. "Bernice Hegdahl might get her feet wet and catch cold."

Norman cleared the driveway with the team and blade. Sundogs guarded each side of the weak sun, a sure sign of frigid temperatures. He noticed with satisfaction how the shelterbelt had blocked some of the snow. The shelterbelt was one thing he had done right. It did what it was supposed to do, and would live beyond his lifetime. He thought of all the trees he had planted in the CCC and wondered how many had survived. Maybe he would go on the bum and visit all the places the trees had been planted.

He thought of swinging by Nels's place to talk about Eddy, but wouldn't take the time that day. Instead, Norman delivered the cream cans, filled the gas tank at the Skelly Station, stopped at the hatchery for a sack of chicken feed, and then headed toward Tolga Lutheran.

Great heaping drifts blocked the entrance to the church. It would take him all morning. No snow drifts in California. With a sigh, Norman lifted the scoop shovel out of his car and onto his shoulder. The snow, heavy and wet, froze into white ocean drifts. Every step broke through the hard crust on top, plunging him into the cold softness below. Snow went up his pant legs and into his boots. He needed snowshoes, something he had only read about in a magazine.

The cold reminded him of Poland. He turned his mind away from those bitter memories. He counted the trees along the edge of the cemetery, the trees that grew around the Polish prison camp and the trees in the grove north of the church. He counted from memory the trees growing in the shelterbelt at home, and then numbered the trees growing in Cincinnati around the hospital. By this time he had cleared the way into the church's side door.

Norman fired the furnace, thankful for the tarp keeping the wood dry by the back door, and shoveled the front steps while the building warmed. He was working on the path to the outhouse when Selmer dropped Mildred off at the gate.

"Hello, Norman!" Mildred called out. She clutched her music folder. "I'm here to practice."

Selmer glared as if reminding Norman to stay away from his daughter. To hell with Selmer. Norman stabbed the shovel into a snowdrift and headed over to Mildred.

"How's your wrist?" Norman said. Mildred's wire-rimmed glasses frosted. "I see your cast is off."

"Finally. I'm back at the organ." She wore a pointed knit cap, the kind they all used to wear when they were kids. It reminded him of the

Norwegian orphans helped by Lutheran World Relief. "How are you?" she said. "I was hoping to talk to you at the box social."

Norman shrugged. "Doing all right." He thought for a long minute. "You traded your green bow." He grinned. "I paid more than two dollars to eat with a married woman."

Mildred's laugh drifted away in the wind. "And I ate with a widow man twice my age."

"Next year," Norman said. "I'll make sure."

They stomped their feet on the doormat and entered the side door of the church. They stood on top of the floor grate as warm air wafting up from the basement melted the snow off their overshoes. It dripped and sizzled on the furnace below. Mildred's glasses cleared and Norman unbuttoned his heavy jacket. The rising air twirled Mildred's skirt in a mesmerizing fashion.

"There's a good picture showing in Dalton," Norman said. "Not Gershwin, but a Jimmy Stewart western."

"Are you asking me out?"

"I get the feeling your father wants me to stay away," Norman said. "Not that I'd blame him."

She raised her chin and spoke firmly. "Ridiculous."

"I don't want to cause trouble," Norman said. He thought about the bottle hidden in the woodshed, his thirst, and weakness. Mildred deserved better than some drunken soldier, a wreck left over from the war. "If I were your dad, I'd sic the dog on me if I came around, and not think twice."

"Don't worry," Mildred said with a laugh. "I'm a big girl."

They agreed on Friday night. Norman shuffled his feet, trying to think of something else to say, wondering if he would have the courage to kiss her on their first date. It had been a long time since he had kissed a girl. Mildred moved toward the organ.

"I'll fire the furnace," Norman said. "It's as drafty as a barn."

The melodies of next week's hymns sounded from upstairs. Norman paused and listened between throwing pieces of wood into the firebox. If he could hear such beautiful music all the time, he might not carry such a great thirst.

"I'm rusty," Mildred said with a laugh when he came upstairs. He sprawled in the front pew next to the organ. "Still working the kinks out of my wrist."

Norman closed his eyes and let the music wash over him. "Pass Me Not O Gentle Savior," "In the Garden," "When Morning Guilds the Sky."

"Do you take requests," he said. "'Softly and Tenderly Jesus Is Calling' is a favorite."

She played several verses, singing along in a sweet voice. She wasn't as pretty as Vera, but she was a good person. If only she had a different father. A car pulled up, and Norman jumped up. Tia needed the car to drive Ma to Ladies' Aid. Norman waved to Mildred and told her he would see her on Friday night. He added one more chunk of wood to the furnace before sneaking out the back door.

He saw Eddy Root hanging around the lean-to, playing with the Hegdahl dog.

"What you doing?" Norman called out and walked toward him.

"Soldiers drink beer." Eddy held up Norman's hidden bottle. "Is this beer?"

"Give it here." Norman reached for the bottle.

Eddy pulled back. The bottle fell onto the cement slab and shattered into a million pieces that sparkled in the bright sunlight. Liquor splashed on Norman's pants and jacket. He bent to pick up the pieces, and flinched as a shard of glass nicked his hand.

Eddy took one look at the blood, jammed the army cap down over his ears and hightailed across the cemetery. The dog followed at his heels, pausing to lift his leg on Old Man Ingvalstad's stone.

"Damn!" Norman knew he should have dropped by Nels's place to remind him to keep closer tabs on Eddy. Harvey always kept a short leash on him.

He thought to go inside for a broom for the broken glass, but Tillie Stenerson and Bernice Hegdahl were just walking into the church. Norman didn't want to explain the smell of liquor on his clothes or his bloody hand. He kicked the larger pieces of glass out of the way. He would return tomorrow and clean up. No one would know a thing about it.

Damn waste of good liquor, though. Norman could spit cotton from such a dry throat. He recalled the warmth and camaraderie of the Lower Joint. It wouldn't hurt to stop for a beer before heading home. Bruce Hegdahl might be there. Sometimes a couple of grass widows from Ashby stopped by after their shifts at the asylum.

He forgot that Tia needed the car. He forgot about stopping by Nels's place.

When he finally came home, it was after midnight. A downstairs light showed across the pasture from the Hanson's. Tillie said Clyde and Vera had the downstairs and his parents had moved upstairs. Norman paused a moment and let himself imagine Vera brushing her hair before bed. Then he pushed into their dark house, scratching a match to light the lantern on the table. A note told him of his supper plate in the warming oven. He wasn't hungry.

He had barely stumbled up the stairs and crawled into bed, when he thought he heard the church bell ringing. Couldn't be. It was his job to ring the bell. He put the pillow over his head, and heard the phone ringing off the hook. Ma ran up the stairs and pounded on his door.

"Norman," Ma said. "Get up. The church is on fire."

Ma grabbed buckets and rakes, and pushed them into the back seat of the DeSoto. Tia scraped frost off the car window and Norman pumped the gas pedal. The church bell rang out over the crusted snow. It pealed as if the end of the world had come, its bright alarm bouncing over the drifted white prairie. It was cold enough to freeze the inside of a man's lungs.

A light showed across the pasture. Sparks burst into the dark sky, like a Fourth of July Roman candle, like the bombardment in Tunisia. Norman wished for another drink.

"It happened before," Ma said. "I was a girl. Prairie fire swept in from the west and took it before anyone knew what happened."

Norman's head pounded from his night at the tavern. Something wasn't right. The bell kept ringing—it couldn't be the church on fire. Billowing smoke and flames poured out from behind the church, where the woodshed flamed. The air filled with choking smoke, burning tar, and the smell of petroleum. The winter's supply of wood, all his work, up in smoke.

Parishioners gathered at the front of the church, out of harm's way while the fire department hosed the back wall of the church, the side in most danger of catching fire. They pulled the small stack of carefully-cut wood by the back door, tossing it across the snow. Great sheaths of ice hung on the windows and walls, doors and sidewalk.

The Stenersons brought their children, wrapped in blankets. They stared out the windows of their truck with wide eyes. Nels prayed on the front steps, begging God to spare their house of worship. Norman lent a hand as some of the men dragged the organ outside, the hand-carved pulpit, the church records, the pews and stacks of hymnals. Better safe than sorry.

The parishioners gathered in the churchyard. Mildred clutched a stack of music to her chest. Ma and Tia held onto each other with bony arms. Norman was surprised at their dismay. It didn't matter to him whether or not Tolga Lutheran burned to the ground.

Mansel and Pastor Hustvedt went back in for the baptismal fount. Clyde and Julius carried out the altar with its huge painting of Jesus in the Garden. Elmer Petterson and Bernice Hegdahl conversed in the warmth of the flames. Someone said Doc Severson was delivering a baby. The Hegdahl dog whined until Tia knelt to scratch his ears. No sign of Blanche Root or Eddy. Ada Jorgenson stayed home to care for Minna.

"Who discovered the fire?" Tia said. She tried to shoo the dog away, but it sat on her feet with its back toward her to be scratched. "Who was out this time of night?"

"Beryl saw the flames from his bathroom window," Pastor Hustvedt said, looking haggard and drawn. Black soot streaked his face and hands. He wore a heavy overcoat with striped flannel pajamas hanging below the sleeves, his hair stuck out from under red ear flaps. "He called me, and then the fire department. He rang the bell to warn everyone else."

"What do you have to say?" Selmer stormed over to where Norman stood with Clyde and Julius. "Explain yourself."

"What do you mean?" Norman said. "I don't know what happened."

"You're the one in charge of the wood shed," Selmer said. He held the broken liquor bottle, and wagged a pointed finger in Norman's face. "You've been drinking on the job!"

Pastor Hustvedt stepped between them.

"There's no time for blame," Pastor said. "The church is spared, thank God." Pastor Hustvedt pointed toward the church belfry. "No one hurt. Only the outhouse and woodpile lost."

"Except Harvey Root," Norman said. "Don't forget Harvey's casket in the storage shed."

Line in the Sand

MILDRED SLAMMED THE CAR DOOR and stared straight ahead. The headlights probed the darkness as their car drove away from the school house. It wasn't fair. The cake walk was still going strong, and she promised Tia help with the clean-up. She had hoped to talk to Norman, at least a little.

Dad muttered vague threats directed toward Eddy Root as the car slid on the icy gravel road. She planned her words, trying to find the ones that would make him understand how she felt.

"That Norman needs to be set back a peg or two." He pounded on the steering wheel with his gloved hand. "Worthless drunk."

Her well-planned words evaporated. "Stop it," she said. The darkness made it easier to speak her mind. "You ruined everything."

"It was Dumb Ed . . ."

"Poor Eddy can't help himself, but you know better." She gritted her teeth. It was now or never. "I'm a grown woman. I wanted to stay."

"Millie-girl," he started. The car hit an icy patch, and he twisted the steering wheel to keep the car on the road.

"No," Mildred said when the car steadied. "I'm not a girl." A feeling of power surged through her. It had been a long time coming. "I'll go where I want and with whomever I wish. Mama is gone . . . and Willy. You don't want to lose me, too."

Dad didn't answer. The headlights glared off slicks of frozen patches. Not a star showed overhead.

This Valentine's Day could have been different. The war over, the boys home again. Mildred tried to figure out what went wrong. Norman bought Vera's box. Dad made a public spectacle. Worst of all, she acted like a timid child. She should have insisted on riding home with Norman.

"Norman was Willy's best friend," she said, her planned words coming back to her. "It's not his fault he survived and Willy didn't."

Dad's silence spoke louder than words. Finally, when they were in the yard, Dad spoke. "You're right. You're not a child anymore."

* * *

They didn't speak of it again. Mildred went shopping at her first opportunity, buying a new tube of lipstick, a compact and a bottle of rose water. Then she marched over to the library, and searched the card catalog. She knew enough to find the travel section. She liked the photographs of lavender fields in Southern France, the vineyards of wine country and the glorious lights of Paris.

Of course, things had changed. Who knew what remained after the Nazis.

She thought about calling Norman, something her mother would have strictly forbade. A lady did not pursue a gentleman. If Mildred were to telephone Norman, she knew the whole township would gossip about it. Rubberneckers a scourge worse than communists.

She thrilled when Norman talked to her at the church and asked her out. But then the church fire when everything turned sour. Dad growled around the house, spending every spare moment on the telephone with Elmer Petterson or other board members, calling for meetings to discuss the details of the near-tragedy.

Mildred didn't understand why Dad let the fire upset him so much. No one was hurt, after all, and the loss of firewood seemed a small consequence.

Mildred overheard him on the telephone when she came back for the chicken scraps forgotten on the table. Obviously, he had waited until she left the house before making the call.

"It's agreed, then," Dad said into the receiver. "We'll meet tomorrow afternoon."

Dad gave her an irritated look, and turned his back toward the kitchen where Mildred gathered the potato peelings and carrot scrapings

175

for the hens. She strained to hear what was being said, and for a brief moment wished there was another phone in the house where she could rubber like Tillie Stenerson.

"What was that about?" she said when he hung up the receiver.

"Nothing for you to worry about," he said. He went straight to the entry and pulled on his barn coat. "I'll be in the hog barn."

Mildred had thought to mention her date with Norman, but it was easier to say nothing about it. She washed the supper dishes on Friday night, and changed her clothes. She warmed her overshoes by the furnace grate, and stood by the window looking out towards the road.

"Going somewhere?"

"To the show," Mildred said. She offered no further information.

"Want me to warm the car for you?"

Mildred shook her head, wondering how she could break the news. Norman had been in their home a hundred times or more, all those growing-up years when he and Willy were pals. Now Dad bristled and sputtered at the mention of Norman's name.

"Not driving," she said. She heard a car, slipped into her coat, buttoned it and was half way out the door before Dad could say anything.

She ran to the car, and hopped in the passenger seat before Norman could open the door for her. Dad's angry face showed in the porch window.

The tires crunched in the frozen snow, and the moon hung overhead like a golden orange. Norman smelled of cigarette smoke and Aqua Velva. He pulled a cigarette from his shirt pocket, and lit it with the lighter. The tip of glowing ember showed in the dark interior.

"You didn't tell your father," he said.

Even though she had been waiting for Norman to say something, she startled at his voice. It sounded low as the bass pedal on the organ, a musical key of G, and yet at the same time a little edgy. Maybe dangerous.

"I don't need his permission."

"That's not how it looked at the box social," Norman said, pulling deeply on his cigarette, and exhaling away from her.

"We've come to an understanding," Mildred said. She thought to explain, and then decided to leave it at that. They made small talk the rest of the way, about the box social, the church fire, the waste of work, and expense of lost firewood.

"How do you think it started?" Mildred said. Dad talked about nothing else since the fire. Maybe Norman could satisfy his questions.

Norman took a deep drag. The glowing tip of the cigarette like a dying ember in the darkness. "Your father says I started it."

"He said that?"

"Yup." Norman took another drag. "Wants me fired."

Dad was angry, but this was impossible. The lights of Dalton sparkled in the darkness. It seemed a silly question, but she had to ask. She took a deep breath, said a silent prayer she wouldn't make the situation worse.

"Did you start the fire?"

Norman didn't answer right away. He parked under a streetlight next to the theatre, and pulled the parking brake. He turned to her. "Of course I did. Got drunk and fired the whole damn place out of pure spite."

He opened the car door, and came around to open her door, slipping in the frozen snow. They stood silently in line for their tickets. Norman stamped his feet and shivered. She didn't believe him. No one would confess in such a flippant manner if he were really guilty.

She sneaked a glance when he bought the popcorn. He looked the same as always. Dad was wrong.

She followed him to seats in the back of the theatre. Other couples snuggled around them, some already necking in the darkness. Mildred hoped Norman didn't have that on his mind.

Then she hoped he did. She wanted to be loved. She was almost thirty years old. She tucked her hand in Norman's arm and leaned close as Jimmy Stewart rode into town.

"Cold?" he said.

She nodded and kept her face riveted to the screen. Norman stretched his arm around the back of her chair. Her heart beat faster. His touch felt like how a jolt from the shock machine in the Lower Joint must feel. Pastor Hustvedt mentioned the shock machine in a sermon one time. Put a nickel in the shock machine, and hang on. The one enduring the electric current longest was the winner. Pastor had scoffed that such a thing could prove a man's courage. All the Luther Leaguers couldn't wait to try it for themselves.

She felt the rough nap of Norman's sleeve on the back of her neck, as the good guys in white hats trounced the bad guys in black. If only all good guys wore white hats, not only in the movies.

She didn't speak until they were back in the car.

"I don't believe you," Mildred said when they were almost out of the city limits. The moon dipped in the sky. The big dipper and Orion visible. "You wouldn't burn all your hard work. If you were going to fire the church, you would have spared the wood pile."

Norman laughed a bitter laugh. "Course I did it. Hate that god-damn job anyway." He lit another cigarette. "Excuse my language."

Norman was protecting someone. Who would be careless with fire, or even start a fire on purpose? Who would Norman care about enough to protect?

"Eddy Root," she said. It was like dropping the last piece into a jigsaw puzzle and seeing the whole picture. "Eddy hanging around where he didn't belong, trying to smoke like a soldier."

Norman slowed the car, and looked toward her. His face almost visible in the glow of the dashboard, and the small glow at the end of his cigarette.

"Don't say anything, Millie," he said, his voice in the Key of C. "Promise. They'll send him back to the asylum for sure. They're already looking for a reason."

He was such a good man, taking the blame for poor Eddy. Her heart swelled with affection, and for the first time in a long time, she felt close to her brother. It came to her as one reason she liked Norman. When she was with him, she felt Willy was still alive.

"Promise me, Millie," Norman said. His voice tightened into a strained Key of G.

"I promise," Mildred said.

"It won't happen again," Norman said. His voice back to an easy Key of C. "I've spoken with Nels, and he's keeping a tighter leash on Eddy."

"But it's not fair to you—"

"Who said life was fair?" His voice rose to the key of A.

Mildred moved closer to Norman's side, and leaned her head against his shoulder. She matched her breathing to his, surprised at how easy it was to find his rhythm.

The porch light glowed against the backdrop of the dark house. Norman walked her to the porch, leaving his car idling against the cold. Mildred tried to imitate Vera Hanson, chatting about the box social and asking if he won a cake after she left. They stood on the steps, their breath pumping clouds between them, teeth chattering.

"Come in?" Mildred said. "I'll make tea."

"It's late," Norman said. "Your dad won't like it."

"Don't be foolish." Mildred took his hand, and pulled him inside.

Dad sat at the table in the dark. He stood when they came inside. His bathrobe gaped open, showing his long johns. Embarrassment and anger choked Mildred's throat.

"Where have you been?" Dad demanded. "Been worried sick."

"Picture show," Mildred said, stumbling for words. This couldn't be happening. The old Dad, before Willy's death, would not have shown such rudeness. "I told you."

"Hello, Selmer," Norman said in a cool tone. "Good night, Millie."

"Get the hell off my property and don't come back," Dad said, with a threatening step toward Norman. Mildred feared he might raise his fists. "I don't want you sniffing around my daughter."

"Dad," Mildred said. "Stop it."

"I'll be going," Norman said. "Thank you for the nice evening."

When the door closed, Dad turned to Mildred. "You'll not keep company with him." He turned the key in the lock and pocketed it in his bathrobe as if he were keeping her prisoner. "Do I make myself clear? He's not interested in you—only in getting his hands on this farm. Heaven knows he'd drink it up if he had a chance."

Mildred couldn't answer. Instead she stomped to her room, slamming the door behind her. She threw herself on the bed, and cried until her mind cleared. It was the middle of the night, dark and cold. She rummaged in the hall closet for Mama's old suitcase, reassured by snores coming from Dad's room.

She must pack wisely for everything to fit into one bag.

As soon as she heard Dad leaving for morning chores, Mildred telephoned Tia. Awkward that Tia was Norman's sister, but Mildred didn't know where else to turn.

"I need you to come over right away," Mildred said. "I'll explain when you get here."

"What's wrong?" Tia's voice sounded concerned. "Is there an emergency?"

"I'd rather not say," Mildred said. One never knew who was listening. "Please hurry."

"If you're too busy," Tillie burst in, rubbering again. "I can help out."

"I'll be right over," Tia said. "No need, Tillie."

Mildred had saved a little money from her job as organist. It wasn't enough. She must swallow her pride, and find work as a hired girl. Then she could rent a room and find a real job, a respectable job. She would save money from every paycheck until she had enough for a train ticket. She would see the world, study music if she wished, and live an independent life away from her father. But working as a hired girl meant starting at the bottom.

Maybe the widow man, Elmer Petterson, needed help with his brood of children. The memory of sitting next to him at the box social made her skin creep. Nels Carlson depended on Eddy for outside work, but she doubted he was keeping up with the housework since Olga's death. Gunda Olson's back was bad. Sometimes new mothers needed help until they were back on their feet. Something would turn up.

Millie looked around the kitchen. She would show Dad. She wouldn't make breakfast or stoke the fire. Let him feel the pinch. She thought to leave without a note, but relented at the last minute. She didn't want him to worry. In the note she said that it was past time for her to make her own way.

She carefully gathered her record collection. Her mother had given Mildred the good china. She would need her patchwork quilts, linens and feather pillows. Mildred couldn't think about those things now. Once she found a room, she would return for them. She grabbed her suitcase and music folder, clutching her pocketbook under her arm.

She ran out to the car as soon as Tia drove into the yard. Tia looked surprised when Mildred shoved her suitcase into the backseat, but didn't ask for an explanation.

"I'm running away." Mildred settled into the passenger seat. She looked into the rear view mirror, and saw Dad standing in the doorway of the barn. Mildred set her jaw. "Want to go along?"

Tia delivered the cream cans to the creamery. Mildred went along inside and asked the butter maker about jobs in town.

He scratched his head and twisted his face in thought. "Can't say that I do," he said. "We'll be hiring another egg candler in the spring."

They stopped at Rorvig's Store, but Mr. Rorvig had gone to a funeral in Wheaton and wouldn't be back until late afternoon.

"I wish I could find a good job," Mildred said. "Like the girls had in the ammunition plants during the war."

"They made good money," Tia said. "Nothing like that now."

As they drove down Main Street, Tia pointed to a sign on Widow Jacobson's ramshackle old rooming house. "Room for Rent."

Tia offered to stay in the car, but Mildred insisted she go along inside. "I'm scared," Mildred said. "I've never run away before."

Widow Jacobson came to the door in a faded nightgown and nightcap. She strained to see who it was and fumbled to put on her spectacles. Several cats rubbed against the furniture in the front room. Mildred's eyes started to water. She had always been allergic to cats.

"The room is two dollars a week with kitchen privileges," Widow Jacobson said, and led them down a short hallway and pointed to a steep set of stairs going to the second story. "It's too hard for me to climb them anymore," she said. "Drummer had it for about a year but he's moved on to Dakota. Sold ladies' brassieres, of all things," she said with a titter. "I haven't been up to clean the room, but you can take a look, maybe do the cleaning yourself to knock a little off your bill. Room at the end of the hallway."

Mildred pressed a handkerchief to her nose to keep from sneezing. The cats were a definite problem. Of course, no mice to worry about with cats in the house. She tried to keep positive. She might learn to live with cats if she tried.

"Are you all right?" Tia said after Mildred sneezed several times in a row.

Mildred nodded and hurried toward the room. They opened the door and Tia gasped. A urine stained mattress drooped half off the bed. Empty beer bottles lined the window sill beneath tattered curtains, gray with dust. A broken dresser drawer hung open, filled with trash, girlie magazines and empty whiskey bottles.

Tia marched over to the bed and lifted the mattress. "I knew it," Tia said, pointing to a scurrying mass of insects. "Bedbugs."

They ran out of the house.

"You'll have to stay with us 'til you find something better," Tia said. "You're not staying there."

"Truth is, I don't have money for anything better," Mildred said. "I'll hire out until I can afford a decent place."

"I need a bath after being in that terrible place," Tia said. "Bedbugs!"

Mildred giggled. "I wish you could have seen your face when you saw the bugs,"

Tia laughed. "Don't tell Ma," Tia cautioned. "She'll have the kerosene out for our hair, if you do."

"Like the time Nedra brought head lice to school," Mildred said, laughing a little too hard. "Willy wore her stocking cap and caught the cooties. Mama almost had a conniption fit."

The mention of Mama and Willy turned Mildred's laughter to near-tears. She was making a huge decision, and so far, nothing had gone right.

"How will you keep your organist job if you're living in town?" Tia said, as she turned the car toward the Fiskum farm. "You ready to give it up?"

Mildred hadn't thought about Tolga Lutheran. Town churches had organists already, much better musicians than Mildred, and no chance for her to find a similar position. What she really needed was a car of her own. More money.

She remembered the time Mama spanked her for picking the raspberries for mud pies. Mildred had packed a paper sack with her best doll and ran away, getting almost to the end of the driveway before Dad gave her a ride back home on the tractor. She hadn't thought it through then, and she hadn't thought it through now.

"Maybe I'm too old to run away," Mildred said. "A grown woman should give it more thought ahead of time."

"A move is different than running away," Tia said. "More sensible."

"Fill your gas tank if you drive me around to find work this afternoon," Mildred said. "Sorry to be such a pest."

Tia broke into a grin. "Sounds like a good excuse to get out of cleaning the calf pens."

Norman raised an eyebrow when he saw her at the noon table, but didn't ask outright what she was doing at their house. Mildred knew the questions would be asked behind her back, not to her face, as was the custom in Tolga Township.

"I'm looking for work," Mildred said while they ate. "Know anyone needing help?"

Mrs. Fiskum said that Ada Jorgenson might welcome an extra set of hands to care for Minna. "I worry so about her," Mrs. Fiskum said. "All that heavy lifting."

"Pastor Hustvedt might know of someone," Tia said. "Or Doc Sorenson."

Norman bent low over his plate, and shoveled in the food.

"I'd like to stay here a few days until I get things settled," Mildred said. "I'm thinking of a room in Dalton if I can find work within walking distance."

"I heard Gertie is quitting at the telephone exchange," Norman said. He looked up from his plate, but didn't make eye contact with Mildred.

"What for she quitting?" Mrs. Fiskum said. "That's a decent job."

"Getting married," Norman said. "Bruce Hegdahl is home and they're picking up where they left off."

* * *

Gunda Olson looked most offended when Mildred asked if she needed help. Gunda assured her she could do her own work. She wrinkled her face as if in deep thought. "You might stop by Ingeborg's place." Gunda pursed her lips in what looked like smug self-righteousness. "She's getting up in years."

Mildred almost burst out laughing. She winked at Tia who stifled a grin. Everyone knew Ingeborg was younger than Gunda by several years, and in better health.

Gunda insisted they stay for coffee and cookies, though they had just eaten a full meal at Tia's house. Julius pulled up a chair and seemed very glad to visit with them. In fact, Mildred noticed he seemed most interested in visiting with Tia. They delved into farm prices and crop rotation.

Julius was younger than they by at least five years. Shy and bookish, Julius had grown into a handsome man with his tall, lean frame and smoky blue eyes. Clyde married a younger woman. What made it be scandalous for a woman to marry a younger man?

Tia might stand a chance of finding a man if she cut her old-lady hair and shortened her skirts. She might even snag Julius. They seemed comfortable together. But then, face powder and a stylish haircut hadn't changed Mildred's marital status. She and Tia were both left on the shelf.

"Are you going live?" Tia said. She mentioned the REA effort to sign up local farmers for electricity.

Julius nodded, but his mother interrupted. "No need. We've gotten by this long without it."

Julius gave a helpless shrug. Mildred suspected she wasn't the only one struggling with a domineering parent. "Dad loves having electricity," Mildred said, feeling a sudden need to defend Julius. "We were lucky to get it before all the rationing started."

"We could afford it month to month," Tia said. "But those darn hook-up charges."

Julius said his brothers did the wiring to save money. Said they learned at the county extension office. "Has Norman any interest?" Julius said. "The GI Bill pays for veterans. We could ride together."

"Probably has more sense than sticking his nose in a book," Gunda said with a sniff. "Too much book learning gets you nowhere."

"Wish I could use Norman's GI Bill," Tia said with a laugh.

Mildred stood and gathered her cup and saucer, trying to shake the feeling of despondency that settled over her.

"Eleanor Roosevelt says farmers need higher yields to win the peace," Julius said, as he gathered their coats. "Farmers and scientists working hand-in-hand for the betterment of mankind."

"What does Eleanor Roosevelt know about farming?" Gunda said with a sniff. "She'll be forgotten soon enough now that her man's gone."

"Thank you for the coffee," Mildred said, anxious to be on her way.

Julius walked them to the car, grabbing a fresh toothpick off the table. "I'm going live whether or not Ma approves."

"Wish I could," Tia said. "Maybe I should work out, too."

"I'll loan you my books when I finish with them," Julius said to Tia. "Help with your wiring if you change your mind. A farmer without electricity won't have a spitting chance."

The rest of the afternoon, Tia was moody and distracted, though she drove Mildred to several more families as agreed upon. After the Olsons, Tia insisted on waiting in the car. "I can't drink another cup of coffee or I'll burst," she said. "Maybe it won't take so long if they know your ride is waiting."

Ada Jorgenson needed help painting Minna's bedroom. Nels Carlson wanted an early spring cleaning in preparation for George's return.

"I'd be glad for the help," Nels said. "I'm not used to batching it."

Mildred glanced out the window where Patsy barked at Tia in the car.

"If you're sure your pa can spare you," Nels said. He seemed to weigh his words. "Something wrong between you two?"

"It's nothing," Mildred said with a shake of her head. She suddenly felt very tired. She'd had a dull headache since being around the Jacobson cats. "Just time I moved out on my own."

"Don't be too hard on Selmer," Nels said. "He's been through a hell of a lot." Gone was the swaggering bravado that had been so much a part of him before the miracle. "Lost his wife," Nels choked back emotion. "Then his boy. Seems to me, you're all he has left." He let out a sigh. "It's easy to hold too tight when it seems you're losing everything."

Mildred knew Dad had changed after Willy's death, but she didn't consider how he must feel.

"I'm praying for your miracle," Nels said. "One for Selmer, too."

Mildred almost asked him to pray for Norman's miracle, too, but hesitated. Such things weren't verbalized in Tolga Township.

She didn't know about miracles, but something good had happened to Nels. No crutches, no more drunkenness, at church every week, but still a little crusty around the edges. In some ways, not so different than before. In other ways, very different.

Mildred looked up at the cold, blue sky as she left Nels's house. Patsy turned away from the car and ran to Mildred. She leaned over and scratched the old dog's ears. Then she prayed a simple prayer.

"We can go home," Mildred said when she climbed in the car. "Work lined up for all next week. If you can put up with me that long."

"Of course," Tia said. "I made a decision. I'm going into the bank tomorrow and try to get a loan." She steered the car onto the snow-packed gravel road.

"For the electric?" Mildred said. "What will your mother say?" She pulled her scarf tighter around her hair and clapped her hands under the heater to warm herself.

"We need to go live, no matter what she says." She turned up the heater. "If Julius can hook up in spite of his mother, I can do the same."

"Think you'll get the loan?"

"I'll put the shoats as collateral," Tia said. "And plant a bigger pickle patch next year. Good money in it." She blew out her breath. "I've made up my mind. Maybe you can hire out to me next summer to pick pickles."

"Good for you," Mildred said. "It's about time we stood up for ourselves."

"It's all upside down," Tia said. "Norman could go to school but doesn't want to. I want to go but there's no money. If only he would take extension classes. I could study with him at night."

"Men get to do what they want and we just sit around waiting for them to make up their minds," Mildred said.

"Then let's change. Let's do something outrageous," Tia said. "Give the old hens something to gossip about."

They drove toward Tia's house. Mildred dreaded imposing on her friends for another week. They wouldn't complain, she knew, but Tia was busy and she must bother her for rides to her chore jobs next week. She was overstaying her welcome. Even after a week of work, she would still need to find a room somewhere, and a steady job. That meant asking more favors.

As they drove by her father's house, Mildred noticed a weak plume of smoke coming out of their chimney. Dad should be keeping a better fire in this cold weather. But how could he work outside and keep the fire going at the same time? She imagined him coming in from the barn to a cold house and empty table. He was a terrible cook.

"Stop," Mildred said. The solution became clear. "Drop me off at home, will you?"

"What do you mean?" Tia braked, and turned the DeSoto into the Moberg driveway. "I thought you were staying with us for a while."

"I thank you kindly," Mildred said. "I'm sick of waiting on the men, but I'm even sicker of acting like a spoiled brat." A plan hatched in her brain as she spoke. There had to be a way. "Time to quit running and begin to act like a grown up."

* * *

Dad came into the kitchen to supper on the stove and a roaring fire. He stood on the doormat, stomping his feet and hitching up his trousers with the insides of his wrists.

"So what's going on?" Dad said in a soft voice. "Are you eloping?"

"Of course not," Mildred said with a snort. "Norman and I are only friends."

"His drinking scares me," Dad said in a matter of fact way. He took off his coat and hung it on a peg behind the door. Then he slipped out of his work boots. His big toe stuck out of his wool sock.

"It scares me, too," Mildred said. She hadn't put the fear into words before. "Don't worry. I'm no fool."

Dad stepped over to the sink and turned on the faucet. "Julius says you're hiring out to the neighbors." Dad lathered his hands and face at the sink, rinsing and groping for a towel. "Not much of a life, being a chore girl."

"Just until I can get enough money to rent a room," Mildred said. "I'm looking for steady work in town." She hesitated, and then added. "They're hiring at the telephone office."

"And the REA," Dad said.

Mildred glanced at him in surprise as she took the hotdish out of the oven and placed it on the table. She grabbed the milk pitcher out of the icebox, and reached for the last heel of bread.

"Talked to the manager when I paid the light bill. Said they need someone, with all the expansion going on." He heaped his plate with tuna fish casserole and grinned. "Good to have you home again."

She had planned her words, but this new information threw her for a loop. She felt her guard go up, in spite of her good intentions to be open and adult. Maybe Dad was trying to fool her into coming home again. "What kind of job at the REA?"

"Office work. Keeping records. Said they'd train the right person. Pay is fair. Chance for advancement."

"You've never wanted me to work before," Mildred said. She wouldn't back down.

"You've never said you wanted to work before."

He was right. Though she'd dreamed of travel, and study, and planned to find a good job, she had never said outright that she wanted one. She had been acting like a child. No wonder Dad treated her like one.

Dad cleaned his plate and took a second helping. Gray strands framed his temple, the balding spot on the back of his head was getting bigger. She knew his mannerisms, his habits, his weaknesses. It was true that she was all he had left. It was also true he was all she had left.

Dad used his bread crust to wipe his plate clean. His face drained of yesterday's anger. It almost killed him to lose Mama. Mildred had been sympathetic, willing to help out because she knew what he was going through. Somehow, she hadn't understood his pain in losing Willy. Dad wept at Mama's funeral, but not at Willy's. She grieved, too. They both were still grieving.

"I won't be treated like a child," she said. She must hold the course. "But I won't act like one anymore, either. We're adults. I don't need your permission or approval."

"I'm sorry. I'll try harder." Dad took another small scoop of hot-dish as if he hadn't eaten all day. "You need a car to be independent. There's a nice little Studebaker for sale in town. You can live where you want. Work where you want." He swallowed hard, bobbing his Adam's apple. "You've earned it."

A job in town. His promise to stay out of her affairs. Her own car. She brought the coffee pot to the table and filled her father's cup.

"I want to ask something," Mildred said. "What would have happened if Willy had come back from the war?"

"What do you mean?" Dad said with a frown. "He would have come home. Back to the farm."

"But what if Willy married and took over the farm?" She had to know. "Where would I have gone?"

"Maybe we would have built a little house on the property. Lots of families make adjustments."

Mildred thought his over. "What if you remarry?"

Dad burst out laughing. "Now who would want to marry an old dog like me?" Then he turned serious. "Everything I have is yours whether or not I remarry, whether you stay or move out." Dad planted both elbows on the table and leaned forward. "All your mother and I worked for . . . and Willy's share. You don't need to work as a chore girl. You don't need to lack anything."

"What if I marry?" Mildred said, "and my new husband hates farming? Or you hate my new husband? What if I never marry? I can't manage the farm when you're gone."

Her father reached for the coffee pot and poured another cup. "Life is hard," he said. "And it tends to get harder with the years, but families stick together. Support each other." His voice was a gentle Key of B, her favorite note. "When the time comes, you'll know what to do."

Mildred washed the dishes and set a bread sponge for tomorrow's baking. Dad took the newspaper into the front room and turned on the radio. Mildred tried to imagine a different life, one with her own car, a job, her own bank account. It seemed not only possible, but desirable. Not out of reach.

The phone rang, and her father answered. She could tell by his voice that he was trying very hard to be polite. "It's for you," he said.

Mildred wiped her hands on her apron and took the receiver. "Hello," she said. It was Norman asking if she needed anything. "I'm fine," she said. "Nice of you to ask, though. I appreciate it."

"How about if I stop by a little later, bring your suitcase." His voice faded and Mildred could hear a baby crying. Those rubberneckers!

"That would be swell," Mildred said. She would soon know if change was possible. She knew it was worth the risk to find out. "I'll make popcorn and get the Monopoly game out."

She hung up the phone, and hurried into the kitchen. Her hair was a mess and she needed lipstick. "Want to join Norman and me for Monopoly?"

"Not tonight," Dad said. He got out of his chair and hitched his trousers with the inside of his wrists. "Think I'll turn in early and let you youngsters have the house to yourself."

The tension eased in her chest. Mildred went over and hugged her father around his neck. "I love you, Daddy."

"I love you, too, Millie-girl."

Tough Old Bird

GUNDA OLSON UNFOLDED from the kitchen chair like a rusty pocket knife, her back stiff and creaky in the damp of March. She clutched the table for support and the kerosene lamp in the middle of the checkered oilcloth shifted and sloshed. She reached a hand to steady the lamp. It was her favorite possession, a wedding gift from her father those many years ago.

Gunda cast a furtive glance behind her, hoping Julius hadn't seen her struggle. She saw him through the north window gathering kitchen wood. Julius wore an ancient barn coat that had belonged to his father, one worn shiny with constant use. It was too small for him—the sleeves rode up on his flannel shirt. Funny, that he would be taller than his father and brothers.

She clumsily gathered the plates from the table, frustrated how her fingers fanned to one side like willow trees in the wind. Lately Julius had been telling her to take it easy. Even hinted that she might be better off going to live with one of his married brothers for a while—to get a rest, he said, though she knew good and well that it had nothing to do with rest.

Lord knew what might happen if she weren't around to give Julius direction. He was a good boy, a man really, but lacked motivation. If she were out of the picture he might find some no-account town girl to step in—a girl as hopeless as the one Clyde Hanson had married.

Gunda scraped dinner scraps into the kettle on the stove where hog mash stewed into a thick slop. The cat meowed and rubbed against her legs. It was gloomy and dark in the kitchen, as it always was when the sun was still climbing the eastern sky. It wasn't dark enough to light the lamp. Once

191

it dropped into the west, there would be light through the kitchen windows. No need for electricity or any other new-fangled invention.

She stirred the slop with a wooden spoon and kicked away the cat. Ground corn, empty cobs, oats, potato peels, egg shells, chicken fat, carrot scrapings, sour milk, rotten eggs, cabbage cores, and beet tops. Gunda was of the firm conviction that hot mash was the key to successful farrowing. The putrid smell of sour milk bubbled out of the pot.

She sprinkled another handful of dried corn into the mixture and pulled the heavy iron kettle to the side for Julius to lug to the pig house. The sow would drop her littler within another week. Gunda already counted the money. If the price held steady.

She'd been saving every extra cent to buy Mansel Jorgenson's low-land pasture adjoining their property. During the dry years, that piece of land had yielded hay and grass when everything else brittled into brown death. It would be an insurance policy in case those bad times rolled around again.

In her experience, bad times always rolled around again. And as everyone knew, a farmer couldn't own enough land.

It hadn't been easy, but she'd talked Mansel into selling the land at a good price. She would surprise Julius for his birthday in September. Gunda could imagine Julius' amazement when she handed him the deed.

Another five acres added to the 170 acres already in their possession meant a 175-acre farm in Tolga Township. Nothing to sneeze at. Quite an accomplishment for a widow left alone in the midst of the Dirty Thirties.

"Julius!" she hollered out the back door. The air heavied with the scent of spring though March was Minnesota's snowiest month, and this year had been no exception. It was also the windiest month though today the windmill blades barely turned. Julius must pump water by hand for the livestock unless the wind picked up. "Slop's ready!"

He stomped his feet on the mat, elbowed his way past the storm door and dumped an armful of wood into the box next to the stove. Julius grabbed a fresh toothpick off the table, reached for the kettle and took it outside without a word.

Without making eye contact.

Nothing unusual about that. Some days they barely spoke ten words to each other.

Gunda dragged a pail of rotted manure mixed with topsoil from under the bench next to the door. It was early to start garden plants but she could hardly wait to get her hands into the dirt. She rummaged in the frigid front porch for the sack of empty tin cans saved for this very purpose. Of course she used them year after year and some of them were rusted clear through. She dipped an old spoon with a broken handle into the rich loam and thought about their argument the night before.

Julius' silence didn't mean he was still mad—but it was hard to tell. Now if it had been one of his brothers, she'd have no doubt of his opinion. Julius was more like Everett that way, keeping things to himself.

Just the thought of her husband brought a fresh stab of grief.

A nervous breakdown, Doctor Sorenson called it, nothing to be ashamed of. Her husband had been fine until the bank failed. And the drought. And the crop failures. Everett had clammed up, gone silent, and given up. Changed into someone she didn't know.

Lots of folks went crazy over the stock market crash. Why, the papers said rich men, educated men, leapt out of windows or blew their brains out. Everett was no weaker than other men. It was nobody's fault, Doc said. She blamed him, though, for leaving her alone with the boys and the farm, and in such hard times.

That day Gunda had been on her way to the garden when Everett stepped out from behind the lilac bushes holding his hunting rifle. He mumbled something about getting rid of her once and for all, that even if he killed her he wouldn't do it well enough to please her.

"You'd kick if you were hung with a new rope," he said. The timbre of his voice stopped her cold. He lifted the gun and pointed it toward her. "I have to stop you before you ruin their lives, too."

She just stood there holding the colander, wearing her garden hat, waiting for him to make a joke and laugh. In their earlier years he was always joking and making little pranks.

Julius came out of the house at that very moment. He was barely out of knee britches, still a boy.

"What are you doing, Dad?" His eyes showed surprise, maybe alarm.

Everett laid aside the gun, and grabbed Julius into a bear hug, sobbing and talking all kinds of foolishness. "Don't let her do it, son, don't let her do it, no matter what."

She had never told anyone about it, and Julius never mentioned it. Sometimes she wondered what would have happened if she had called for the doctor—or the minister. Surely someone could have stopped him.

Instead, she decided to wait a while, at least until the beans were put by. Back then it was so dry the corn scorched and withered in the fields and their hay barn sat empty. Black, dusty clouds rolled in from North Dakota, covering the windows and getting through the tightest screen. The garden did almost nothing, and they were lucky to have the acre of cucumbers for the pickle factory that the boys had watered by hand.

Everett had seemed more like himself at noon. He told Joyce, their oldest son, to start on the calf pens and directed Marion, their middle son, to herd the cows to the lake to save on the well.

Joyce said he saw him walking into the woods with his gun. Even a mess of squirrels was welcome meat during such hard times. When Everett was late for supper, Gunda had felt a clench in her stomach that left her stone cold and hollow. Joyce found his body next to his favorite birch tree overlooking the lake.

Gunda sighed and opened the envelope of tomato seeds, pushing a few into the center of every container, pushing down the sadness with each seed. She never mouthed the word, suicide, in front of the boys. Always called it an accident.

It had happened, and nothing would change it.

Ingeborg Hanson's second cousin suffered a nervous breakdown, and ended up in the Fergus Falls Asylum. Harvey's boy had spent a few years there when Sofus Ingvalstad caused a stir. Gunda didn't wish Everett in such a place even if he had turned lunatic. She only wished that he'd tried harder to come out of it.

She'd been fifty-one years old. Too old to start over on her own. Harvey and his boy came over after the funeral and helped in the pickle patch. Nels and Olga brought enough food for a week.

When they were having afternoon lunch, she had voiced her doubts that she could make it on her own. Spoke her fears out loud, though it wasn't like her and she hadn't done it since.

Nels had looked at her over the rim of his coffee cup. He paused as if weighing his words. "You'll make it." He'd looked at her and winked. "You're a tough old bird."

It was the nicest compliment she'd ever received.

Gunda reached for a folded paper of yellow tomato seeds. They had been her mother's seeds, brought from the Old Country, and saved year after year from the strongest plants. Her mouth watered at the thought of fresh tomato slices sprinkled with sugar.

Marion and Joyce took after her. They'd met sensible farm girls who knew their way around a barnyard. Marion and Gladys farmed a nice piece of acreage north of Underwood. Joyce and Ethel lived with her parents west of Dalton. They had their wits about them and both feet on the ground. She didn't worry about them.

Julius was different. More like his father. He was weak, maybe, not able to take charge and be a real man. Marion said Julius should have been born a poet instead of a farmer. He would surely ruin his eyes the way he read every book he could find. Julius insisted they subscribe to the *Fergus Falls Journal*, of all things, though Gunda had to admit the papers were handy for more than just reading. Good for fire starting, and better than the Monkey Ward catalog in the outhouse.

If he had his way, Julius would have gone to high school—or even college. Of course, with the Depression in full swing, there was no money to humor such whimsies. It would have meant boarding out in Fergus Falls, a terrible expense. Besides, after Everett's death, she needed him on the farm.

Everyone knew a farmer didn't need more than an eighth-grade education.

Why couldn't he find a decent girl from among their neighbors? Tia Fiskum could drive a car, milk cows, and plow a furrow straighter than a man. Even Millie Moberg knew how to work though she spent far too much time with that music foolishness. Julius said they were too old for him. What were a few years?

When Tillie Stenerson told her that Julius had taken a shine to a Battle Lake girl named Annabelle Swenson, Gunda told him in no uncertain terms she would not welcome a lazy, good-for-nothing town-girl into their house. Why she'd just as soon he married a Catholic.

Gunda lined up the tin cans on an old door salvaged from the old summer kitchen, one end balanced on the sewing machine and the other on a small table by the south window. It was a little precarious but should be all right unless Gladys brought the grandkids over. Nothing was safe with them around.

She considered again how many plants were needed. She had started a second garden during the Depression, and kept it out of habit, she guessed. One on high ground for wet years and the other on low land if it turned dry.

Bugs, hail, drought, deer, or renegade stock could take a crop in minutes. She had a vivid recollection of the grasshoppers that almost starved them out in her girlhood. She remembered the feel of sharp wings on her bare feet, the way they spit tobacco on her dress.

Gunda scrounged for more cans. She planted watermelon and muskmelon, onions, broccoli, cauliflower, and pickling cukes. She would sow additional seeds directly into the garden for a second crop. It was a wondrous thing to see a Minnesota garden in August. The corn, potatoes, pumpkins, squash—a thing of beauty. Almost as pretty as a field of ripened wheat or a flock of Ingeborg's white geese.

She chuckled to think about Ingeborg's new daughter-in-law. Tillie Stenerson said that Vera didn't know how to wash an egg, stitch a seam or churn butter. Said she was afraid of chickens and useless as teats on a boar. But what could you expect after the outlandish airs they'd taken on? First the electric and running water. Then a new barn. The tractor.

Julius called it progress.

Last night out of the blue, Julius brought up the electric again. Said the REA wanted everyone on their road signed up. Said it was less expensive if they all hooked up at once. After years of rationing, copper wire was back on the shelves. Julius said having the electric would profit in the long run. They could run more animals. Said electricity was safer.

"You'd like it, Ma," Julius said, and looked at her with those eyes so much like his father's. She almost weakened when he looked at her that way, but caught herself in time.

"We can't afford it." She shouldn't have said it so plain. He didn't know she was saving money for land. She should have eased him down, discussed it a little more before giving her reply.

Julius hadn't answered. Just got up and went into his bedroom and closed the door. He hadn't spoken since.

"Good Lord, Ma," Julius said behind her. She hadn't heard him come in, so wrapped up in her thoughts she was. "You're planting enough for the whole township."

"We've got to eat."

"Already enough in the cellar for next winter." His face wore a look of disapproval. "There are only two of us. I was hoping this year to cut back."

"Rorvig needs plants for the store," she felt defensiveness rise up in her. Why should she explain anything to her son? "Ingeborg wants yellow tomato plants. Tia might take some cabbages."

"I'm going into town." Julius took off his barn coat and slipped into his mackinaw jacket. "Won't be home for afternoon lunch."

"Take the eggs."

She watched him climb into the old Ford and pull out of the driveway. She should have asked him why he was going. They had kerosene. Flour bin full. Sugar still in the sack. Root cellar held potatoes, cabbages, and beets. Jars of home canned beef and chicken, pickles and tomatoes filled their basement. They had enough coffee, all the milk and eggs they could use plus more left over. He wouldn't have thought of the eggs except she reminded him.

197

A sudden weariness fell upon her. Maybe she'd sneak upstairs and take a little rest. Julius wouldn't know a thing about it. Just a half hour.

* * *

The next morning, Gunda's back was killing her from bending over the seedlings. She'd had a restless night, and felt tired and cranky. A crick in her back forced her to lean to the side when she walked.

She refilled both cups on the breakfast table. Her crooked fingers made pouring awkward and took her full attention.

"Feeling all right?" Julius wiped his plate with the corner of his toast. "You're walking funny."

"It's nothing," Gunda said. She lost her grip on the pot and splashed coffee on the table. Julius reached over and wiped it with the forearm of his shirt sleeve.

Julius didn't make eye contact. "Joyce called."

Something was amiss. "I didn't hear the phone." She set the coffee pot back on the stove and straightened her back, biting back a grimace of pain.

"You were in the hen house," Julius said. "He's taking Gladys to Elbow Lake to get her tooth pulled." Julius drank the rest of his coffee, first blowing on it to cool it down. "Needs you to watch the kids. He'll pick you up after breakfast."

Julius looked like he did the time he stole a pound of butter from the ice box and ate the whole thing while hiding in the outhouse.

"I can eat in town," Julius said on his way out the door to finish the chores, "if you don't have time to cook dinner."

Would he never learn?

She'd been in her mid-forties when he was born. The other boys were finished with country school and working on the farm. Of course, she hadn't been happy at first. But she'd gotten use to it and had been glad ever since. She still chuckled every time she remembered how Inge-borg's jaw had dropped when she found out.

There had been a quilting party at Ingeborg's only a month before he was born. Gunda never said a word about the baby coming and no one thought it amiss that she'd put on weight. It wasn't until she and Everett walked into church for the christening that anyone knew. It was hard to pull anything over on Ingeborg, but Gunda had done it. It still made her smile.

"I've already put a roast in for noon dinner," she said. "No need to go into town. Pickled beets on the work table. Molasses cookies and bread in the icebox. I'll be home before supper, I'd guess."

* * *

Gunda knew something was wrong when Joyce didn't stop in the house when he brought her home. That and Nels's old truck sitting in the yard. The grandchildren had worn her out with their constant bickering and questions. She'd missed her usual nap. She wasn't up to cooking for company.

The smell of sawdust was her first warning. A pair of legs stuck out from under the kitchen table. Nels was down on the floor pulling wires through a hole in the wall.

"What the hell are you doing?" Anger made the swear word pop out of her mouth before she could stop it.

"Hello," Nels said. "Pretty much done. Be out of your way in a minute."

Gunda slammed her pocket book on the table, and stood in the center of the room. She felt like crying. She had told Julius they couldn't afford it, yet he had gone ahead. Sounds of a hammer came from upstairs.

Nels pulled himself to his feet, and she marveled at the ease of his movement. Why just a few months ago he couldn't have walked up the hill to their house without a struggle. It was a miracle, after all. No matter what Pastor Hustvedt might say about it. A fleeting thought reminded her that with her crooked fingers and aching back needed a miracle, too. She was too angry to think about it.

"Thank God for our boys," Nels said as he took off leather gloves and leaned back against the cupboard. "Did you hear George is coming home?" His eyes teared and big drops traveled down the creases of his wrinkled cheeks. "Finally earned enough points."

Gunda stood without speaking. If miracles made a blubbering idiot out of people, she wanted nothing to do with them. Why, Nels cried at the drop of a hat. Couldn't even sing a hymn in church without bawling like a heifer in heat.

"Your Julius is smart. Could be an electrician. Knows it backwards and forwards."

Gunda felt tears pushing behind her eyes. She swallowed hard. The last thing she wanted was to make a scene in front of her neighbor.

"When you think of the terrible war and so many boys taken . . ." Nels choked the words. "Everett would be so proud of him."

Julius walked into the kitchen wearing a carpenter's apron with a hammer hanging through a loop. His rolled-up sleeves showed bulging muscles. A toothpick dangled out his mouth. His jaw was shadowed with the growth of beard, his face locked in stubbornness.

The same look Everett used to get on his face when they argued.

"And thank God for the electric," Nels said. "Make your life easier."

Julius had gone ahead and made the decision and somehow got the money . . . no money except from their bank account. The money saved for the land. Her money. The money they had worked for, sacrificed for and saved in spite of everything. Money that could have given them the extra acreage to make more money, enough to make life easier. Everything gone because Julius wanted highfalutin' inventions to give him more time to ruin his eyes reading. Anger blazed like white fire down her spine.

The cat rubbed by her legs and she kicked him away, harder than necessary. She jerked her coat off and hung it on the hook, and reached for her apron. She had to get busy, had to do something to stop herself from airing family problems in front of the neighbors. After Nels left, she would have words with Julius.

Gunda grabbed the broom and swept the wood shavings into the dust pan and dumped them into the wood stove. Nels laughed as the cat yowled and scurried out of the way. He asked Julius if their sow had dropped her litter and offered to help with the chores since Eddy would be doing them at his place. Dusk darkened the kitchen. Gunda lit the lamp as the men bundled in their coats for chores.

Julius soon returned with a baby piglet tucked inside his jacket. "Eleven piglets, Ma," he said with a cautious grin. "Here's the runt."

Gunda wiped the squirming pig with an old rag. It was sickly looking and shivering with cold. She swaddled it in an old blanket, almost like a baby, "Fetch a crate with a little straw in the bottom."

She didn't give Julius the comfort of conversation. Anger swirled as she fished in the drawer for the eye dropper. Let him stew. She could give the silent treatment, too. She poured milk into a saucepan on the stove while holding the piglet in her left arm. He was too weak to squirm but squealed a little now and then.

"Shhhh," Gunda said. "You'll be all right."

Julius brought the crate and positioned it on the open oven door. There was a small fire going in the wood range and the oven door was warm but not too hot. She'd have to watch that it didn't catch fire.

Julius stood beside her, shifting his weight from one leg to the other, something he always did when he was nervous. She didn't look up at him. If he wanted to run things, then let him. She'd keep her mouth shut. She was an old woman. He didn't care for her advice anymore.

Gunda pulled a chair next to the wood range after Julius went back to his chores. She placed the warmed saucepan on the oven door beside the crate and dipped the eye dropper into the milk. She poked the dropper into the corner of the piglet's mouth and squeezed the rubber bulb. The piglet choked but swallowed a little milk and poked out his tongue for more.

"You'll make it, "Gunda crooned. "You're tough."

She worked the dropper until the pig drifted into a contented sleep. She placed it in the crate. Maybe she wouldn't make supper at all. Let him fend for himself. She was sick and tired of doing everything.

Gunda creaked up from the chair, but as she turned away from the stove, the cat tangled in her feet and she stumbled, falling sideways to the kitchen table where the lighted lamp swayed and tipped. Kerosene spilled and fire followed it across the table and onto the floor, catching a stray bit of straw.

She panicked. She backed away from the table, knocking over the board holding the plants. Tin cans crashed to the floor, rolling in all directions. Gunda pulled herself back to her feet, and reached for the pan of warm milk beside the piglet and doused the flames.

It happened so fast. She wasn't hurt. Thank God for that. The oil cloth melted and ruined. The lamp cracked in two. Her father's face so young when he gave it to them on their wedding day. Julius' fault. The spilt milk, ruined cloth, broken lamp and tipped seed containers. It wouldn't have happened if he hadn't gone ahead with the electric.

By God, that her life would come to this.

She gripped the back of the chair until her breathing returned to normal. Then she remembered. How could she have forgotten? She lit a candle and went into the basement, taking care not to trip on the rickety stairs. Her knees wobbled but she had to find out if it was still there. She placed the candle on a wall holder and brushed cobwebs away from her face. Then she reached behind the potato sack. In the back corner of the bottom shelf sat a small crock.

Gunda cackled with relief. Julius hadn't taken everything. She stuck her hand inside the crock, pulling out a handful of tarnished coins, and a wad of folding money secured with string. It was her hedge against starvation and bank failures, her secret hoard.

Her fingers worked the knot. The bills showed mold around the edges from the damp cellar. Gunda ran her fingers through the coins, sniffing the musty smell of the basement. Maybe she wouldn't buy the land, after all. She might not have an eighth grade education, but she was smart enough not to put all her eggs in one basket.

Vera Hanson

T HE MAILMAN WAS LATE AGAIN. Vera kicked at a frozen clod at the
end of the driveway, pulling her jacket tighter around her body, and
tucking cold hands under her armpits. She hadn't worn her winter
coat though it was only March. She was almighty sick of the burden of
winter coats and overshoes. She strained her eyes up the lonely gravel
road where Clarence's old truck should be coming.

All morning her thoughts had been on Selma. She had read her coffee
grounds after breakfast, making sure that Clyde was out of the house. She
wasn't an expert at coffee ground readings like Selma, but it seemed she saw
a trail of coffee grounds on the rim of her cup that suggested something coming from far away. Selma and Anton had moved to California at the start of
the war and liked it so much they stayed. Surely a letter would come.

Vera glanced back toward the building. Mrs. Hanson trudged toward the hen house carrying two buckets. Vera stuck out her tongue once
her mother-in-law was over the rise of the hill. If Vera was even half an
hour late for one of her chores, the old lady was quick to pounce. It
seemed Mrs. Hanson just waited for Vera to slip up on some small task,
so she could take over and do it herself.

Tillie Stenerson said that Mrs. Hanson had entertained the
Ladies' Aid by telling about Vera's attempt to butcher a chicken. "Said
you started out chasing a rooster with axe in hand but ended up being
chased by that same rooster."

Vera gritted her teeth. That rooster was mean! Anyone would have
been afraid of its talons.

She jumped up and down to get the blood flowing through her cold feet, still keeping her hands under her arms. The baby was hardly more than a swelling under her jacket, but it was just a matter of time. Soon she'd be big as a house and wearing aprons to cover the gaps between buttons. Her pretty dresses wouldn't fit. There was no money for anything new.

Mrs. Hanson had been sewing the most hideous maternity clothes for Vera from her collection of old flour sacks. It wasn't what Vera wanted, though it would have to do. Every cent they earned went back into the farm.

If only she had her own money. Clyde wouldn't hear of his wife working outside the home. Said he'd be the laughingstock of Tolga Township if she did. With even a small wage she could buy a lipstick or *True Story Magazine* without feeling the silent disapproval of her in-laws. She had to answer to them as much as she answered to her husband. A little money of her own would make all the difference.

Vera kicked the frozen clod again and yelped with pain as Clarence chugged over the hill, and finally stopped at their mailbox. She plastered on her brightest smile.

"Missus." Clarence touched his hat brim, and pawed through a box of bundles tied with string. "Still winter."

Before the thank you was out of her mouth, she was talking to the back of his truck as he drove away again. Her smile turned to a frown as she rifled through the small stack of mail. Nothing from Selma. Nothing from her cousin, still in the Philippines. Bank statement. A post card from the creamery about the annual meeting. Then she saw it.

Real Estate Gazette for California Properties.

California. She shivered and hunched her shoulders. Warm and sunny. Selma and Anton slept with their windows open to inhale the fragrance of orange blossoms and ocean breezes. Selma earned extra money picking fruit and almonds during the harvest. Anton worked steady at a filling station right on the coast, and could look up any time he wanted to see the mountains in the distance. California had lots of jobs. In California it wouldn't matter that she didn't know a thing about farming. In

California she could spend time with Selma, and maybe get a job at the same candy store. At least until the baby was born. In California they'd be away from Clyde's parents and the local busybodies. Far away.

She leafed through the catalog as she started back to the house. Mrs. Hanson had taken care of the hens, so she had no reason to hurry. Clyde was fixing fence in the farthest field, and had taken a lunch with him to save time. The day stretched out in agonizing slowness. Like solitary confinement.

Vera numbered the town friends she might visit. Considered window shopping in Dalton or visiting her grandma in Fergus. But though rationing had finally ended, thank God, Clyde would never let her take their car. That left the old pickup with bald tires and iffy brakes. Their money was needed for tractor parts and seed for the coming season. It was only right—but darned inconvenient.

She could phone her mother but she suspected Mrs. Hanson rubbered in on her conversations. She couldn't prove it, but it seemed no telephone call was private. Always there was extra static, a distant tone, strange sounds, and even breathing. Clyde blamed Tillie, but Vera thought otherwise. No, Mrs. Hanson listened in on Vera's conversations like a jailer.

If only she were the woman of the house instead of just an add-on daughter-in-law. Why if she weren't under such scrutiny she might be a better cook. She'd clean when she wanted, and to heck with the brooder hens. She'd spend money the way she wanted, and have company every day. She'd go to town church instead of stuffy old Tolga Lutheran. It wasn't that much farther to drive into town, only a couple of miles. Clyde wouldn't consider it because the town church met every Sunday while the country church could only afford a preaching service every other Sunday. Clyde said this was the best part about membership at Tolga Lutheran.

But Clyde would be different if they didn't live under the same roof as his parents. Under their thumbs.

The thought of bringing their child into such a stifling environment was more than Vera could bear. She flipped back to the beginning of the flyer. *Chicken farm with three-room bungalow. Quaint and private for discerning buyer.* If only they could move somewhere else before the baby came. Vera would love chickens if they could be on their own.

Vera startled when a horn sounded behind her and stepped to the side of the driveway. Tia Fiskum waved from the driver's seat of their old DeSoto and brought it to a stop beside her. The partially opened trunk lid revealed two cream cans on the way to the creamery secured with strands of baling twine. Through the backseat window, Vera saw a case of eggs ready for market. Vera dropped the mail. She scrambled to retrieve it from the frozen ground.

"Want a ride?"

Vera stumbled into the car, though it was only a short walk to the house, and rubbed her hands before the feeble warmth of the heater. "How nice to see you."

Tia wore a questioning look. "Shouldn't you be wearing a heavier coat?"

Vera mumbled something about a quick dash to pick up the mail. It was crazy, she knew, and she'd never admit it to anyone, but somehow Vera had thought to rebel against Mrs. Hanson's constant evil eye by wearing her spring jacket. Foolish. Tia must think she was crazy. Maybe she was.

Mrs. Hanson came out of the hen house with empty buckets. Her face lit up when she saw who it was. "Tia! Come upstairs. I made ginger snaps."

Vera looked at Tia and then at Mrs. Hanson. She felt like a mouse in a trap. Did Tia come to visit her, or Clyde's mother?

"No time today, Ingeborg," Tia said. "Just stopped for a quick chat with Vera on my way to the creamery." Tia reached into the back seat and pulled out a newspaper-wrapped bundle. "Ma sent the brains and kidneys from the butchering."

"*Mange takk,*" Mrs. Hanson said. "Be sure to thank her."

Mrs. Hanson smiled, but Vera could tell by the crimp in her mouth that she wasn't happy. Triumphantly, Vera led the way to the side door while Mrs. Hanson went around to the backdoor and staircase leading upstairs. She should have invited Mrs. Hanson to join them, but it was just too awkward.

Tia was the first of the neighbors to drop by and see Vera. Of course, Tillie often visited, but one couldn't really count her. She was always looking for any reason to get out of the house.

Clyde hated when Tillie came around. "Even if she is my relative, be careful. Anything you say will be all over town before dark with elaborations you never dreamed of."

Tia was different than Tillie. Tia was smart and nice and had the potential of being a real friend. And she was their closest neighbor.

Vera dropped the mail on the table and went directly to the range, and lit the gas burner with a kitchen match. First the sulfur smell of the match and then a whiff of propane before the gas whooshed into blue flame.

"Hang up your coat," Vera said. "I'll cook coffee." Her mind whirled in a thousand directions. They were out of jam and the bread was on its last heel. Vera should have set a sponge that morning but had forgotten. She had no cookies, nothing baked. At least there was plenty of Arco coffee. It would have to do. She hurried to fill the speckled pot with water from the faucet. "Is your mother well?" Vera said loud enough to be heard above the running water.

"Ja," Tia said. "Thanks for asking."

Something in Tia's voice made Vera turn. She caught Tia gazing out the window toward the cow yard, across the far pasture to where Clyde drove in from the fence line. The tractor was a green dot, but the faint sound of its chugging engine penetrated even this far away.

Tia's face carried the ragged yearning of a starving person, like one of the DP's in a European newsreel.

It was true then. Tillie was right. It was no secret that Mr. and Mrs. Hanson had wanted Clyde and Tia to marry. Mrs. Hanson still joked about it, though lately, Mr. Hanson flashed quick looks of disapproval whenever the conversation drifted in that direction.

Vera knew that Clyde held no feelings toward Tia, but now Vera knew for certain that Tia loved him.

If only Tia lived here, with the folks upstairs, and Clyde in the far field. Tia would call the Hanson's by their first names, and think nothing of it. Tia would feed the chickens before dawn, and set the bread sponge before breakfast. Tia knew how to butcher mean roosters, gather dirty eggs and plant a garden. If Clyde got behind in his field work, she could help him with that, too. There was nothing Tia Fiskum couldn't do if she set her mind to it.

For the first time, Vera realized her mistake in marrying Clyde. She was the interloper, the town girl intruding where she didn't fit in, where she wasn't welcome. Where she would never be welcome. Vera had a sudden impulse to thrust it all at Tia and run away to California.

Vera poured coffee into Tia's cup, the strainer shaking and slopping over onto the clean tablecloth. She blindly returned the pot to the stove and wiped her eyes with the corner of her apron before taking her place by the table. She doubted Tia even noticed, as she was still looking out the window toward Clyde.

The kitchen looked strange as she saw it through Tia's eyes. The running water, electric current, refrigerator, and gas range. Clyde said the Fiskum farm still had an outdoor toilet, water carried from the well, and kerosene lamps.

Surely Tia envied her for the house, her man, and the baby coming.

Vera pulled herself straighter, and patted her stomach, just a small reassuring movement that calmed her back to reality. The baby was hers, and no one else's. Not Tia's in spite of how she felt about Clyde.

Tia made small talk about the butchering and the weather and news from Europe. Terrible all the refugees. Had she heard about the Luther League's plans to raise money for World Relief? It seemed she bounced around from one topic to another—one second talking about the Luther League, and the next asking how the calves were doing, and the price of cream. Finally her voice died away, and they sat without speaking.

The only sound was the clink of cups on saucers, the hum of the icebox in the corner, and the scraping of chairs upstairs. A rooster crowed and Rex barked. The fragrance of fresh coffee filled the room.

"Nels Carlson is having a Bible Study," Tia said. "Next Thursday at eight o'clock."

For the life of her, Vera could think of nothing to say. Nothing at all.

"I'd like Norman to go." Tia took a sip of coffee. "Norman needs . . . something."

Of course he did. After what he'd been through in the war, he needed a miracle. Maybe as much of a miracle as the one that healed Nels Carlson.

"I've come to ask a favor," Tia said, and Vera had the distinct impression Tia had planned what she would say before coming over. "He'll not listen to me . . . but if you and Clyde were to ask him to go with you. . . ."

So there it was. Tia hadn't really come to visit. She didn't come as a friend.

Vera swallowed a harsh retort, as Norman's face came to mind. He had been painfully shy when he used to bring his mother's grocery list into Rorvig's Store. She sometimes teased him, trying to get him to talk.

Once she had asked him what size bloomers his mother needed. His cheeks flamed fiery red, and the words tangled on his tongue. Of course, she had known the list said bananas, but it had been a good joke. Another time she held his hand while giving him the change, just to see what he would do. He had run out of the store, almost forgetting his box of groceries.

Looking back, she hoped she hadn't been mean. She hadn't meant to be cruel. She had always liked Norman. Even written him a letter or two while he was away at war. It was the thing to do.

She let out a long sigh and reached for her cup. If only someone had helped her father before his drinking got out of hand. All the sadness and trouble that could have been avoided if her father had stopped drinking.

"I don't know what Clyde will say." Vera thought she did know. He wasn't much interested in Sunday church, let alone religious gatherings during the week. But Clyde's opinion of the Potato King was one of admiration, at least the Potato King he'd known before the miracle brought such changes. Besides, Norman was his oldest friend. He might do it, just for those reasons. "I'll let you know."

* * *

It was a cold Sunday morning, and heavy frost covered the windshield and painted the trees in the shelterbelt alongside the Fiskum driveway.

"What the hell has Nels come up with now?"

"It's a Bible study." Vera wasn't really sure what that meant, but it sounded harmless. Boring but harmless. "That's all."

"Lordy, Lordy," Clyde wiped the inside of the windshield with the back of his sleeve to clear the glass, "What's George going to say when he gets home and finds his old man turned into a Holy Roller?"

Clyde took another swipe at the windshield. "Is he inviting his friends from the Lower Joint?"

Vera handed him her handkerchief. Clyde rubbed it across the steamy interior of the windshield. "How's a man to get any work done if he's gadding about every night of the week?"

"Norman needs you." Vera placed a hand on Clyde's shoulder, and took back the soggy handkerchief. "Plain and simple."

The car jolted in an icy rut, and Clyde struggled with the steering wheel to keep them on the road and out of the ditch. "Shit."

Vera knew then that he would go. She understood how Clyde felt about staying back on the farm when his friends went to war. During the war it had been easier to believe the slogans that praised farmers for winning the war with food. Now with the boys home, hearing their stories, seeing their wounds, it seemed they were the only heroes. He wouldn't like it, but Clyde would go to Nels' Bible study as penance for sitting out the war on a tractor seat.

Tolga Lutheran came in sight, and its chimney blossomed dark clouds of smoke. Norman was clearly on the job firing up the church furnace. The burned shell of the woodshed and privy building stood stark reminder of the recent fire. New outhouses had been nailed together to make do until spring.

"So you'll ask him?"

"You want to go so bad." Clyde pulled a cigarette out of his shirt pocket, and fumbled for a light. "You ask him."

* * *

Mrs. Hanson had been dark as a thundercloud all day. Vera figured Clyde must have told her about the Bible Study. Vera was feeding the calves when Mrs. Hanson waltzed into the barn, and made a big deal about sweeping the alleys, griping about how some people weren't content to do their work, stay home and keep out of trouble. Complained that Nels's miracle shouldn't cause other people more work.

"Quit your bitchin', Ma." Clyde always hated whining except when he was doing it. "I'll pull tits without your help."

Mrs. Hanson closed her mouth with a snap, and swept until dust rose like a small whirlwind, then left the barn in a huff.

Clyde straightened his cap. "Could have ridden that damn broom back to the house."

Vera knew better than to say anything. Clyde was allowed to complain about his mother, but if she said anything remotely critical, he would be all over her. They finished the milking, and Vera ran the separator as Clyde made one last check on the drinking cups.

"Damn it!"

"What's wrong?"

"Pipes froze up in the northwest corner."

Vera's heart sank. It was already past seven.

"You go," Clyde said. "I have to thaw the pipes."

Vera told herself he wasn't glad about it, that he would rather be going to the Bible study with her as planned. But he did have a smug look about him. A rather smug look. She timidly suggested that Mr. Hanson might do it.

"Good God!" Clyde said. "Pa's eighty years old and near crippled with lumbago."

So in the end Vera bundled up in her good coat, rubber overshoes, wool scarf and mittens, and left without him. It put her in a terrible mood, though Clyde let her take the car. She would have rather done anything than go to the meeting. In fact, the hopelessness of her situation made her think of liquor. Of course she wanted nothing to do with alcohol after living with her father's problem all her life, but it made her think of it all the same. Think how nice it would be to just take a drink and forget it all: the farm, the in-laws, Tia Fiskum, Pa, and Clyde. Forget about being a town girl and not fitting in. Forget how helpless she felt, and how it seemed she no longer had a voice.

Of course, even if she found a voice, there was no one to listen.

"Baby." Vera rubbed her belly. "Promise you'll always listen to your mama."

Stars glittered across the expanse of black sky. There must be a million of them. As she drove around the curve to Norman's house, the full moon hung suspended over Dane Prairie like a giant balloon, like another sun, only pink and red. Vera gasped at its beauty. She could almost reach out and touch it.

She was still gaping upward as she stopped the car in Norman's yard, and beeped the horn. Their lab ran out from the barn, wagging his tail. Norman came out of the house buttoning his plaid jacket. He stopped when he saw she was alone.

"Barn froze up," she said through a rolled-down window. The excuse sounded feeble, even to her, but it was the truth. "I'm driving."

He hesitated. But then he walked around to the passenger side, and climbed in. He smelled of bacon grease and shaving soap.

"Beautiful moon," she said to make conversation but he didn't answer. "And the stars!"

They drove along in silence. Clarence Stenerson's barn showed the soft glow of electric lights in every window. The windows were dark at Gunda Olson's place. Already in bed, she supposed. Odd, Julius didn't have a lamp lit somewhere. It was early for him to go to bed. She didn't see his car in the lean-to. Maybe he'd gone to a picture show.

"Funny how much we can tell about our neighbors just from driving by their places at night," Vera said. "Who goes to bed early, and who's still milking cows."

"Everyone knows everyone else's goddam business in Tolga Township," Norman said. "And nuthin' about nuthin'."

The blackness folded like a cocoon around them. The gravel road to Nels's place shone like a golden path directly into the moon. The heater cranked out a feeble ray of warmth, and the insides of the windows frosted with their breathing.

"I hate the cold," Norman said. "After freezing in Poland I vowed to move to warmer country if I lived through it."

Vera almost drove off the road. She wasn't the only one wanting to escape. She smiled in the darkness, glad he couldn't see her grin.

"Selma loves California." Vera told him about the citrus and almond groves, the sea breezes, and the jobs available. She knew she was talking too much, chattering actually, but she couldn't stop herself. All the thoughts she'd had about California poured out. All the words she had tried to tell Clyde, but couldn't.

She mentioned the chicken farm in the real estate flyer. Norman listened without saying a word until they were parked in Nels's yard, and she pulled the emergency brake.

"I have a California map," he said as he opened the car door. "I'll look it up when I get home. Where did you say it was?"

"Merced."

"You been there?"

"Not yet," she said, "Maybe next year if the wheat does anything."

The moon hung over Nels's house, and the yard glowed beneath it. Other cars parked in the yard: Julius Olson's, Clarence Stenerson's old truck, Millie Moberg's new Studebaker, and others. She was surprised at how many were there. Nels's dog barked from the doorway.

"Hush, Patsy," Norman said. He petted the old dog's neck and ears. "Good girl."

"Come in out of the cold!" Nels threw open the door and gestured inside with exuberant enthusiasm. "*Welkommen!*"

They stamped the snow off their feet, pulled off overshoes, and laid their coats across the bed in the bedroom next to the kitchen. The house had the tumbled look of a bachelor's quarters. It was clean enough, but a box of oatmeal, bar of Ivory soap, jar of pickled pigs feet, and a sack of coffee beans sat on the kitchen table beside a rumpled newspaper. A woman knew to put groceries away before company.

The house, plain and simple, hardly seemed the place where a miracle would have taken place. Vera looked around the kitchen. Chairs lined the walls of the front room. Millie Moberg sat on the piano stool in front of an ancient pump organ. Her dad sat beside Tillie Stenerson. Julius Olson jumped to his feet, and offered his chair to Vera, pulling a toothpick out of his mouth.

"I'll sit on the floor," Julius said when Vera protested.

Vera thought to explain why she was there without Clyde, but there was no opportunity. Millie began a wheezy version of "Pass Me Not Oh Gentle Savior." They were half way through the first verse before Vera dared glance at Norman.

Norman sat on the floor with his back against the wall, and his eyes closed. "Savior, savior, hear my humble cry . . . while on others thou art calling, do not pass me by." The words sounded different, sweeter, than they did in church. Maybe Nels's miracle had made it a holy place.

After the song, Nels opened a large black Bible on his lap. Then he bowed his head and prayed out loud. At least he tried to pray. The words garbled in his throat, and his voice cracked with emotion. "Thank you, Dear Lord." Nels tried several times but finally just sat in silence. His foot tapped on the floor, and he gripped the Bible with such force that Vera feared he might tear the pages.

Millie launched into "Sweet Hour of Prayer." Tillie Stenerson's voice rose above the rest, and Vera was surprised at her beautiful soprano. Norman hid his face between his drawn-up knees. Julius covered his face with his big hands, and Mrs. Hegdahl sat looking with sharp eyes that reminded Vera of an old hen looking for a way out of its cage.

The song ended. Nels blew his nose with a loud honk.

"I didn't deserve it," he said. "It should have been Olga." His mouth worked and his chest heaved. Vera felt the need to look away. "God did a miracle . . ." He shook his head and handed his open Bible to Millie, and motioned for her to read.

Millie read from Psalm 25. "Remember, O Lord, your great mercy and love, for they are from of old. Remember not the sins of my youth and my rebellious ways; according to your love remember me, for you are good, O Lord."

The words melted the room, and Vera caught her breath as she felt the Presence descend upon her. It was around her, beside her, over her. The Presence in every breath, every blink of her eye, as tangible as the feeling of love she had for her unborn baby. As real as the smell of coffee, or the chair beneath her. She had never known such peace. She had never felt so unworthy, and yet so accepted. It made no sense. It made all the sense in the world. Joy filled her, soothed her, and encouraged her. Everything would somehow be all right.

She peeked around her and realized they all sensed it. Norman opened his eyes. The lines on Tillie's brow relaxed. Mrs. Hegdahl sniffed into a handkerchief.

No one said anything.

"He's real," Nels said, and his mouth crumpled like a rotten apple. "Real."

They sang "In the Garden," and the words came alive. "And He walks with me and He talks with me, and He tells me I am His own. And the joy we share, as we tarry there, none other has ever known." Never before had Vera understood how God called her away from life's struggles and trials.

"Don't you feel Him?" Nels's lower lip trembled, and his voice dropped to a whisper. "He's here."

They sat for what seemed like a few minutes, but was actually half an hour. One by one, they stood up, and crept out of the room. No one speaking, not even Eddy Root who had fallen asleep lying on Patsy's back. The patient dog lay there as if it was the most natural thing in the world to be Eddy's pillow. Nels fetched coats, bid quiet farewells and warm handshakes.

Norman greeted Mildred and her father in the kitchen. It sounded like Norman had plans to call on Mildred later in the week. They made a cute couple. They were lucky to find each other. Mildred had found a swell job at the REA office. What Vera wouldn't give to have a job in town, drive her own car like Mildred.

She and Norman were the last to leave. He seemed far away. Vera felt tongue-tied in the aftermath of the experience.

"Does this mean we're saved?" Norman said when they were almost to his house. "A soldier in the camp kept telling me I needed to get saved."

"I don't know," Vera said. "Maybe we don't need to know the name of it."

"I never thanked you for the letters," Norman said.

"Norman," Vera said. She paused for a moment. "My father drinks too much."

"I know," Norman said. "Lot of that going around."

"I'm going to pray for you."

He didn't answer. Just opened the door as soon as the car stopped. Vera watched him head toward the dark house. She was just leaving when Norman trotted back to the car, and tapped on her window. She rolled it down.

"I count trees when I feel like I'm going crazy," he said. "I do it all the time." He hesitated before turning to jog into his house. Their dog got up from the stoop and followed him into the house.

* * *

"How was it?" Clyde asked when she got home. The pipes were thawed. He was smoking and reading Zane Gray. "Handle any snakes?"

"Of course not." Defensiveness rose up. She felt very tired.

"Did Norman get religion?" Clyde chuckled and turned the page.

Vera hung up her coat and scarf, slipped off her overshoes. One thing for sure, she would not discuss it with anyone who had not been there to see for himself. She tried to remember the Psalm they had read, but couldn't recall what it was. Something about the Lord being good, and helping those who hoped in Him.

She rifled through the books on the dining room shelf, looking for her confirmation Bible. How long had it been since she'd opened it? When she finally found the black leather book, she tucked it under her arm and went into the bedroom.

"I listened to that quack on the radio," Clyde called after her. "The Holy Roller miracle worker."

Vera didn't say a word.

Mansel

MANSEL JORGENSON REACHED for a rusty Arco coffee can from the garbage heap behind the steer shed, taking care to avoid a tangled roll of rusty baling wire. A musty smell wrinkled his nose as he emptied the can of rotted leaves and a dead mouse.

Thank God, the war was over and the squint eyes finally beaten. He could use scrap metal again without feeling like a criminal. He pawed through the mound of old junk: broken glass, tin cans, an old washtub, and his daughter's outgrown wheelchair.

He snagged the baling wire, and it uncoiled with a zing, and nicked his thumb. He could have lost an eye! He cursed a steady stream of words his wife, Ada, did not allow in the house, and popped his thumb into his mouth to suck out the poison before his jaws locked up for good.

He had more important work to do, but Ada wouldn't let up about the drafty front room. She said that Minna would catch pneumonia if he didn't patch the cracked siding. She threatened to take matters into her own hands. That meant she'd hire Norman Fiskum and hand Mansel the bill. As if they could afford to have someone else do their work.

The northwest wind confirmed the prediction of the *Farmer's Almanac*. Snow lurked within the gray cloudbank hovering on the western horizon though it was late for snow, even in Minnesota. The Dakota's treeless expanse to the west did nothing to shield Minnesota from winds that threatened again and again to blow them right off the map.

Spring planting would soon be upon him, and he needed to clean out the barn in order to spread manure on the fields before he did the plowing.

Mansel sucked his thumb hard, and pulled work gloves from his pockets. A man had to die of something, and if for him it was the lockjaw, he would just have to bear it.

If only Ada were the one with jaws that wouldn't open.

Mansel kicked a molasses can, and immediately repented for his criticism. He didn't wish anything bad on his wife, of course he didn't. Ada had enough troubles in her life. Besides, there would be no one else to care for Minna if Ada were stricken with lock jaw or anything else.

He kicked a mound of dried leaves and uncovered the mother lode of cans: beet, corn, peach, and apricot. He added them to the basket until he had enough for the job.

In their first five years of marriage, Mansel and Ada Jorgenson buried four babies. The first, a healthy boy named after his father, died from diphtheria before he learned to sit up. Mansel's throat thickened with the memory of little hands reaching up to his beard, the hopes buried with him. The next, another boy, was stillborn. Mansel remembered the way dark curls had folded around his tiny ears. Then a year later the newborn twins, Edna and Alma, caught the Spanish influenza. Edna died first, and they'd almost dared to hope Alma would be spared. Alma was the larger and stronger of the pair. But then she was gone, too, in spite of Doc Sorenson's labors.

Mansel hefted the basket waist-high, and trudged into the empty steer shed. No reason to freeze when there was shelter. He pulled a straw bale before the only window where light spilled in and showed a silvery stream of dust mites in the frigid air. The shed stank of manure and damp earth.

The dirt floor churned into frozen black waves littered with old corncobs, stirred up by the hooves of the young stock sent to the stockyards before the ground froze solid.

He'd almost lost Ada, too, with the influenza. One day she was the healthy mother of twins, milk bursting from her ample breasts, and the next she was weeping over dead babies, too sick to raise her head off the pillow.

He was no doctor, but Mansel blamed everything else on the influenza. Ada had been sick for weeks, and when she finally recovered, was different. It was as if a new person moved into her body. Though she looked like the old Ada, the similarities ended there.

One by one he cut the cans with a tin snip, and smashed them flat with the back end of a ball peen hammer, taking care to avoid the sharp edges of tin, enjoying the manual labor that left his mind free to wander.

God, Ada had been beautiful. Her chestnut hair had fallen below her waist when he first removed the pins on their wedding night, cascading like a golden waterfall down her back. Ada was witty and quick and loved dancing and parties. It was as if she couldn't get enough of the world. She had dragged him to Whist parties, progressive dinners and canasta tournaments. She taught him to schottische and polka. They attended cake walks in the school basement and ham suppers at church.

But after the twins, the new Ada took over, and he was the one coaxing her out of the house to do things.

He was rarely successful.

Ada didn't tell anyone when she conceived again. Not her mother or sister. Hell, she didn't tell him until he noticed her puking every morning, and demanded an explanation. Even then, Ada didn't want to talk about it.

Finally, he sat her down at the kitchen table, and wheedled an answer. She cried and fussed, but finally said their happiness had jinxed them. They had been too open about their joy. It had brought the evil eye upon them. Surely it had, she said. She begged him to understand.

This time would be different. She had a plan, and her eyes glittered as she told how she'd trick the devil. She'd fool all the devils in hell. She wouldn't show happiness, wouldn't tempt fate, wouldn't tell a soul until the baby was born, and off to a good start.

And she didn't.

Ada hunkered down in their farm house, and refused to leave. She wouldn't show herself to company, not even to the hired man during silo-filling. She skipped church, and missed Great Aunt Sarah's funeral. She'd repeat her plan in the voice of an old crone until he thought he'd lose his mind.

The strangest thing was that Ada almost convinced him. Stranger things had happened. Maybe she was right. He dared to hope for a son. A healthy, strapping boy who would work the farm beside him, and take it over when he was too old to continue. The dream bolstered him through those long months when Ada was crazy as a hoot owl, and he not much better.

Minna was born in the middle of a January snowstorm. He'd gone for Doc Sorenson, though Ada begged him not to. She didn't want anyone to know about the baby yet. Mansel waited too long, hoping the baby would come easy, and on its own. When it didn't, he made a mad dash for the doctor, risking his team. They got back just as the baby crowned.

At first Mansel looked away to hide his disappointment at a daughter, but the delight in Ada's voice was enough to change his mind. A daughter wasn't so bad. She would care for them in their old age, and give them grandchildren. Someone to brighten the years ahead.

For a half hour they reveled in the new baby. Her dark hair, perfect fingers and Aunt Sarah's nose. But when Ada drifted off to sleep, Dr. Sorenson pulled Mansel into the porch with a face as solemn as sin. "The baby won't live a month," he said, "something wrong . . . her heart . . . maybe more."

As he felt the words cut into his consciousness, Mansel gathered what little sense he had, and asked a single question. "Should I tell Ada?"

The good doctor had looked at him long and hard, then shook his head. "She'll figure it out soon enough."

Mansel built a little coffin, sanding away his grief as he smoothed and stained the wood. The coffin, still hidden behind a stack of boards in the barn, was now far too small, but he couldn't part with it. There would be no more babies in their family. No grandchildren. No hope.

Their only child fooled Dr. Sorenson. She survived. One month, and then another, and then a year, then five years, and then a decade. Then two. Though Minna lived, she was feeble-minded and crippled, mostly blind, and deaf in one ear.

In twenty-five years she had yet to say a single word, or take a step. Mansel hammered a lard can so hard that the hammer bounced up and almost hit him in the face. What had they done to deserve such cruelty? What kind of God would play such a joke?

The animals had done well last year. For once there had been enough rains for good pasture, and he had fattened them with ground corn mixed with a little oats. With the end of the war there was a sudden demand for everything, and the prices were good. He hadn't told Ada how much they brought in. She'd just get her mind set on new parlor paint, or other such nonsense if she knew of extra money.

He doubted Ada even noticed when the stock shipped. On shipping day she had been too worked up about Minna's hat to notice anything else.

"She won't quit asking about it," Ada said, "It wears me down, I tell you. She wants a new hat with a blue ribbon. Not pink, mind you, not white, but blue and only blue."

Mansel listened like he always did, and hid the astonishment from his face. What else could he do? He nodded in what he hoped was a sympathetic manner, fumbled in his pocket and brought out a dollar bill.

"That ought to be enough," he said, knowing full well that Minna never left the house, never went to church, and never spoke a word.

Dr. Sorenson said it was Ada's way of coping. Good God. What would he do if his wife ended up in the asylum?

Mansel gathered the pile of flattened cans, and carried them to the north side of the house. Ada would have a conniption fit if she saw that he was repairing, instead of replacing, the siding. He took care to keep hammering to a minimum. As if it would matter, it being on the side away from the driveway. Who would see, or care if they did see, the tin patches over the ancient siding to keep out the north wind.

But Ada didn't like the old ways. Why, when his parents were still alive and running the farm, they had used empty cans for water glasses, insulation, measuring feed for the cattle, picking berries, holding bacon grease, a million ways. But tin cans were just a nuisance to Ada, something to throw out in the junk heap, and clutter up the scenery. Attitudes like that had fueled the Japanese war machine! But she wouldn't listen when he tried to tell her so, wouldn't give him the time of day.

Since Minna was born, Ada thought only of their daughter.

Mansel dug around in his overall pocket, and fished out crooked nails. He laid them across a rock, and tapped them straight before pounding the tin pieces onto the wall. He looked with satisfaction at the multicolored patchwork growing across the siding. He took care to have all the letters right side up. Arco Coff . . . Lard . . . Pea . . . could be peaches or peas or even pears . . . but who would care, or take the time to read. Pretty though, like a quilt. He kept at it until he finished, just as the weak sun stood straight overhead.

"Mansel!" Ada called from the side stoop. "Dinner."

Mansel surveyed his project, hooked the hammer into the loop of his overalls and walked around the corner of the house to the side door, scraping his work shoes on the metal scraper imbedded in the sidewalk. She'd have a fit if he tracked on her clean floors. Ada's floors were always clean.

"Getting colder."

Ada gave a distracted nod and hurried to take the roast out of the oven. She was dressed both for town—a clean apron, and the milk house—a dishtowel over her hair. Mansel wondered which it would be.

"Butter or gravy?"

Mansel started to answer, but realized the question had been directed to their daughter who sat half-reclining in a wheelchair by the kitchen window. Minna rolled her eyes when she saw him, and flailed a clasped fist while squealing a high-pitched sound that always reminded him of a mouse caught in a trap. Her mouth gaped open, and drool dripped down her chin.

"Hi, sweetheart." He bent and kissed the top of Minna's head. "How's my girl today?"

"Gravy it is," Ada said, as if Minna had answered.

Mansel drank a dipper of water from the bucket on the sink. He washed his hands and reached for the bottle of iodine on the kitchen shelf. He dabbed some on his thumb.

"Hurt yourself?"

"It's nothing."

Mansel ate in silence while listening to his wife's one-sided conversation with Minna, as she spooned potatoes and mashed peas into her daughter's mouth. Minna choked, coughing potatoes over the front of Ada's apron.

"Sorry!" Ada said. "Mama's going too fast."

Mansel's meat and potatoes were gone, and sheets of fat had hardened across the top of the gravy bowl before Ada finally turned to her own plate.

"Good dinner."

She picked around her peas with a tentative fork, and used her butter knife to carefully cut her meat into identical squares before lifting them to her mouth.

"Cold wind."

Again no answer. Mansel looked up from his plate, and was surprised to see his wife teary eyed.

"What's wrong?" Nothing drove Mansel crazy as much as a bawling woman. "What did I do?"

She shook her head, as Mansel searched his mind. She'd been fine at breakfast. He hadn't bothered her since. It must be the tin cans.

"I'm going into town to see Mama." Ada dug an embroidered handkerchief from her pocket, and sniffed loudly. "Minna insists I go."

Mansel looked up in surprise. Ada rarely left Minna for any reason. He thought of the calf pens, and the manure pile waiting to be forked into the spreader.

"She's worried. Says she won't rest until I check on Mama."

Mansel thought to mention the pens, but decided against it. She wouldn't be gone long. He nodded, and Ada put the handkerchief down.

"Minna naps after dinner," Ada said in an almost breathless voice. "She'll be fine till I get back."

Ada leapt to her feet and pushed Minna's wheelchair to the master bedroom she shared with Minna. Mansel had shifted upstairs to the spare room after Minna's birth. It was easier that way. Besides, Minna was scared to sleep alone. At least that's what Ada always said.

Mansel tuned out the one-sided chatter from the bedroom, and gathered up the dirty dishes. He was a stranger to dishwashing. The china cups fumbled in his farmer-thick hands. He stacked them in the dishpan, and poured scalding water over them from the simmering tea kettle, sprinkling a handful of soap powder under the stream of water, and watching the bubbles grow until they spilled over the top of the pan.

"How nice." The dishtowel was off her head, and another apron tied around her second best dress. "Let them soak—I'll be right back."

"Think you can handle the Studebaker?" Mansel was of the persuasion that the world would be a safer place if women drivers kept off the roads. "You could take the team."

"I'll keep to the back roads," Ada said, as she pinned her second best hat over her braids. "It's cold for the buggy."

He watched through the window as she backed the old car out of the shed, and ground the gears into forward motion. He'd forgotten to remind her to lay off the clutch. Too late now. He shook the coffee pot, and poured another cup and sliced a sliver of pumpkin pie from the pie plate. Then he sank onto the kitchen chair.

Strange, so quiet. Like the air had been sucked out of the world. Minna asleep in the bedroom, and Ada away. He stuffed the whole piece of pie into his mouth, and washed it down with the lukewarm coffee. The clock ticked from the front room side board. A strange weariness came over him though he had done nothing strenuous. Weary of living, he thought. Weary of getting up every day, and listening to Ada's imaginary conversations. It wasn't her fault, he reminded himself.

But it wasn't his fault either. Pastor Hustvedt once said that the troubles of this world weren't God's fault, but the devil's. Mansel knew nothing of such things. He only knew that their life had started out good, but ended up down a rat hole.

If only the babies had lived. If only Minna had died when she was supposed to. If only he and Ada hadn't gotten married, hadn't met at all. He understood how a man could just pack up and leave. Of course, Mansel would never do it, but he understood how it might happen. One morning he would pack his good suit and a change of underwear, and buy a train ticket with the money from the steers. No, he'd buy an airplane ticket. What freedom to finally be released from the ties of the earth. And everything else.

A car chugged into the driveway, its engine changing gears with the reduced speed. What did she forget? Leave it to a woman to waste gas chasing after forgotten items. Mansel was surprised at a knock. Who would come at dinnertime in the middle of a workday? He reached for the doorknob ready to slam it in the face of some sonofabitch Fuller Brush salesman or Jehovah Witness.

Nels Carlson stood at the door wearing his barn coat, and a wool cap with the ear flaps down.

"Hello Mansel," Nels said, "I had you on my mind so strong that I decided to visit."

Mansel's first instinct was to slam the door in his face. Goddam Bible thumper. Nels had been impossible since his knee got better. But he and Nels went to country school and confirmation classes together. It wasn't as if he could turn him away.

Nels took a chair by the kitchen table while Mansel poked more wood into the stove's firebox. He explained that Ada had just left for town. He poured hot water from the tea kettle into the coffee pot, and set it on the hottest burner to boil. Damn woman was never where she should be. He searched and found the coffee can filled with ground beans. He grudgingly admired how she kept everything in order. He had no idea how many grounds to use, and finally dumped most of the can into the speckled coffee pot. He stood watch, so it wouldn't boil over onto Ada's clean stove.

"Spring's late this year." Mansel wanted to catch up on the *National Geographic*. He didn't want to talk to anyone, much less a religious fanatic. Why, Nels didn't even walk with a limp anymore.

"I had a dream," Nels said after a long pause. "That's why I come."

Mansel's mouth dropped open. A dream. God had heard his thoughts, and sent Nels to rebuke him. A chill went through him, and he closed his mouth.

"In my dream I saw how hard it is for you." Nels rubbed his stubbled chin. "And Ada." His pale eyes brimmed with tears. He pulled out a red bandanna handkerchief from his overall pocket, and honked into it. He worked his mouth, and spoke in a whisper. "And hardest of all on Minna."

Mansel choked at the sound of Minna's name. Most people acted like she didn't exist. Her name brought a lump to his throat. Mansel suddenly realized his love for Minna. She was his daughter, after all. Of course he loved her.

"But as much as you love her," Nels continued, as if reading his mind, "the Heavenly Father loves her more. In my dream He called her his little lamb."

Boiling coffee overflowed onto the stove. Mansel pulled the pot off the burner with his bare hand, yelping with pain, biting back a curse.

"He has a hell of a strange way of showing it," Mansel said.

He was suddenly as angry with God as he had been afraid of Him just moments before. He slopped boiling coffee into two clean cups, not bothering to use the strainer, and set one before Nels, and the other by his chair. The sound of the saucers on the table clanked louder than he expected.

Nels pulled the steaming cup and saucer closer, and blew across the top of the cup. "I used to think the same." He took a cautious sip and poured coffee over the lip of the cup into the saucer to cool. "I was so mad at God I would have throttled him had I the chance." He slurped from the saucer. "What you don't know," his voice cracked again, and he set the saucer on the table beside his cup, "is that God's heart breaks over your situation." Tears made his eyes glisten. "I saw it in the dream."

Mansel didn't know where to look. He sank into his chair while all the time wishing he was out in the cow barn pitching manure.

"I'll get to the point." Nels cleared his throat, and wiped his eyes with his sleeve. "After the wife died, I planned to end it all. Couldn't see a reason to go on."

Mansel stood up and walked over to the kitchen window. He pulled back the curtain. He was mortified to feel tears in his eyes, too. He was no better than Nels. Crying like a girl.

"Then Jesus healed my leg."

Mansel had heard the story before. How Nels had sent for an anointed handkerchief from a radio preacher, but it arrived too late to save his wife. How God healed him while he was drunk and cursing His Name. The miracle had spread through the township like wildfire. Nels Carlson, drunken reprobate, walking without crutches.

"It was one helluva surprise." Nels pulled a cloth from his shirt pocket with great reverence. "Scared the shit out of me, knowing I didn't deserve it."

Mansel looked at the cloth. It really happened. He'd known Nels all his life, knew of his war wound, the arthritis.

"I've come to pray for Minna," Nels said. "In my dream she was healed, too."

Mansel had expected a lecture that God was punishing him by making Minna feeble-minded. That it was his fault.

What would Ada think? But then, what could it hurt? Finally, after a long pause, Mansel nodded, not trusting his voice, and led Nels into the bedroom.

Pictures of baby lambs decorated the yellow walls. White lambs with blue ribbons around their necks. Black lambs with white ribbons. A wooden plaque hung over her bed with the verse *He Careth for You* painted in black letters beside a lamb wearing a pink ribbon. Another over the dresser said *God's Little Lamb*. Minna slept snuggled in a pink quilt embroidered with little lambs, holding a toy lamb close to her chest and sucking the back of her hand. She smelled of urine.

"Innocent," Nels said, and his voice trembled. "A gift from heaven."

It was as if Mansel saw Minna for the first time. Gentle. Helpless. Yes, she was innocent. He vaguely remembered Ada asking about lambs. Said Minna wanted one for a pet. He had agreed to buy one. He remembered something about a promise—one he hadn't kept.

Nels spread the handkerchief over the sleeping girl's hair, then closed his eyes and murmured a quiet prayer. Mansel hadn't known what to expect, but certainly not the simple prayer. If Nels had spoken in tongues, or swung from the light fixture, Mansel would have been less surprised. Mansel struggled to hear over the loud thump of his heart, but caught only a word here and there, his name and then Ada's.

A peace, thick as honey, settled over the room. Minna smiled in her sleep. A knot started again in Mansel's throat, and only with great determination did he keep the tears pushed down.

After a long moment, Nels put the handkerchief back in his pocket, nodded and left the room.

Mansel followed into the kitchen, not knowing what to expect, or what to say. He thought to ask if they would have to wait for results, or if it would happen all at once. What would it be like to have Minna whole and normal? It was too good to be true, but Nels was living proof. And the dream. . . .

Mansel's thoughts were interrupted by the ringing phone, two shorts and two longs.

"Hello." Mansel craned his neck to speak into the mouthpiece. Static filled the receiver. Tillie Stenerson rubbering again. "Jorgenson's," he said louder.

Ada's voice always pitched higher when she was anxious. "Mama's sick." More static. "I'm over at the Madsen's to call Doctor Sorenson. He's gone to Elbow Lake," her voice faded out, and then came back at the end of her sentence, "won't be back 'til suppertime."

"What's wrong with Ma?" Mansel said. Ada's mother was a hypochondriac of the worst kind.

"Got a cold on her chest, running a fever. Minna was right." Ada's voice cracked. "Hope it's not pneumonia."

Mansel checked the clock on the side board. The day was getting away from him. He sighed. It couldn't be helped. He was stuck inside until Ada got back. The peace from Nels' prayer already gone.

"I'd hoped to finish the calf pens." He struggled to keep the irritation out of his voice.

"Betty will come soon as Harold gets home."

Mansel hung up the phone, just as the door closed behind Nels on his way out. Strange he didn't say goodbye. He listened but didn't hear the car. Mansel looked out the window. The car still parked in the yard, but Nels nowhere to be seen.

"Sonofabitch." Mansel pulled on his coat, mittens and went out to the barn where Nels pitched manure from the calf pen into the litter carrier.

"*Nei!*" Mansel said. "You have your own work."

"Not so much with Eddy working every day." Nels stopped long enough to remove his heavy jacket. "You'll help me out sometime."

"But . . ."

"I remembered something." Nels leaned on the fork, catching his breath. "In my dream Minna told me how hard it is to be trapped in her body without being able to communicate with people. She said it's the hardest part."

Mansel looked toward the house. He couldn't chance leaving Minna alone, as tempting as that might be. There might be a fire. She might fall out of bed. It didn't seem proper to suggest that Nels sit in the house with Minna while he did the work.

"*Mange takk*," Mansel said at last. "Many thanks." As he trudged back to the house, he decided to help Nels as soon as possible. He wouldn't be beholden to anyone.

Minna slept. No change that he could see. He walked over to her bed and touched her hair. He sometimes heard A.A. Allen on the radio while he was trying to tune in a baseball game or a boxing match. He'd never listened more than a minute now and then. Mansel made a mental note to listen to the radio preacher all the way through. It couldn't hurt.

He paced the floor in the kitchen, picked up a magazine and threw it down again. He looked out the window, and saw the mound of manure rising in the spreader. In the quiet of the house with Minna asleep and Ada gone, it seemed Mansel had been to church. The prayer for Minna. The help with the manure pile. And Nels's dream. Somehow, it all seemed holy. Each fork full of cow shit seemed as holy as the prayers of the preacher.

Ada roared into the yard about an hour later, heavy on the foot feed, riding the clutch. She left the car by the sidewalk, and hurried into the house, her face flushed and her braids falling down beneath her hat.

"I hurried as fast as I could." Ada's eyes wore the same pleading look they sometimes did when she tried to explain what Minna wanted. "Betty will stay with Ma until Doctor Severson gets back. Let's hope Ma doesn't wind up in the hospital."

"Who's here?" Ada glanced out to the yard. "Is that Nels's car?"

Mansel nodded, pulled on his barn coat and headed for the door. He stopped half way. He went back to Ada, and put his arms around her. He kissed her nose and gave her a gentle squeeze. "It will be all right," he said.

She was too surprised to say a word.

Mansel finished spreading the load of manure on the field, and got back to the house in time for supper. The clouds moved directly overhead, and he nosed a whiff of snow in the air. Mansel rubbed his hands together, stomped the dried clay off his boots on the doormat.

Minna sat in her chair in the corner, flapping her hands and squealing as he walked by.

"How's my girl?" His mind was on the plowing, and the strange conversation with Nels. No changes yet in Minna. Another broken dream. Good thing he hadn't told Ada, and gotten her hopes up about it.

Mansel washed up at the sink, soaping his hands and face, bending over the wash basin to splash water on his face. He groped for a towel. It seemed the kitchen was noisy. Too many voices. Too much commotion.

"Give her some jelly, for God's sake," Mansel said, as he rubbed the coarse towel over his clean face.

"I'm going as fast as I can," Ada said.

Mansel straightened up, and dropped the towel. Ada spread chokecherry jelly on a small bit of bread, and popped it into Minna's open mouth. She cooed with delight.

"I heard her," he said. It was as if church bells were ringing. It was as if the angels sang. "I heard her say, 'I want jelly.'"

"I know," Ada continued as if their world was still the same. "She must have asked ten times."

He looked at Minna, watched her flap her hands, and heard her squeal like a mouse caught in a trap. But through it all the words came, "When can I have my pet lamb, Daddy? When can I get my lamb?" The words weren't actually spoken, he had to admit, but somehow he heard them inside of him. In his heart.

The tears started then, and wouldn't stop. He sank onto the kitchen chair, pulled out a handkerchief and mopped his face. Through it all, he heard the silent voice chatting about pet lambs, and what she'd name one. Sobs boiled up from a deep place, one that had been kept locked away too long.

"What's wrong, honey?" Ada laid her hand on his shoulder. "What is it?"

A door had opened. A light had turned on. He put his arms around Ada, and buried his face in the crook of her neck.

Lingering

H IS FATHER'S DEATH had been quick and violent, a rug jerked from beneath his feet, stunning in its ramifications, a ragged wound that never completely healed. But this, his mother's death by inches, was worse.

Julius Olson hitched up his overalls, found a toothpick tucked in his shirt pocket, tugged at the cuffs of his blue chambray work shirt and steeled himself to enter his mother's downstairs bedroom. He ducked his head to go through the doorway. His father had built the house for himself, never dreaming his son would outgrow him.

The smell hit with the open door. Ingeborg Hanson had been over every day since the stroke, but no amount of bleach could disguise the reality. Ma was dying.

Doctor Sorenson said there was no hope of recovery.

Of course, Nels Carlson would disagree. Julius didn't put much hope in miracles.

His mother's rocking chair sat next to her bed, its wooden seat cushioned with an embroidered pillow made by his grandmother. White curtains covered the single window. His mother lay curled like a pink shell, gray hair twisted into a loose braid, her skin as white as the underbelly of a baby calf. Her eyes fluttered beneath closed lids, a strange ripple beneath the thin skin.

He turned the cool rag on his mother's forehead—her skin hot and dry as the dust storms of the thirties, parching and scorching. Her breath smelled of death itself. She moaned a low groan, and Julius leapt back as if she had slapped him.

Her breathing stopped.

Julius thought it was finally over, but his mother gasped, her mouth gaping like a hooked fish on the sand. Ragged breathing refilled the room. A strange relief. Julius leaned over, kissed her cheek and patted her hair. How often she had done just that to him when he was a boy with some childish ailment. She had worried he might catch polio at the local swimming hole, fretted over every sniffle when he sneaked out and went anyway, certain he had caught the dreaded disease.

How small she looked. Doc Sorenson predicted she wouldn't last a week, but here it was almost two. Dear God, if she could just close her eyes, and go to sleep. She hadn't eaten for days, and barely choked drops of water.

"How is she?" Ingeborg's voice startled him from the hallway.

"The same."

Ingeborg stepped to his mother's bedside, and spooned a few drops of water into her open mouth. She held a washrag to Ma's lips, as she coughed and sputtered. Ingeborg shook her head and turned the rag on Ma's forehead.

"Come," Ingeborg said. "You have to eat."

He followed her into the kitchen, and slumped down at the table. Smells of onions and bacon wafted across the room. Julius' stomach rumbled. Maybe it was wrong to feel hungry at such a time. Ingeborg placed a bowl of steaming dumplings before him.

The bulb dangled from the ceiling. Julius had a sudden longing for the old lamp, the way the shadows had gathered in the corners. The way things used to be.

"It's my fault." Ingeborg twisted the corner of her apron, "I was mean about the tomato plants."

Julius stopped blowing on a spoonful of dumpling and looked up in surprise.

"Gunda was bold to set them out so early. When the frost nipped them, I was gleeful." Ingeborg put the jam jar on the table. "Thought for once I'd win the ribbon."

Julius choked. His mother's stroke had nothing to do with tomatoes. Ingeborg and his mother had shared a terse relationship. Always quick to criticize each other, competitive in quality and quantity of garden produce, but always there to help as needed.

"I was mean-spirited." Ingeborg sat in a kitchen chair. "She deserved better."

"You've been a good friend," Julius said at last. "Nothing to feel bad over."

"I telephoned to gloat—that day she took sick."

"It's not your fault." Julius bit back the explanation that would have assuaged her remorse.

He had forced the electric against Ma's wishes, took money from their account to pay for installation, and then accepted an invitation to Annabelle Swanson's house for Sunday dinner.

No, it wasn't about tomato plants. That day of his mother's stroke he had announced his intention to go to Annabelle's house after her family got home from Sunday Mass.

Ma hadn't known Annabelle's family was Catholic.

Actually, he hadn't known either. It mattered little to him. Martin Luther had started out as a Catholic, after all.

A sudden knock sounded. Ingeborg motioned Julius to keep eating as she opened the door for Nels Carlson and Eddy Root.

Julius stood up. "Will you have supper?"

"Smells good," Nels said. "We've already eaten but won't turn it down, will we Eddy."

They hung their jackets on hooks by the door and pulled off their overshoes. They smelled of stale sweat and cow manure. Chairs screeched away from the table. Eddy watched the light bulb dangling over the table like a snake charmer with eyes on the cobra.

"Is your Ma dead yet?" Eddy said, real sudden like.

"Quiet now," Nels said, with an apologetic look toward Julius. "Eat."

Ingeborg bustled back and forth, dishing up soup, and standing watch to keep the bowls filled. The smell of cooking coffee filled the room. No conversation until the men finished eating.

"Now, then." Nels pushed away from the table. "We've come to lend a hand."

Sudden tears filled Julius's throat. Ma always said that a man with good neighbors knew true wealth. The Carlsons and the Hansons neighbored on opposite sides of their land. Julius recalled the many games of Whist played around this table, the canasta and checkers, the shared troubles with dust storms and tragedy.

"Thanks," he whispered.

"We'll start the milking." Nels reached for his overshoes. "Anything else to be done?"

"No," Julius said. He wouldn't take advantage of these good people.

"Water the young stock," Nels said to Eddy. "And check the hogs. I'll be out in a minute."

"It's sad," Nels said as Eddy slammed the door on his way out. "Another one of the old guard passing."

Julius nodded. Ingeborg whisked the dishes off the table into the sink.

Nels was a changed man. Of course the healing took away the crutches—but there was more to it than that. Nels had never been soft hearted before the miracle. Now he went to church more, and cared about other people more.

"She always was full of spunk," Nels said. "Can I see her before I start the chores?"

They trudged to her bedroom, their feet heavy on the worn rug. Ma lay with closed eyes and gaping mouth, gasping for air, her face pale, and her lips blue.

"Gunda," he said, "It's Nels."

Julius watched the rise and fall of her chest beneath the blankets. She looked shrunken, like a wet bird he had once rescued from a mud puddle. She would hate having people see her this way, her mouth hanging open, the groans that came when least expected.

Julius had done this to her as surely as he had put in the electric. He had pushed her into her grave with the news of Annabelle Swanson's religion. He might as well have taken a gun to her.

"I'd like to pray," Nels said. "Is that all right?"

Julius nodded. It wouldn't change anything. It was too late for him. The years stretched ahead. He'd live alone or maybe marry Annabelle. It wasn't what he had dreamed. It wasn't a college education and a life spent teaching history. It was dirty hands, manure-caked boots, and backbreaking labor until he was too old to do it any longer.

Nels pulled out a folded handkerchief and placed it on top of the covers. No doubt, it was the handkerchief that had carried his healing from Miracle Valley, Arizona. Nels placed his hand lightly on the top of his mother's head and prayed quietly.

In the kitchen, dishes rattled in the sink, and Ingeborg's quick steps tapped across the floor.

"I've seen a lot of death." Nels's chin quavered. "The Great War, my parents, our babies, and Olga . . ."

It seemed wrong to speak the word, death, in the presence of the dying. Julius searched his mother's face in hopes she hadn't heard, and felt a need to protect her.

"There's death and then there's life," Nels said. "One breath in this world and the next in heaven."

"Do you really believe that?" Julius said with an unexpected sharpness. "That there's something more?"

"I know it, son," Nels said. "As sure as I stand in this room."

They stood awkwardly by her bed, until finally Nels pocketed the handkerchief.

"Gunda," Nels said. "Quit struggling and go with God. He's calling your name."

Julius wished he had the excuse of chores to allow him to leave. It seemed his mother rested easier. Maybe there was something to Nels's prayer cloth, as he called it. Gratitude welled up in him that she rested, no matter what the reason. If only she could fall asleep, and never wake up.

Julius felt guilty for wishing his mother's death, even in these circumstances.

It had been years since he spent any time in his mother's bedroom. The small room was like a shrine to the ancestors. Photos of unsmiling grandparents, stern soldiers, and drooling babies covered the walls. His parents' wedding photo hung over the bed with their framed marriage license on one side of it and his parents' baptismal certificates, also framed, on the other.

How young they looked. Of course, Julius's parents had been young when they married, younger than Julius was now by several years. Julius saw himself in his father's face. Recognized his brown eyes in his mother's image. He tried to imagine Annabelle's and his photo on this wall. Tried to imagine Annabelle cooking in his mother's kitchen, sleeping with him in this bed.

He was getting ahead of himself. First bury his mother and then think about Annabelle. It was hard to push Annabelle out of his mind.

Annabelle wasn't exactly beautiful but she laughed like tinkling bells. She had a wonderful sense of humor and was always telling funny stories about her little brothers or people she knew. He liked that she made him laugh. All his life he had been too serious. She was respectful to her parents, and the oldest in her large Catholic family. She wasn't afraid of work.

But the religion difference.

His mother cried out and her breathing stopped for a long minute. Julius stood to his feet, and was about to call for Ingeborg, when his mother gasped several uneven breaths.

A car drove up the lane. Julius heard Ingeborg welcome his brothers, Joyce and Marion.

They stomped their feet on the rug by the door, and came directly to Ma's bedroom.

"How's she doing?" Joyce bent over his mother's bed and kissed her cheek.

"'Bout the same." Julius saw Joyce's tears when he straightened up again. Marion went to fetch kitchen chairs.

Their mother had wanted girls. It was the family joke how she had insisted on naming her first two boys the names she had picked out for daughters. Joyce and Marion were anything but feminine. They looked alike, muscular with thick necks and big hands, short and stocky like their mother's side of the family, balding with families of their own. Julius towered several inches over them, more like his uncles on his father's side.

Ma said she gave up on girls by the time Julius came along. The truth was that his father had put his foot down when Julius was born. Joyce told Julius about the argument, how his father said he couldn't bear the embarrassment of having all his boys named like women.

"Remember the time she raised cucumbers for the pickle factory?" Marion dragged two wooden chairs behind him. "We filled a box car."

"Hauling water in that drought," Joyce said. "Those heavy buckets stretched my arms—to this day I have a hard time finding shirt sleeves long enough."

"Wasn't that the summer Pa died?" Julius remembered how they picked cucumbers after the funeral.

No one answered him. They sat listening to Ma's rasping, and the squeaking chairs.

"Always knew she'd work herself to death," Joyce said. "Never slowed down."

Again the awkward silence.

"I'm thinking of planting flax in the lower forty," Marion said. "If the spring rains do anything."

They discussed crops, prices, crop rotation, and weather. Julius hated the way every conversation linked to weather. The rain or lack of it. The heat. Frost. Snow. Always the weather.

If he were a history professor, he would start every conversation with something related to history, and discuss weather only if it pertained to the facts. The snow that defeated Napoleon, or Washington's cold Delaware crossing.

Another car turned into the yard. "Must be the doctor," Julius said. "Promised to stop by."

But Pastor Hustvedt's voice sounded from the kitchen.

Julius and his brothers stood and shook the preacher's hand as he entered the bedroom, and stood solemnly by the sickbed.

"Well, well," Pastor Hustvedt said. "Gunda's leaving us."

The kindness in Pastor's voice reminded Julius of his father's funeral so many years ago. Pastor Hustvedt had been a young man then, just out of seminary. Julius remembered how the preacher had taken his hand, and looked him straight in the eye.

"Always remember what a good man your father was," Pastor Hustvedt had said. "He loved you very much."

Those words had carried Julius through more than one dark night when he had worried about his father's soul. A suicide did that to you. Never quit tormenting you with the what-ifs and might-have-beens.

"*Mange takk.*" Julius pumped the preacher's hand, soft in his own callused mitt.

His mother had given the pastor grief on more than one occasion. Like the time she stormed into the deacons meeting, and complained about the switch to grape juice instead of communion wine. And the time she talked the board members into vetoing indoor plumbing—even after the church had gone live with the REA.

Julius had a strong urge to confide in the reverend about the conversation with his mother before her stroke. But he hesitated. Not only because his brothers were there, but also because his mother wasn't dead yet. All her life, his mother had been like the sun and moon to him— constant and unyielding. Maybe she would yet recover.

The talk drifted to the weather, the Pentecost Dinner, the school board elections at the rural school across from the church. They discussed the men returning home after the war, the Nuremburg Trials, relief efforts for suffering Europe, and veiled funeral plans.

"The church is available any day this week," Pastor Hustvedt said.

He never said the word, funeral, and for this, Julius was grateful.

"I've spoken to the Ladies' Aid and put them on standby," Pastor said. "Just let me know what works best for you."

Julius walked Pastor Hustvedt to his Ford. The air felt moist, the snow turned into spring mud. At least they could dig the grave without hitting frozen ground. They could be thankful for that.

"Ma always said she wanted Tia Fiskum to sing at her funeral." Julius pushed the toe of his shoes into the soft ground. "Still, Still With Thee."

238

"And her favorite Scriptures?"

"Psalm 121," Julius said. "Lifting eyes to the hills." His voice cracked

Pastor Hustvedt nodded, and gripped his hand again. His Ford churned through the muddy driveway, slipped and slid to the township road.

Julius watched him leave, dreading his return to the death watch. His brothers would soon leave for chores. He was the one left to watch over the dying. His sister-in-laws had taken their turns, but Julius knew their friction with his mother. Ma wouldn't want them there at the last. She would want him to be there.

He would get some work done while his brothers were still there. Julius trudged past the pig house where Eddy watered the hogs, and walked down the steps into the barn built into the side of the hill. As his eyes adjusted to the darkness Julius headed toward a cow and pulled a milking bucket from the ledge on the wall. Nels Carlson milked Old Doll.

The comforting sounds of the animals calmed Julius, as he leaned his cheek against the Jersey's side, and stripped milk into the bucket. Maybe Annabelle would turn Lutheran. It would be easier, there being no close Roman Church. If he turned Catholic, they would stick out like a sore thumb.

"It's hard." Nels's voice startled Julius from his thoughts. "Olga lingered, too, you know."

"I don't know how Ma lasts."

"She's a tough old bird," Nels said. "Plucky."

They milked in silence except for the clucking hens scratching in the dirt floor.

"I went to school with your father," Nels said.

Julius turned on the milking stool to look at Nels. "I'd forgotten."

"Friends until I went to war. Your father stayed back to help with the farm."

Of course, Julius had known this, but hadn't thought about it in years. His father stayed home to farm while his friends went off to war. Just as Julius had done.

"He never wanted to be a farmer." Nels poured the bucket of milk through the metal strainer into the milk can. "He dreamed of studying music."

Julius had not known that. He held his breath.

"Of course, no money back in those days." Nels turned to the next cow to be milked. "When I got home from the war, Everett had married. Seemed to have forgotten all about an education."

It was early May, cooling down as the weak sun dipped behind the shelterbelt to the west of the house. Julius pulled his cap over his ears, and hunched his shoulders closer to the warmth of the animal's flank.

"But when he died . . . that way . . . I thought about his dream." Nels stopped stripping the cow. The only sounds were the frogs starting up in the cow yard, a symphony of chirping that usually pleased Julius. "I always figured the dream killed him more than that old rifle."

A chill shuddered through Julius. Killed by a dream. Only a heartsick man could suicide himself.

"That's the thing about a dream," Nels said. The sound of milk pinged into the bucket again. "You've got to follow it and grab it by the tail . . . or else let it go and make your peace."

They finished milking. Nels and Julius returned to the house, as Eddy headed home across the pasture.

"You go right home," Nels called out to Eddy. "Your ma needs you."

Marion and Joyce stood and readied to leave the sickroom.

"We've got to go," Marion said with a clear sound of relief in his voice. "Call if something changes."

"Strange how death always comes at the wrong time," Nels said as he and Julius settled into the vacated chairs. "Too early, mostly, but sometimes late."

They sat together in the falling shadows. Julius lit an old lamp that had sat on his parents' dresser since he was a baby sleeping in the crib.

"I suspect it's because the strong are used to having things their own way and don't appreciate the Good Lord stepping in and interrupting their plans," Nels said.

Nels leaned forward, and rested his chin on his hands. Maybe he was praying. Julius didn't know whether to fold his hands, or leave the room. He had just decided on the latter when Nels lifted his head, and spoke to Julius's mother as if she were perfectly well, and able to converse.

"Gunda." Nels leaned closer to her face. "You've got to think of your sons. They're worn out with the death watch. I suspect you're scared to go because you'll have to account for your part in Everett's suicide."

Julius's eyes almost bugged out of his head. It was as if Nels were chastising his mother, blaming her while she lay on her deathbed.

"Just admit to God you drove Everett too hard and say you're sorry." Nels seemed emboldened by his words. "Ask Him to forgive you— He will." Nels straightened and spoke louder, more confidently. "It's your time, and I command you in the Name of Jesus to do the right thing and let go. Everett is waiting."

Julius's mother took one shuddering breath, and then nothing. Her body relaxed. Her face took on the look of peaceful sleep. Julius felt for her pulse. Nothing.

Relief washed over him. It was finally over. He turned to say something to Nels, but he was already gone. Julius heard Ingeborg's voice in the doorway, "Dr. Sorenson's here."

Julius called his brothers, phoned Pastor Hustvedt, and the undertaker in Dalton. He rang Tia Fiskum and asked her about singing at the funeral. Ingeborg tearfully cleaned the kitchen, and changed the sheets on her old friends' bed before leaving. She hugged Julius although she was so short she could only hug his chest.

"Thank you," he said, and his voice wheezed like the old pump organ in the church basement. "I'll never forget what you've done."

He watched Ingeborg step over the fence, and cut across the field to her farm. The path had connected the two friends for decades. Julius suspected it would be the last time Ingeborg used it. The evening grew chill. He hoped Ingeborg was dressed warm enough. The last thing they needed was for her to take sick.

Julius had rarely been alone on the farm. His mother and her strong presence had always filled the place. Now the air felt thin and empty. Julius gave a fleeting thought about calling Annabelle, but decided against it. Then he wondered why he wouldn't want to call her—if he really loved her.

He looked across the yard toward the wooden fence between their place and the Carlson farm. He saw the old corncrib, the hens scratching and the young stock nosing in the hay. The pile of rocks on the corner. The windmill fluttering with a swishing thunk. Nothing tied him to the farm any more. He tried to imagine what it would feel like to have hands as soft as the minister.

He could go to high school. He'd attend night classes. Then college. He couldn't bear the thought of selling the old place, but he could rent it out. Lots of returning soldiers were looking for a startup.

Pastor Hustvedt's dirty Chevy slipped and slid up the muddy driveway.

"My sympathies."

Julius considered telling him about his plans, but decided against it. Instead he invited the minister into the house. Ingeborg had left a pie standing on the table. They drank warmed-over coffee, ate pie, and sat in silence. Julius refrained from turning on the electric light. The gloom of the evening suited him.

"Feels like a north-west wind," Julius said at last. "Hope it doesn't mean a late frost."

Sheperd of the Flock

Pastor Melvin Hustvedt pushed back in his chair at Tolga Lutheran, and reread the words on the page. He clenched the tip of the pen between his teeth, oblivious to the drip of black ink on the cuff of his second-best shirt.

Not a sound in the church except for the squeak of his chair, and the rumble of the wood furnace.

An unpleasant chore troubled him. He glanced out the narrow window of the study to see the Hegdahl dog digging into Gunda Olson's fresh grave. Pastor Hustvedt rapped on the window. The dog barely hesitated before digging again.

It would never do for the grave to be disturbed on Sunday morning when the parishioners came to church. Such impropriety would leave a stain on Tolga Lutheran not easily erased.

Pastor Hustvedt stepped outside, and breathed in the freshness of the morning. Thank God, Harvey Root's marker sat next to Willy Moberg's stone. A relief, although he never allowed himself the luxury of complaining about it to his parishioners. A marker meant the whole fiasco of the burned coffin was over. Plain and simple.

"Get away!" The dog just looked at him. "Go home!" He convinced the dog to leave with a couple of well aimed stones.

"Pa says not nice to throw rocks."

Pastor Hustvedt twirled around to see Eddy Root huddled in the small concave where the church steps connected to the sanctuary. Eddy wore an old wool coat and an army cap. One hand was bare, the other a wool mitten. His nose showed red from the breeze, but maybe he had been crying. It must be hard on someone like him to understand the abstract issues of life and death.

"Eddy," Pastor said. "How are you doing?"

They made small talk, though Pastor Hustvedt wished Eddy would be on his way. He had work to do, important tasks that required his immediate attention. Besides, maybe Eddy really did belong in the asylum. Eddy seemed harmless, but one never knew.

"Angels talk to me," Eddy said as his bright eyes darted from one side to the other. He pointed up to the clouds. "About Ole Stenerson in heaven."

Nels Carlson would go right along with angels in the sky and such nonsense. He swallowed hard as Eddy prattled on about snakes at the asylum and soldiers drinking beer.

"You'd better go home," Pastor finally said when he was tired of talking to poor Eddy. "Your mother needs you."

With that Eddy got up, and brushed the seat of his pants. "Do you wrestle?" Eddy looked him full in the face and there was something unnerving about his clear blue eyes in his stubbly face. "Norman doesn't like to wrestle."

Something wasn't right. "I did a little wrestling at Concordia years ago," Pastor said. "Why do you ask?"

Eddy looked down, put his hands in his pockets and mumbled something into the top of his jacket.

"What did you say?" Pastor said. "Tell me again."

"Old Man Ingvalstad said men wrestle women when they're in heat." Eddy's words came out in a rush. "Said they like it. Nosy old sonofabitch. Pa said don't talk about it or they'll send you back to Fergus."

Pastor Hustvedt's shook his head in disgust. He remembered Sofus Ingvalstad, and had no doubt the man capable of planting such vile thoughts into Eddy's simple mind. Sometimes he wondered if he had accomplished anything in his thirty years at Tolga Lutheran. His Concordia professors had not prepared him for such situations.

"Your pa was a smart man," Pastor said after a long moment. "Don't talk about wrestling. It will only get you in trouble."

What was the world coming to? The papers groaned with the bad news of the war's aftermath. Displaced people, bombed out cities, starvation, halted economies, the Nuremburg trials, and the death camps. Willy Moberg wasn't the only young man in his parish killed in the war. And others, like Norman Fiskum, damaged and suffering. Pastor Hustvedt felt powerless to help them or their families.

Eddy trotted off across the cemetery followed the Hegdahl dog. The dog reminded Pastor Hustvedt of his need to contact Bernice Hegdahl about the Pentecost Dinner.

The dinner raised funds for the church. With the way the offerings had been lately, and the dire condition of the roof, it was even more important that the dinner prove successful. His wife, Harriet, said that desperate circumstances demanded immediate action. She said that Bernice had the needed enthusiasm to see it through to the end.

The writing was on the wall. Bernice would take over like Patton on the way to Berlin, and alienate all the other women in the Ladies' Aid Society. He dreaded the phone calls, the petty complaints and jealousies. But Harriet had been firm. Bernice was the only woman for the job.

He dragged himself back into the church office, careful to wipe the mud off his shoes. The call to Bernice must wait. He sat down in his desk, and picked up the pen and a fresh sheet of stationery.

Dear Bishop Nielson, There is a delicate situation in my parish that I need to discuss with you.

He penned a dark line through the sentence, pressing so hard that the ink blotted and the nub of the pen pierced through the paper.

Dear Bishop Nielson, I'm having a problem with a parishioner who was healed by a radio preacher.

Perhaps it unwise to admit to problems with parishioners and then there was the ethical question of whether or not a healing had really taken place. There must be a more delicate way.

Dear Bishop Nielson, I suspect that one of my parishioners has suffered a mental collapse.

It was no use. Pastor Hustvedt crumpled the paper and tossed it into the waste-basket beside his ancient roll-top desk. It wasn't a problem to be discussed with the bishop or anyone else.

Nels Carlson had been crippled and miserable. Now he was healed, and extolling the Reverend A.A. Allen from Miracle Valley, Arizona. Nels, almost giddy with delight, lit with an unseen fire that radiated from his work-worn face.

Impossible. Pastor Hustvedt put no stock in radio fly-by-nights. Why, there were rumors that the Reverend A.A. Allen was a drunkard. Even so, the man preached a lively sermon—though of unsound doctrine. Mr. Allen twisted the Holy Bible, lifting verses out of context, and obviously putting more store in experience than theology.

He was quite a salesman if he could convince Nels Carlson to send a whole dollar to Miracle Valley, Arizona, for any reason. This, an offering unseen by Tolga Lutheran until after the miracle, when it suddenly seemed Nels's pockets knew no limits. The man dropped a ten dollar bill into the offering plate one Sunday. Harriet saw it with her own eyes, or Pastor Hustvedt would not have believed it possible.

Harriet worried that others in the struggling parish might send their meager offerings to Reverend Allen in hopes of a similar miraculous result. Surely God would not allow the true church, the Lutheran Church, to suffer. But anything might happen. God had chosen to heal Nels, and let Olga die. And she had been the Sunday School Superintendent. Who could know the mind of God?

There was no denying the change in Nels. He radiated exuberance for the things of God. He was reading the Bible from cover to cover, and cornering people after worship services to tell them what he'd been reading. His face glowed with ecstasy when the Old and New Testament passages were read during the services. He entered into the hymn-singing with gusto, though he tended to sing a half-step flat of the organ, and was known to burst out weeping in the middle of the message. He was the first at the communion rail, and never missed a service. The man hinted several times of his desire to use the pulpit to share his glorious healing and conversion story.

Martin Luther would roll over in his grave.

Years ago, Old Man Johnson became so enraged by the preaching of an early minister, that he took an axe from the woodpile, and hacked the pulpit in two. The story was a well-known part of Tolga Lutheran Church history. One never knew where the road to heresy might lead. Or where it began.

And now the last straw.

Nels Carlson hosted a weekly group meeting at his house, a Bible Study, as told by Mildred Moberg. She fairly beamed with the telling of it, how the Scriptures opened up to them in near-miraculous ways. Even her father, a deacon, attended. Pastor Hustvedt could easily decipher the hidden truth—Mildred was just happy to have somewhere to go, or anything to do. She would be as exuberant about a husking bee or a quilting party.

But there was another issue entirely. An important issue that could not be overlooked. Nels had invited Pastor Hustvedt to attend the Bible studies—not as the leader, as it should be, but as a participant. He, the ordained pastor! What could Nels Carlson know about the Holy Scriptures? And where might it lead? A church split? Scandal?

He had seen enough. Pastor Hustvedt shook his head and gathered his papers. At a time like this a man needed strong coffee and lots of it. A pity the church had no indoor plumbing. No water for a mile even if he had the resolve to fire the ancient range in the church basement kitchen. He shook his red thermos and a small measure sloshed in the bottom. It would be lukewarm and stale, hardly worth the effort.

He glanced out the window where a robin pecked around Olga Carlson's grave. It pulled a pink worm out of the ground. Eddy Root said the worms talked to him. The sky was as blue as a robin's egg with only a stray wispy cloud. Pastor restrained himself from prying open the only window of his dusty study.

At the Hegdahls there was sure to be coffee on the stove. If he left soon, he would get there on time for afternoon lunch. Bernice boasted blue ribbons for her date cookies.

But first things first. Harriet had told him in no uncertain terms that he must deal with the issue of Nels Carlson. It was affecting their marriage, all the stress and confusion. Surely a miracle from God should bring people together instead of driving them apart. Further proof that Nels was unbalanced.

If only Nels would just shut up about it. God knew there was not a person in the parish unhappy with his miraculous recovery. But to keep talking about it!

"I'll not be like the nine lepers who left without a word of thanks," Nels said. "I have been healed and will give God the glory for the rest of my days."

Though not a young man, Nels would undoubtedly outlast them all. Just thinking of the years ahead, listening over and over to Nels's "testimony" brought a hopeless feeling to Pastor Hustvedt. What kind of message was Nels sending to the Confirmands? That it was all right to smoke and drink and avoid God's table, and still receive healing in a miraculous way?

Harriet said he was comparing himself with Reverend Allen. Ridiculous, although he had felt compelled to listen to his radio program several times since Christmas. How could he dispute erroneous doctrine if he didn't know what was being said?

When Mildred Moberg broke her arm, Nels called for Pastor Hustvedt to pray for her. The woman needed a doctor, not a preacher. He prided himself on serious, intellectual discourse. Harriet said the parishioners wanted sermons more like Allen's. The "rip-roaring, Holy Ghost-filled sermon," or whatever nonsensical phrase touted by WOW out of Omaha.

Such notions could not be tolerated at Tolga Lutheran. What would be next? Handling snakes? Casting out demons? It was too much.

Of course, God was God, and if He wanted to heal someone, it was none of their business. Melvin Hustvedt would not correct God. For some reason He had seen fit to bless the sinner, and take his sainted wife. But faith in anointed cloths smacked of Catholicism. He wanted none of it.

He dipped his pen in the bottle of black ink. He tapped the nib against the lip of the ink bottle, and wrote another sentence in his best hand on a clean sheet of stationery. In spite of his unrest of spirit, Pastor Hustvedt paused briefly to admire the slant and grace of his penmanship. Beautiful. Short and succinct. The perfect answer to this problem, though he was not sure of Harriet's approval.

Dear Bishop Nielson, I am requesting a transfer to another parish.

Frieda

A DISTINCT ODOR OF COW MANURE wafted from a plowed field to the right of the farmhouse. Frieda Carlson shifted her purse to her other hand while her young husband, George, pounded on the door.

"I'm home, Pa!" George, at six feet, towered over her by a foot.

Frieda stood in the chill of April gaping at the ramshackle house with peeling paint, hay bales stacked around the foundation, and a boarded porch window. Melted snow puddled in the low spots of the yard. A few dirty drifts gathered in the shade of an evergreen stand. A winter's accumulation of downed branches, bits of kitchen wood, a naked ham bone, a flat tire, empty coffee cans, and an overturned bucket scattered across the yard. Chickens scratched and pecked in the dirt alongside the porch steps.

Behind the budding lilac bushes next to the house sat a small building with a moon-shaped carving. Frieda had never used an outhouse before.

Then sounds of frenzied barking as a dog came running across the pasture. Frieda stepped away from the stinking animal, trying to avoid the chickens, the ground spongy beneath her best shoes.

"Patsy!" George knelt and stroked the top of the dog's head. "Did you miss me, old girl?" He pushed his face into the dog's neck and hugged its wiggling body, oblivious of its muddy feet.

George had never mentioned a dog—or an outhouse. Frieda wasn't exactly sure what she had expected, but she had not expected this.

"We're home," George said through a huge grin that made him look younger than his twenty-five years. His brown eyes glistened. "I never thought I'd live to see this day."

"We should have told your father we were coming." Frieda spoke in German and pushed a lock of blond hair behind her ear. A knot of panic cramped her voice. She straightened her blue velvet hat with the fashionable net, and smoothed the wrinkles from her blue skirt. George always said the blue veil accentuated her eyes.

"The truck is here. Pa's around someplace," George said, as he headed toward the barn, leaving Frieda standing alone.

The granary door swung open, and George's father stepped into the melting morning, shielding his eyes with the side of his hand. Mr. Carlson was an older version of George with his long legs and broad shoulders. His shock of gray curls contrasted to George's dark hair. They carried their bodies the same way. Anyone would recognize them as father and son.

"George, is that you?" Mr. Carlson came running. "Thank God!"

Frieda stood timidly to one side as the men hugged, slapped each other on the back, and hugged again. A cat rubbed against Frieda's legs, leaving black hairs on her silk stockings. She pushed it away with the side of her shoe. It hissed and swiped a paw, snagging a run down the front of her leg. She kicked again, harder this time, and it ran under the porch.

"If only your mother were here," his father said. His mouth worked, and Frieda could see he was fighting back tears.

"Pa," George motioned for Frieda and pulled her close. George squeezed her tight. "I want you to meet my wife."

"*Guten morgen.*" Frieda could have kicked herself when she realized she had spoken in German. She and George had agreed to speak only English once in America. "Good morning," she repeated hurriedly. She reached out to shake Mr. Carlson's hand, and saw a look of shock and confusion cross his face.

"Wife?"

"Frieda's the only good thing about the whole stinking war," George said. "It's over—and now we're home."

Frieda felt her cheeks color as Mr. Carlson's eyes rested on her growing middle. They should have told George's father about their marriage, she thought, but it seemed wrong to share their joyous news. They married the day George received permission from his commanding officer. They hadn't dreamed their wedding day would also be the day of his mother's death.

* * *

A few weeks later, Frieda reached into a nest and pulled out a manure-encrusted egg. She placed it in the basket, and shuddered as a rat scampered up the stone wall of the coop. It looked down at her from the safety of the eaves, its taunting eyes pinpoints of fire.

Of course, she was grateful to be in America. Germany lay in ruins. There were no jobs, no hope. Her father, a professor of literature and art history, earned his soup by clearing rubble from the streets of Gottingen. Disgraceful for a man of his education and position, though there was talk of re-opening the university. Her younger brother, Otto, had disappeared on the Eastern front. They prayed that he had been captured, but the cruelty of the Russians toward the Germans offered little hope of his survival.

Hitler had ruined everything. She steeled herself, and reached under another hen, pulling back when it pecked her hand. She shoved it roughly aside, and stole the eggs amidst clucking and flapping red wings.

So many *todt*. So many dead. All for nothing. *Nicht*.

George was handsome, a kind man, and good husband. But George had clearly exaggerated his status. In spite of the acreage that made him sound like a wealthy man, the farm was a hovel compared to the flat once owned by her parents in Gottingen. Of course, Allied bombers destroyed the flat, and everything else she had known.

It could be worse. She could be stuck in Germany under the Reds. The raping and killing. She counted her lucky stars that Gottingen had fallen under British control. Even so, her parents insisted she leave Germany. There was a chance Russia would find a way to take over the British sector as well. Nothing was certain. When she and George met, her father pushed for marriage. "Germany is a graveyard," he said. "Leave while you can."

She added eggs to the basket. Hitler claimed Norwegians as Aryan brothers. She was not so naïve to believe all that now, but surprised to find nothing akin to the good folk of the Fatherland in these dull and dim-witted people of Scandinavian heritage. They seemed preoccupied only with weather and crops.

"Sweetheart," George called from the door of the hen house. "I'm heading into town for tractor parts. Magneto on the fritz. Need anything?"

Frieda looked down at her muddy overshoes and filthy finger-nails. She knew George was in a hurry by the way he shifted from one foot to another. She refused to go into town looking like a peasant. If only the library carried books written in the German language. Sometimes Frieda felt she would die without something to read.

"Yeast," she answered flatly. "Two cakes and a jar of brown mustard. Two pounds of sausage. Five pounds of sauerkraut."

She returned to the hens as angry tears gathered in her eyes. She boasted a degree in Library Science. Her life once overflowed with music and literature. Her father enjoyed a career as a loved and respected professor. Even during the hardest years of the Great Depression, her family enjoyed a comfortable life.

Now her days filled with farm chores, cooking and scrubbing. She was glad her parents could not see her. In America she was no better than a Pole or a Jew. The bottom of the heap. Even their servants back home never dirtied their hands with barn filth. She trudged back toward the house, heavy on her feet with the growing baby. Patsy, sniffed her apron and tangled between her feet.

"Go," she kicked the dog away. "*Schweinhund.*"

Bending awkwardly over her large stomach, Frieda placed the egg basket at the door and removed her overshoes. She hung up the shapeless barn coat that covered her clean clothing. It was the only coat that fit.

Her father-in-law worried over a ledger at the kitchen table. He mumbled something she could not understand.

If only she and George lived alone. Mr. Carlson made life difficult. Not that he was unkind. He was polite and patient with her failed attempts at farm chores, and running the house. Even though he picked around the sauerkraut, he thanked her for cooking.

The trouble with her father-in-law was the way he looked at her stomach when he talked to her. No doubt figuring the months on his fingers. Let him think what he wanted. Their baby, not due until mid-summer, was conceived within the bounds of wedlock. Sometimes she wanted to shout out that the baby was legitimate. In spite of everyone's opinion on the matter.

She was the outsider, the foreigner, and the enemy. People at church smiled but did not welcome her. Once, she overheard Tillie Stenerson telling Bernice Hegdahl that German girls took desperate measures to get into the United States. They looked her way and did not lower their voices.

Only Vera Hanson called her by her Christian name. Vera once invited her and George over for Whist, a game unknown to Frieda, and one she had no desire to learn.

Frieda washed the eggs, kneaded the rising dough, peeled potatoes for dinner, and fired the kitchen stove. She was thinking about Otto, worrying if he had enough to eat, when Mr. Carlson's voice interrupted.

"Did you hear the news?"

"*Nein.*" She shook her head. Radio announcers talked too fast. Her English was improving, but it was easier to read the newspaper when it arrived later in the mail. At least then she could refer to the dictionary to figure out what was said.

"The Nuremberg Trials. The Auschwitz murder of millions." Mr. Carlson stacked his paperwork and returned it to the wooden secretary. His face like an angry stone. "You're lucky to be out of that hole."

He was right, but his words cut like a knife. She had chosen America. She envisioned Broadway, theatre, symphonies, plenty to eat, culture. There was plenty to eat in Tolga Township, thank God, but nothing else was as she had hoped. Still, Mr. Carlson's criticism of her fatherland made something rise up in her to defend it.

"It's a helluva indictment against civilized people," Mr. Carlson said. "What's wrong with those people?"

The truck chugged into the yard, and Frieda hurried to set the table. Her nation's actions could not be explained. Her father said that though Hitler's Thousand Year Reich lasted only a short time, the shame of it would last more than a thousand years.

She hurried to put food on the table. She added vinegar and caraway seed to the cabbage salad, pulled a dish of homemade butter from the icebox, and poked the potatoes with the tip of a knife. Pork filled the kitchen with its rich aroma. Frieda spooned drippings over the top of the roast covered with sliced onions and apples. Sauerkraut nestled around the beautiful cut of meat.

Fleisch, meat, was the one thing that did not disappoint. The farm provided all they wanted, and then to spare. The smoke-house groaned with hams and bacon. Jars of canned beef lined the cellar shelves. Just thinking about the luxury of meat after so many lean years made her mouth salivate. If only she could send some to her father. To Otto.

"What's for dinner?" George hung his coat and pulled off his rubbers.

"Smells like kraut again," Mr. Carlson said.

Frieda stood by the stove, uncertain what to do. Her mother used sauerkraut in almost all recipes. Frieda didn't know how to cook without it. An old cookbook that had belonged to George's mother sat in the kitchen cupboard, but Frieda stumbled over the unfamiliar English words, and the measurements in cups and quarts instead of grams and kilos.

The anticipation of the meal drained out of her. She placed the food before the men, stood to the side ready to serve them, frustrated beyond words. She was a slave, a servant, almost a prisoner. She should have stayed home with her ffamily and taken her chances with the Russians.

"Frieda, did your father fight in the First War?" Mr. Carlson said around bites of food.

"*Ja*, he was a *kaptain* at Verdun." She thought to mention that he served in the same unit as Adolph Hitler, but Frieda knew better than mention the man so hated by the West.

At first, her father admired Herr Hitler's improvements to German society. Her father applauded the better roads and new jobs. Of course, her father's enthusiasm waned when the great purge of 1933 emptied the university of life-long Jewish friends. Her father hated the book burnings, though he participated lest he lose his position. What else could he have done? Any protest meant deportation to the hideous camps.

Mr. Carlson and she conversed haltingly about the Great War, the battles, dates, and years.

"To think, we fought each other in the trenches and now share a grandchild." Mr. Carlson carefully scraped away a bit of sauerkraut. "Life is filled with surprises."

It was his first open acknowledgement of the coming baby.

"He named you *Frieda*, peace," Mr. Carlson said with a gentler voice. "I remember that word from the Great War. Your parents must have hated war as much as we did."

"They're so far away." Frieda swallowed a lump in her throat. She felt tears pushing into her eyes. "It's their first grandchild, too."

"We'll take photographs," George said as he reached for the potatoes. "And your parents can visit."

The conversation drifted to crops and weather, never ending speculations of hog futures, and the price of wheat, while Frieda tried to imagine her father using the outhouse. Some things were impossible to visualize.

* * *

Vera Hanson dropped by the house with a German chocolate layer cake. Vera handed her the cake, and refastened a bobby pin holding back her curly hair. Vera expected a summer baby, too, and her belly pushed against the buttons of her dress.

"Come in." Frieda deposited the cake safely on the table. "I'll cook coffee."

"I thought you'd like German chocolate," Vera said with a breathy voice. "A bit of home."

"How kind." Frieda appreciated Vera's thoughtfulness—even though coconut always gave her the hives.

They talked about gardens, fair ribbons, and the upcoming Pentecost Dinner at Tolga Lutheran.

"It's our annual fundraiser," Vera said. "I'm bringing two white layer cakes with lemon filling and seven-minute frosting."

"Everyone must cook?"

Vera nodded. "Didn't Bernice Hegdahl call you?"

Frieda shook her head.

"Anyone with names c through h brings cakes."

"So I must bake?"

"Bernice decided." Vera nodded, and laughed a high-pitched laugh that reminded Frieda of Irma Muller from Hitler Youth, a fat girl who tried too hard to fit in. "Said she knew I couldn't cook and you might bring sauerkraut."

A cold stone settled in Frieda's stomach.

"Isn't that funny?" Vera's blue eyes shone like a bright bit of summer sky. Her lips quivered, and Frieda had the distinct feeling that Vera was near tears. "I've been learning to make all kinds of things." She pulled a Betty Crocker Cookbook from her handbag. "Clyde's mother gave it to me on my birthday." Vera sniffed and swallowed hard, pushing her lips into a smile, though her chin quivered. "I thought you might like to borrow it for a cake recipe."

Frieda looked in dismay. They could make their own damn cakes. They didn't welcome her. She was despised by George's people. She wanted no part of Tolga Lutheran. She didn't even know if she believed in God anymore. A fleeting memory of singing Christmas hymns flitted through her mind. She wasn't the naïve child she had once been.

"Keep the cookbook for a few days if you'd like." Vera's lips stretched again into a smile. "You're expected to bring at least two cakes, three if they're small."

George walked into the house, interrupting their conversation. "Hello, Vera. How's Clyde's winter wheat?"

Frieda gritted her teeth. Always crops and weather, weather and crops. Not ever a discussion about music or literature.

"Frieda and I are baking cakes for the Pentecost dinner," Vera said. "They're raising money for roof repairs."

* * *

George, usually so kind and genial, put his foot down.

"We're both going and that's all there is to it," he said that evening with crimped lips and crossed arms.

Frieda had never seen him so obstinate. What difference would her absence make? She opened her mouth to protest, but he cut her off.

"This is the way it is. We're going to the Pentecost Dinner tomorrow night and you're going to bake cakes to help fix the church roof. It's the least we can do. We have to get along with our neighbors." George uncrossed his arms and lowered his voice. "They may not seem friendly, but give it time." He looked at Frieda with pleading eyes. "They're decent folks."

Frieda wanted to stamp her feet and refuse, but she could not deny her husband's request. He had been so kind to her. She sighed and nodded. George kissed her nose, and left the house to work on the corn planter.

She wished Hitler had never been born. Then she wished that she had never met this blond Norwegian American—Aryan brother or not. She imagined Bernice Hegdahl gossiping how Frieda cooked nothing but sauerkraut.

A thought came to mind. As a young girl, Frieda had learned to decorate cakes from one of her nannies. She enjoyed creating flowers and ribbons out of icing, even birds and people. If she must bring cakes, she would create works of art. Frieda reached for Vera's cookbook. She'd show Bernice Hegdahl. She would show them all.

* * *

There was a God, Frieda decided, when she unloaded her cakes in the church basement the next night. The cakes had survived the trip across rough country roads covered with upside down mixing bowls, and packed in an old peach crate found in the cellar.

Her cakes stood in tall chocolate layers, neatly iced in butter frosting. Yellow blossoms and pink ribbons danced across the sides. A little boy and girl danced across the top of one, a bouquet of roses on top of another.

Vera helped Frieda place them on the dessert counter. The counter already crowded with cakes of every kind and description: spice cakes with brown sugar glazes, angel food with whipped cream, and a lopsided white cake with peanut butter frosting. Vera's lemon-filled cakes with fluffy frosting stood to the side. Vera positioned Frieda's cakes on either side of a bouquet of fragrant lilacs in the center of the table.

"Gorgeous!" Vera gushed. She swiped a finger at a spot of frosting on the edge of the plate. "Like wedding cakes." Vera pointed toward her white-frosted cakes and whispered, "Mine fell a little. Think anyone will notice?"

Frieda shook her head. "They're beautiful. I can't wait to try a slice."

The kitchen bustled with buxom farm women wearing sturdy shoes and colored aprons. Mrs. Hegdahl stood on a stepstool handing down orders like a drill sergeant, along with serving dishes from the highest shelf. Tillie Stenerson mixed coffee grounds with eggs, and added the mixture to huge speckled coffee pots of boiling water. Mrs. Fiskum sliced loaves of home-made bread, and Mrs. Sorenson buttered each slice. Vera's mother-in-law stood by the range, her face red from the hot fire, swirling a wire whisk in a large pan of gravy. Tia Fiskum lugged huge roasters of meat from the ovens, and wielded a sharp knife to slice the beef and hams. Mildred Moberg trans-ferred pickled beets, dills and chowchow into pickle dishes. Mrs. Hustvedt covered a dishpan of mashed potatoes with a cookie sheet. Mrs. Root stirred Watkins nectar into pitchers of cold well water.

Such abundance. If only Frieda's parents could share the feast. Since the war, Frieda vowed she would never take food for granted.

A few of the women nodded Frieda's way, but only Vera spoke to her. A large pitcher of nectar stood beside empty glasses and stacks of cof-fee cups. Long tables stretched across the basement. Luther Leaguers wiped them with wet rags dipped in soapy water.

"Vera," Mrs. Hegdahl said, "Can you two cut the cakes?"

Frieda's cheeks warmed at the slight. It was as if she weren't there.

"Of course." Vera turned to whisper in Frieda's ear. "Who died and made her the boss?"

Vera handed Frieda a serrated knife, and as Frieda cut the cakes, Vera placed the slices on small plates until every surface of the dessert counter was filled.

Frieda cut cake at her brother's wedding during the summer of 1942. Somehow her mother scrounged enough sugar. Otto looked so dashing in his uniform, and his bride lovely in silk. But now Otto was gone, and his wife dead in the Dresden raid. Frieda chased the bitter memories away, and concentrated on the task at hand.

A long line of hungry Lutherans stretched up the stairway, and out into the cemetery. Pastor Hustvedt led in singing the table prayer, and the church ladies struggled to dish the food as people filed by the serving counter.

Each person carried a heaping plate in one hand, and a dessert plate in the other. As they found an empty chair, they were met by Luther Leaguers with coffee, silverware and nectar. Frieda noticed how quickly her cakes were chosen.

"We need more ham," Tia called from the serving line in a loud enough voice to be heard above the clatter of dishes. Her mother hurried to fill another platter. The entire operation ran like clockwork. Frieda admired efficiency, and grudgingly admitted that the Pentecost Dinner was a wonderful success.

"Can I get another piece of that chocolate cake?" Mr. Hegdahl held out his empty plate. "Who brought it? It's the best I've ever tasted."

"Frieda made it." Vera poked Frieda in the ribs with her elbow.

"Thank you," Frieda said with a demure nod, as she passed another slice.

"Bernice needs your recipe." He turned to go but then stepped back toward the dessert table. "I'll be sure to remind her to ask for it."

Frieda smiled. Yes, there was a God. Only God could have given her the idea to make sauerkraut cake for the Pentecost Supper at Tolga Lutheran. Her mother always said it made the tastiest, moistest cake possible. She could imagine the look on Bernice's face when she learned her secret ingredient.

Till Death Do Us Part

TIA FISKUM PAUSED in the middle of the cramped kitchen with the jam dish in her hand, half-way between the icebox and kitchen table. "Elmer Petterson visited with me yesterday," Pastor Hustvedt said. "He's lonely. Needs a mother for his children."

Ma quit pouring coffee, and Norman got up from the table, and left the supper table without a word, slamming the screen door. Through the open windows came a chorus of chirping robins, crowing roosters, clucking hens, and buzzing flies.

"Asked about Tia." Pastor Hustvedt sipped scalding coffee from a white cup with a delicate slurp. He wore a threadbare suit with a white shirt and tie. Pastor Hustvedt was the only pastor Tia had ever known. He had baptized her, confirmed her, and she had always hoped he would be the one to conduct her marriage. But Pastor Hustvedt was leaving Tolga Township in another week. He wouldn't be marrying her or anyone else.

Tia put the jam in the icebox, her face feeling hot and sweaty. Sweat trickled under her arms, and dampened her housedress and faded apron. Humidity frizzed her hair, and she pushed loose strands behind her ears. She reached over and turned on the electric fan, enjoying the cooling breeze.

All afternoon she had worked with her brother, hoeing the acre-sized cucumber patch that would repay the bank loan for the electric hook-up. It was worth it to get the electric. Her socks were blackened, and she must look a sight, but she still knew it was worth it to get electricity.

Elmer's wife had died of some vague, female complaint. Lucinda, a mousy woman with buck teeth and crooked smile, had been eighteen years younger than Elmer. Tillie said Lucinda wasn't very bright, but Tia always admired the way she tended her family. Six Petterson children filled a whole pew at Tolga Lutheran, and sniffled and squirmed through every sermon. The little girls wore braids so tight that Norman declared their faces in perpetual grimace.

Elmer kept his farm neat and tidy, and never hung around the Lower Joint like some of the men. He was a churchgoer and on the deacon board, known as a decent person and hard worker.

But Elmer Petterson went to school with Tia's father. His oldest son, Willem, already hired out and the twins, Roy and Ray, had just started reading for the minister. Manfred and Hilda still in grade school. Little Lucy only three.

The children were lately frayed looking, their clothes ragged and scanty. Last Sunday, Lucy came to church with uncombed hair and a dress with missing buttons.

Ma and the preacher made small talk about the Ingvalstad place being sold, the progress of field work, and the weather forecast. Tia busied herself at the kitchen sink, washing the supper dishes, glad for an excuse to avoid the conversation, trying to focus instead on the meadowlarks singing in the shelterbelt, the bawling of the cows in the barnyard, and the clucking hens outside the window.

Marrying Elmer would mean a family, and a chance to stay in Tolga Township. The Petterson farm nestled in the shadow of the big hill just down from the churchyard, next to the Hegdahls. Tia could live close to home, visit Ma all she wanted and see her at church every Sunday and at Ladies' Aid. Ma would have grandchildren to spoil. Surely if Norman had nieces and nephews, he would feel more settled.

Even though it meant being married to Elmer, and Tia had to admit the thought made her queasy, it might be her only chance. Suitors weren't exactly pounding down the doors. Of course, Mr. Petterson was up in age, and maybe wouldn't live much longer.

Being Elmer's widow appealed to her more than being his wife. If he died, she could take over his farm. He had some nice acreage and a nice tractor. Tillie Stenerson once said the best man to marry was a rich one with one foot in the grave, and the other on a banana peel.

Even so, it was too bad she couldn't marry the children instead of their father.

"Well, Tia, what do you think of that?" Ma said after the preacher left.

Tia felt heat rise up her face to the roots of her hair. She didn't answer. Instead, she fumbled with the wooden comb holding her hair, and stuck it deeper into her braids, tightening them into a steadier crown. Lots of women married older men. Of course, she could do it—if she set her mind to it. She had killed that calf and secured a bank loan on her own credit for the electric. She could do anything.

It was just that she had never considered any man except Clyde.

Just the thought of leaving the fields and rolling prairie of Tolga Township gave her a panicky feeling. Although she couldn't explain it, even to herself, Tia knew that her life entwined with the good black dirt of Tolga Township. The dreams of her father and grandfather tied her to the land as tightly as steel chains.

Elmer came calling later in the week. He had a mole on the side of his cheek, a brown blotch shaped like the state of Oklahoma, and a wart the size of a pencil eraser on his chin. His neck corded with age, and his fingernails looked dirty and ragged. His voice wheezed as he rasped a hello, and commented on the weather, and need for more rain if they were to have a chance at a good pickle crop.

He and Ma talked easily of the electric, and how nice it was to have it. He'd heard that Nedra had taken a job at a cannery in California, and intended to stay out West where her parents remained. A shame to sell the old place, but they agreed times were changing, and it was unlikely Nedra would find a California man to take over the farm.

It came to Tia that Ma was closer his age, and that maybe Elmer was courting the wrong Fiskum woman. The idea of Ma marrying again was too absurd to consider. It was Tia who Elmer wanted. She knew it by the glint in his eye, and the way he looked at her chest when he thought she didn't notice.

Elmer stayed long enough to eat a dozen molasses cookies, and empty a pot of egg coffee. Ma smiled, and thanked him for his compliments. Tia heard the words as through a thick veil, the whole time remembering how Vera had smiled at Clyde. When Elmer turned to her, and asked about the church choir, Tia smiled back at him. It wasn't a flirty smile like Vera's, but a smile, nonetheless.

He put a fresh toothpick in his mouth, puffed up his chest, and reached over and patted her hand. The touch of his skin reminded her of the wet paw of a stray dog once found in their pasture.

After he left, Tia hunted around the farm until she found Norman in the shade of the shelterbelt. She plopped next to him.

"What the hell do you think you're doing?" he said at last. "Slimy bastard is old enough to be your pa."

He looked at her with unclouded eyes and seemed more like the old Norman, the one before the war. He hadn't been drinking lately, at least not that Tia had seen. "It would be the biggest mistake of your life."

"I won't leave Tolga Township," she said. "Marrying Elmer would be a chance to have a family, and stay here."

His heels dug gouges in the weedy soil.

"You want to stay?" His voice sharpened.

Tia expected him to go into a tirade about moving to California and getting away from Tolga Township. Instead she had to lean forward to catch his reply, he spoke so softly.

"I'm getting used to the idea."

* * *

Next week at the June Farmer's Union meeting, Tia admired new curtains hanging on the hall windows, sewn and donated by Tillie Stenerson. Tillie recounted the yardage bought from Rorvig's Store, its price, and how she patched the cloth on the east window curtain because the material ran out, and there was none to be found in all of Otter Tail County to match the dye lot.

"I have something to tell you," Tillie said. Her smile spread ear to ear. "We're expecting. Baby due around Christmas."

Tia should be happy, but instead felt only jealous. Even Tillie, the flighty, fickle gossiper, found happiness. Tia escaped Tillie's wagging tongue, and joined Bernice Hegdahl by the lunch table.

Tia poured a glass of Watkins grape nectar, and sniffed it to make sure it wasn't spiked, watching Norman talking to a stranger at the back of the hall. They stood beside a table heaped with dishtowel-wrapped bundles of buns and doughnuts to be served after the business meeting.

Tia could tell by Norman's posture that he liked the man. He wasn't particularly handsome, wore wire-rimmed glasses, a plaid flannel shirt, and overalls with the hems rolled up. His hair, what he had, showed red around a bald spot the size of a saucer on top of his head. He puffed a cigarette, smoke curling over his head in graceful spirals.

Tia made her way over to gather the bundles to bring into the kitchen, half hoping Norman might introduce her. But when she came close enough to hear their conversation, Tia heard them speaking about a wedding. She wanted to run away, but her feet stuck to the ground.

"Tia." Norman waved her closer, holding a drink of something that did not resemble Watkins nectar. "Meet Russell Lindquist."

Russell shook her hand with a strong grip. His eyes looked gentle and he didn't wear a wedding ring—most farmers couldn't afford such luxuries. She glanced around, but didn't spot a wife anywhere. No female strangers at all. He was older than Norman, maybe in his mid thirties.

"Russell bought the Ingvalstad place," Norman said. "He's George Carlson's cousin, and served with him overseas."

"How nice." Tia didn't care where he lived. The good ones were always taken. But then she felt guilty for being so selfish. Norman could use a friend. There was no reason to be rude.

"Your raspberry patch is the best in Tolga Township," she said. "Last year I picked fifty quarts so they wouldn't go to waste."

"Pick again if you want," he said. He reminded her of her father, maybe the way he held his head. "I'll have enough work with the crops."

No wife. He would ask a wife before giving away the berry crop.

"Could trade jam for berries," Norman said. "Tia's jam wins blue ribbons at the county fair."

Their talk quickly turned to spring rains, tractor parts, and taxes. Russell had already signed up for Extension classes through the GI Bill. He urged Norman to reconsider taking part. Tia excused herself and collected the baked goods.

"Let me help." Russell dropped his cigarette onto the floor and snuffed it out with the toe of his boot. He took the bundles from her arms. "George told me so much about Tolga Township I feel as if I know everyone already."

Tia didn't know what to say. Tillie Stenerson ogled them from across the lunch table. Out of the corner of her eye, Tia saw Elmer Petterson looking her way. The meeting was about to begin.

"It's peaceful here," Tia said to Russell. "Some folks think it's too quiet."

"I'm looking for quiet." Russell placed the bundles on the serving table. "It's all I thought about overseas—just find a quiet place to settle down and raise a family."

Tia felt her ears warm.

"Save me a dance?"

Tia hesitated, and then nodded before hurrying back to the kitchen and busying with the coffee. Nels Carlson brought a pan of apple kuchen to the serving table. He walked straight and tall without crutches, still a surprise every time Tia saw him. Tia felt strangely tongue-tied around Nels since his miracle. It didn't mean she wasn't happy for him, but confused why God would heal him, and not others.

"Frieda's learning the language so quickly," Nels said. "Why don't you stop by for a visit? Hard for her with just men around."

Tia promised to stop by, as she emptied a white bag labeled *Carston Bakery* of its fat sour cream cookies. Only Vera Hanson would bring store-bought cookies.

She added them to a serving platter half-filled with Bernice's date bars.

"I see you met Russell Lindquist," Nels said. "Eddy and George did his chores while he was at his friend's wedding yesterday. Has a nice little place there."

Tillie Stenerson edged closer to hear what they were saying, and Elmer Petterson waved and motioned for her to come and sit in the empty chair next to him. Tia pretended she didn't see him.

Elmer started walking over to them. Eddy Root reached for a cookie and Nels pulled him back from the food. "You stay close by me, Eddy. Those are for later." All heads turned to watch.

"Who can dream what great things God has in store for us?" Nels's eyes carried a piercing light, and reminded Tia of a religious zealot with a message from the Almighty. "The future brighter than we could ever imagine. The boys home. Progress on every side. We settle for less than His dream."

Tia agreed. Pastor Hustvedt's final sermon to Tolga Lutheran had said the same. Endless possibilities belonged to those who trusted in God. What seemed like a closed door was really an open door to another adventure.

Elmer started a conversation with Nels about the price of wheat, and Tia saw her opportunity to join Vera Hanson and Frieda Carlson at the back of the room. They chatted about baby blankets and crotchet patterns. Their babies would be born with the wheat harvest. Tia and Norman would stand as godparents for the Hanson baby. Out of the corner of her eye, Tia saw her brother laughing with Clyde.

Russell turned his head, and Tia felt him looking at her. Selmer Moberg called the meeting to order, and Bernice's snotty daughter sang "Good Night Irene" as entertainment.

Through the open kitchen window, orioles sang their haunting melody. They weren't the only ones singing, Tia thought. If a person really listened, she would hear the background of wrens, sparrows, frogs, and crickets. All had reason to sing now that the war was over, and the spring grass turned lush, the fields freshly planted and sprouting green waves of promise against the backdrop of good, black dirt. Not everyone's song could be as glorious as the oriole's, but without the symphony of all of them joined together, the world would be a stark and lonely place.

Tia squared her shoulders, and held her head high. Who could know what God might do? She left the kitchen. Frieda and Vera could finish what was left to be done.

Tia walked over to the back row of folding chairs, and sat beside Norman and Mildred. Clyde Hanson and Russell Lindquist sat on the other side of them. The air filled with stale cigarette smoke, egg coffee, and the honest sweat of hard-working farmers.

She could hardly wait until the music started.

The End

Acknowledgements

Workshops with Jonis Agee, Robert Olen Butler, Judson Mitcham and Sheila O'Connor inspired *Shelterbelts*. Thanks to Patricia Weaver Francisco and Angela Foster for editorial expertise, and to Five Wings Arts Council and the Minnesota Legacy Program for much appreciated financial assistance. Critique partners, Martha Burns and Teddy Jones, persevered through countless revisions. Krista Soukup from Blue Cottage Agency, Chip Borkenhagen from River Place and North Star Press made publication a reality. A special thanks to the Benedictine sisters at Annunciation Monastery for writing space and support. Thank you!